# IT FADES, IT FLIES, IT LIVES, IT DIES . . .

The shell of darkness and light the sphynx had conjured around herself and her victim pulsed with the power of the Riddle. If he answered correctly, she would lose, as she had lost only once before the sorcerer had bound her.

But this one was no sorcerer. He was like all of them she had stalked since escaping her magical prison.

"Answer me," she said, leaning toward him, the gilded fingernails beginning to curve into tiny sickles. The power of the Riddle held him captive. Through it she began to sense the draining of his spirit into hers as the unanswered riddle drank him down.

"I am not human," she said aloud as she knelt beside his corpse. Her body crouched, furred and winged and taloned, freed of her human disguise. "I am merciful. . . ."

PQ-BWS-247

# SPHYNXES WILD

Esther M. Friesner

A SIGNET BOOK

NEW AMERICAN LIBRARY

NAL BOOKS ARE AVAILABLE AT QUANTITY DISCOUNTS WHEN
USED TO PROMOTE PRODUCTS OR SERVICES. FOR INFORMA-
TION PLEASE WRITE TO PREMIUM MARKETING DIVISION, NEW
AMERICAN LIBRARY, 1633 BROADWAY, NEW YORK, NEW YORK
10019.

 SIGNET TRADEMARK REG. U.S. PAT. OFF. AND FOREIGN COUNTRIES
REGISTERED TRADEMARK—MARCA REGISTRADA
HECHO EN DRESDEN, TN, USA

SIGNET, SIGNET CLASSIC, MENTOR, ONYX, PLUME, MERIDIAN
and NAL BOOKS are published by NAL PENGUIN INC.,
1633 Broadway, New York, New York 10019

First Printing, May, 1989

1  2  3  4  5  6  7  8  9

PRINTED IN THE UNITED STATES OF AMERICA

# DEDICATION

Motherhood is a hard gig to play. Rehearsal time is minimal, the audience is tough, the critics show no mercy, and no one goes out there to warm up the house for you. Flop-sweat is proverbial.

Therefore, this book is dedicated to two of those unsung artists who have turned in (in this reviewer's humble opinion) a great performance:

Beatrice C. Friesner and Geraldine J. Stutzman.

# ACKNOWLEDGMENTS

Special thanks to Dr. and Mrs. Luis Roberto Gonzalez, for the loan of their books on Taino mythology and Puerto Rican culture, and to Professor Emeritus José Juan Arrom of Yale University, who first introduced me to pre-Columbian Caribbean myths.

# Prolog

The wizard awoke in the abandoned motel and found his companion gone. It was not unexpected. Ever since they had come to this place, she was forever running off, pretending to still possess the freedom his enchantments denied her. He lay on his back, the silk sheets cool and slick on his bare brown skin, and stared at the ceiling while he thought about her.

Roaches scurried overhead, mistaking the darkness of boarded windows for the familiar shelter of night. It was simple enough for a spell's whispered utterance to let him see them, in spite of the dark. His magic could give him a cat's eyes, and more. Another weirding, as easily uttered, and the scuttling vermin would drop from above in a rain of fire-crisped chitin. The wizard smiled his indulgence, eyelids drooping lazily. He was feeling generous; he would let them live. Sometimes it was enough to know you had the power to do a thing without actually having to prove you could do it.

"Not like the old times," he murmured. His eyes closed completely. A dream of painted marble pillars sprouted from the cold green linoleum. The cracked mirror opposite his bed swirled with a hastening vortex of spangled light, drawing out the dimensions of the squalid room like a master glassblower twirling his bright bubble of molten glass into a never-ending thread of rainbow.

Light danced before him, he followed after; light, that knew the figures and the steps that could lead a man back down the spiral of the years. The pillars were more solid now, exquisitely fluted, their capitals banded with gold. Rose petals fell from silken canopies stretched between them, just beneath the ceiling. The courtiers laughed, tilting back their heads to welcome the fragrant rain. Some opened their mouths and tried to catch the tumbling petals on their

9

tongues. He had seen children in Pannonia behave so, in the winter snows. In the alcove, flute girls played, and a melancholy Jew from Samaria lured exotic harmonies from his harp. The emperor was amused. He motioned to his favorite freedman and commanded further entertainment.

The freedman blanched at the emperor's words. His hands were trembling even as he spread them helplessly, making excuses. The emperor's face seemed to soak up all the blood that left his servant's features. The outraged roar of his thwarted whim could be heard down all the galleries of the ages.

*What do you mean, my sorcerer has gone?*

"He meant exactly what he said, old toad." The wizard's words were a sigh. "Elaboration and rhetoric never were poor Varo's strong points, if he knew they existed at all. You never could stand to have your servants smarter than yourself. I became weary of holding the glass up to your nonexistent intelligence, and so I went, that was all. As Varo told you, I was simply gone, and prudently gone forever, or at least until word reached me that you were safely dead and deified."

A ghost of himself from a past yet more remote hung in ashen silence behind the emperor's divan. The phantom of a phantom ran through the mage's whole repertoire of hollow tricks—tricks just clever enough to make men say how wise the emperor was to have hired such a sorcerer, never *too* clever, lest men wonder why such a sorcerer wasted his time in service to such a bay-crowned fool. Then the emperor struck his freedman across the face so hard that the blood ran from Varo's smashed nose, and the ghostly magician vanished. The summoned dream flew with him.

The living mage opened his eyes again. "Those days are lost, and well lost," he said. "Some things are best left sleeping." He yawned and stretched, the outline of his long-limbed body a spare and lanky shape beneath the sheets. The silk showed every hollow between the ribs when he arched his back—a habit he had picked up from her. The small tightnesses of sleep banished, he swung his legs over the edge of the bed and sat up. The silken sheet became a makeshift himation.

She had roamed enough. It was time to call her home.

Outside the motel, cars and buses sped past on the highway. The sun was still low in the eastern sky, and the early-morning freshness lingered. Every breath he took filled his lungs with the familiar salt smell of the sea, filled his heart with the same eternal regrets for how debased and adulterated that oldest memory had become. The smell of this ocean was more waste than water. All of the promise had gone out of it. He knew the true scent of the tides, and all their secrets; this was a sad parody of that. Oh, he knew! He had been born at Cumae, where the famed sibyl dwelled. The smell of his mother's milk was inextricably blended with the indescribable perfumes of the sea and of sorcery, each powerful, each beautiful.

The sea spoke in riddles, and the sibyl's answers were enigmas for every petitioner to untangle for himself. He had been bred to the business of interpreting puzzles, reading plain truth out of other men's mysteries. The sibyl herself had foretold his fate:

*Thou, Vergilius, on an alien shore, as immortal as thy choice shall make thee. Master of all answers, master of none and one, ever to seek it until it may find thee. The riddle bound shall bind thee, the riddle loosed shall free thee, the riddle answered make or unmake thee.*

Something like a movie marquee hung from the same aqua-and-silver pylon that supported the derelict motel's neon sign and its *Vacancy/No Vacancy* shingle. It was years since the stylized pink conch shell had been illuminated, or the red-and-yellow *Sea-Side Inn*.

"Marsh-Side Inn, more like it," the wizard said to himself, leaning against the pylon and shielding his eyes from the sun. Across the highway, the reeds and wetland grasses grew tall and dusty gold, the waters of the Thorofare shimmered. The motorists never seemed to notice that wild beauty any more than they did the lone man wrapped in white and silence. They had no time, and their sights were distracted by another goal.

"You are right, my pet," Vergilius said to the sea breezes. "We men are blind enough without the need to claim our own eyes in sacrifice."

He looked beyond the reeds and the water, seeking to read the answer to the riddle of the unseeing travelers. It was easy enough, though his powers had never been very strong in taking the omens. But here there was no need to

11

consult birdflight, or the steaming entrails of a sacrifice. The answer towered clean and golden and silvery on the island beyond the marshes. It sparkled by day and shone by night with a multicolored glow so bright that one could almost hear the music that played on that strange shore.

"To hear with our eyes . . . such magic," the sorcerer mused. Sweet music, the clink of coin. Powerful music, that had lured the wizard's companion to this spot and made her content to remain here so long. Music easily mastered, for those creatures who lived outside the laws of chance and were proud to think that they could lose no mortal game.

"But you did lose," the wizard murmured. "Outplayed at your own game by an ordinary boy. But was it game or gamble? Did you never suspect that in all the world, someone might come to you with the answer? Did you always hold us in such scorn? Well, we have taught you a different lesson, that swole-foot youth and I."

The sorcerer spread the white silk sheet to the wind, and a seagull soared over the highway, the wetlands, the water, circling, seeking . . .

From on high, she was ridiculously easy to spot. But then, hide and seek was not the game she preferred. She lay curled up for sleep in a nest of plume grass. The seagull alit on a nearby hummock of fairly dry ground and watched the slow, regular rise and fall of her tawny sides. A few curling strands of blue-black hair lay across her face, and one incongruously long lock of gray the same color as her folded wings. She stirred in her sleep and rolled partway onto her back, covering her face with her paws, the tufted tip of her tail twitching in a dream-hunt. Sunlight and shadow described the too-perfect roundness, the too-icy whiteness of her breasts.

Without realizing it, Vergilius was in human form again. Casting aside the sheet, he crept toward her on hands and feet that metamorphosed into lion's paws to match her own. Try as he would, he had yet to find the way to limit his own shape-shifting abilities to something midway between beast and human.

It was as a lion that he stood over her, lowering his blunt, square-muzzled face to one delicately made ear. Her smell was keener and more pungent in his nostrils when he wore this shape, all the more compelling and urgent. Lacking the means to use human speech as he was, he snorted sharp and hot in her ear to rouse her.

Very lazily, the sphynx opened her amber eyes. The pupils were slitted like a cat's, but the thick lashes above and below were quite human. She smiled, and though her lips were more sweetly curved than those of any woman he had ever known, the tearing teeth between rivaled the lion's fangs for cold, keen power.

Her thoughts drifted into his brain slowly, like the languid heavenward trail of incense burnt to the gods. *Again?* The thought of a sigh. *Very well.*

She rose abruptly, whipping out her gray goshawk's wings, knocking the lion into the water. The wizard heard her harsh, coughing laughter as he hauled himself out of the muck by claws and paws; it had been no accident. His mane was matted with mud, his glorious golden coat streaked with brown and green. The sphynx beat her wings once, twice, not enough to lift her that far from the ground if she had been anything natural. But her whole being defied nature and all its rules, and so she hovered there, riding a wind that did not rustle the delicate reeds, and taunted him.

*Shall I fly away, Magician? This time of all times, why should I not fly from you now?* It was no jest, but an open challenge.

It was not the first, but they had been coming too closely, one after the other, of late. Vergilius no longer found such pranks amusing. He answered without delay, in his own way, immediately. Yellow fire burned in the wetlands. The lionskin seared away, the wizard stood free of the mire and raised his hand, speaking a single word.

The gray wings stiffened outward suddenly, their tips crackling. The sphynx pawed the air madly, yowling as unseen bars stabbed into a cage around her. The woman's head atop the hawk-winged lion's body bowed slowly, under the pressure of an invisible hand whose might she fought every inch of the way. Defiance was useless. Her whole body was brought inexorably back down to the earth, and the spell upon her compelled an unwilling obeisance before the sorcerer.

"You will fly from me when I say," the magician said. "Not before."

*And when will that be?* Thoughts hissed and burned.

Vergilius had seen what the sphinx's thoughts could do to the unprepared mind. In the little Theban village where legend had lured him, they showed him a young shepherd whose flock had led him too near a certain forbidden cavern in the hills. That shepherd now lay naked on a straw pallet, so that the charitable souls who cared for him might clean him of his own wastes more effectively. Saliva ran from the corners of his mouth as he babbled in a tongue neither Latin nor Greek; saliva mixed with blood when a periodic frenzy shook him and his own teeth pierced cheek and tongue. The villagers said he was fifteen.

Fifteen was too young to wander near that cave where the sphinx's dreaming thoughts hung shadowy and hungry about the vine-overgrown adit like bats. They were only the thoughts of her healing-time dreams, the thoughts of her slumbering rage, yet they were enough to destroy the young man whose mind was not prepared to hold so much horror. Had he met her waking thoughts, death would have been mercy.

Ordinarily, the peasants would have guarded the secret of this unlucky boy as closely as they did the location of the cursed cave. But how often did they host a man of magic, the emperor's own pet sorcerer come on a wanderer's holiday from great Rome itself? Opportunities were few, in this rough land, and not to be missed. Could the gracious magician try to heal the boy? They could not offer much, but if he would name a price . . .

The price he named was not the one he took. He gave the lad a semblance of health that lasted only until he was a week's journey away from the village; a shell that crumbled in upon itself because there was nothing of the boy's self left to sustain him. The monster had devoured the rest without even knowing she did so, without waking.

But if the peasants cursed Vergilius for a charlatan, they should also have blessed him for a savior. They would lose no more of their number to the dreaming nightmare. The cave was empty, the magician paid in full. He had set them free.

*And when will you set me free, Magician?*

"When?" Vergilius stroked a beard he no longer had. "When you are less fearsome, less deadly."

*I, fearsome? You do not seem to fear me, Magician.*

"I am only one."

14

*True . . .*

"Not all men are like me, to face you and subdue you when all your powers are awake."

*Did you?* The question was as casual as the caress of an April breeze. More insistent came the next thought: *Answer in truth, Magician! What is the real reason you refuse to let me go?* Her head thrust up sharply, breaking his sorcerous hold. He saw cold hate flash in her eyes. *Let me go. While you still can.*

He tightened the spell's grip, felt her pushing back against it with all her power. Sweat dewed his face and body, chilled him in the cool wind blowing in from the sea. The emerald ring on his left hand paled to the color of dying grass. From all the cities he had seen and the lost lore he had studied, he called up a new measure of strength and hurled it against her.

She battled a moment longer, then broke. All her limbs collapsed under her, and she crouched submissively at his feet, head bent, face burrowed deep between her forepaws. The sorcerer laughed, and whirled the lion-form back around him like a golden cloak. While the sphynx mewed and moaned with fear, a strange note of teasing invitation seemed to run beneath her protests. Vergilius' pale yellow eyes saw her flanks quivering in anticipation. Her song vibrated in the magician's ears, rippled down his body, set his every muscle humming until he loosed a triumphant roar and leaped upon her. Spells of shielding splashed out to veil the sight and sound of their wild coupling from any who might happen to pass by.

But who would wander in these marshes? Who would turn aside from the highway that led so straight and true to the waiting city of dreams?

*Who?* The question touched the sorcerer's mind as he slept in the motel bed, human again. Afterimages of love-making came creeping into his mind, timid and tentative as midnight mice. *What was that harsh smell on her breath? What was that dark red stain dappling the fur beneath her breasts?*

*A seabird,* the reassuring answer came. *She must have caught and killed a gull. There is good hunting in the marshes, and she was born a hunter.*

The sphynx leaned over the sleeping magician. Her wings

15

were gone, her lion's body melted away into the cold, white, graceful shape of an ordinary woman. Resting her weight on hands instead of paws, she bent over her lover and her captor to breathe away all further thought of those few unfortunate details he had noticed.

*I must be more cautious,* she thought. *He is not entirely blind.*

She closed her eyes, but even so she felt the enchantment Vergilius had laid upon himself: a shell of complete protection while he slept. The magician had not lived so many ages—so many centuries of that time with her—by being careless. He might look vulnerable, naked and unconscious, but he was walled safe from her in a fortress of sorcery.

*Walls crumble,* the sphynx reflected. She forced her mind more deeply into the trance that let her see past seemings. The spell protected him from bodily harm, but there were lines, cracks, crevices through which the willing mind might slip and seek whatever it had the will to find.

The sphynx smiled, guiding her thoughts through the labyrinth of the magician's hoarded knowledge. *I shall learn from you, my master. Even now I know more than you suspect. And did you think it was your own whim that brought us here? Have you never sensed me so near, my thoughts so much a part of your thoughts that you could not tell one from the other?*

She laughed softly, the sound still a beast's throaty rumbling in spite of the human form he had given her.

*The form he thinks he gave me. But I take.*

A slim hand whisked a mystic sign on the air, and a young woman with black hair and amber eyes stood beside the road where the cars and buses continued to whiz by. She watched them fly in much the same faintly amused way as her kin had observed the useless, desperate evasions of their landbound or airborne prey before a kill. She had not yet thought it worth her while to learn the barbarous tongue of this place and time, and so the words ATLANTIC CITY on every passing bus's destination sign meant nothing to her.

But the city did. She sensed the power and the life emanating from it as surely as she could sift the air for the scent of human helplessness. What she had sought for so long lay there, in the shining towers. Other places, other cities had possessed that same aura, but here there was less chance of being detected or disturbed. She was a hunter who preferred to hunt without help or competition.

Her tongue slid over her teeth. She could still relish the memory of the hunt, cherishing the chase itself more than the sweetness of the blood. To hunt secretly was best. She would never have dared to take that lonesome fisherman she had surprised among the reeds if there had been the slimmest chance that anyone would overhear or see her. Oh, the look in his eyes as she sprang!

*Payment,* she thought. *Poor reparation for the old wrong. But I am only one.*

The distant towers sang their song of power, which can make one a number to fear. She tilted her head back, and in the ancient tongue crooned her dead mother's lullaby tune to the unknown gods of men:

"What goes on four legs, two legs, three?
What holds a world but cannot see?"

The songs met and mingled in the wind from the sea.

In his sleep, the magician dreamed of an enchanted halter that frayed and broke, loosing a fire on the world.

# CHAPTER ONE:
## Magic in America

Sanchi tugged up the worn plush collar of his phony bombardier jacket and wondered whether it would be blasphemous asking the Virgin's help to make Alonso's bus reach Atlantic City faster. The damp, chilly weather of early spring made him antsy. He still wasn't used to a seaside resort having any other season but summer. There had been too many promises of warm weather to come, too many hints of new greenery and flowers. In winter, you expected it to be cold and nasty—Nature's own package deal, like the twenty-bucks-credit-back the casinos all offered—but spring wasn't supposed to let you down this way.

*"Como si fuera toda la vida garantizada,"* Sanchi muttered, digging his hands deeper into his pockets. *As if you weren't used to letdowns by now,* a thought added. The brown leather jacket was cracked in places, and both pocket linings sported plenty of holes. It would be some time before Sanchi could buy himself a new one, on what he made at Dionysia.

But the wait would have been a damned sight shorter without Alonso being wished on him.

*A fine way to talk about your brother!* The pang of guilt hit Sanchi right under the ribs. His mother's voice stabbed in on the thin, sour wind from the sea. He could feel his cheeks reddening, and not just with cold. No matter how old he grew or how far from her he roamed, he never could escape the power that his mother commanded to make him feel nakedly young, plainly unworthy.

*But he's not my brother.* Stubbornly he tried to beat down an opponent who wasn't even there. *My half-brother, OK, but nothing more.*

*And so? What were you to José María, eh? Not even half a tie of blood to bind you to him and his family, not even one thin drop! But still he took you in when your uncle Carlitos died. He raised you with his own kids, he shared out the little he had equally among you, and never bothered to ask whether you deserved it more or less than Berto, or Manuel, or Mike, or little Elena. If Alonso were his kin, and his own mother asked him to help the boy out so little—so very little!—you think he'd be quibbling about whole-blood, half-blood?*

It was all an approximate mental replay of the phone conversation Sanchi had had with his mother last week, when she had first asked him for this favor. The only difference was that his memories didn't shrill, "Damn you, why do I have to beg for every little thing? You're as selfish as your stinking father!"

A sly little needle of winter's retreat jabbed him through the worn spot in his jeans. Would Alonso's bus never get here? The sun was shining, but it could do little to banish the aching feeling of emptiness in Sanchi's belly—emptiness that had nothing to do with the fact that he'd skipped breakfast.

*You have a short memory, Mama. I never did anything for you and 'Lonso? It's been years, but even so . . .*

The letter crinkled in his pocket, under his frosted finger-tips. For lack of anything better to fill the waiting time, he took it out and read it again.

It was postmarked Godwins Corners, Connecticut, wherever under hell that was. Good, heavy, respectable paper the color of top cream was ruined by Sandra Horowitz's enthusiastic, illegible scrawl with a very outspoken magenta felt-tip pen:

*I'm trying to understand why you won't keep in touch. Lionel says it's normal, you wanting to forget New York. Everybody else has—part of the magic, sayeth Lord 'n' Master, who made him the big sorcery expert?—except us, the ones who experienced it most. Maybe you do just want to pretend it never happened. But how can you? Even though it's all long over and done with, there are times I still feel as if you and I were standing together under Persiles' shield, ready to fight, maybe ready to die.*

"No, Sandy." In spite of time and sorrow, Sanchi still had a young boy's soft, delicately shaped lips. They curved up at the corners in a smile that had nothing to do with joy. "I was never ready to die, not even for Persiles. I was a kid, then. No kid ever believes anything really bad can touch him. Other people die, not him."

Other people die.

*Then there are times I feel he's still with us. I saw him die, the same as you, but still . . . how much do we know about such things? Not proven, Your Honor; take it straight from the lawyer's mouth.*

Sanchi grimaced as another lick of cold air slipped down the back of his neck. Or was it something else that gave him the chills? Lionel was right. There was a reason he never answered Sandy's letters.

*If you want my opinion—which I've got no reason to expect you do, but what the hell—I'd say that we can't choose to forget. We have no choice any more. Magic has touched us, and now we're marked out from the rest of the world for good. If you got any of my other letters—and José María claims he gave me all your proper forwarding addresses—you know what I mean. There's magic here, now, in this country, this time, in you, in me, and we never had to look into other worlds to see it. We only had to learn how to use our eyes in this—*

Sanchi crumpled the letter and jammed it back into his jeans. He made an impatient sound, eyes sweeping up and down the street for some sign of Alonso's bus. He had no stomach for putting up with Sandy's phony-mystic ramblings. Some people believed in the Harmonic Convergence; Sandy had twelve pastlife-pileups on the Psychic Expressway. He could count on the fingers of one hand the number of her letters he'd managed to read all the way through. Lately he was likely to toss them as soon as he recognized the return address, or the fancy-lawyer stationery.

"Oughta take a hint," he told the inside of his collar. "How many times I ever wrote back? Think she'd catch on that I don't want to know her anymore and why the hell she'd want to know me . . . ." He laughed. She'd come a long way since New York, since she'd been that flibbertigibbet redhead college student who thought she was going nuts every time reality threw her a curve. A lawyer now! Successful, too. And if he could believe some of the stuff she wrote him, life in Connecticut was one solid screwball after another, with Sandra Horowitz batting .999.

He remembered how badly she'd freaked when they'd first met—him a little snotnosed Puerto Rican kid who didn't even know his own age, her the big-deal Ivy Leaguer. It wasn't the supposed social inequity that had unhinged her, but the fact that a brat who should've been in Times Square panhandling spare change was instead in the Columbia University library asking her all about dragons.

The wind from the sea blew colder. The towering casinos fronting the boardwalk always seemed to block out the best of the sunlight. They had sprung up in all their glittering glory as if to answer the economic prayers of a city that had known better times. Like this small, elusive springtime, they were all promise. The glamour of the casinos was like the tide, washing prosperity ashore only so far and no farther. Farther inland, nothing much had changed. Sanchi worked amid the flash and sparkle of Dionysia, but after his shift was over, he went back to sleep in a tatty boardinghouse where he had a cheap room with a washcloth floor rug and broken plastic blinds at the window.

Nothing had changed. He was the same person who once heard a knight speak of wondrous and terrible quests, the same Sanchez Rubio who had stared in awe as a figure out of legends had named him squire and friend. He was the same boy who had stood by his beloved master's side and seen impossible horror put on a dragon's skin and stalk city streets. And when the beast's inexorable evil drew Sanchi's long-lost mother and unguessed baby half brother into its power, he remained the same boy who stood with Sandy and Lionel over his master's corpse and brought the dragon down.

"Never do anything for you and 'Lonso, Mama? Only saved your lives."

And that was where the fairy tale was supposed to end. He'd dreamed about his mother's return almost from the day she'd run off, and always the dreams were gold and rose, Sanchi triumphant, his mother's face shining with love and gratitude, her heart aching with remorse as she explained the very good reason she had had for abandoning him.

Only none of it came true. Her gratitude was a reflex that lasted only slightly longer than the standard knee-jerk. She took him back, but shrugged off his every question about why she'd gone away and left him in her brother's care.

When he grew too insistent, she told him to shut the fuck up, and smacked his face. She never raised a hand to 'Lonso.

"Where's the magic, Sandy?" Sanchi said under his breath. "How come you got your happy-ever-after? Why not me?" He wished that he could ask her, face to face. She had an education. Maybe the answer he was after was something you learned in college. But every one of her letters that José María sent on to him only added to the deadweight of envy in his heart. Not even the natural happiness he felt for his old friend's good fortune could begin to melt that away.

He was cold. Alonso's bus was acting a lot like Alonso—getting in on its own time, schedules go hang, doing what it damn well felt like, suiting itself. Could be it was too good to stick to a timetable. That was for ordinary buses.

He heard a large vehicle pull up behind him, but when he turned he saw that it was only a steel-blue stretch limo. The dream on wheels glided past him, its driver and passengers a riddle behind impenetrable black glass.

Sanchi watched the limo sail down the street. A block away, it almost nudged old Zorro headfirst into the garbage can he was rummaging through. Zorro was one of the street people, his real name as much a mystery as his life. Sanchi had given him the swashbuckler's honorific for the weird black cape the old man wore and his cracked spectacles so repeatedly mended with black electrical tape they looked like a bandido's mask.

*There's your magic, Sandy,* Sanchi thought, watching the old man hurl a curse at the indifferent limousine, then go back to his dumpster diving. *Those people in that car, they're going to come back and wave a wand over old Zorro and change his life, give him money, a home, food, warmth, respect. Might even take pity on mine.*

Another rumbling noise announced the long-awaited bus. It pulled up right in front of Sanchi and started discharging passengers. Alonso hopped off the steps, jostling the few people with the temerity to get in his way.

*Madre de Dios, was I ever such a pushy punk at that age?* Sanchi thought. Though 'Lonso was so much younger than Sanchi, their mother's dark looks dominated both faces. It was impossible to pretend no kinship to this scrawny, gawky, perpetually snarling clatter of bones and sarcasm.

Alonso was now complaining loudly about having to take such a long bus ride with a bunch of whacked-out old farts out to blow their pension checks on the slot machines. He didn't bother modulating his voice. Sanchi couldn't escape. He had to witness the effects of 'Lonso's words. Every lined face that twisted with hurt feelings, every spoiling shadow 'Lonso's scorn cast over an older person's holiday made Sanchi's face burn. He snatched his half brother's luggage from the bus driver as soon as it came out of the compartment and struck off up the street as fast as he could go.

He left too quickly to see the blue limo come back by the same route it had followed before. It stopped a judicious distance from old Zorro. One of the rear windows whispered open two fingers' breadth.

*Dominic.*

The old man jerked his head out of the trash, his expression as incredulous as if some herald angel had called his name. In the blur of his mind he wondered how this stranger knew who he was without ever realizing that nothing had been spoken aloud. Amber eyes regarded him through the slitted window. The car door swung open.

\*　　\*　　\*

"You see that, Yolanda?"

"What?"

"What I saw getting inta that big limo. A real eccentric millionaire. You know, like Howard Hughes."

"Get outa here!"

"Yeah? And I suppose every bum in this city has a limo pick him up outa the garbage?"

"Why not?" Yolanda shrugged. "This ain't Brooklyn."

# CHAPTER TWO:
## Land of Opportunity

"A busboy?"

Sanchi couldn't decide whether 'Lonso's eyebrows went up higher than his voice or vice versa. The kid was still in bed, showing no intention of getting out in spite of the fact that Sanchi had told him a dozen times that they were both going to be late.

"What did you want?" Sanchi replied. "They're not hiring vice-presidents today."

"Ha, ha. *Muy chistoso.*" 'Lonso pulled up his knees to form twin mountains of rumpled bedclothes. "Someday you're gonna just kill me laughing, big brother." His legs straightened out again and he closed his eyes, giving every sign that he intended to go right back to sleep.

It was a gesture meant to enrage, like a cat flaunting its hindquarters at a toothless dog. Nobody with a working set of nerves could possibly want to spend more time than necessary in that cruddy boardinghouse bed. After a night on the rump-sprung leatherette sofa, Sanchi would have been glad to get his bed back, but even nostalgia didn't change the facts: the bed was a slab of sheeted peanut brittle.

'Lonso's luxurious yawn ended with an abrupt whump as Sanchi yanked him out of bed by the ankle.

"Shit, man—"

"Get up, get dressed, and get out." Sanchi jerked a

thumb at the door. "Right now. I have to lock up my room." He stressed the possessive a shade too strongly for 'Lonso's liking. The kid had a crooked, skinny grin on an equally crooked, skinny face.

"Sure," he said, picking himself off the linoleum and rustling through his still-packed valise for clothing. "Lock up. Wouldn't want anyone to steal anything." *As if you had anything worth taking,* 'Lonso's eyes added. *Because I'd take it.*

It wasn't much, as digs went, but 'Lonso had been jabbing Sanchi at short, sharp intervals ever since his arrival, and hard memories stood behind it. *Just like the good old days,* Sanchi thought when the kid first started in. *The minute you learned that Mama'd let you get away with ragging me, but come down hard if I even raised my voice to you, you bit hard where it hurt and never let go. Jesus, sometimes it seems like you learned how to rub me raw before you learned how to talk. It hasn't changed. Just like before, at home.*

Home.

Why wasn't it his mother's face he saw whenever he heard that word? No, the little apartment Mama found for them up in the Bronx never surfaced. His few years there were a smear of time, dirty, easily and eagerly wiped away. In their place were other faces, different years, and a dreamy warmth that lingered until guilt seeped in and pushed it aside. But while it lasted . . .

*"This is your home now, Sanchez."* José María's voice, *deep and comforting, the man's strong arms around him, the broad chest against which he could hide his eyes and blot out the sight of his uncle, dead, murdered.*

*"Papi, you're kidding! How we gonna feed—?"*

*"Shut up, Manolo. You don't look like you're starving,"* Roberto said, carrying himself with the full dignity and authority of the eldest son.

*"Bobby's right!" little Elena chimed in.*

*"He is!" Miguel backed up his baby sister before Manuel could demand who'd asked for her opinion. "Papa knows what he's doing."*

*"Yeah, Mike, sure." Manuel's words dripped sarcasm that Alonso might have envied. "Anything Bobby says, you can't wait to agree. You'd trip over your own tongue racing to lick his—"*

*"Manuel!" Papi's voice was the finality that sliced away every objection. Manolo cringed, made apologetic sounds completely bereft of sincerity. Papi ignored the boy's phony whimperings. He was a finder of strays, a nourisher of souls, a healer of hurts that others never saw. He had work to do. His whole heart focused on the newest foundling. "Everything will be all right, San— No, we can't call you Sanchez, that's our family name, and we'll all get confused. Sanchi, OK? You'll stay with us, Sanchi."*

*And a child slowly lifted tear-filled eyes from the sheltering shoulder, feeling brave again, being the small man his uncle had always taught him to be. A man doesn't cry. "Only until my mama comes back. Then I'll have to go."*

*"Of course." In memory, Sanchi saw Papi's pitying look for the first time. "When she comes back, of course you'll have to go with her."*

*"She'll come soon."*

*"Seguro que sí, Sanchito. But until then . . ."*

"Hey!" Fully dressed, 'Lonso leaned back against the door and jiggled the knob loudly, irritated. "First you tell me to haul ass, then you sit there like a jerk. I'm ready. Let's get the hell outa here."

They walked the few blocks from the boardinghouse to Dionysia. 'Lonso was loud in his comments on everything and everybody they passed. There wasn't any room for gray in 'Lonso's world; either he approved or disapproved. His hate list included everything about the boardinghouse, the shabby street, and the people who did their best to live decently there on what they earned. Like Sanchi, most of them made a living directly from the casinos. 'Lonso seemed to prefer the indirect route. He didn't find anything he liked—with the exception of a passing pimpmobile—until they crossed Pacific Avenue.

"Now *this* is it." 'Lonso pulled his hands out of his jean pockets and tried to grab the widest vista of boardwalk property his arms could hold. His stingy, lopsided grin burst its bounds, turned into a broad, brilliant smile.

"You like it?" Sanchi's inquiry lacked real interest or enthusiasm. It was an old, old scene to him. He could still remember his first sight of the boardwalk, the casinos, the waves. He had smiled then, too. For a moment, he wanted to draw closer to 'Lonso, to try to recapture what he'd lost or else warn the kid not to let the glitterwalls blind him.

Then he saw the difference between his then-smile, 'Lonso's now. His half brother's happiness was neat, narrow, and very specific, not at all what his had once been. Even the little honky-tonk stands peddling saltwater taffy made him happy, and the hustling wicker pedicabs, all that energetic life around him. It took him a long time to see some of the ugly things hiding under the shine and the noise and the smells of perfume, candy, sunwarmed planks, open sea.

*Don't waste time warning him, friend. He doesn't need a guide. He's seeing just what's there. And he's hungry for it. Man, he wants it all.*

"Come on, *hermano.*" 'Lonso snapped his fingers. "If starting out as a busboy's what it takes to stay here, I'll bus my butt off."

They strolled along the boardwalk, past most of the more famous casinos. 'Lonso tried some of the names on his tongue, relishing each one: "Bally's, Caesar's, Trump's, Tropicana, Atlantis—all *right!* Hey, what's that thing?" He pointed to a square-pillared colonnade fronting the Convention Center.

"Kennedy Memorial." Sanchi paused, letting his eyes follow the graceful curve of the twin rows of pillars. The late president's solemn, sculpted face looked out of place in the shelter of those lotus-carved capitals. Someone had left an iris at the pedestal's base, a purple spear.

"Oh." 'Lonso dismissed it all with one twitch of his lips and slouched on ahead.

Sanchi quickened his pace to catch up. As in a bad cartoon, he kept hearing coins pouring into a slot-machine tray every time his half brother showed interest in something new. No possible way to turn it into a profit, end of interest. 'Lonso was young, but he had a firm grasp of practical philosophy.

*Maybe you're the smart one,* Sanchi thought, watching the kid stride on up the boardwalk. *Maybe I should learn from you.*

A wayward thought made him chuckle. 'Lonso heard, and wheeled around sharply. "You laughing at me, man?" His dark eyes had the smallest sliver of feral yellow light. Sanchi imagined he saw stiff barbs shoot from his half brother's skin, and those tight, ungenerous lips curl back to show dog's teeth. The ridiculous conceit—man/beast, boy/beast lurking under 'Lonso's paler skin—forced him to stifle another laugh.

"No way, 'Lon; not at you. Just at myself."

Was it his warped way of perceiving things, or did he hear the velvety sound of talons retracting into their muscled sheaths? *Touched by magic, am I, Sandy? Plain touched is more like it.* 'Lonso was showing all his teeth in what should have been a friendly expression.

"Hey, OK, big brother. You got plenty to laugh at there. Gonna let me in on the joke?"

"Like you said, there's plenty of them. I'm wall-to-wall funnies. Let's get you to that interview."

Somewhere between the springtime sunlight of the open boardwalk and the cool darkness of Dionysia, Sanchi lost his sense of humor. *Learn from 'Lonso, yeah. The way I learned from Persiles, from Sandy, from Lionel . . . all I do is learn. But what could anyone have to learn from me? All my life it's like I've been in training. For what, dammit? The eternal student, the forever squire, always ready to follow, never fit to lead. Always carrying the shield for the real warrior, never ready to hold a sword of my own. Never.*

"OK, Rubio, I've got a special job for you. Feel up to learning something new?" Sanchi's manager on the casino floor was only a little older than he, but had a self-assured way of carrying his big-shouldered body that gave the impression of extra years.

"If you think I can do it, Mr. O'Connor."

"Oh, you can do it. If I didn't think so, I'd ask someone else, now wouldn't I?" O'Connor patted Sanchi's sky-blue blazer. Everyone working the casino floor at Dionysia looked ready to ship off on a fancy yachting party, the women in pleated white skirts, the men in crisp cream flannel trousers and modified ascots, both sexes sporting identical blazers. The Great Gatsby might have gasped appreciation at the cocktail waitresses' ensembles: radically abbreviated versions of Daisy's gauziest garden dress. Sanchi just thought he looked ridiculous.

"Yes, sir." Sanchi moved just enough to be outside the compass of O'Connor's friendlier gestures.

O'Connor shook his head. This was an old dance of Rubio's, one the big Irishman couldn't quite understand. He liked Sanchi. More than once he'd invited him to join a crowd of other Dionysia staff for a couple of drinks after work, a weekend fishing expedition, a movie. Every time Sanchi begged off, pulled away, hid behind the excuse that work and friendship shouldn't mix.

Still, O'Connor persisted, maintaining an attitude of amused indulgence. Sanchi wished the man would give it up. He felt like a brick-shy alley cat his boss was constantly trying to coax into the open. It only made the bars roll down harder between them.

"It's simple stuff, Rubio," O'Connor told him. "A little surveillance work, OK? Over at the baccarat tables."

"Up in the booth?" Sanchi was puzzled. What with all the cameras and the trained security staff to man the one-way mirrors, he would be a fifth wheel; a square one.

"No, right here on the floor. I think we've got trouble."

They could have had disaster on tap and no one but Sanchi and O'Connor would have been aware of it, even though they spoke well above whispers. They were standing in the midst of the hullabaloo surrounding Dionysia's fleet of craps tables. It was almost as safe a guarantee of privacy as being locked in a soundproof closet; safer. If you weren't the croupier or the shooter, no one cared what you were doing.

"Trouble?" Sanchi frowned. "What kind?"

"The worst; the quiet kind. Take a look over there and you'll see who I mean." O'Connor gestured to where the baccarat tables stood in their elite separation, on a raised platform behind a gilded white marble balustrade.

Sanchi had observed that there was a sort of natural order of things inside the casinos. In the wild there were hunters and hiders, eaters of grain and eaters of meat, day-dwellers and night-stalkers. So too here. By day, most of the action centered on the slot machines, with a gradually growing crowd drawn to the craps tables and the other games. Baccarat was the exception. Baccarat belonged to the night-prowlers, and it wasn't too strange to see the tables deserted, the dealers idle for most of the daylight hours. The occasional daytime players were either hangers-on from the night before or casual passersby who tried the game for a lark before returning to more familiar territory.

Sanchi had it down to an unwritten code in his mind: Little old ladies played the slots and yuppies rode the roulette wheel and blue-collar types hit the craps tables. James Bond played baccarat. Exquisitely. And he won.

He spotted the man O'Connor meant at once. He looked more like one of James Bond's string of insidious foes; he was winning anyway. Perhaps Bond would win with more panache, but Dionysia wasn't concerned with flair. The word had come down—as passed to Sanchi via O'Connor and to O'Connor from on high—and the word was that this man was winning far too big, far too consistently.

"He's been here a week," O'Connor said, steering Sanchi even farther away from the baccarat tables. They made a slow circuit of the casino floor, paused to consider the showcard advertising Pia Zadora's coming performance in the Bacchante Room. "Every day at opening time, like clockwork. He takes maybe an hour or two off for lunch and a couple of potty breaks, then exits for good around six o'clock."

"Good credit?"

"Who knows? He hasn't needed any all the time he's been here. He put down some cash at the cage his first day, hasn't had to sign a note since."

"That good?" Sanchi couldn't believe it.

O'Connor's face was one of the reasons he inevitably lost at poker. Lies always showed, and none showed now. "Yeah, that good, when nobody's that good. He doesn't lose. I'd say the man needs looking into, wouldn't you?"

"Sure, but don't they see him up in the—?"

"Some scams the camera misses. Just help keep a human eye on him. You're not the only one I'm tapping. Let me know what you see."

Sanchi nodded once, briskly, and drifted back toward the baccarat tables. The man was still there, though he had begun to consult his watch. It was getting close to lunchtime, and O'Connor had said this type wasn't one to miss a meal. Sanchi scrounged himself a clipboard and a pad from a nearby floor boss's station to serve as props. He started making efficient, important-looking notes as he edged nearer and got his first really good look at the man.

*Black ice,* Sanchi thought, and wasn't sure how he'd come by such a weird way of tagging a total stranger.

But it was true. Everything about the man was coldly elegant, with none of the dazzling glitter of sun striking blue-white sparks from ordinary frost. This was a far more discreet glamour, a sleek refinement that went much deeper than the glitzy veneer other high rollers seemed to spray-paint on themselves with flashy clothes, fashionable hairstyles, eye-catching jewelry, and bedmates to match.

This man was neatly dressed and groomed, but current styles hadn't touched him. Neither did he look eccentric or affectedly antiquated. The single emerald ring he wore said wealth by its size and purity, muted good taste by its unostentatious setting.

*Timeless,* Sanchi thought, and his mind filled with an image of the sea.

From beneath skillfully lowered eyelids, Sanchi simultaneously jotted down more nonsense on the pad and watched his target at play. There were no swift or distracting moves, no manual byplay to distract the dealer, not the veriest hint of legerdemain in action. Still, the man looked an awful lot like the prototypical stage magician, down to the tidily trimmed black mustache and Mephistophelian beard. If there was any trickery helping this person to Dionysia receipts, Sanchi couldn't see it from where he stood.

A sideways glance and he caught sight of his coworker Gemma, tall and blond and coolly at home in her Dionysia rig. To judge by the way she managed to find so many small tasks to do in the baccarat section, O'Connor must have put her on the case too. Sanchi decided to leave the floor-level observation to her and go up to the booth to see whether his unjaded eyes could catch anything the regular security personnel had overlooked.

The booth was really a large room that roofed the entire casino floor, a mezzanine not mentioned on any regular elevator's indicator panel. Sanchi reached it by sprinting up one of two private staircases. He knew he got too little exercise as it was to justify taking the special elevator. Besides, it was too close to the vault. Getting near so much money in one place gave him a creepy feeling, perhaps another legacy of his time against the dragon—the beast had had the fondness of its kind for acquiring unreasonably huge piles of wealth.

They eyed his badge carefully when he came in. Up in the

booth, security guards monitored the batteries of closed-circuit televisions giving a full panorama of the gaming area. There were also more direct observation posts: one-way mirrors set in the walls and ceilings, made to blend in with the decor. Most players were too rapt with their own pursuits to care about the mirrors, and those who were aware of their watchful presence couldn't tell a snooping glass from an ordinary part of Dionysia's high-sparkle interior. Some wag who'd seen too many grade-B horror flicks had even slipped one-way glass behind the eyes of the plaster masks of Comedy and Tragedy near the roulette wheels.

It didn't take Sanchi long to find the mirror he wanted, the one with a clear view of the baccarat table where his mark still sat. A word to the woman at that post and she grudgingly ceded him her seat. Sanchi had the dizzying sensation of peering down from a great height at a precarious angle. The one-way glass was so well maintained that it was like leaning over an abyss with nothing to stop you from plummeting to the casino floor should you slip. Sanchi found himself holding on to the arms of the chair for the first few moments before he could relax.

He watched the man play three more hands of baccarat. He won them all. Nothing about his manner of play hinted at underhanded doings. He looked quite bored, indifferent to the fortune in chips that was piling up before him. As Sanchi watched, a slim young woman in a dark wine-colored sheath approached the table. Her auburn hair was impossibly thick and wavy, her skin luminous against the heavy satin of her gown.

It was too early in the day for such a dress, or such a professional huntress. Word must have leaked to the street about this big winner. The successful pimps played their ladies as a wise hunter played his dogs. If the game was big enough, you didn't waste time waiting or send in the untried pups.

The weird perspective of his ceiling roost made Sanchi lose all sense of reality. His assignment was forgotten, and he let his mark play another hand without bothering to watch out for tricks. Like the worst addicted soap-opera fancier, everything else could go hang; he wanted to see this episode's resolution.

It resolved itself quickly, briefly, and not to the lady's

satisfaction. No sooner did she insinuate her supple body into the chair beside him, yet refuse to play, than the man turned to her and said a few words. Sanchi couldn't hear them, but he could guess. The lady's face went from ivory to scarlet. She spat something back, her delicate features suddenly hard and twisted, burning with rage and shame. The man didn't even bother to pay her the compliment of a shrug. He had dealt with her offer and was now indifferent to everything but the game. The lady was about to add a few additional curses, but Gemma materialized at her elbow. Sanchi knew the drill: a polite suggestion to move along. The lady moved.

And in that moment between moments—while Gemma was seeing the lady to the door, while the dealer was getting a new shoe full of cards for the game, while a yawn interrupted the security woman who was asking Sanchi if he'd be sitting there all day—it happened. The man looked up. He looked straight at the surveillance mirror, unwavering eyes the color of his emerald penetrating the glass. There was nothing vague about his glance; it held cold purpose and had unerring aim. He looked right into Sanchi's eyes.

And nodded.

And winked.

*I know you,* the eyes said.

Sanchi pushed himself out of the chair and stammered thanks to its rightful tenant. His heart was beating fast as he hurried from the observation booth, the borrowed clipboard still tucked under one arm. By the time he reached the baccarat table, the man was gone.

O'Connor told him not to sweat it. "He'll be back after lunch; the usual. Why don't you go on break now too?"

Sanchi set the clipboard down on the same counter where he'd gotten it. He decided to detach the top sheet he'd scribbled on—no sense leaving a lot of stupid doodles and Spanish gibberish for someone else to toss.

His hand stopped over the page. There were words there he hadn't written—could not have written unless his pen had changed color from black to brick red. AVE, AMICE MEO. He didn't even know what that meant.

But he knew the drawing beside it, and he knew he had not—would never have—drawn it.

A dragon.

# CHAPTER THREE: Get a Job

"Where'd you get it?" Sanchi's voice trembled from the effort he made to keep it level. Dolmades was the most casual of Dionysia's eateries—a glorified snack bar, at best—but it still wouldn't do to start a shouting match with Alonso on company property. For the first time he understood what people meant when they spoke of fingers that itched to kill. There was a prickling sensation crackling like a myriad hornets' stings over both his hands, and only wrapping them tightly around 'Lonso's windpipe was going to salve them. "Who bought you the booze, goddammit? Who?"

'Lonso gave his half brother a liquor-mangled grin. Leaning one elbow on the restaurant counter, he propped his chin on one hand and replied, "Hey, chill out, *hermano*. It don't matter. I didn't get the fucking busboy job anyway, so if I had little drink, what the hell?"

"You're underage, that's what the hell." Sanchi lowered his voice, pressed his fingertips into the countertop as if trying to pry out one of the fake Greek coins imbedded in the Lucite surface.

"So B.F.D. I can hold it. And if I can't, I promise not to puke all over your pretty work clothes, *de acuerdo?*" Abruptly, 'Lonso stopped smiling. He took a pull from the cup of coffee in front of him, and all the booze-borrowed softness left his eyes. "Look, Sanchez, cut the crap. You don't really give a damn what I do with myself as long as none of it splashes on you. I could turn up like—like—" He dragged an abandoned newspaper across the counter and stabbed a finger down on the article describing the black-caped corpse that the police had found on the beach that morning "—like this old gomer here, and you'd be relieved." He couldn't help reading a line or two of the story in question, and went a little yellow. "Sure, that could've

33

been me lying in the sand with my throat cut, bleeding like a pig, and you'd never—"

Sanchi placed his hand over the story. He didn't want to read about poor old Zorro again. It made him sick, thinking of the kind of human trash that could get kicks from killing a harmless street person so readily, so inhumanly, and for what? No money, a few rags, a battered knapsack; Zorro had nothing to steal but his life.

"Alonso, you're wrong," he said. "I'll be honest: I don't like you—"

"Big surprise."

"—but that could change. It *should* change. You're my brother, we're family, and we don't have that much kin for us to go wasting what we've got. I *want* to love you, 'Lonso."

'Lonso snorted into his coffee cup. "Bet you do." His eyes twinkled with nasty mirth as he regarded Sanchi over the blue-and-white ceramic rim. Slowly he replaced the cup on its made-in-Korea Wedgwood saucer.

"After you left for good, Mama talked about you. Hey, you look like you don't believe it! But she did. Once you went out that door, it was like you died and got canonized. Every fucking day, Sanchez this and Sanchez that and how you'd done some kinda incredible shit in New York City when you were just a kid and I was a baby—saved our lives, hers and mine." He took another sip. "Bullshit."

Sanchi looked into his own cup, lacing his fingers around it tightly, and said nothing.

"Every time I turned around, she was comparing us. Always it was how I was a disgrace to my father's memory, but you almost made her believe that she was wrong about who popped you inside her." Alonso snickered. "Stupid bitch didn't even realize what kind of a whore that made her sound like."

"You don't talk that way about our mother, 'Lonso." An unarticulated threat lay beneath his muted tone, his carefully controlled voice.

'Lonso only twisted his mouth into a more skeptical expression. "Why not? Who made you her knight in shining armor?" His lips quirked sharply, responding to the way Sanchi's whole body jerked involuntarily at those words. "A knight in shining armor, yeah," he repeated. "She told me about him, too, and a whole lot of other stuff no one in his right mind would swallow. I told her she was full of it, and then she showed me this."

'Lonso dipped into his jeans pocket and pulled out a battered vinyl wallet. Wrapped in a scrap of newspaper and tucked into one of the empty credit card windows was a lone gold coin. 'Lonso unveiled it with a magician's stage flourish, held it up to his right eye like a monocle.

"Today it's a Krugerrand. Ma said it was a Maple Leaf when she dug it out, that it could change itself, but half the time she so busy mining six-packs, she doesn't know which way her head's screwed on. I wonder where she got it?"

"I gave it to her," Sanchi said. From the corner of his eyes he noted the restaurant clock, a contemporary dial linked to a working clepsydra. His break was almost over, but he couldn't get away.

"Sure you did." 'Lonso wrapped it up again. "Part of the haul your friend the knight gave you, right? And you passed all of it on to Ma, and she went through it like a drunken sailor until there was just this one left to prove how much better you were than me. When did I ever bring home one lousy dime, let alone a magic Krugerrand?"

" 'Lon, you're so much younger than me, she couldn't have expected you to earn—"

*"What the fuck do you know about what she expected of me?"* 'Lonso's outburst made heads turn. One of the waitresses made a discreet call on an in-house phone. "You make it with some rich uptown dude, turn yourself into twice the whore she ever was, and she doesn't care what kind of a line you feed her so long as you pour the gold into her lap."

" 'Lonso . . ." Sanchi knew it wouldn't take long for the waitress' call to get action. Swift, subdued, efficient security was the key to a successful casino, and Dionysia was one of the best. He made a halfhearted effort to shush his brother. Part of him secretly longed to see the kid get taken down a couple of pegs by experts, part wanted to spare Alonso the humiliation of being thrown out of Dolmades.

*And spare me too,* he thought. *Guilt by association. I guess you're right about me after all, 'Lonso. Don't splash anything more on me.*

'Lonso was off the counter stool, hunkered over in a belligerent crouch, as if he expected his brother to spring for him then and there. When no attack came, it infuriated him further. "What's the matter with you, man? You hand over your balls when you put on that pretty blue coat? Didn't you hear what I *called* you? That mean nothing?"

Sanchi saw two security people stroll into the restaurant, playing it casual. The waitress who had made the call hurried over to brief them—not that it was necessary. Alonso's continued loud posturings would have tipped off a deaf man.

Sanchi let out a long breath. Weariness made him feel old. "I know that what you said isn't so. If I beat you to a pulp, will that convince you? You won't believe the truth about how I got that gold, and I can't really blame you for that, but I never did anything shameful to earn it. There's no reason to fight you over a lie."

*"Who are you calling a li—?"*

A heavy hand fell on 'Lonso's shoulder. "Excuse me, sir, but would you please come with us?" The security agent had no need to raise his voice. Like O'Connor, his size alone was argument enough for instant cooperation. 'Lonso was drunk, but he wasn't stupid. He shut his mouth and let the men escort him from the restaurant. Sanchi made no move to follow, and 'Lonso didn't bother with goodbyes.

"Don't worry, Sanchez." Like a shadow, Gemma had stolen up behind him. Her cool, clipped words were gentled by a smile. "Every family's got one." She slipped onto the stool beside him, ordering coffee as if she were a British peeress instructing her butler to pour the wine.

"Maybe I'd better go after him." Sanchi felt ready to be evicted from his own skin. Gemma's golden perfection always had that unsettling effect, made worse whenever she acted friendly. "The kid's crazy. God knows what he'll do."

"He'll go throw up and head for home when he's hungry. Relax, enjoy what's left of your break. He's living with you now, right? How did you ever get roped into that?"

"Long story." He tried leaving, but Gemma laid her hand on top of his on the counter and pressed down.

"I'll bet you could tell it to me in three minutes if you tried."

There was no way out but surrender. "It's a favor to my mother. He was getting in trouble at home, running around with a gang, skipping school. When he dropped out altogether, she called me. His father's dead, there's no man in the house, and Mother can't manage him." He couldn't call her "Mama" with those blue, blue eyes watching him.

"So she wished him on you. Too bad. Well"—she acknowledged the arrival of her coffee with an automatic nod to the waitress and drank it black and steaming—"if you need to teach the little whelp manners, I'll lend you my gun." She relished his startled expression—could anyone who looked like Gemma wield more than a rolled-up copy of *Town and Country*?—but said no more and allowed him to leave the counter.

Sanchi went through the rest of his shift in a daze. She had come too close, too deliberately. Why? He wasn't sure what it meant, if it meant anything. Old dreams of his returned, left over from the time when he'd imagined that a college education would purchase his mother's admiration.

There had been women like Gemma there, at the school where a scholarship could do nothing to open the unseen doors. What he felt for them—so white and golden, so much the product of "classical education" families—was an unformed yearning that left only shame and humiliation in its wake when they looked right through him. He was not unacceptable, merely inappropriate.

The few who did acknowledge his existence did so with the self-conscious air of anthropologists in relentless pursuit of the ethnic, missionaries out to convert the heathen, or social workers self-bound to condescend or die. He reached his limit on the day that one of those long-limbed daughters of Wall Street asked him to join her for coffee, only to try engaging him in an earnest discussion of subway graffiti. She was doing a sociology paper and it wasn't every day she could corner a native informant.

"Why do you do it?" she asked. "Really?"

"I never did."

She laughed away his denial. *Everybody* knew certain unassailable truths. "No, really. You can tell me."

"Look, I am telling you. I never went in for that. I never wanted to, and Papi would've had a fit if I did."

"Oh. Really." She looked at him as if he were a liar, or a traitor.

He couldn't live like that. He left school because it taught him too much.

But Gemma hadn't seemed to lower herself or to treat

him like a 7-Eleven store of the Minority Experience. He didn't know what she wanted, and he couldn't begin to sort out how he'd feel if—*milagro!*—she saw him as nothing more than a man.

O'Connor noticed Sanchi's distraction, as he noticed everything, and took him off surveillance. Besides, the mysterious big-time winner hadn't deigned to come back from lunch today. He might not be back at all.

Gemma was fascinated. There was nothing more diabolical about Dolmades than an unreliable egg salad sandwich. That changed immediately, astonishingly, when he came in. It was more than his subdued, expertly tailored wardrobe, the trim black beard and mustache, or those burning blue-green eyes. Something hovered about him, woven of shadows and silence. She was drawing out the consumption of a second cup of coffee and darting more and more frequent glances at the clepsydra when he sat beside her.

"Well?" From his pocket he took a handful of the many chips he had won at baccarat that morning, made them into a neat stack, and pushed it near her elbow without looking at her directly.

"You know that those won't do me any good," Gemma replied just over the lip of her cup. "I'm an employee."

"You mistake an offer of price for actual payment." He cleared half the stack's substantial height. The chips didn't even click in his fingers. "I hope the accuracy of your report is not similarly affected by greed."

Gemma's pale, fine face tightened. He knew where to insert the blade better than any surgeon. If she had half the pride she pretended to, she should have gotten up and thrown the chips in his face or, less melodramatically, swept them onto the floor and let him crouch to recover them.

Ah, but would he?

"His name is Sanchez Rubio. He was raised in New York City, probably born there too. He's living in a boardinghouse here—do you want the address?"

"Unnecessary."

"With his brother. *Half* brother," she corrected herself. "When he talked about him, it sounded as if they have the same mother, but different fathers. I'm assuming his father's

38

dead; the half brother's definitely is. And that kid is a son of a bitch."

"I am not paying you for character analysis of Mr. Rubio's family." The dark man let the chips pour from his fingers back atop the stack. "What more did you learn of his past?"

"Nothing. Yet." Gemma couldn't keep the resentful snap out of her voice. He had no right to address her like that, like a servant. "I've hardly said two words to him that weren't strictly business before now. Do you want me to become his confidante in five minutes? 'Hi, Sanchez, glad to see you, let's go to bed'?" She wanted to use a more vulgar term, to shock this man, but breeding was too strong a bridle on her tongue. Her mother's icy disapproval of all things common, from linens to language, was still there.

"No, of course not." The gentleman pocketed the chips and produced a more satisfactory-looking roll of bills instead. He counted off the value of the chips, slipped it into an empty traveler's-check wallet, and set it between them. "I beg your pardon. My interest overwhelmed me. Discretion is more important than my impatience. But if you can tell me more, you'll find me suitably generous."

"Why are you so interested in Sanchez?"

"That is something that need not interest you."

There being no further need for conversation, he left. Gemma pocketed the black plastic billfold and put down a precisely percentaged tip.

She did not return directly to work. She still had some time left on her break, and she could put it to good use.

The glassed-in elevator gave her the sensation of flying, even more so when it seemed to break through the roof of Dionysia into the open air. The view of the boardwalk, the beach, the ocean, the other hotels, was breathtaking. She could almost believe that she was free of the earth and all its importuning voices.

The feeling didn't last. She sighed as she stepped out onto the penthouse level and rang the doorbell of the Daedalus suite.

The door peeled open to the width of an eyeball. "What do you want?" The gatekeeper didn't sound as tough as Gemma remembered him. The first time, she had actually imagined that she was going to be murdered if her answers weren't exactly correct. This time he sounded less powerful, more human, even a little shaken.

"I have something to report. May I come in?"

"I don't know . . ." Again that impression of strength, once present, now drained away. "She's sleeping."

"For this, I am awake. Let her in, Tri." The other voice rippled through the crack in the door, sending tremors through the small hairs just below Gemma's tight chignon. The door opened farther, and a long white hand tipped with gold-painted fingernails extended itself invitingly. "Tell me, my child. Enter and tell me everything."

Gemma stepped inside and the door whispered shut.


# CHAPTER FOUR: News from Home

It was evening when the girl finally found Sanchi's address. Her legs ached, not so much because of the distance from the bus stop as from the fact that she'd foolishly chosen to wear high heels.

*"Como si ser adulto fuera solamente cambiarse de ropa,"* she murmured, awkwardly lugging the battered suitcase along beside her and trying not to knock herself off her own teetery shoes. "You'd think that by now I'd know myself. This is all stage-dressing; I *hate* heels. *Madre de la Virgen,* is Sanchi going to need to see me staggering along on these things to know I'm grown up? Papi, I don't know where you get some of your ideas." It was an honest complaint, but in spite of pain and weariness and irritation, she couldn't keep the love out of her voice when she said her father's name.

She waited on the porch for what seemed like a week before Sanchi's landlady deigned to answer the doorbell. "We're full up" was that lady's way of greeting a visitor. The thin whinny of a sitcom laughtrack wafted out the door.

"I don't want a room, I want to see one of your tenants."

"Yeah?" Blatant suspicion. "Which one?"

"Sanchez Rubio."

The landlady snuffled something that might have been assent or dismissal. She closed the door without bothering to ask the caller to wait inside. Only the fact that the door opened again fairly quickly kept the girl from taking off one of her high heels to do a little impromptu percussion on the aluminum.

It was Sanchi, and there was nothing hesitant or doubtful in the joy that bloomed across his face when he saw her.

*"Elena!"*

His arms hooked under hers and swirled her around and around on the porch in a wild reel. "Elena, Elena, Elenita!" Every reiteration of her name made him swing her higher and higher until one of the despised high heels went flying over the porch rail.

"Sanchi, my shoe!"

That made him set her down and look shamefaced. He bounded down the steps, vanished around the side of the house, and returned with the flying piece of footwear. "Sorry. I was just so glad to see you."

Elena giggled as she hopped on one foot trying to reshoe the other. "So I gathered. Can you have visitors in your room if you vouch for me? The way the landlady looked at me, I bet now she thinks streetwalkers make housecalls."

She wasn't sure if she entirely liked the way Sanchi looked at her—a look that defied anyone to believe that *his* Elenita even knew the meaning of the word "sex."

"You're family," he said. "If she doesn't like it, too bad. Come on in."

On the way up the stairs, Elena sifted through the many scents of the boardinghouse: too much cabbage and not enough ventilation, too many cats and not enough attention to the litter tray, too much reliance on flower-scented aerosol sprays to cover the ubiquity of liquor, urine, sweat, human stagnation, and not enough plain cleaning. Elena decided that if Mama could smell how Sanchi was living, she'd haul him back to New York by the ear, and forget about how old he was!

"Hey, *hermano,* what's this? You finally getting lucky?"

Elena froze in the doorway. So Papi had heard right.

The kid sprawled on the one bed in the room and looked as if he owned the place. Elena's scowl slackened a little when she saw the packed grip beside the bed. Could she hope that he was leaving, or was he just so damned lazy that he hadn't unpacked yet? Earnestly she prayed to be right on the first count: Let her only see him safely out of Sanchi's hair and she could go home with head held high, mission accomplished.

"Watch your mouth, Alonso. Someday one stupidity too many's going to slip out. This is Elena Sanchez."

"*Papi's* little girl?" The mock marvel in his voice made Elena's lips compress hard. Mama could deplore her only daughter's temper all she wanted, Elena had never managed to develop any patience for smartasses. Her first impulse was still to kick them right where they were smartest. "Not so little, now," 'Lonso added. He did everything but lick his lips.

Elena fixed her thoughts and her eyes on the pitiful ghost of a mustache straggling across Alonso's upper lip one bristle at a time. It was physical evidence of how young he was, but he'd taken adolescence as an excuse for obnoxiousness. Sweat dewed it, plastered down his hair. He could have been attractive without that leer, those shameless eyes that made no secret of how he was looking at her.

*So, another Cristóbal Colón of sex,* Elena thought. She managed to give Alonso a polite smile, then turned to Sanchi as if they were alone.

"Listen, Sanchi, I hate to do this to you, but I need your help, OK? I need somewhere to live."

"How about right here, *chica?*" Alonso patted the mattress.

Elena looked at him and did her best to put on the same gently condescending martyr's mask her grandmother—her beloved Mamacita—used whenever another one of Papi's stray cats got sick on the kitchen floor. "Honey, would you run downstairs and ask the landlady if she's got a phone book we could use? Thanks." Whether he went for the book or not was immaterial. In her eyes he'd been pigeonholed as a second-rate fetch-and-carry, and she'd let him know it.

Alonso didn't move, but he didn't try opening a wise mouth anymore either. Elena let him sulk, and Sanchi tried hard not to smirk over the way she'd handled the kid.

"Well, Sanchi?" she asked. "Can you help me?"

"Sure I can," he said. "But first things first. What are you doing here? Last I heard, you'd finished college, you were maybe going on to nursing school. Atlantic City's not exactly famous for that kind of education."

Elena took a deep breath, cleared her mind for the first of many lies. "I'm not so sure nursing's what I want anymore. I thought maybe I should take a year off, think about it. But you know how it is at home. Mama would be asking me every second day whether I'd made up my mind yet, and Mamacita would take over asking on the days Mama missed."

Sanchi's eyes half closed. *Home.* He remembered: the old kitchen table where everyone worked and ate and quarreled and loved; the ever-present sound of cats and kittens meowing as they were fussed over, nursed back to health by Papi and Mama, Mamacita and Elena, sometimes by some of the boys, until Papi took them away to the new homes he magicked up out of thin air and persuasive words; Mamacita hovering over him as he did his homework, hushing anyone who dared to disturb her Sanchi's concentration. Not even Papi was immune. He was Mamacita's own son, and she wasn't shy about shushing him so that Sanchi could work in peace and become something, be somebody. . . .

*I've let you down, Mamacita.* Bitterness filled his heart. *I was nothing when Papi took me in and I'm still nothing.*

Elena didn't notice how his face suddenly lost all joy. She was only partway through her carefully prepared recitation. "So anyway, I had to get away, get out of New York City to think—just do some plain work to support myself until I have this figured out."

"Live away from home? On your own?" Sanchi had to laugh. "Maybe I'd better open the door right now, before Papi breaks it down and drags you back to the city. If you ran away, I don't want to be your accomplice."

Elena made a wry mouth. "Listen to you! Want a refresher course about what century this is? I'm a full, legal adult, a college graduate, and you're acting like I'm still six years old."

"Because that's how Papi sees you, Elena. Seriously, how did you give him the slip?"

"Papi knows I'm here." The words came more easily. At least that much wasn't a lie. "We compromised. I could go somewhere out of town so long as it wasn't that far away and I had relatives there who could look out for me. So how about it, Sanchi? Do you feel up to playing the watchdog?"

"You sure you want that, *chica?*" Alonso had gotten his second wind. "That one follows so close, he drools on your shoes."

"You won't have too worry about that much longer, 'Lonso," Sanchi replied. "Soon as you get on that bus tomorrow, you're free of me, drool and all."

Elena went limp with relief inside. *So the little brat's going back to Mother. Good. That'll make it easier to talk to Sanchi and get him straightened out, then it's back to New York and—*

"I changed my mind, *hermano,*" Alonso said. He sat upright on the bed, hooked his bag over with one foot, and released the catch. "I'm going to stay."

He spoke to Sanchi, but stared at Elena. He showed her that she wasn't the only one who could communicate without words. The difference in their ages, the plain fact that she couldn't stand him, Sanchi's rising anger, all meant nothing to him. The wicked flicker in his eyes told her: Now there was something in Atlantic City worth staying for.

# CHAPTER FIVE: Promenade

The view of Atlantic City that Gemma had so enjoyed from the glassed-in elevator car was a poor cousin to the panorama visible from the penthouse suite itself. It was beautiful, especially at night, and therefore the more precious, the less to be shared with the unworthy. The sphynx had banished all her unwitting human servants. She sat alone at her desk overlooking the sea.

Gold-tipped fingernails slit open the last of the envelopes addressed to Ianthe Apeiron. It was from Damion. Amber eyes swept over the pleas of a man in the last stages of financial desperation. Were the rumors true? he demanded. A strange demand, when she could almost hear the pitiful whining in his voice. Was she truly bent on ruining him? Didn't she know that the company was his heritage, his family's pride, his very life? Couldn't she call off her agents, give him a little more time?

And then, what he no doubt considered to be the unanswerable argument: Didn't the past mean anything to her?

The sphynx smiled. She was fond of questions that carried several possible replies but only one true answer.

When he spoke of the past, he meant those trifling few years she had spent alternating between his bed and the gaming tables, likewise the beds of other fools as blind to her deliberate philanderings as he. How alike, how remarkably alike they were, all of her lovers! Each flattered himself into believing that he was, if not the first, then the best, the most memorable, the sole experience she would cherish even after they parted.

In a way, each was right. The sphynx did not forget. Her memories had no limits, for they fed her dreams, and her dreams were eternal. From each lover she stole a measure of his self—knowledge, strength, cunning, insight, whatever best suited her desires—and left him lessened. Such gifts were memorable indeed. They had made her what she was.

Lamias only drank blood. So did she, when she could get it, when she wished to do so, as the whim touched her. But she did not need human blood to survive. She could live as long on broiled mullet, steamed beet greens, raw windfall apples. She had even developed a fondness for Godiva chocolates, of late. Blood and flesh, bone and marrow of mortal creatures were mere symbols for what truly fed her, just as the words of their ineffective human languages were only symbols for things whose true nature they would never understand.

Didn't the past mean anything to her? Oh yes, Damion, more than you will ever know. The past was built out of visions of broken wings and breast fur split by the shafts of stone-headed spears, fangs clenched in useless snarls as the mothers fell dead over cubs already slaughtered. It was walled by the death-glazed eyes of her kin and the staring eyes of men—first fearful, then confident, then gloating in their triumph at how easily they exterminated the race of "monsters" in the hills.

*We were all young,* she thought. *Young as the earth was young. If they had let us live, we would have come into the true strength only I have lived long enough to achieve. We were forged of the hidden powers, meant to grow and learn the wondrous magic of the Riddle. So long as we hold the Answer, let their silly weapons try to harm us!*

*We* . . . The word came back to mock her solitude. Winged ghosts drifted past the curved glass wall, riding the briny air. The lone years never lost a single grain of bitterness for her. A mind trained to perfect memory, to hold so many riddles, had its disadvantages.

Only half aware, the sphynx allowed her human face to show the signs of weariness. Faint smudges, blue-gray, appeared beneath her glowing eyes. *We might have taught them so much. So young, we were! Why did the gods not set us down on this world earlier than men, to let us mature, to wrap our rightful strength around us like wings of stone? An ignorant child can kill a new-hatched eaglet, but when the bird has grown—Neither race knew the other's limitations. We were surprised by the attack, overwhelmed by their audacity and their numbers. I thought that they were gods, come to destroy us for some offense we had commited without knowing. Gods do not explain their cruelties.*

Her perfect mind relived the horrors of the slaughter, the desperation of her flight. Her tender wings were not yet strong enough to bear her weight. That might have been the saving of her, for the men had come with nets as well as spears. Chubby baby paws scrabbled up a narrow path on the cliff's face. Thorns tattered her fur, still stippled with the marks of extreme youth. The pads of her paws bled freely. It was a miracle that the men did not think to follow the blood trail.

The sphynx did not believe in miracles; only the whims of chance. It was a small cave the orphaned creature discovered and made her own. Her nose twitched, again breathing in the scents of bird and bat droppings.

*I was still just a cubling when I first suspected that perhaps they were not gods after all.* The taste of first blood returned to her tongue. Her wings were stronger. She had stooped to kill a spring lamb that had wandered too far from one of the humans' herds. Soon she learned that she could take other prey as well.

*I grew, I watched them from the cliffside, and knew that I was older, stronger, wiser than they. From gods they dwindled into cattle; there is a riddle. And what a measure of their smallness it was when ignorance of their own nature made them my victims for so long.*

The sphynx closed her eyes. She had dismissed her men to patrol the gaming tables downstairs, to watch for the coming of the sorcerer. She doubted he would be fool enough to appear at night, when her strength was greatest, but you never knew. And that tow-haired wench had claimed she had the means to lure him to Dionysia after sunset.

Well, let her try. She fancied herself very sly, that one. No doubt she thought that she would gain more than a spy's wages from her mistress, given time. It was laughable, how easily that Gemma allowed her own riddle to be read—for each mortal was just that, in the end: a riddle to crack open like a bone. What was Gemma's riddle, then? Only a variation on the Great Riddle of this land.

> "Three there are and three there be,
> Each will gain the rest for thee:
> Flesh to flesh in burning hold;
> Song of silver, chink of gold;
> Power to make others bend.
> None the Answer in the end."

Softly she crooned the Riddle of Three Answers she had woven ever since the sorcerer Vergilius had brought her oversea. Money and sex and power, and the conviction that mastery of one would inevitably fetch its master the other two. Gemma was a mirror of that Riddle; a very small and tarnished one. Most likely she thought that her beauty would seduce the wizard, and in gratitude for bringing him down, "Ianthe Apeiron" would open the coffers of her fortune to the faithful servant, perhaps even take the wench into one of the many multinational companies she controlled.

The sphynx opened her eyes and saw two tawny paws lying atop the letter on her desk, claws pinning the paper to the powder-blue blotter. She reforged her human guise and jotted a few lines across the bottom of the page. The acquisition was to go through. If at all possible, the stockholders in Damion's endangered company were to be made aware of the affair he had had with her. He was a married man. Let envy of his wealth couple with false moral indignation to win them over to her side. The gambit was cheap and obvious, but it might save her agents a few dollars per share in their tender-offer maneuverings. This battle was hardly a challenge, so why not make it that much easier?

To hold the Riddle was strength; to speak the Answer, salvation.

She was tired of playing the little game. She took a silk coccoon-jacket from her bedroom closet and let the twilight folds of blue and gray and muted green fall about her.

The stir she made downstairs was satisfactory. She never tired of their attention, though she alternately assumed the correct celebrity roles of fearsomely bored and dangerously irritated. The moment she entered the lobby, two of the handpicked men assigned to watch for her arrival strode up and flanked her, with professional indifference to begging the pardon of lesser beings who happened to be between them and their employer. They were too large to make argument wise, large enough to belong to an era when courtesy consisted of merely crippling your rival for life.

She went to the roulette table first, and chose to lose heavily for effect. Beneath thick wings of black hair secured with diamond clips, her ears could swivel with more than human agility, unperceived, to catch the faintest whispers. Covertly she observed her fellow players.

They in turn observed her. A blade-cheeked creature in unbecoming yellow taffeta was nudging her elderly escort's attention back to herself by swearing that Ianthe Apeiron was no more a Greek heiress than a codfish. The silver-templed gentleman replied, "Shut up," and wasted a slavish smile on the sphinx as he offered her a cigarette.

"No thank you." The sphinx never took her eyes from the wheel as yet another stack of her chips was raked away. To the pinch-mouthed yellow moth she added, "But Leila, darling"—how easy to overhear a stranger's name at the tables!—"I thought you told me you'd *ordered* him to stop smoking!" She left the table while the couple began to sort out just who had the power to order whom.

She spotted the young man playing blackjack. Even at the crowded table, with smoke hanging in dusty ribbons from the ceiling and the dealer fast passing from starch to rumples, he stood out: bronze skin, honeyed hair, eyes that incredible shade of deepest amethyst.

*Beautiful.* She had been born with an appreciation for

beauty. Mortals who imagined that they shared that same appreciation knew nothing. In them, the taste had to be learned, cultivated, forced into being. If it had been a natural part of their souls, they never would have destroyed so much loveliness with their repetitive stupidities.

Oh, what a face that young man had! Eyes that held the soul accessible, lips she could taste with a glance. She wasted no time in taking the stool beside him, after first dismissing her attendants. They made no demur. Though they now wore tuxedos instead of denim jackets, most of their education had taken place in the streets, where the first lesson was when not to ask questions.

A few moments by his side, and the sphynx saw grace of movement matched to beauty. But what a waste, such riches scattered in the midst of mortals! *Like a Corinthian vase turned into a pisspot,* she thought. *Cathay silk wrapping a dunghill.*

It didn't take long. It never did. When she left the casino with him, her attendants fell into the disciplined drill that diverted anyone from following her out with her latest acquisition.

He didn't ask her name, because every habitué of Dionysia knew Ianthe Apeiron, and she did not ask his because it was irrelevant. Within moments after she had directed him to remove his shoes and stroll the beach with her, he was trying to impress her with his own wealth, his casual disinterest in her as a person but his willingness to bed her, if she insisted.

*Money and sex and power,* the sphynx thought, watching him preen. *Not one of your kind but lives in the heart of that Riddle. If your beauty does not place me in your power, you are making sure that I know you have money too. Poor toy. But you are very pretty. If there is more to you than this small dance, I may relent.*

The ancient song rose in her throat, a purr of melody. All the magic she had stolen from Vergilius blended with her own ancient mastery of the Great Riddle. Reality heard the song of the sphynx, and slipped gracefully from one disguise into another. Appearances shifted softly.

He did not notice how the moonlight hazed away as they meandered arm in arm into the lee of the boardwalk. The supports rose gradually, steel becoming flower stalk. The salt-bleached and wind-worn boards stretched out like sheltering hands above their heads to hide them from sight. The lights from the hotels, the neon signs, the streetlamps all merged into a warm glow that was neither darkness nor light.

In the heart of the shining shadow around them, she maintained the illusion that she was Ianthe Apeiron—very rich, very beautiful, and entitled by reason of wealth and beauty to be as capricious as she pleased.

"Tell me something," she said to him, settling her arm closer around his waist, lifting her mouth to be kissed.

"Anything at all," he answered, still playing quite a different game.

His mouth tasted hot and sweet. Her hands had no trouble undoing his tie, and the buttons of his shirt. She felt his heart lurch, then leap into a faster beat as she caressed the warmth of his bared chest with knowing fingertips. His smile broke on a jagged breath. His arms were crushing her urgently against his lovely body.

"Tell me something," she repeated, having stripped away his frivolous shell as easily as wresting a ragdoll from a child. "Tell me." And mind to mind she sang him the Riddle she had made for him:

> *It fades, it flies, it lives, it dies,*
> *And only gone, it treasured lies*
> *In its possessor's memory,*
> *And in the seed once sown cries, "See!*
> *The everlost, the used-to-be."*

The shell of darkness and light she had conjured around them pulsed with the power of the Riddle. As much as she hated the race of man, she had evolved into artist enough to cherish their most lovely creations, whether these sprang from the hands, the imagination, or the mere blind act of begetting a being who looked like this. Her eyes were silver mirrors. She let him see his own image in them, even though such a flagrant hint might cost her this play. In the great gamble that underran the great Riddle, she often took such chances. If he answered correctly, she would lose, as she had lost only once before Vergilius had bound her. She consoled herself with the thought that at least now she was wise enough not to go flinging herself over cliffsides in a tantrum.

But he was like the rest of them. His eyes stared bleakly into hers and saw his own face without seeing anything more. "I—I don't know what you're talking about, Ianthe," he stammered. "What do you mean?"

"That is for you to answer."

"But I can't—" Fear rose in his voice as he stared at her, though no man would see anything extraordinary about the lady except her exotic beauty. Indeed, the longer he gaped at Ianthe Apeiron, the more beautiful she seemed to be, beautiful within, beautiful without, beautiful in a way that was more precious because beauty itself was such an evanescent thing. There was beauty in her looks and in her movements, beauty in her voice and in the very air that touched her, beauty so strong that all the world seemed to thrum with the word in an endless chant of *beauty, beauty, beauty* . . .

And it terrified him.

"Answer me," she said, leaning towards him expectantly, the gilded fingernails beginning to curve into tiny sickles. The power of the Riddle held him captive. It twisted into a travesty of the cord linking mother to unborn child, and through it she began to sense the draining of his spirit into hers as the unanswered Riddle drank him down.

It was a kindness to kill him. The same claws that had traced teasing patterns around his nipples now opened his chest from one to the other, flesh and bone. What little light the Riddle had left in his eyes went out, but before it was entirely gone she told him the answer, so that his spirit could go free.

"I am not human," she said aloud as she knelt beside his corpse. Ianthe Apeiron's body crouched, furred and winged and taloned as the pale face dipped down to lap blood. "I am merciful."

# CHAPTER SIX:
## Lady's Choice

Everyone noticed Ianthe Apeiron's return to the casino, but
no one thought it very remarkable that she returned alone.
There were a hundred possible explanations, the most logical of which was that she had found the merchandise unacceptable once she got it out into the moonlight. It happened.
As for the handsome young man, there were so many of
them hanging around the casinos, different but interchange-
able, like Cabbage Patch dolls. It was so easy to forget the
particulars of his appearance, and so convenient to do so.
At Dionysia, you paid attention to the games, not the people. The sole exception was Ianthe Apeiron; she was worth
watching.

As always, it gratified the sphynx to have the humans
stare at her. What piqued her peculiar sense of humor most
was the thought of how much harder they would stare if
they only knew. She saw her bodyguards hurrying to meet
her, but warned them off with the subtlest of hand signals.
They were paid to be perceptive as well as obedient; they
hung back to let their mistress indulge her thirst for the
spotlight.

If the sphynx's mind had not been so pleasantly abstracted
by thoughts of her recent escapade, she would have moved
less languidly and not lingered to strike smug poses in the
doorway to impress the gawkers. She also would have seen
the young person racing straight for the very exit she so
charmingly blocked. He showed no care for how stunning
she looked or how rich she must be. Likewise he showed no
visible intention of slowing, stopping, or even swerving. The
boy jostled roughly past the lady without a by-your-leave,
giving her a startlingly firm elbow to the ribs in his haste to
leave Dionysia. Ianthe Apeiron uttered a little gasp and
staggered aside as he hustled through, out into the night.

Her bodyguards saw, and started spewing apologies even

as they sprinted across the casino floor to reach her. Within seconds of the minor assault, the largest man was snapping out commands for a team to follow the kid and teach him some manners.

Ianthe laid an apparently gentle hand on the big man's arm. If he seemed to wince at her touch, perhaps it was some trick of the casino lights.

"No, Tri," she told him. "I think that one is too young to endure one of your 'lessons.' But do follow him." This soft command was addressed to the six other men now surrounding her. "He is fast and he is young. Also bold. He might be interesting. Perhaps he will be worth some of my teachings."

The men wasted no time in obeying, though the sphynx thought she detected a look of pity in more than one departing face. She shrugged it off and decided to try the dice for a change.

'Lonso ran out of the casino and across the boardwalk, hating every loud reverberation of his pelting feet over the planks. Maybe the cops were after him, maybe not, but it didn't pay to stand around and find out. He cursed his own clumsiness and stupidity. The purse had looked so perfect, so tempting! The twirling lights of the ceiling mirrorball made a rainbow twinkle from the rhinestone clasp, the gold lamé fabric.

Just because the lady had laid her purse on the table beside her and wasn't paying attention didn't mean she hadn't asked someone else to keep an eye on it.

*Damn!* 'Lonso's shoulder still hurt. A fresh throb of pain shot through it with every other step. Jesus, the size of that security guy! He'd never seen a set of shoulders that wide on anything human, or felt a hand with all the pliability of a leghold trap close on his arm. If not for a quick twist that nearly dislocated his shoulder and a damned lucky kick, he'd still be in there, waiting for the cops to come collect him. Even so, with his captor doubled over in pain, it had taken a real wrench of his bones to escape.

'Lonso vaulted the boardwalk railings and dropped to the sand. He scuttled under the planking like a crab seeking the sea and ran on, but with self-satisfied stealth, the sand absorbing his footfalls. Overhead he could hear passing feet, a few voices, the occasional wayward strand of music from the hotels. As long as he didn't hear anything like deliberate pursuit, he was happy.

He came out from under as soon as he thought it was safe. He was too smart to stay under the boardwalk longer than he had to. The things you found down there had better reasons than his for keeping out of the light. He had enough troubles without doing heavy shopping for more.

Down the beach from Dionysia, he climbed back onto the boardwalk and took his bearings. There was the Atlantis, and there was Caesar's; swell. Irritably he shifted his shoulder. The hell with it—he should've had that purse. Back home, he'd developed just the right edge for a snatch like that, checking out all possible watchers, getting away clean. This time, not only had he come near to being nabbed, he'd bumped that woman in the doorway. Any delay could make a difference. He was losing it, getting soft, turning into just the kind of pussy his old friends used to trash for the fun of it.

He felt secure enough to lean back on the boardwalk railings and have a smoke. OK, so he'd missed; there'd be other times. He was still fast, and stronger than he looked. Just let Sanchi try throwing it around with him once too often and he'd show him how a man could fight. Age didn't mean crap, and size only counted when he was taken off-guard.

Sanchi. He had to laugh, sending out little ragged puffs of smoke on the night air. There were times he found it impossible to believe that his big brother had actually lived in New York City for so many years and survived. Trusting? Gullible? Downright dumb? Any and all of those terms applied to the man. When 'Lonso came in and told him he'd gotten a night-shift kitchen job at another hotel, Sanchi swallowed the story whole.

*"Good for you, 'Lonso."* That's all he'd said, hadn't even asked which hotel. *"You won't regret it. Want to call Mama and tell her? It'll make her happy."*

'Lonso lifted his lip a little at that idea. *"Nah, I think I'll save it; surprise her with my first paycheck."* Mama wasn't half the jackass Sanchi was. If he told her he had a job at some hotel, she'd be on the phone so fast, checking out his story, that it'd melt the wires. It was her damned double-checking on the stuff he told her back home that had landed him here. She found out about the gang, about school, and she raised a five-borough stink. He could've told her to stick it, but she was like a bulldog: When she had something in her jaws, she held on. She meant it when she threatened to bug hell out of the cops until they cracked down on his friends, and she was expert at being an ass-pain. The cops would start riding the gang hard, just to shut her up, and the gang would find out who was behind all that sudden attention.

She was still his mother. He didn't want them coming after her. He knew too well what they did when people got in their way; he'd helped do it. So he caved, let her think she'd won. No more running with the gang, she'd said. She wasn't going to have a son of hers doing that.

But when it came to giving him something else to do—to paying attention to him long enough to help him find a good place in the world—that was another story. The only half-way positive thing she ever did for him was ship him off to Sanchi and wash her hands.

*"You're a big boy,"* she used to say. *"Your father made something of himself out of nothing, and he wasn't always whining around asking someone else to fix up his life! If he were alive, he'd knock that whining right out of you, make you a real man. Not like that punk trash you hang out with. He caught you with them, he'd—"*

Yeah, what wouldn't his old man do? What *couldn't* he do? Somewhere in back of Mama's screaming and nagging and bitching lay the truth about 'Lonso's father. To hear her go on, he was too good to be human, but human enough to smack hell out of a disobedient son. Half the time 'Lonso wished the old man were still alive just so he could see whether his father would try beating respect into him. He didn't want to believe that. He liked to think his father had been too smart to go for something that stupid; it never worked. If it did, Mama would've had him whipped into line long ago.

'Lonso finished his cigarette and flipped the butt over his shoulder onto the beach. The night was too beautiful to clutter up his mind with unpleasant thoughts. He watched couples stroll past, caught the glimmer of sequins, the sub-dued gleam of satin, the wink of gold. They acted as if he wasn't there—you needed a certain minimum income to make it into their reality. That made him smile, the way some of them figured property was a permanent part of them, like an arm or a leg, something they'd take to the grave because they owned the world and that was how they wanted it run.

Clearly they'd never heard of amputation. He made deliberately obnoxious mouth sounds and comments at the couples as they passed, ignored the angry, empty threats the men tossed after him. Blindsight worked two ways.

The boardwalk turned boring fast if you didn't have anything to spend or anyplace to go. 'Lonso left, only pausing long enough to shake the sand out of his sneakers. Back in the city streets, he lost some of his jauntiness. It hadn't been so much of a fun night, and baiting all the bozos in the world wasn't going to give him back his self-respect after that botched job in Dionysia. He didn't want to go back to that piss-poor boardinghouse and watch Sanchi snoring on the sofa. He toyed with the idea of finding Elena, playing up to her, apologizing for how he'd behaved. Women were suckers for a good apology. They were trained from birth to rush right in and tell the man never mind, it's OK, just don't do that again.

Of course you did it again. Then you apologized.

On second thought, he'd give Elena more time to forget their first meeting. She looked smart, for a woman. He knew it would be a different story if he had money. Then he could suggest they go somewhere, really impress her. So she was older; so what? He'd known older women before, thanks to his city friends. The women treated you like a kid until you showed them you could put down a man's stack of cash. Enough bills on the table and you could wear a Sesame Street bib and they wouldn't care.

Always the money. Like it worked on Mama, turning Sanchi into some kind of hero. Like it worked on turning no into yes, a sarcastic laugh into *Anything you say, 'Lonso, honey*. Like it would work on Elena.

He saw the old woman about a block off. She had a plastic shopping bag on her left arm, her pocketbook tucked up safely against her body on the same side. She probably imagined that anyone trying to snatch it would think twice—the purse strap would tangle with the shopping-bag handles and make the job too inconvenient.

What was a little inconvenience? And why guard something so closely if there wasn't something worthwhile inside? 'Lonso grinned for the invisible audience of his absent friends and took off. He hit the old lady hard from behind, knocked her to the sidewalk. She screamed, but one kick in the head convinced her not to do that again. Blood spurted from her nose; broken. She lay on the sidewalk, staring up at him, terrified. He recognized that look; it always made his smile a little wider.

*Probably thinks I'm going to rape her, too. Stupid old bitch.* He blew her a kiss and laughed at how she shook. As he yanked the pocketbook away, he noticed that her right arm was hanging a little funny, crumpled up. He noticed it the same way he noticed that the neon BUDWEISER sign he ran past had a burned-out U.

They were waiting for him. He didn't have a chance to wonder how they got there or why there were so many of them. A fist the size of a grapefruit slammed into his cheek, and that was all he took with him into the darkness.

The police officer was polite, but suspicious. "You saw him grab the lady's purse?"

Tri shrugged, a truly impressive gesture. "I thought I heard a scream and then I saw this kid come running around the corner with that in his hands." He pointed to the recovered pocketbook. A second officer was simultaneously trying to comfort the victim and explain to her that they had to take her purse down to the station to be registered as evidence. She was still begging to get it back when the ambulance arrived.

"And what were you doing in the neighborhood, sir?"

Tri liked the way the cop almost choked over calling him "sir." Not so long ago, he would've been the one the cops were booking. Reflectively he ran his tongue over three front teeth that had been broken stubs when the sphynx first hired him, lost in a judicial dispute with one of Atlantic City's finest; Tri had won. Cosmetic dentistry, expense no object, had restored a perfect smile. He showed it off to full advantage, enjoying the whole charade, as he replied:

"I work for Ms. Ianthe Apeiron, as a bodyguard. I live in the hotel, but I'm off duty right now. I was visiting a friend. You want her name?" He gave the name and address of a hooker who could be trusted to swear to anything, sometimes on credit.

The cop shook his head. "What a night. Everything from petty crime to that body on the beach. OK, thanks for all your help."

"My pleasure," Tri said.

"Hey, Frank!" the second cop called to his buddy. "The victim told me she saw five other guys."

"What, with the perp?" Frank regarded Tri levelly. The bodyguard was big, but not big enough to take on six.

"Nah, with him." A jerk of the thumb indicated Tri.

The first policeman's brows came together. "So where's your friends?"

"Disneyland." Another shrug. "I was the only one, I swear. After what that punk kid did to that poor old lady, I wouldn't be surprised if she saw seven of me."

The cop wasn't quite ready to buy it off the rack, but it had been a rough night. His stomach still lurched at the description of the corpse Bill and Conrad had radioed in from the beach. It was gruesome enough to be a mob hit, and that's how it would probably wind up in the files—the UNSOLVED files. But what a way to kill someone. What kind of strength did it take to rip open a grown man's rib cage like that? Not even this creep looked powerful enough to do it.

"If we need more information, we'll call you," he told Tri.

"I'll be glad to help. That's Ms. Apeiron's number I gave you, but she won't mind. She's not American, but she's a great believer in our system."

"You don't have your own number?" The suspicion was back, triple-strength.

"I told you, I live in the hotel, part of Ms. Apeiron's suite extension. That's the best way to reach me, through her. Even when I'm not on duty, she knows where I am."

The cop wasn't paying much attention, and it was dark. Easy enough to miss the cornered look on Tri's face as he added, "She always knows." Impossible to hear the wraith of laughter that sounded for Tri's ears alone.

# CHAPTER SEVEN:
# Back-Alley Wizard

Sanchi woke up early, after a bad night. His back and legs were a dependable map of every crease and sprung spring on the sofa, and his mind felt like a crumpled washcloth. A glance at the untouched comfort of his rightful bed made everything hurt worse. 'Lonso hadn't even bothered to sleep at home.

Consciousness was too muzzy for him to feel more than vaguely worried about the kid's whereabouts. Resentment and a thousand bodily aches and pains pushed away the very real concern that something might have happened to his little brother. He decided to head for work, maybe pick up a bite of breakfast in the hotel, and coffee. Definitely, inescapably, vitally coffee. Dolmades was open early, for the red-eye crowd, and if he was feeling upscale, he might hold off on real food until break time, then treat himself to one of the fancy breakfasts Sybaris was famous for. But this above all: coffee.

Elena was standing between him and the caffeine. Even if she hadn't seen him for years, the girl should have known better. She was waiting for him just outside the male employees' lounge, looking pretty and fresh in her maid's uniform. Usually large quantities of well-bleached and starched linen on a woman were an aphrodisiac—witness the myth of the nurse-*cum*-temptress—but at this hour and in this condition, Sanchi would have bypassed the Playboy mansion and headed straight for Maxwell House. He grunted something bisyllabic at her and tried to forge past.

"Hey, what's with you, Sanchi? No hello? No 'Good morning, drop dead'?"

"Sorry," he said, with a face that said something else.

"Aha." Elena nodded wisely. "No breakfast yet, right? OK, go do what you have to in there and I'll bring you some take-out down from Dolmades. Large coffee and what with it?"

"Another large coffee. And a doughnut."

"So now you're a health freak. Plain or sugared? Never mind. Coffee-flavored if they've got it, *ya sé*."

She was gone and back in a satisfactorily short time. They sat together on a cushioned bench in the passageway while she unpacked two white paper bags and set out breakfast between them. She had bought him a couple of doughnuts and a fresh buttered hard roll to help anchor the morning brew. A quarter of the way down the first Styrofoam cup and Sanchi made an attempt at rejoining the human race.

" 'Lonso got a job," he told Elena.

"Great." Her response was about as sincere as his pre-caffeine greeting. "So did I, as you can tell." She fanned the skirt of her uniform. "And the place your landlady referred me to isn't half bad. The woman's even got an extra spare room that looks better than where you are now. Why don't you move?"

"Oh, it's OK where I am now."

"Yes, but this is better. Why not improve?"

Sanchi drained more of his coffee. He didn't like the soft but unmistakable sound of insistence in Elena's voice. Somewhere there was another shoe about to drop, and if he knew anything, it was poised right over his head.

"My place is OK," he repeated. "I'm used to it."

"You can get *used* to anything. That doesn't make it the best you can do. Sanchi, what's wrong with taking a step up, if you can? You could do it. You've got the brains."

"Since when do you need brains to move house? Somehow, *hermosa*, I get the feeling that you want me to change a lot more than just where I'm living." His smile was sad. "Confess, Elenita. Papi put you up to this, didn't he?"

Her face darkened like a thundercloud as she tried to drum up impromptu indignation. "What are you talking about? Put me up to what? If you want to live in a dump, live! I just thought you might want to do better. Where does Papi come in?"

"Nowhere, nowhere." The first cup of coffee was gone. Sanchi was able to make peace with the world. "My mistake." But he knew he hadn't been mistaken. *Improve* meant the same as *do better*, and Papi wasn't the man to smother his opinion that his fosterling Sanchi could do a lot better with his life than he was doing now.

"Look, I've got to get ready for work," Elena told him, rising from her seat. "Why don't we meet for lunch? When do you get off?"

"Sorry, Elenita, no can do. I'm being switched to the night shift. I just had to come in early today to get the details straightened out. I'll be going home at lunchtime, then coming back here much later. Sorry. But look, if you need me for anything . . ."

"I know where you live." Elena didn't sound thrilled to hold that information. She made one last stab, saying, "This new shift, it's nothing permanent, right? It'll last how long— one week? Two?"

"Until further notice. Which is to say, as good as permanent. I'm really sorry, *chica*. Now that you're working here, it would've been nice to see you more often, but—*qué va!*" He tried to sound mournful and resigned. A sigh helped.

Elena's mouth tightened into a bud of carefully contained sarcasm. "Yes, it would've been nice." She didn't give him the chance to add any more layers of gloss but made an exit as crisp as her uniform.

*Now I've done it* Sanchi thought. *Pissed her off, talked down to her. . . . When am I going to learn that she's not a little kid anymore? And she never was a stupid one. But she shouldn't think I'm stupid either. Papi's behind this, I know why, and I don't want any part of it.*

He cleared away the breakfast trash and went looking for O'Connor. Having unloaded the lie about his new work schedule, just to avoid Elena, he knew he'd better make it true.

O'Connor looked bemused by Sanchi's request for a transfer to the night shift. "Suits me, Rubio. I'll bet there's more than one family man on night hours who'd be glad to switch. I'll look into it." He made a note on his pocket pad.

"I want to start tonight," Sanchi blurted.

O'Connor's eyebrows rose. His Papermate hovered over the open pad in his palm. "Tonight? Kind of sudden, isn't it? It's not that easy. You can't pull your day shift now and still be at your best tonight."

"I want to go home now, rest, and come back later."

"Right. Leaving me short-handed."

"It's not a busy day, not many people, not like the week-

ends. Mr. O'Connor, if it gets heavy later, call me at home,
I'll come in earlier, but please—"

"What's with you?" O'Connor's mistrust grew in direct
proportion to the escalating rate of Sanchi's pleading. "Something the matter at home?"

It was a microscopically thin straw, but Sanchi nabbed it
with both hands and hung on. "Yes. It's my brother, Mr.
O'Connor."

"Your brother . . . you were with some rowdy kid in
Dolmades; was that—?"

Sanchi should have known. Nothing could ever happen
privately at Dionysia. Miserably he nodded. "That was
Alonso. He didn't come home last night. Maybe it's nothing—
he's old enough to take care of himself—but he's still only a
kid."

Now O'Connor was honestly concerned. "You called the
police?"

Sanchi managed to laugh. "I don't think—I hope I won't
have to. See, he's getting less wild; got a job for himself the
other day and maybe he went off to celebrate. It's on the
night shift too, not here, another hotel. I bet he's back at
the room right now, sleeping. I just want to be sure, and I
want to work the same hours he does, so I can keep tabs on
him better. I'm responsible for him."

O'Connor snapped his pad shut and tucked it into his
breast pocket right behind the sporty white handkerchief.
Every doubt was banished. "That's real nice, Rubio. From
what I heard, you've got your work cut out for you, baby-
sitting that one."

"What you heard—?" It hit him, sharp and sour: the
incident at Dolmades. Of course. Sanchi wondered whether
he was blushing like a woman, just from the remembered
shame.

If he was, O'Connor made no comment. "OK, you're
right, we're not expecting a big crush until evening. The
only thing is if that big winner comes back today, but— Oh,
what the hell, I'll have Gemma cover for you. And good
luck working with Jorgensen for a manager. He's not a
pushover like me."

That night, Sanchi found out that O'Connor was a shameless understater of facts. Tom Jorgensen was a native of

Minnesota and seemed to bring an aura of Minneapolis February everywhere he went. Sanchi's first impression of the man was an icicle with a crewcut. The New Yorker didn't have to wait long to learn that Jorgensen's first impression of his new man wasn't as complimentary as that, and he didn't hesitate saying so. In the Twin Cities, being plainspoken was a virtue. Bad enough getting a five-minute lecture on the shameful condition of his uniform, but Jorgensen was so tall that Sanchi got a crick in his neck just trying to look his new boss in the ice-blue eye during the harangue.

"I'm sorry, Mr. Jorgensen. I'll have it cleaned and pressed," Sanchi muttered. *Sure I will. And how am I going to manage the time for that?*

"See that you do." Jorgensen's thin nostrils flared once, smartly, scrupulously. Like every one of the man's gestures, it looked carefully calculated and meticulously rationed. "Welcome aboard." Warmth having been allotted, he turned on his heel and went back to important things.

Sanchi was too tired even to shrug. So what if his new boss would look more natural wearing a coat of scales and a layer of lake ice? It was a fitting ending for a day like this. After securing his escape from Elena, Sanchi had returned to the boardinghouse. Alonso still wasn't back, and Sanchi didn't wait for him. It took less than ten minutes for him to learn that the only thing more depressing than coming home to those shabby lodgings in the evening was hanging around them in full daylight.

He'd spent the day walking the beach, reading books in the public library, checking out an afternoon movie. By the time he showed up for work, his uniform had its own tale to tell. As he headed for his post patrolling one sector of the slot machines, he wondered whether it had all been worth the effort.

*Come on, you know it was!* His eyes burned with fatigue, but his thoughts remained clear as he watched Dionysia's assorted clientele at play. *Elena's here because Papi sent her. It'll be her voice, but his words: "Sanchi, go back to school, you've got brains, don't waste them. Sanchito, you can make something special of your life, I know you can, I've got faith. . . ." He means well, but he wouldn't know he was whipping a dead horse if he smelled it. Maids work days, so I just stay on the night side until she gets tired and goes home.*

Worn out as he was, he still had to smile. Judging from what little he'd seen, Elenita had inherited all of Papi's stubbornness and none of her mother's compliant disposition. She wouldn't be here, urging him back to a better life, if she didn't want to be.

The smile was weak. It froze and shattered easily when he saw the man come in. Sanchi knew him at once—O'Connor's mysterious big winner, now playing the odds by starlight. In the full tenue proper to accompany a black dinner jacket, he strolled calmly through the crush of old ladies, young couples, and slot-machine zombies, making for the baccarat tables. Sanchi couldn't help thinking how natural the dark man would look in a red-lined black satin cape with a faithful bat flapping over one shoulder.

It wasn't a bat that followed him, though. A red dragon writhed through the haze above the casino floor, floating over his head like a trained kite until it unraveled into streamers of ordinary cigarette smoke. Sanchi squinted his eyes shut and rubbed the bridge of his nose with pinching thumb and forefinger. When he looked again, the man was seated and hard at play, with no attendant phantoms.

More than anything, Sanchi wanted to turn and run, find Jorgensen, ask for the day-shift job back, claim he was sick, quit, anything. No one else in the casino had seen the dragon, but that didn't mean it was any less real. Eyes that had once witnessed magic, a life touched by enchantment, a young boy who had walked the streets of New York City as companion to a legend, these could not be blinked away.

In Sanchi's mind, a knight in armor stood tall, looked down sternly at his squire. *"Why do you tremble, Sanchi? We faced worse together, you and I."* Ghosts are only memories made visible, and more vulnerable therefor because banishing the sight likewise banishes the memory. The ghost of the knight Persiles dwelled only in Sanchi's mind and heart. Exorcism? Impossible.

The remembrance of the boy he had been replied to the ghost of Persiles. *"What is he, my lord? What sort of man spins dragons of smoke?"*

The knight's battle-weary eyes crinkled at the edges. *"So now I am 'my lord' to you, Sanchi? How you have changed. Before, it was 'Hey, Boss!'—was it not?"* Shadowy shoulders rose and fell with a breathless sigh. *"You and I both know it is not the dragons of smoke we must fear. Why fear their makers, then? I taught you many things. Bravery cannot be taught, but duty can. You were told to watch this man. Well, then, do it."*

"I'm afraid . . ."

*"You are. But you are still my squire, bound to me with ties that neither time nor space nor death can wholly sever. Sandy is right. What magic touches, it changes for all time. Watch him, Sanchi. Follow him, if you must."*

The child of memory screwed up a pugnacious face full of boldness the present-day Sanchi hardly felt anymore. *"You giving me orders?"*

*"Of course."* Again the laugh lines without the laughter. *"You were the one who called me Boss, remember?"* Then he was gone, and Sanchi felt as if his ribs enclosed nothing but ice and darkness.

He went about his normal duties, feeling a growing lassitude from lack of rest. Still, he managed to keep a more than cursory eye on the mysterious gentleman. Sanchi wasn't the only one paying attention to him. It didn't take many heavy wins at baccarat before a discreet signal attracted Jorgensen's notice. Sanchi watched as something approaching human interest made those glacial eyes open a bit wider, watch a little harder.

An opportunity was an opportunity. Sanchi moved in swiftly when his break came up. "Mr. Jorgensen, did you see that high roller at the baccarat table tonight?" In as few words as possible, Sanchi told his new manager about O'Connor's measures. "Maybe he didn't like being watched so much daytimes, so he's switched MOs." Sanchi wouldn't know an MO except on a Halley's bottle, but he'd heard the term on *Hill Street Blues* and it sounded good.

"Possible. I will ask for special attention upstairs." Jorgensen pursed his lips a moment, then added, "You are familiar with the situation. Keep an eye on him here."

Sanchi did as he was told, forcing himself to draw nearer to the baccarat game. It was easier now, with someone *real* giving him the order. Who obeyed the commands of ghosts except madmen?

And who but a madman would see such a sight, such a long-buried horror? The dark man looked up from his cards, straight at Sanchi. Sea-colored eyes met brown, and became mirrors of the color not their own, then more than mirrors. A new face spread suddenly over the magician's features, an explosion of illusion unsoftened by any slow gradation of change. Two realities changed places too abruptly for a normal mind to accept without the world jerking out from underfoot. This wasn't the B-movie werewolf transformation; it was scrimless, merciless, heartstopping.

"*Tío.*" The new face tore Sanchi out of his skin, made him a child again, naked in fear and sorrow, helpless. The photograph was in one of those cheap tabloids that battened on calamity. Papi had tried to shield the boy, hide the newspapers, but he had no way of preventing Mrs. LeBeau across the hall from buying her regular copy of the issue with Uncle Carlos' face on the cover. It had been a slow week for New York journalism. The story of the innocent victim who surprised some junkies in his apartment and died for it was news. The deathmask photo was excellent. Its clarity was forever acid-etched in Sanchi's brain. Only now it was where it had no business being. Uncle Carlos' face, caught in the instant of death's violation, on a living man.

Sanchi ran from the casino. The faces between him and the street-side doors were blurs, the voices indistinguishable wailings. He heard his own breath, rasping, sobbing, and the sound of his voice made small, trembling with an unceasingly whimpered chain of *no, no, no, no* . . . He bolted from the boardwalk's protective curtains of gold and silver light, through the garish red and blue neon of the true city, on into the dark of lesser streets.

Footsteps pounded behind him. In his ear, a voice unknown spoke: "Stop. Please." Then, more firmly: "If you don't, I can stop you."

Maybe it was a lie. Maybe the voice was just his own insanity. Even if it was madness he sought to outpace, Sanchi didn't stop. Old training snapped back. *When someone on a dark street yells 'Stop!' that's when you keep going!* He saw a shadowy driveway between two houses, ran up it, clambered over a picket fence behind the garage, jammed splinters into his palms, landed in a tangle of early pea plants on the other side. He caught his foot on the chickenshit chickenwire fence around that scruffy backyard garden, tore the pants cuff of his already abused uniform, but kept running: down another driveway, across a street, straight for the narrow alleyway between two CLOSED: COME BACK SOON shops.

But into that alley would be his expected route. A quick glance over his shoulder told Sanchi that if his pursuer was real, he was still negotiating the backyard obstacle course. A chance was a chance. Sanchi saw the green pickup truck just three cars down from the alleyway. He was over the tailboard and lying flat on his belly in the back, hidden from anyone except the searcher who might think to double back and deliberately peer into the rear compartment. Most chasers would keep going right down the alleyway first, and as soon as Sanchi heard the alley's echoes swallow any telltale footsteps, he intended to leap out of his temporary earth and take off in another direction.

Instinct held. Sanchi heard the sound of running feet—very light, very rapid—almost at once. He pressed himself even flatter, his nostrils filling with the stench of dog piss and sawdust. He waited, and was rewarded by hearing the pelting sounds go on unslackened. He readied himself to spring up and away.

Something stopped him. It could have been a trick of sound, it could have been the odd way echoes warped in a city, it could have been his own heartsounds pounding in his ears that sounded like the beat of other feet, more feet coming through the same way as the first pursuer. He peeked over the top of the tailboard just in time to see two men vanish into the alleyway.

*And will you run away now, my squire? You can, you know. A man who weaves dragons has no need of your help.* The ghost in armor wavered at the borders of sight.

*Help?* Sanchi thought the word in the very instant that the sounds from the alleyway turned loud, ugly. The fleeting thought that perhaps those other two runners had come to help his unknown pursuer died quickly. Sanchi knew what a streetfight sounded like, even at a distance. He ran, but not away.

He had only seen the last two of them enter the alley; there were six, all told, and they had the dark man up against the brick wall at the alley's blind end. Two of them were working him over professionally while two more held him pinned. One stood back, shoulders slumped, like a disappointed little kid waiting a turn at bat. The sixth man, the largest, was doing something very strange: He was holding the victim's right hand. Just that, with a glove that twinkled silver and green in the borrowed light of the alleyway.

Sanchi glanced around quickly, then cursed to himself. *Who the hell ever heard of an alley this clean? Jesus, not even a trashcan lid, let alone a good-sized two-by-four. And rocks? Forget it!* In his mind's eye, the ghost of Persiles shrugged.

*It would seem that all you have to use is yourself, my squire.*

*And it would also seem that I'm going to get my stupid ass kicked good, my lord. But here goes.*

He breathed in, switched on his *Let-me-see-proof-of-age* voice, and shouted, "Hey! What are you doing?" It was a dumb question, so for the same money he simultaneously linked it to a dumb gesture: Knotting his hands together into one outsize fist, he brought it down as hard as he could on the nape of the unoccupied goon. Hey, it worked on television.

Miracles happen. The man went down with a grunt just as his teammates turned. In that strange aura of dissociation that comes in crises, Sanchi was able to hold on to two superimposed thoughts at the same time:

*They're all wearing tuxes!* and

*What the fuck do I do now?*

Before he could pick up on the implications of black-tie muggings, he caught a sweep of silver and green, a gloved hand falling back to its owner's side as the biggest man went into his fighting stance. *Instincts of the streets. When you hear something come up behind you, something loud, something unexpected, your first instinct is to drop what you're doing, wheel, and face it. If all you are holding is a hand— the hand of a man your boys have already beaten halfway unconscious—it doesn't seem like you're doing such a dangerous thing.*

*Until the whole alley seems to explode like an oil refinery going up and throws you and five other men three stories high before you come down into streets seven blocks away and light and life snap out together.*

Sanchi stood in the mouth of the alleyway and felt something hot flow down his leg. His thoughts fled for shelter to what Mr. Jorgensen would say: *Rubio, it is not suitable for employees of Dionysia to piss in their pants.* Imagining his new boss's severe expression as he uttered that pontification was the only thing that kept Sanchi standing when the dark man approached him, one hand extended. An enormous emerald ring glittered.

"Your servant, sir," he said. "And your debtor."

Sanchi watched his own hand rise under its own power to return an automatic clasp. The handshake he gave was almost damper than his pants. A stranger's voice came out of his mouth as he replied, "No problem. My pleasure."

"Was it?" A black brow lifted as sea-colored eyes darted discreetly, briefly down to assess the state of Sanchi's trousers. A word was spoken and the pants dried.

"You're a wizard . . . aren't you?" He was cheeping like a duckling, but Sanchi had to ask. The answer would be either yes, no, or *I'm a dream and you're crazy, Sanchito.*

The dark man flicked his hand, and a snowy handkerchief appeared. He dabbed the blood streaming from his split lips and badly cut face, then flourished the cloth once. The bloodstains vanished; he made a dancer's bow. "I am Vergilius, called the sorcerer. I am master of many spells, commander of countless unknown forces, wizard of unguessed powers."

"Uh-huh." Sanchi nodded, then looked down at the wrinkles and rips in his partially restored uniform. The reality of things was still too dicey for him to resist adding, "You Martinize too?"

# CHAPTER EIGHT:
## Previous Experience Helpful, Not Necessary

Vergilius speared a bite of grilled salmon and used the morsel like a schoolmaster's pointer as he gazed steadily at Sanchi. "Then you will help me?" It was more declaration than inquiry.

Sanchi kept his eyes down, but with two broiled trout on the plate before him he was stared at no matter where he looked. At least the sorcerer wasn't garnished with lemon and parsley. On the other hand, the trout weren't trying to louse up his life as it had been similarly, thoroughly loused up only once before. "What help can I be?" he countered. "I told you, I wasn't anything more than a squire, an extra, a spear-carrier. Literally."

Beneath the black mustache, an ironic smile flashed with snake's-tonguelick brevity. "That's what you tell me now. You forget, I've read your memoirs." He chewed the salmon and followed it with a sip of very good Cabernet Blanc.

"That's another thing!" Sanchi's head came up sharply, his eyes afire. "You can read minds, you can launch full-grown men like they were Ping-Pong balls, you can change faces—"

"Not always," Vergilius said, a brief bitterness shaping his words. "Not dependably anymore."

"Well, even when you're *un*dependable, you're a one-man firefight. Christ, you can rig it so you *never* lose at the tables—"

"An injudicious error on my part," the sorcerer murmured. "Unseemly haste to raise the necessary funds, and the private joke of doing so at *her* expense, under her very nose. I should have contrived to lose once in a while. She might not have noticed me so quickly that way." Expertly he detached the final morsel of fish from its succulently crisped skin. "Pride has ever been my undoing."

Vergilius' calm was not contagious. Sanchi felt his collar chafe as if his neck had swollen two sizes. "Pride, hell. It doesn't change the fact that you can do so much, all those things I said, and you want me to believe you need *help?*"

"Yes." The sorcerer lightly touched the clotted gash under his left eye as if by chance. "As you yourself witnessed tonight, I do need help . . . on occasion."

"All right, OK, undependable, I forgot, wrong question." Sanchi waved past mistakes off with his knife before commencing the decapitation of the first trout. The fish was tepid by this time, but he ate it to exorcise Mamacita's living spirit. Like all grandmothers, she wouldn't mind if the world ended so long as everyone cleaned his plate first. "You're not almighty. You can use help. What I'm asking is, *why me?* And I want a straight answer!"

The magician remained unruffled. He did not respond at once, but hailed the sommelier. A knife-edged twenty cut the air beneath that serviceperson's well-educated nose. "Another of the Falernian, I think." The man looked bemused, but unwilling to contradict money. Vergilius smiled and patted the upended Cabernet bottle in its silver tableside cooler. "The Falernian," he repeated.

"Yes, sir." The sommelier plucked the double sawbuck from Vergilius' fingers with the finesse of an experienced artichoke-eater removing the virgin leaf. He hastened off and returned with a fresh bottle of Cabernet Blanc.

After the usual rites of examining label and cork, approving the first sip, and refilling the glasses, the sommelier left Vergilius to resume his conversation with Sanchi. "You see?" the sorcerer said, indicating the sommelier's departing back. "He only *thinks* I said Cabernet because that is the only rational supposition he can make. He knows nothing of Falernian, or Chian, those dear, departed vintages; Chianti, perhaps. Just so with you, *señor* Rubio. You only *think* you are asking 'Why me?' because it is the only sensible objection to voice. What you really mean to ask is 'How can I escape again?' "

Sanchi bristled. "That's a lie!"

Heads turned. The sorcerer made a hushing gesture. "Please, *señor* Rubio. We are not in Dionysia now. I doubt your employers would like to learn that one of their own was asked to leave Caesar's finest restaurant for unacceptable behavior."

Sanchi settled down fast. Still smarting, he said, "I'm not afraid. If you're such a hotshot mind reader, you ought to know that."

"I know what you have faced, in your time," Vergilius replied. "I cannot read all minds, merely those that—how to describe so that you can understand?—those that refuse to remain unread. A sorcerer gains much of his power from observation, meditation, study, seeking the heart of things. To see beneath the surface soon becomes second nature, and some surfaces are more yielding than others. We comfort ourselves with the illusion that our thoughts are our own, secrets that will never out; this is only a relative truth.

Your recollections scream so loud that I am amazed people do not follow your every step, pointing and whispering. To have helped to slay a dragon . . ."

"No one follows me." Sanchi's voice kept dropping lower and lower until it was a wonder that the magician did not lean across the table to catch the words. "No one remembers what happened, except the people it really happened to: me, Sandy, Lionel . . . I'm not even sure Papi and the others still believe it was all true."

"How many horrors are in danger of oblivion?" Vergilius asked the air. "The sphynx capitalizes on our forgetfulness too, in her way. *She* does not forget. It is more comfortable for us to pretend that we are a kindly race, to let bygones be bygone, to let the dust of history mingle with the ashes of the dead and to sweep both under the same rug. Often I regret that one of the demands of high sorcery is memory. I have seen much in these flying centuries that I would pay to forget."

It was a mistake to look into the sorcerer's eyes; a mistake Sanchi was still unable to avoid. He looked, and in a distant jungle smiling adults passed out cups of poisoned fruit drink to trusting children; in a parched land mothers laboriously, uselessly groomed their children's thinning hair as they watched the babies' bellies swell with hunger; on a flower-decked railroad siding a band played while cattle cars discharged their latest shipment of souls to learn the final lesson: *Arbeit Macht Frei.* Slave ships sailed over the waters of every age, and children filled the holds. They sang hymns of joy as they were led off on a crusade that ended in the slave markets of Africa. They stood on the block in a Roman market so that a pope might admire their golden beauty, name them angels, send missionaries to convert their tribe but make no move to end the trade that bought and sold them. The wonder of the world filled their eyes for such a little while before they died.

"You see, my friend? I do not forget." The wizard's words were a cold breath over the sweat bathing Sanchi's face. He felt pain in his right hand and saw that he had grasped his knife so tightly that his fingernails had gouged red half-moons into his palm. Mamacita or no, he pushed his plate away. He heard Vergilius add, "Nor do you. That is why you, *señor* Rubio: for what you have experienced and not forgotten. For the fire-hardened edge that memory has given you. For what has touched your soul and someday may wake it."

Sanchi's breath came out with a shudder. He took a long drink of wine before speaking. "I guess you won't take no for an answer, huh?" He managed to grin.

Vergilius returned the smile with his own half-bitter twist. "I wasn't planning to, no."

"Then I guess it's a deal. Nothing I haven't done before, anyway. Only, what's it called when you help out a wizard? Not being a squire . . ."

"Why?" A new scar on Vergilius' temple made his wry look seem more comic than condescending. "Were you planning to have business cards printed up? You are not the sorcerer's apprentice, if that's what you're after."

"Who cares, as long as I'm on the sorcerer's payroll." Sanchi's grin widened. "Which, if you'll dip into my mind some more, was just the sort of arrangement I had with Persiles."

"Indeed." Vergilius pursed his lips. "Was that all it took, the offer of money? I might have saved us both some time, and you some anguish. For a man so concerned with cash, I am surprised that you are not presently in a position offering greater opportunities for advancement."

This sounded too much like Papi's song, Elena's version too. "Look, a lot of people got in on the casino business from working the floor," Sanchi spoke hotly. "With an MBA you can really go places in management!"

"Pardon me, I was unaware. When and where did you receive your MBA, *señor* Rubio?"

All the heat subsided instantly into sullenness. "I don't have one. Not yet. But that doesn't mean I couldn't go back and get one!" One excuse linked to another neatly. "Yeah, but business school costs money, so how much are we talking here?"

Vergilius dispatched the last of the wine and folded his napkin into a prim little sailboat shape. "No fear, you shall be paid." He lifted the sailboat to give Sanchi a flash of golden disks beneath, then whisked them from sight.

"Then I'm with you." Sanchi thrust out a hand over the mangled trout. Vergilius shook it once, for form's sake. "Just tell me what we've got to do."

"As easily as that." The wizard was definitely amused. "I have told you my story. You know that there is a monster loose in your world—a monster worse than any dragon because colder, more cunning, educated by more than an accidental brush with sorcery. And half human. I kept her by my side for centuries, as if numbering the years mattered. Time was only another riddle to her—one which I, a mere manling, had solved. Riddles are her blood and bone, and from the first, the theme she weaves them to has been Man."

"Sure, I know that one." Sanchi nodded. "What goes on four legs in the morning, two at noon, three at night. That's simple. Oedipus solved it."

"Ah. A man with a classical education." Sanchi was unsure of whether the sorcerer was making fun of him. Vergilius sounded too much like a kindergarten teacher coaxing the alphabet from a backward student when he asked, "And what happened to Oedipus, *señor* Rubio?"

"When? In *Oedipus Rex* or *Oedipus at Colonus?*" Sanchi shot back. "Or do you mean the whole house of Oedipus and anyone who fell in with them? Antigone, Eteokles, Ismene, Polynikes, Kreon, the Seven Against Thebes, which ones? If you're trying to catch me out, you'd better do it on details."

"My apologies." Vergilius did seem chastened. "If I've offended you, perhaps you would prefer to reconsider our agreement."

"The agreement stands. I just want two things straight: One, I'm not some dumb PR, not an extra from *West Side Story*. I know more than the streets."

"More than you think," the wizard said very softly. Sanchi kept talking right over Vergilius' words, and they were lost.

"And two, if we work together, don't worry about me remembering my place and don't keep putting me down to remind me. I know what I've got's next to nothing compared to your powers, even if you think they're undependable. You give the orders, I take them, but if I think they're stupid, I kick. And you can drop the *señor* Rubio. Call me Sanchi."

Vergilius leaned back in his chair. "Look in your pocket, *señ*—Sanchi."

It was not the response Sanchi had expected to his diatribe, but he did as asked. Tucked into a small leather drawstring bag were five gold coins, Canadian mintage.

"For a well-deserved lesson in manners," the sorcerer said. "And I will be obliged if you will call me Vergilius. I do want your experience, and your insights. I need them far more than your subservience. It also never hurts to have a friend at your back, particularly one of proven courage. Note that I have said *a friend*. I want that too, Sanchi. In all the centuries of my life, I did not think I needed one. Perhaps if I had harkened less to my intellect, more to my soul, I should not be in my current predicament. Nor should your world." This time he was the one to initiate the handshake, and it was more warmly done.

Over coffee and dessert, Sanchi asked, "So when do we start?"

"You'd do better to ask *where*," the sorcerer replied.

"That's easy. She's right here in Atlantic City, at Dionysia."

"So we just take the elevator up to see her—after announcing ourselves on the house phone first, eh?" Fresh berries drenched in amaretto and *Schlag* assisted in an admirably efficient vanishing act. "We take out her bodyguards, destroy her, and tidy up the place in time for an early supper." He shook his head. "No, Sanchi, I am not deriding you. I only want you to know that it will not be an easy battle. I have magic and you have the experience of supernatural combat, but she has all that and more. She is not just virtually immortal and sorcerously wise; she is mistress of an earthly fortune, and all the powers of this world that wealth can buy. That includes soldiers in all manner of strange uniforms who will willingly bar the way between us and her with their own bodies."

"They don't know what she means to do to humankind, I guess."

"Or else they know her plans to the last detail. Do you think they care what she does to others, so long as she continues to supply their own immediate wants?"

Sanchi remembered. He was a child again, watching Uncle Carlos read the morning paper at the kitchen table. *"Here's this drug kingpin finally up on charges—Jesus, the photos of the house he lives in, that wife of his, a couple of cute little scrubbed-up angel kids in private schools—and people standing up to say what a nice guy he is, a family* man. A nice guy! Damn him. God damn him, him and his house and his precious kids, all standing on a mountain of smack, someone else's kids buried underneath, and what does he care? What the hell do any of them care?" Uncle Carlos threw the paper down and stormed off, slamming himself solitary in the bedroom. Some funny noises came from behind the closed door, but what could they be? If Sanchi didn't know that men don't cry, he'd have been able to name them. Uncle Carlos never cried, not even last week at Cousin Francisco's funeral, and Francisco had been only seventeen.

"You're right, Vergilius," Sanchi said. "Like they say, money talks."

"Louder and longer than a fledgling lawyer; that is so. You would not be here with me now, if not, though I still do not see why that frostbitten manager of yours thawed so readily at my request for an extended interview with you. I had not even progressed to the stage of offering a bribe."

"You wouldn't need to. You're a big player and a heavy winner; casino policy says give you anything you want."

Vergilius' mouth twisted over a private joke. "I wonder what sort of 'anything' your superior imagined I wanted with you."

"Hey!" The suggestion cut too close to the bone, touched a spot still raw. *Persiles . . .*

"You loved him." The words struck Sanchi like a fist to the chest. The shock left him too stunned to register whether Vergilius spoke them as fact or question, uttered them with pity, envy, or scorn.

"I didn't! He was—I worked for him, that was all. We got to be friends later, and—and I want you to *stop* reading my mind!"

"I've already explained." Vergilius laid his hands palm up on the table. "I cannot help it."

Something disturbing occurred to Sanchi. "The sphinx . . . can she read minds too?"

"I would not be at all surprised. Invade them, more likely. But the skill must be imperfect, or else you and I would not be here now, undisturbed by her minions." The mage settled back in his chair and sighed, replete. "I think she has decided that the rules of this game will be played out with as little drawing upon her own sorceries as possible. We humans are not worth the effort. Why swat a fly with a piledriver? A good thing; I abhor having my dinner interrupted. Moreover, the sphynx's wisdom has led her to invest much of her power in creating a fortress of finance rather than enchantment. Her future prey become her present allies. People believe in money more readily than in magic, and belief adds its own strength. She has built an empire, and empires are not easily brought down."

"An empire . . ." Sanchi considered the problem. "Well, there's you for magic and me for battle. Now all we need is someone who knows empires and we're home free."

The sorcerer laughed and motioned the waiter to fetch a telephone. His fingers dashed out a number on the buttons. "Hello, may I please speak to Mr. Trump?" he said.

It took several cups of coffee and much eloquence for Vergilius to convince his new aide that Romans had a very peculiar sense of humor.

# CHAPTER NINE: Phone Home

The night was dreaming into morning when Sanchi got home. He was just fitting his key into the lock by the yellow light of a flyspecked porch lamp when the door opened for him. Blue knuckles knotting a pink seersucker housecoat together, Sanchi's landlady glowered at him.

"A woman wanted you."

The hour had nothing to do with her brusqueness. She always unburdened herself of boarders' messages with the same attitude most people would bring to the burial of a long-dead, just-discovered rodent: Get rid of it quick and no questions asked.

No questions answered either. Sanchi had learned that it was useless pressing the landlady for the time of any call or the identity of the caller. All he ever got from her was a rough shrug. It was none of her business. He should be thankful she bothered to mention the mysterious caller's sex. If it was important, they'd call back.

Sanchi grunted one of those polite neutralities—an acknowledgment of nonservice rendered—and tried to go up to his room. A hard hand fell on his arm.

"You tell whoever it was not to call you here at all hours. She called five times! I had to get out of my bed to answer the phone."

That was an arguable truth. Though phones were forbidden in the individual rooms, the landlady enjoyed extensions in her own apartment and all the common-use areas. The sole exception was the bathroom. If she'd had to get off something to answer the phone, it hadn't been a mattress.

"I'm sorry. I'll tell her when she calls back."

The landlady snorted. "*If* she does. Clear crazy, she sounded. And the tone of voice she used with me, the language—! *When* I could understand her with that accent. I swear, someone ought to teach you people how to talk good English. That *is* the language in this country." Having done her bit for patriotism and linguistics, she flounced back to bed, leaving Sanchi with the fairly certain knowledge that his mother had called.

She would call back, that was certain. But why? Something to do with Alonso, probably. Upstairs, there was still no visible sign of his brother's return. Sanchi let himself topple backward onto the bed and flung one arm over his eyes. Maybe the kid had gone back to New York and sprung a surprise on Mother. That would be enough to set her off. Oh yes, she'd be calling back to let him know how he'd failed her again. It was only a matter of time.

The gold coins from Vergilius were a weight of hope in Sanchi's pocket, a potential counterbalance to offset any and all harshness from her. It had been a long time since he'd had gold to give her, but he remembered the grateful look she'd lavished on him when he first showed her the wages Persiles paid and the short period of peace it hired.

Gratitude and love. He wasn't the only one who lived with the pretty lie that one must necessarily lead to the other. Thanks for the lovely time, dinner and a movie, a rock concert, that SRO Broadway show, I was dying to go, here's a kiss, here's more. Oh, what a gorgeous necklace, sports car, ticket to Martinique, of course I love you, come inside and I'll prove it. You went to bed with me, you let me do things no other woman ever allowed, it felt so wonderful, I don't know whether I'll ever find someone else who'll give me so much, let's get engaged. Sanchi had said or heard variations of those themes many times. He knew what they were worth, how long thanks-purchased love lasted, how sincere it was. Knowledge was not wisdom. Even ghosts knew that buying the mask of love was better than remaining entirely unseen.

He heard a phone ring down the hall, a door open, the scuff of shuffling feet on thin carpet, and a peremptory rap on his own door before the landlady started jiggling the knob. He unlocked it to hear, "It's for you again. Take it downstairs. And *tell* her."

The living room was dark and smelled of stale cigarettes and fried onions. The leatherette armchair near the phone creaked and farted when Sanchi sat down. He heard two sets of heavy breathing when he picked up the receiver—the caller's and the landlady's. "I'm on," he said, but got no sound of the upstairs extension being replaced in its cradle. All right. Let her listen. He was too tired to fight little battles. "Mother, is that you?"

Oh yes, it was. The landlady would eavesdrop in vain.

You can never hide from the language you first know. Somehow the insults are more vicious, burn through all the defenses, have a sulfuric reality that later-learned tongues never quite acquire. *Like when you're on vacation, spending foreign money. It's not as* real *as dollars,* Sanchi thought, while his mother tore into him in rapid Spanish. *It's Monopoly paper, play bills, funny money. It doesn't count. And curses are only words that shock other people when I hear them in English. They mean nothing to me. I can tune them right out.*

Not these. He had nowhere to hide from all the things she was calling him. Vergilius might be an adept with the enchantments of ages at his beck and call, but Sanchi's mother was mistress of a voracious, merciless spell of destruction that took a grown man and stripped him down to a hungry child begging at a gate that would never open.

"—in jail! Why don't you watch him? Did I ask that much? He's a baby, your brother, he doesn't know what he's doing! How come you can't keep an eye on him? You're such a big deal down there, such an *important* man, you don't have the time, is that it? God damn you, you selfish pig! You're worse than your stinking father!"

Very calmly, very softly, his voice restrained to the safe, monotonous register where neither screams nor sobs could break free, Sanchi assured his mother that he would go down to the police station at once and get Alonso out.

"I try and try for hours to get you. Where have you been? What were you doing, and my Alonsito in such trouble! Don't you care? My poor baby, he's locked up there this long and it's all your fault. Oh Jesus, protect him!" She was weeping. He could hear her take in the air in huge, ragged gulps. The landlady's breathing ran in badly muted continuo beneath. "God help my sweet son!" She slammed the phone down so loudly that the landlady forgot herself and gasped.

Sanchi caught a slivered glimpse of pink seersucker as he returned to his room. No doubt the landlady was watching, waiting to see if he turned right around and went to the police station. *Probably going to slap me with an ultimatum when I bring 'Lonso back. No criminals in her boarding-house. Not without a fat rent hike, I bet. I wonder how she's going to manage explaining how she knows the little shit's a criminal without admitting she was listening in.* He gave a short, humorless laugh. Love would find a way.

If she wanted to see him go after the prodigal immediately, he cheated her of it. He had been up since the previous morning, with a bad night's sleep backing that and the backstreet chase to top it all. Exhaustion claimed him, and the bed was guaranteed his so long as he put off that trip to the precinct house. He fell asleep wondering how he was going to keep 'Lonso from learning about the Roman wizard.

"Turn'm into a toad, Vergilius, and I'll give you a week's work free," he mumbled as dreamless sleep came on.

Elena forced herself to sit still on one of the gray steel chairs while Sanchi continued to argue with the policeman at the desk. She had no business being here—Sanchi was her lookout, not 'Lonso—but it was almost as if she'd never had a choice. When she called Sanchi that morning just to touch base before leaving for work, he'd sounded awful. If she hadn't known him better, she'd have assumed he'd cooked his brain cells on something.

But how well did she know him? The thought made her frown. They'd lived like brother and sister under the same roof for years, until he went back to his real mother. Elena had been only six when he left, and the visits since then had been frequent but not long. Maybe it wasn't so many years she'd known him after all; just hearing Mamacita's constant repetition of how Sanchi had loved little Elenita, how Sanchi always had time for her, how Sanchi was often nicer to her than her real brothers.

Now, while Sanchi thrashed out matters with the desk sergeant, Elena had the chance to study the real person instead of the memory. For the first time she noticed that he wasn't as tall as she remembered. *How could he be? I was only six, and he was—what?—twelve? No wonder I thought he was tall!* Her legs, long in proportion to the rest of her body, gave her the illusion of height. The truth was, she was a small woman. He was scarcely a few inches taller than she, and so dark and slight-limbed that he seemed smaller than he really was, and younger. The desk sergeant was a mastiff beset by a bantam cock, and he wasn't doing a very good job of hiding either his annoyance or his amusement.

*What right does he have to look at Sanchi like that?* Elena wished there were some way she could protest other than in her mind, but she'd been too thoroughly trained: When a man talks, a woman sits still. *Sanchi doesn't even have to be here, getting talked down to. Why should he care who bailed out that rotten brother of his?* she wondered. *Alonso wouldn't give a damn if Sanchi fell through a hole in the world and vanished, and Sanchi knows it. But there he stands, trying to find out what's become of Alonso. Why?*

She knew about Sanchi's mother, about the hysterical call he'd gotten, but there was more to it than that. He could have told the woman to get off his back, leave him be. He could tell her a lie, say that Alonso was fine, great, out of jail—which he was, that much would be the truth. Fate had given Sanchi the perfect excuse to shuck all further responsibility for the boy. But he persisted, trying to find out where his half brother was now, and with whom. He didn't need to know. His rump was covered, as far as reporting to his mother went. Why was he insisting? Why did he care?

A vagrant thought whispered through her mind, light as a moth's breath: *And why does Papi care for the strays?*

The desk sergeant got in the last word and Sanchi threw his hands up in surrender. They came down as fists when he returned to Elena. "He beat up an old lady," he said. "Can you imagine that? Tried to steal her purse but didn't get away with it. Some guy who works as a bodyguard stopped him; hard, I hope."

"I overheard. So what happened? Where is he?"

Sanchi twisted invisible rings. "They don't know. Someone bailed him out—"

"So fast? On an assault charge?"

"No charge—I don't know—maybe 'bailed out' isn't what I want to say. The old lady came in with two more bodyguard types and a younger woman and said she wasn't going to prosecute. She was walking a little wobbly, but she'd been all patched up and she was smiling like 'Lonso did her the biggest favor of her life by knocking her down."

"That's weird," Elena said. "Even for Atlantic City."

"Not so weird." Sanchi gave her a hand out of the chair and escorted her from the precinct house. "I'm betting that whoever came for Alonso had plenty of money and spent enough of it on the old woman. Talk about your miracle cures!"

"Yes, but why? Who was it?"

Sanchi shook his head. "I just got through getting told it was none of my business. Maybe that's so, maybe a little more money went into making it so. All I know is that 'Lonso's free. The rest's a mystery."

"When we find him, we'll solve it." Elena spoke as if using the first person plural in this case were the order of the universe.

Sanchi didn't share her cosmic vision. "Whoa." He hooked a hand around her elbow and stopped her in midstride. "What do you mean *we*, white man?" He held his wristwatch up so that she could read the LED display. "Mickey's big digit is on the nine and Mickey's little colon is coming before the forty-eight. I'm doing night work now, but aren't you supposed to be over at Dionysia right now? Finding yourself?"

His smile was the one treasured memory of which time hadn't cheated her. When nothing held it back—no secrets, no regrets—it warmed everyone who saw it. Elena had to laugh just as much as she had to give in. Intrigue just wasn't her line, and she thought he'd appreciate her more if she turned honest.

"OK, Sanchi, you win. I'm not exactly putting in a strong showing at my new job."

"*Me dices lo evidente.* What? You're letting that passion for hospital corners go unslaked?" His hand flew to his chest. The man had sustained a grievous shock. "That could be dangerous. Tell me, young lady, have you been getting your MDA of fresh towels and shampoo samples, or should I call a priest?"

"*Ya me rindo!* Enough, you crazy!" Her first impulse was to give him a genuine New York noogie, but her knuckles didn't cooperate. A second thought said *Wait*. He was wonderful and infuriating and her brother and not, all at once, and suddenly she wasn't sure whether he was the crazy one. *Who are you, Sanchi?* That she cared so much to know the answer had become, impossibly, most important to Elena Sanchez.

"Enough? You're ready to confess?"

"Easily." She was still laughing, but her eyes studied him deeper than skin. "If they fire me for showing up late, that's that. I am *not* here for the sea air or to *find* myself, as you so pop-shrinkily put it."

"So it comes out at last. Damn, I'm good. Nobody expects the Puerto Rican Inquisition."

"I'm here for you. It was Papi's idea." He looked patient, hearing out what he already knew, but he also seemed let down. More words came, faster. "I came because he sent me, I admit it, but once I got here, saw you again, I wanted to stay. I wanted to help you, Sanchi."

"Help me back on the right path? The one Papi thinks is right for me, you mean. Thanks for all your kindness. I can get you a ticket back to New York real soon." He pulled out his wallet and handed it to her.

She smacked it from his hand, but swiftly followed up the dramatic gesture with a New York practicality: stepping firmly on the fallen wallet. "Don't try shipping me off until *I* say I want to go, Sanchez. Papi is my father; he can order me around, but only so far. You don't get even that. And Papi hit his limit when he sent me here. I've changed my mind—not about staying, you're stuck with me—but about what I'm here for."

Sanchi stooped to recover his wallet. He couldn't resist a little streetcorner appreciation of Elena's legs on the way up, but the murmured trill, the softly spoken *Ay, me muero, chica!* were swallowed down hard when he saw how high the fires leaped in her eyes. She was not in the mood for humor, and he seemed to recall something Papi had said about Elenita's temper and keeping the Civil Defense phone number handy.

"So . . . you're really staying for yourself?" he asked.

"I'm staying for you, like I said. Not for what Papi thinks you ought to be, or Mama, or Mamacita, or even your own mother. You. As you are. And I think that right now you wouldn't mind some help finding Alonso."

*"De veras? Nada de sermones ni—?"*

"I don't get paid to preach. Anyhow . . ." She didn't like having to drop a new bombshell on him, but he'd have to know. "The sermons are going to be in the hands of the experts, starting Friday. They're coming to get you, Sanchi."

"They—?"

"Papi, Mama, the boys, Mamacita, everyone except the current crop of homeless dogs and stray kittens, and that's only because Papi wouldn't force an animal to ride some of those tour buses."

She looked so harried, on his behalf, that Sanchi lost all thought of her as being on anyone's side but his own. When she'd been four, he'd helped her sneak around Mama's rule about no comic books for little kids, pretending that he harbored a bottomless thirst for Donald Duck, Richie Rich, and the occasional X-Men extravaganza. *Qué va*, it got her reading at least two years above her grade level when she finally went to school! Now they were conspirators again, and the feeling that came flooding into him was a whiskey glow that didn't dribble away.

"They're not satisfied with the job you're doing on me?"

She gave a rueful smile. "My first mistake was telling them how you gave me the slip by changing to a night job. They took away my Beretta and revoked my espionage license right there. Now they bring in the hard stuff—Mamacita—but they'll hit you with the rest of the arsenal too. They're going to *claim* it's a family weekend excursion. They're not going to bother explaining how come Bobby's on vacation with them while his wife and daughter are down in Florida visiting her folks." She laid one hand on his shoulder. "Do us both a favor, Sherlock, and don't ask. They want only good things for you. It's not their fault that they love you."

"I know." The change that swept over his face when she spoke of his foster family was appalling. She had never seen all light and happiness extinguished so rapidly from a man's eyes, to be replaced by longing, and the ashen fear that longing would lead only to despair. "I know they love me." He said it like a man mouthing fairy tales, the impossible. *Who could truly love me?*

*I do.* Her thought was not romance, but realization. He was her brother, just as much as Mike and Bobby and Manolo, and more than that. It would have been easy to say as much, to recapture his smile. Something forbade it. Again, *wait.* Some things a properly reared woman was not supposed to say.

They walked on, heading back to Dionysia, formulating between them a plausible excuse that might save Elena's job. A rattletrap car zoomed past, a phantom out of every '50s Teen Death ballad, its tailfins doing wicked things to jetstream the street dust right into a lady's nose. Elena started sneezing violently. Reflex made Sanchi yank out his handkerchief without remembering why this was no longer a good idea.

The gold coin twinkled in the sunlight, then bounced three times on the sidewalk. Sanchi gave a hoarse cry and slapped it underfoot, but Elena had seen. She asked the obvious question as soon as she had blown her nose.

Sanchi puffed out his cheeks as he exhaled the last breath of a condemned man. No prevarication. Remember what Papi said about Elenita's temper, and Ground Zero was a bad place to test its limits.

Delaying tactics, however. "You meant what you said before?" he asked. "About being on my side?"

"You're suggesting I'm a liar?" Her brows were dangerously close together.

No escape. Let her think he was crazy. He picked up the gold coin and saw the face of Caesar. It winked at him and shifted shape to his own laurel-crowned features, then back to a mundane Maple Leaf. Vergilius hadn't been joking about the Roman sense of humor.

"Elena," Sanchi said, "I've got this new job . . ."

After he told her, he took the gold coin from his palm and studied it. "Like the knight," she said.

He stared.

"You know, the knight you used to work for," she repeated. "Perseus or something. The one Papi found. When you and he and those others saved your mother and Alonso and the city—" Her lips twitched. "Everyone's allowed one mistake."

He grabbed her arms. "You remember!"

Now it was her turn to stare. "Well, of course I do! All these years I kept wanting to ask you about it, what it was like working for a real knight, killing a real dragon, but— this is so weird—Papi always told me not to bother you with made-up stories about things that never happened. I don't understand; he was *there*." She lowered her eyes. "Mama said I had an overactive imagination and it wasn't such a good thing. She made me give away all the comic books you got for me, the whole collection."

He was doing more than smiling; he was laughing out loud and hugging her. "Probably threw out books worth more than this!" His hand closed over hers, sandwiching the mutable gold coin between them. "And they called *me* impractical! But if you remember—if you really remember what happened to me, Elenita—then this time there's such a chance, such a chance for us . . . !"


"Look at that," the vision in pedal pushers said to her equally blue-rinsed traveling companion. "Disgraceful."

"What?" It wasn't easy getting off the tour bus in ladylike fashion after you reached a certain age, especially when sporting a clingy polyester skirt, and the last step was so *high*! Dearly she wished she'd worn stretch pants, no matter what Charley said about her hips. People who walked behind beer-bellies shouldn't throw stones.

"Over there, across the street."

Charley's lady adjusted her glasses. "Just two people."

"*Kissing* like that! In public and in broad daylight!" She yanked down the seat of her pedal pushers, which had had the effrontery to get wedged in an intimate locale. "Hmph. What can you expect from *their* kind?"

She would have said more, but she was blocking the bus door and was told to move it by general consensus of the backlogged passengers.

"Well, I *never*."

"Maybe that's your problem."

# CHAPTER TEN: Night City

The sphynx licked the feathery tufts of fur between the toes of first one hind paw, then the other. It was as good as a backrub for freeing her mind when she was in a reflective mood, even better because she needed no *other* to achieve the proper state of pure thought.

So Tri was dead; he and his team too. Their loss was immaterial. They could be replaced—already had been, in fact, cheaply. It was what that loss signified:

Vergilius. The sorcerer was stronger than she'd thought. Or had she merely misremembered his powers? Memory could be the ultimate trickster, posing a riddle even she might stumble over to her death. Just because she had escaped Vergilius once, eluded him, defeated him, nearly killed him, was she recalling him as less than he truly was?

A bad mistake, underestimating an enemy. She knew. She was still paying for her last mistake. That swole-foot stripling prince from Corinth had looked too beset by his own Furies to be a threat, and see what he had done to her! She could picture him now, staggering up the Theban road to her aerie, blood spattering his bare legs, his short traveler's mantle. The day was hot and she was bored with how little challenge humans presented her. Meat with eyes, the lot of them. She would ask this one the Riddle, give him the minimum time to reply that its spell demanded, and kill him.

So much for expectations.

"Ianthe!"

She heard her name called from the bedroom. She thought

87

the boy might have slept longer, but again, expectations . . .
Feathers and fur melted into a woman's body, veiled and
visible in a translucent peignoir of honeyed satin. Silvery
gray feathers framed her face—she liked private jokes the
best—as she went back to bed.

"Did you miss me, little one?"

Alonso never was very good with words, once he got past
dares and curses. He grabbed for her, and she let him. It
was the last action he would ever take of his own volition,
so she could afford to be indulgent. He was young; educa-
ble. He would have fewer bad habits to break than Tri, and
he would obey better. Not so strong, but more vicious; less
smug, more cunning. It wasn't a poor trade.

*Such a waste, Tri,* she thought as Alonso made intense,
clumsy love to her body. *The glove I gave you should have
done the trick. Placed over the wizard's source of power, it
would mute every spell. What did you do, Tri? Lose your
grip? I think not. Scorned my gift, more likely. Thought you
were strong enough on your own to defeat him. Pure force
against pure magic? When magic comes from powers mastered by the mind? Not an even match, poor brutish Tri,
though not imbalanced in the way you thought. And the
glove lost too. It will be ages before my spells can weave
another. The police are saying it was a drug deal gone bad.
How else to explain the bodies in that parking lot? So torn
. . . knives, of course. We explain things in language we can
accept.*

As an afterthought, she sent a holding spell into Alonso's
mind at the moment he climaxed, shuddering and whispering love-words he never meant. The enchantment struck
him stunned, gaffed him like a game fish. She had to roll
him off her and wait until he came back to his senses.

A finger to his lips touched away his sheepish grin, his
apology for "just turning over and going to sleep." She took
him by the hand and guided him from the bed to the outer
room, where she had him gaze out the window.

"I want you to do something, Alonso," she said.

Gemma sat on an exquisitely needlepointed chair, making
her knees be "good neighbors" as per her distant ballroom
dancing teacher's coy instructions. She had been told that
Ms. Apeiron would see her shortly. That was nothing new;

she often had to wait for an interview. What was different and disturbing was the creature who had given her this information.

She knew him at once: Sanchez Rubio's half brother. She remembered him from Dolmades, and she hadn't liked what she'd seen then. Now he had changed; for the worse, measurably. He slouched back on the white settee across from her and weighed her every possibility with his eyes before discarding her for something better in his mind.

*The arrogance* . . . It could only come from one thing: money. Ms. Apeiron's favor, too, which also meant money. But what was the gilded witch doing, hauling off infants to her bed? The boy couldn't be out of his teens, and Ms. Apeiron was . . . how old?

It occurred to Gemma that she had no idea at all of this employer's age, a thought hastily followed by the fact that she had an equal information gap as to how old her other patron was. All she had was an inner nagging that insisted both of them were older than they looked, but when it came down to specific sums of years, the voice went silent. She told herself it didn't matter, so long as both of them continued to pay her for what she could tell them.

Seeing Rubio's brother here, so unexpectedly, changed a number of items in the report she had brought, foremost among these the price. She was formulating the counterreport she would peddle to the dark man when Ms. Apeiron motioned her into the library.

That was what Ms. Apeiron called it, even though there was only one book to be seen, a child's illustrated introduction to the Greek myths. It was the smallest room in the suite, having no windows and just enough floor space for a diminutive Queen Anne escritoire and two chairs. A lingering smell of lilac air freshener made Gemma think it had once been a walk-in closet.

Ms. Apeiron was gracious, as always. Inside the escritoire were three Mont Blanc fountain pens, a Waterford crystal inkwell, a stack of cream laid letter paper, a small rosewood tea caddy, and a silver-trimmed decanter of Frangelico with attendant glasses. Following ritual, Gemma accepted a taste of the sticky, fragrant liqueur before mentioning the fact that she had something pertinent to pass on, though she preferred less subtle, more potent spirits. Custom likewise demanded that further details wait until Ms. Apeiron drained her own glass.

"So much more civilized this way," Ms. Apeiron always said, her head tilted to one side and those extraordinary eyes fixed on Gemma. "No information is so vital that it can not wait upon the courtesies."

Personally, Gemma wondered whether Ms. Apeiron believed this or simply liked to see how far she could make others conform to her whims. The answer would keep. As long as Ms. Apeiron was paying the reckoning, she could have Gemma's reports delivered naked in a vat of vichyssoise.

No sooner had Gemma uttered the last word of her latest report than she wished for something cold to dip into, with or without a snipped chive garnish. The rage on Ms. Apeiron's face looked hot enough to slag granite. The air conditioning in the closet-turned-library was suddenly inadequate to its task.

"So that is what he has been hiding," the lady hissed. "A helper. And he would not choose just anyone. That must mean he is ready to—" She clipped off her own words and gave Gemma a hard stare.

For the first time, Gemma felt uneasy about the consequences of her double game. Something not human faded over the older woman's face, a wash of cold, alien apparition that startled and was gone. Whatever it had been, it left Gemma sure that it would be more than a personal inconvenience if Ms. Apeiron learned of her other source of income. She started up from her chair.

"Where do you think you're going?" The question snapped her back down. More slowly, Ms. Apeiron added, "Don't you want your pay?"

She pulled the tea caddy toward her as she spoke. "I think this calls for more than money. You have earned a bonus, my dear Gemma. The news you bring me concerning Alonso's brother is most fortunate. I apologize if my initial reaction to your report was disconcerting. You know how passionate these business rivalries can be."

Gemma did not know, but she preferred to be agreeable. "No bonus necessary, Ms. Apeiron," she said with practiced sincerity.

"No?" For one awful moment it looked as if Ms. Apeiron

had believed her. "But I insist." Her fingers dipped into the tea caddy and plucked out something richer than Earl Grey.

Gemma regarded the brooch in wonder. It was nearly the size of her palm, of solid gold painstakingly wrought into a Medusa head. The monster's eyes were sapphire chips, and every one of her snaky locks sported a diamond eye. It must have cost a fortune but at the same time was so big that it was impossible to wear without looking gauche and tacky. It might be melted down, yet that would destroy half the value. The jewel was only good for hoarding away, or using as a bargaining chip. Ms. Apeiron's so-called "bonus" was at once fabulous in terms of hard value and worthless in terms of plain enjoyment. When Gemma looked up she thought she caught her female employer smiling over that very thought.

"I hope I've made clear how much I appreciate your work, my dear," Ms. Apeiron said, gracefully shepherding Gemma to the door. "I am willing to pay you even better for any further information that deals specifically with the young man you mentioned."

"Sanch—?"

"Hush." A gold-tipped finger touched Gemma's lips, cool. Ms. Apeiron's eyes darted meaningfully to the settee where Alonso still sprawled. "Discretion is an art, and you are too pretty not to be an artist. I may take the liberty of contacting you by telephone. You won't mind?" Ms. Apeiron closed the suite door on Gemma's answer. There could be only one.

In the elevator, Gemma pondered the ways of the very rich and decided it would be prudent not to mention Alonso's new position to Sanchez. Not yet.

The anchorman assumed the proper expression of controlled shock and sorrow as he finished reading the story of the old woman found dead in her Atlantic City apartment, strangled. Robbery was not a motive. The police had found large sums of cash in her bedside table. The senselessness of her death was just as bewildering as its execution: The dingy little apartment had been locked. Patrolmen acting on an anonymous tip had had to break through a door secured by lock, deadbolt, and chain.

"Only one chain?" the sphynx mused, munching popcorn.

"And at her age. One would imagine she would know better. The cities are not safe anymore."

Lying next to her on the sofa, his head resting on her hip, Alonso giggled. Images from the television swam over his eyes, reflected there in miniature perfection. Nothing of his own soul was left to drive them away. "Cities never were," he said.

The sphinx ruffled his hair without wasting a glance on him. "You are too young to know how wrong you are. It was not always so. Once the cities were your proudest creation, reared by the strong for the sake of the weak, sanctuaries of power against the night. In the safety of walls and numbers, you found the time to learn many things; too many. A true Riddle dies under the eyes of wisdom. In the cities you grew too wise, too strong, too certain of having a wall at your back instead of a shadow."

Alonso was not paying attention. He cared more about the long-legged models striding through a blue-jeans ad than about the cities. His lack of interest should not have mattered. He was no more than a sounding board to his new mistress, but tonight she felt like demanding more.

*Vergilius thinks I do not know the worth of a helper; a true-bonded one. I will teach him to scorn my intelligence. This one will do as well as any other*—she regarded Alonso as one would a lapdog about to be turned useful animal —*and if I can have him as well as steal the one the mage has chosen . . . oh, a rare touch, that! You will see, Magician; you will learn.*

She made no mystical gestures, only continued to munch popcorn. The spell she called upon was the most casual creation. The pictures on the television bled off, and a new panorama scrolled across the screen.

Empire. Alonso blinked, rubbed one eye, then sat up to watch more closely as the sphinx pulled electronic strings to send her video puppets through their dance. He saw huge office buildings, real estate holdings, ships, ranches, mines. Sleek men and women dined in luxury and leisure, chased down the sun or the snow at their pleasure, knew only choices and the freedom fortune gives. Numbers trickled down the screen, stock market quotations, commodities reports, bank accounts domestic and foreign, the financial statements of the interwoven corporations whose many threads braided themselves into a leash that ended in Ianthe Apeiron's grasp.

The screen went dark. Only a flicker of brightness showed in the lower left-hand corner. By slow degrees its light grew until Alonso saw the faces of homeless men by its flare: a trashcan fire stoked against the cold. It was the world away from what he had just seen, this poverty where the only choices were live or die, yet awareness came that here too were the gossamer strands of his lover's web just waiting to be plucked up and plaited into the whole.

*What do you think these people would* not *do for a chance to possess what I've shown you?* The sphynx's thoughts were his. *Poor as their lot is now, how much poorer do you think it would be if I were to toy with my holdings sufficiently? Money is easier to manipulate than men, but then it manipulates them for you. Human lives are bought and sold daily, Alonso. Some I purchase directly. . . .* She showed him a vision of herself passing among the shivering men, money changing hands as she picked and chose the ones she wanted to serve her just as if the Roman slave markets had never closed.

*Some I shall take, though they will never know I claim them.*

On the screen, panic. Somewhere, huge blocs of investments had been withdrawn suddenly, without explanation. More followed, so swiftly that no one had time to learn that there was only one hand behind this turn of the cards. And then a tumbling market, an avalanche of fear to sweep away the small with the great, a government promising miracles, a wave of action and reaction girdling the globe and lives cast up broken in its wake. Desolation.

The second stage, coming on gradually, imperceptibly, inevitably—a new leader here, another there, a third, a fourth, all murmuring the same hypnotic spell of comfort to the people who were learning hunger and cold: *We are not to blame for our troubles. We are the virtuous few, victims of our age-old enemies. We must not let them triumph. We must destroy them now, before they can harm us more with their evil color, faith, nation, politics, sex. We will feast and be warm when they are dead.* The flame of the trashcan fire grew, leaped up, roared across the screen and left darkness.

The sphynx sighed, and let the network reclaim the television. She trailed two fingers across Alonso's smooth cheek. "Alas, the only war that I can wage now is to send my people into the streets, adding to the terror in their small ways, letting the night into the cities. It is a minor pleasure, but in time I will taste a greater one. If I am not disturbed," she added.

Alonso shifted himself closer against her side in just the way she remembered her littermates nuzzling more deeply into their mother's warmth. "I did what you wanted OK?" he asked.

The sphynx stroked his neck. The slim cord of black silk he wore there looked unremarkable; impossible to tell that it concealed a core of flexible wire, unless you knew. The plain zinc disk hanging from it looked ordinary too. It was when you touched it to a lock and spoke the words of sealing or opening that you valued it more.

She wiped a slick smear from the pendant charm, pleased with how scrupulously her new one had followed instructions, though he'd taken forever to memorize the applicable spells. If Tri had been half so obedient . . . The cord felt slightly greasy and was dappled here and there with white streaks. Only she could smell the fading fragrance of cold cream and muguet dusting powder still clinging to it. Only she could scent the even more elusive perfume of an old woman's terror and death.

"You did fine, Alonso," said the sphynx.

# CHAPTER ELEVEN:
## Family Matters

The Burger King on the boardwalk was a far holler from any description of a wizard's lair Elena had ever read. For one thing, the indispensable collection of flasks, vials, and bubbling alembics might have gotten mixed up with the Diet Pepsi dispenser. For another, the stuffed crocodile would have had to hang right over the french-fry baskets. This aside, it was as good a place as any to grab an early bite of breakfast and encounter a legendary mage at the same time. Elena was practical.

When Sanchi had brought her along to meet the sorcerer, she had anticipated being awed by his noble bearing, his innate wisdom, his aura of controlled power, and his virtual immortality. She never expected to be the butt of one obnoxious remark after another while watching him shovel down hash browns and scrambled eggs.

"Must she be here?" Vergilius asked, giving Elena a once-over that simultaneously assayed and dismissed her from the scheme of necessary things.

On her side of the table, Elena pursed her lips hard and rolled several sharp replies around the inside of her mouth until she wore the edges off. Much as she wanted to jab one or more right into the sorcerer's face, she held back. Sanchi had told her about Vergilius' powers, as demonstrated in that alleyway battle, but that wasn't what bridled her tongue. She wasn't afraid of him, just of *el qué dirán*—Mamacita's universal bugbear—the *what will people say* about a supposedly well-bred girl who says rude things to a man.

If he insulted her, well, that was a matter for another man to settle. That was Sanchi's function. He was right there beside her, his hand pressing hers beneath the table, and he didn't let her down.

"Yes, she must be here," he said. "I've told her everything. She's in this with us; she wants to be."

"How brave." The magician was patently bored by Elena's theoretic bravery. "And will you tell me, Sanchi, since you've taken it upon yourself to start recruiting me an army, why this person qualifies?" To Elena he said, "I beg your pardon for speaking the truth, girl, but I fail to see anything special about you. You are pretty, probably capable in your own way, but definitely ordinary. You *do* know what Sanchi and I shall be attempting?"

Elena swallowed another good verbal wallop and simply nodded.

"And you believe it? All that he's told you?"

She nodded again.

The wizard finished his coffee. "Then I'd like to interest you in a vacation-home time-share scheme at the Empire State Building. No pets."

"Of course not," Elena said calmly. "Considering how

poorly you watched your last one, Master—that *is* the right way to address a sorcerer, isn't it?"

"It will do." Vergilius' gritted teeth barely moved.

"Elena . . ." She could tell Sanchi was scandalized without looking at him. She shook free of his sheltering grasp and folded both her hands on the tabletop.

"Master Vergilius, *was* any of what Sanchi told me a lie? You and he are teamed against a monster, he says; a real one."

"Real enough, if the destruction of humanity is any sort of real possibility. He told you the truth."

"He told me what you told him. Has he even *seen* this monster for himself?"

"Not yet." More irritation crept into Vergilius' voice.

"Then why are you calling me gullible just for taking his word when all he's done is take yours? I've known him longer than he's known you."

A cold smile flickered over the mage's lips. "I've given him . . . some proofs of my sincerity."

A scarlet dragonling the size of a walnut materialized on the table. Unfortunately for the effect Vergilius hoped to create, Elena chose that instant to smack her hand down on the Formica for emphasis. The squeak and the splat were drowned out by her raised voice. "Why don't you want my help too? Are you afraid I'll divide Sanchi's loyalty? Then you don't know him very well; or me."

"What is there to know?" The magician's tone implied *not much*.

"I'll tell y— What *is* this stuff on my hand? Ketchup? They ever wipe down these tables?" Vergilius passed her a paper napkin and she went on: "Listen to me, Master Vergilius. I was there the first time Sanchi touched magic. I was only six, but he wasn't that much older, and I can still remember how he acted then. When Sanchi chooses to serve, he does it with all his heart. If he's chosen you, don't worry about me diverting him."

"He serves for loyalty . . . not gold?" Vergilius let the lightest of taunts tinge his words. "Is that what you remember, lady?"

"Oh, he'll take the gold too. He's not a damn fool." Elena leaned back in the hard plastic seat. "I am. That's a fair warning. You don't need to pay me to stay and you won't be able to conjure up enough gold in this world to make me go." She smiled at him, a dare.

The sorcerer smiled back. "If he's told you everything, you know I don't use gold to get rid of supernumeraries."

"I also know you don't do too well on that score without Sanchi to help you. I see the cuts are healing nicely. You should let Mamacita have a look at you, though. She's got all these wicked folk remedies from the island. Papi calls her *la brujita* for a joke. Maybe you two can trade recipes."

"Elena . . ." Sanchi was squirming. "Elena, I wasn't lying when I told you what he did in that alley."

"Then be just as honest when you recall what I do here and now!" the sorcerer cried, and lunged across the table to kiss Elena heartily on the lips. She jerked back, a hand rising automatically in a slap that never landed. Instead her fingers explored tentatively around her lips.

"Don't grow a beard, Sanchi," she said. "It stings."

Vergilius laughed until he caught the glare Sanchi aimed at him. He patted his assistant on the shoulder. "Do not play the basilisk with me, my young friend. I have met the genuine article, and they are dull-witted beasts. First you insist the lady be with us, then you snarl when I welcome her to the cause."

"I'm in?" Elena asked.

He grabbed her hands and sandwiched them between his, "Forgive me for my earlier behavior, my dear; it was unavoidable. The peril we three shall face together is quite real, and I could not have you tagging along if you were in any way under the impression we were going to play hide-and-seek with a George Pal plaything. I had to try you, to provoke you, to bring the truth of you nearer to the surface of your mind where I might read it."

"Read what? My mind?" Elena was dumbfounded. She looked to Sanchi for confirmation.

"He can't do it all the time, Elenita."

"He'd better not try." To the sorcerer she said, "Don't do it to me again. Mental trespassers will be shot."

Vergilius appeared delighted by her declaration of embargo. "I shall respect that. Your thoughts were no easy fortress to assail. I'll reserve my strength for more vulnerable adversaries. Ah, but what riches I did see in you! I read truth in you, sweet lady, devotion, a steadfast heart, and all the courage you claim. As for memory . . . that is as I have already told Sanchi, the heart of high magics."

"Magic?" Elena echoed. "I'm not magical. I'm just offering another pair of hands—you know, someone to reload the rifles."

"Elena, we're not going to skeet-shoot the sphinx," Sanchi said.

"Well, what will we do about her?" Elena asked, regarding first one man, then the other. "I thought it was going to be straight search-and-destroy."

"Hm. No experience, I see." Vergilius stroked his beard. "Another candidate for proper training. My lady, I shudder to meet so much blind enthusiasm in one soul. It is dangerous when bravado envelops bravery."

"What do we do, then? Wait for her to strike first?" Elena shook her head. "I don't like that."

"Your pleasure doesn't enter into it." Vergilius twisted his emerald ring. "The sphinx decides. This battle is waged on more fronts than you know. At present she is the only one in a position to decide when we shall confront her."

"Or *if?*" Sanchi didn't look any more pleased than Elena. "If she's this powerful, maybe she doesn't have to fight us at all."

"But she will fight." Vergilius sounded sure of it. "She will fight because we will force her hand—with your help, sooner than she expects. We will nibble at her precious plans like mice, making them unravel from beneath her hands, until she has to face us. And then she will fight out of fear."

"So we keep walking down dark alleyways, waiting for her to get scared enough to spring out at us? Boss, I warned you; this one I kick on."

"She will not spring from the darkness." The sorcerer's bitter smile quivered for an instant. "That is too crude for her these days. I know her well, you see, and one more thing I know: When the time comes for her to seek our deaths, there shall be a Riddle in it, as always. When she thinks the time is ripe to summon world's end, there shall be a Riddle. So it must be, and we must answer or perish."

"I don't get it," Sanchi said. "Not now and not since the first time I read the myth. Why the Riddle? Why couldn't the sphynx just kill Oedipus without asking it? Why can't she be killed by someone who doesn't know the answer?"

"I think there must have been a time when she could be slain without so much formality," Vergilius answered. "When the serpent is in its eggshell, a child's naked heel can crush it. When it has hatched and grown, its death must come in another guise. If I were to explain the rite of Riddle and Answer so that you might understand, Sanchi, you would end as a wizard or a very old man, and this sweet world would have ended long before."

"You're a magician; make it short."

"Such faith in my powers . . . Well, I'll try. The sphynx is a creature bred out of a different beginning than ours. Her existence outside the realm of myth is an impossibility to most people, yet she exists. Just as you are ruled by natural limits you can temporarily evade but not escape forever—gravity, weariness, age, death—so the sphynx and her kind are subject to other rules with the same inevitability. They constrain her, set boundaries to her powers, bring her into the realm of mortal weakness and vulnerability for an instant. The cycle of the Riddle and the Answer is one such rule. In the moment of the Riddle, she and her prey are as open to one another as two lovers, but only one can emerge holding the Answer. The one who does gains the power to steal the essence of the other; *if* he knows how."

"Essence . . . do you mean like . . . the soul?" Elena asked timorously. She touched the small gold crucifix at her neck.

"Name it yourself. Whatever it is, vitality flows with it from mortal men, and existence. The killings afterward are ritual; all true life is gone."

"But after Oedipus, why didn't she—?"

"—die?" The sorcerer sighed. "She might have, had he remained to finish the job. He assumed that a fall off that cliff would do it; he always did take too much for granted. Have I not said she is not like us? Given time—ages—she recovered. The sphynx comes away strengthened by the force her Riddles drain from the victims. She thinks it worth the risk, gambling her one moment of vulnerability against what she may gain."

"So that's all we'll have to do? Wait for her to come to us, then answer her Riddle?"

Something sharp and steely blue winked in and out of

being under the magician's hand. "How disappointed you sound, Elena! Be comforted. Give the sphynx the Answer and you only purchase the opportunity to kill her. She will still have her lion's body, her hawk's wings . . . and perhaps a measure of her magic. Solve her Riddle and she will still fight back until the time of the Answer has passed."

Elena exhaled slowly. "Suddenly I do feel needed on this little expedition."

"As you are, my dear; as you are also, Sanchi."

Sanchi looked dubious. "I still say it wouldn't hurt to try a .357 magnum right off the bat and not dick around with Riddles. It just might work."

"Not a sword?" Vergilius' eyebrows rose. "And here I thought you were the romantic sort, the swashbuckling don."

"I don't know how to use a sword—much."

"You don't know how to use a magnum either," Elena put in. "But you're going to need one. It's almost eight."

"So?"

"So Papi said the bus gets in before eight-thirty."

*"Ay, Dios!"* Sanchi shot out of his seat. "Come on, we'd better run."

Vergilius cocked his little finger while Sanchi was helping Elena from her chair. The cobra was a subtle shade of lime green and not too ostentatious in size, but having three heads helped it make an impression. It coiled in the aisle between their table and the doorway, hissing in harmony.

"I think that I would like to know the reason for this haste," Vergilius said casually.

Sanchi didn't sneer too openly at his employer's bit of conjury. "Nice try, Boss, but I'm betting it's only an illusion." He walked right through the creature and halfway out the door. "Bingo; I win. Coming, Elena?"

"You go on." She kept her eyes on the cobra. "I—Master Vergilius does deserve some explanation; *por cortesía.*"

Sanchi shrugged. "Later, then."

When he was gone, Vergilius regarded Elena with new respect. "You hold the amenities in high esteem, my lady. I have not seen the like for centuries. I am impressed."

"Get rid of the snake." Elena sounded like a mouse on its deathbed.

"But it is as Sanchi said, an illusion—"

*"Get rid of the goddam snake!"*

"Have it your way," said the sorcerer, and vanished the serpent just before the manager asked them to take their culinary custom elsewhere.

Mamacita had just finished telling Sanchi that he looked wonderful, but much too thin, when Elena showed up.

"I can only stay a moment, *querida*," Elena said, kissing her grandmother even before her parents and three brothers. "I have to get to work. I've been late once already."

"We wouldn't want *that*." Manolo jammed his hands in his pockets and nudged Mike, the youngest brother. He liked to get his audience's attention before delivering what he thought of as zingers. "No gold star on your Do-Bee chart."

"Shut up, Manolo." Mike relied on the traditional family way of dealing with Manuel's wit.

"*Vete con Dios, angelita*." Mamacita patted Elena's cheeks, nearly going on tiptoe to do it. Age had dwindled her to a cricket, small and dark and ever lighthearted. "We'll have a nice talk with Sanchi instead."

Elena saw Sanchi tense up, and her own skin itched in sympathy. Here came the sermons, the well-intentioned prying and prodding. As if to shoot the bar across any retreat route, Papi said, "Yes, he's just told us that he works nights at Dionysia now, so we can steal a little of his time for a visit."

"Unless he has better things to do," Mama murmured demurely, looking down at her red patent-leather handbag. "This is our first time in Atlantic City, and we only have this one weekend. It's such a big place. Still, I'm sure we can find our hotel without too much trouble if Sanchi is that busy."

As Sanchi protested that he was now and always at their service, Elena had to admire Mama's dexterity. Why use a knife or a needle when pulling the right string works so well?

She knew it would fail, but she had promised to take his side. "Sanchi's too polite to say, Mama, but since he does work nights, he really ought to go home and sleep now."

"I haven't stopped him." Mama's eyes were as luminous and guileless as when she'd been young. "If we are interfering with your life, Sanchi, you must tell us. We can manage

101

on our own." She proved this by grabbing for the heaviest suitcase and trying to pick it up singlehanded, though the piece had wheels and a pullstrap. Her softly uttered "Ay!" had just the right dying fall to it. Elena silently acknowledged a master of the motherly art.

"Allow me, my dear lady!"

This time Mamacita put some force behind her cry of distress as the dark stranger swooped into the midst of the family Sanchez and whisked the suitcase from her hands. "Now, which hotel are you seeking?"

"Why, *Mr. Roman!*" Elena eeled her arm through the sorcerer's, forcing him to set the suitcase down. Pumping sincerity on all cylinders, she heard herself actually gush for the first time in her life: "Mama, Papi, everyone, I'd like you to meet Sanchi's new boss and our dear friend, Mr. Rhett Roman."

"Rhett?" Manolo sneered. "Isn't that the name of that big-time dude in *Gone with the Wind*?"

Vergilius stood tall and stared the snottiness off the young man's face. "It was my late mother's favorite book."

"What a coincidence!" Papi exclaimed. "Elena's, too."

"I'd never have guessed." Vergilius gave Elena a teasing sidelong glance. She affected to ignore it, even though she could not control a brief blush. .

"What is this 'new boss,' Sanchito?" Mama demanded. "You just told us you are still at Dionysia. Are you lying to us?"

Lying. That was the line no one crossed in the Sanchez family, except at his own risk; not even Manolo. Elena braced, then flung herself into the storm of words instantly pouring from Sanchi's mouth to explain "Mr. Rhett Roman" to the others. By the time the two of them finished a verbal tap dance, fireworks display, and royal white elephant stampede, there were only three questions Papi had to ask:

"So when is the soonest Mr. Roman will get you into that MBA program?"

"Where *is* Mr. Roman?" and

*"Virgen santísima!* Where is Mamacita?"

Elena and Sanchi had about even odds of answering any one of these on the money. Mamacita and the magician were gone.

# CHAPTER TWELVE:
# Collective Bargaining

"I think I want the other too." The sphynx spoke offhand-edly, as if she were purchasing a mate for the strand of black pearls now dangling from her fingers.

"Yes, Ms. Apeiron?" Gemma watched the smoky drops swing back and forth before her weary eyes. She was still suffering from a disrupted sleep schedule, brought on by new working hours. Though it was the peak of the after-noon, it felt like midnight to Gemma. At Ms. Apeiron's wish, she had been transferred unexpectedly to the night shift. The lady had not elaborated on her reasons initially—nor did she have to—but still she'd made it clear that Gem-ma's foremost duty now would be to observe Sanchez Rubio. And the dark man? All interest in him had faded.

Gemma hoped the sudden disinterest wasn't mutual. She was doing very well for herself on the double-sided trade.

"Yes, Gemma. I think it a great pity that brothers should not be friends. You know how pleased I am with dear Alonso's progress in my employ. However, I fear that some-thing holds him back from his full potential. I do not know much of your—how do you say it?—*pop-psyche* theories, but I do know people. This sorrowful breach with his brother may be the cause."

"Has he mentioned Sanchez to you, Ms. Apeiron?"

"No." The sphynx's long lashes swept her cheeks. "But you have, and so I realize how deep the rift goes without Alonso knowing that I am aware he has kin. To not so much as hint that he has blood ties in this very city!" She sighed prettily. "I must see to that. It is my duty."

Gemma did not question Ianthe Apeiron's desires. She sensed that there would be no profit in it, and possible termination of employment. Not just her impromptu spying activities, but her commonplace job as well would go. Ms. Apeiron never spoke about the full extent of her holdings, but

Gemma didn't wait to be told everything. She had friends in New York, friends who knew where to look for information. Their reports, which Gemma elicited so casually, had opened her eyes to the full scope of Ianthe Apeiron's empire. It would have been frightening if it weren't so exciting. The lady held Dionysia—and so much more—as surely and as unconcernedly as she held those pearls.

But if she had been paid to speculate, Gemma would have wagered the pearls and the Medusa brooch as well on that one word: *want.*

*I think I want the other too.*

Gemma knew where dear Alonso was making his much-vaunted progress; her employer had no discretion outside of business. She wouldn't put it past Ms. Apeiron to want to sample both the brothers. At once? Perhaps. One whim was as much a possibility as another for those with the means to make their playgrounds to personal specification.

"Shall I tell him tonight that you want to see him, Ms. Apeiron? I'll see him on the floor."

"Oh no, child. An order would not do. It would put him on the defensive, not at all open to reason. I don't want that. Alonso may have hurt his feelings. They are so passionate, these people! So sensitive."

The pearls relinquished their hold on Ms. Apeiron's fingers and fell seemingly by chance into Gemma's upcurved palm. The younger woman touched her tongue to her upper lip. How cool, how smooth the pearls felt against her skin. Already she dreamed their rainkiss touch between her breasts. The strand glowed, each misted globe a tiny crystal ball where the future swirled up out of the stormclouded depths.

*Gemma was the one who held the silken reins of empire. Gemma was the one whose merest wish before breakfast was reality before noon. Gemma was the one who cried halt to all the tiresome games, the mating rituals that had to be obeyed if life was not to end in loneliness. She desired, she demanded, and she was given all she desired and more.*

The black pearls rippled through her finger and flowed into her lap. From far away, she heard Ms. Apeiron tell her, "You will find a way to mention Alonso to him tonight, Gemma. A subtle way; I have faith in you. And then you will draw his attention to me. I will be waiting at the blackjack tables. You will not disappoint me."

Gemma's hands folded over the pearls in her lap. It was like cupping them above a flame. She shook her head.

"Mamacita! *There* you are!" Elena sprinted down the length of the oceanside shopping arcade, nearly colliding with a photobadge cart in her haste to reach her grandmother. Sanchi came after at a more subdued pace.

"Where else should I be, *tesoro?*" The old woman dipped her fingers into the plastic bag Vergilius held for her and munched a pinch of pink cotton candy. Elena might have looked more scandalized if her grandmother had chomped down a live lizard, but not much.

"And what are you doing, eating that junk? *Basura!* Papi told me that your doctor said—"

*"Ya me basta lo que dicen los médicos. Que yo tengo más años que un montón de ellos!"*

*"La señora* Sanchez is correct," Vergilius remarked. "I have seen few doctors reach her age. She should be giving them advice."

"You see?" Mamacita looped her arm through the sorcerer's and fused the link shut with finality. "You should listen to Mr. Roman, Elenita. He is a man of experience!"

"Please, *señora* Sanchez," Vergilius murmured. "I thought I asked you to call me Rhett."

Sanchi wondered what Elena was thinking of calling Vergilius. The look on her face boded ill for anyone not wearing protective gear. Even though he knew that in reality Elena had about as much chance of doing the sorcerer any real harm as a midge had of injuring a lion, still he was glad he wasn't the object of her ire. Anyway, one determined midge, properly placed, could drive the biggest lion bughouse.

He felt a surge of vicarious relief when Elena used the threat of losing her job to pry Mamacita away from the sorcerer and hustle the old woman back to her family.

"Narrow escape there, 'Rhett,' " he commented as the two women walked off under the brightly painted eyes of the carved circus girls and diving horses hung like figureheads from the arcade pillars. The boardwalk mall was shaped like a great ocean liner, its interior decorated to remind the tourist of Atlantic City's first heyday as a resort. It was a little disconcerting for Sanchi to realize that Vergilius might easily have known that Atlantic City too.

"I didn't."

Sanchi jerked his head sharply and gave the wizard an accusing stare. Vergilius' seaborn eyes remained calm as a sheltered bay. "Your pardon, Sanchi. Your thoughts should remain your own. Again, I could not help it."

"Maybe I should apologize to you for being so transparent," Sanchi sniped. "Or charge you a fee-per-read. Eh, forget it; your mind reading's probably all my fault, too." His sigh was the sign that he had categorized Vergilius' occasional clairvoyance as another of the inevitabilities that kept life out of his control. No use fighting what would be. "I just wish you could read 'Lonso's mind that easily. Then I could find him."

"Who is 'Lonso?"

Sanchi was genuinely surprised. "You mean you can't get that from me without asking?"

"Shall I try a Vulcan mind-meld?" the wizard asked in a too-sweet voice with a thread of steel under it. "And before you ask, *she* was the one who watched that show."

Ticklish knowledge, that, that the sphynx had once been a trekkie. Sanchi tried to stay serious, but forcibly swallowed laughter always gave him the hiccups. Vergilius made a face and offered his protégé a piece of saltwater taffy from a white pasteboard box.

"Your grandmother's purchase," he said as Sanchi unsuccessfully tried the old hold-your-breath cure. "I suppose I should be in trouble with Elena for this as well." He looked from the hand holding the taffy box to the one clutching the cotton-candy bag. "I saw no harm. Your Mamacita is a delightful woman and we were having a fascinating conversation until that female *Huracán* bore down on us."

"*Hura*— what?"

"Oh, just a being out of your folklore. Not a very nice one."

"Couldn't you have had this—fascinating conversation on the—'scuse me—way to their hotel?" Sanchi demanded, thoughts of Alonso momentarily shoved aside. All the fear and frustration of the past half hour with Mamacita missing came back to him. "If Papi hadn't—sorry—hadn't said that Mamacita kept talk—pardon—talking about saltwater taffy and diving horses the whole wa—ay down here, we'd still be all over the board—*damn!*—boardwalk looking for you!"

"Is that how you think you found us?" Vergilius said quietly. "Here, those hiccups will drive us both mad. Let me; I have a unique cure."

Under guise of patting Sanchi on the back, the sorcerer stepped behind him and placed both hands on his shoulders. His touch was gentle at first, like the beginning of a backrub. By the time Sanchi sensed those powerful hands tightening at his neck, it was too late.

The pastel decor of the arcade blurred suddenly, then dimmed. In the strange sideways thoughts panic often brings, Sanchi mused, *Oh yeah, I know what this is: the Vulcan nerve pinch. Two-handed, huh? What did he do with the packages? Mmmm, sent 'em on to Mamacita's room by Phantasmal Express: when it absolutely, positively has to get there bibbedy-bobbedy-boo. No tips, please, we're dead. Me t—*

*Persiles.*

The knight was the first thing Sanchi saw, tall and magnificent as he remembered him, clad in a mantle of light. It's glory cast Persiles' features into shadow. Behind him, in the penumbra outside the blazing mantle's aura, Sanchi could just discern the familiar shapes and colors of his narrow room in Papi's apartment. The knight leaned forward, bending toward Sanchi from a great height. His lips moved, but all the sound they made was inside Sanchi's head. The words rang and reverberated like the tolling of a great brazen bell, somber, significant:

*Open the third eye, and see.*

And then there came the memory of that first vision, shining for Sanchi's eyes alone: Persiles' lost lady, and the world of Khwarema dragon-lost with her. Stately figures of lords and ladies, human and elfin, moved in ponderous majesty beneath the gleaming banners of a feasting hall. It was all as Sanchi had seen it before; it had to be, frozen in the vaults of memory. An exultant warmth rose in his blood as the boy he had bccn saw a world more wonderful than his dingy life as just another NYPR kid. It was real, open to him; by Persiles' grace, it was his. Here he was wanted, not wished-on. He would never leave it. He was home.

But as the past rushed over him, stubborner memories sprang up in a hedge of thorn to tear the miracle to shreds. *Where'd he get that mantle?* Sanchi's reason protested silently. *When Persiles touched me that time he was still wearing Papi's spare clothes; brown polyester, man! And why is he so tall? I was a kid then, but this feels like I was only up to his waist. Hell, he never even sounded like that! Not like some voice-over in a fifties Bible flick. Persiles was human! And he gave me the gift of the Sight just like that, a present. He'd never be one to take back a gift, once given. Could I still—?*

Sanchi shook his head, trying to lay a name to what most bothered him about this enforced vision of the vanished world. *Khwarema . . . it wasn't like this at all. This is phony, a sideshow. The people there were like Persiles: They were human too. These—these move like dolls, like cardboard kings.*

"Of course they do," said a voice whose first word broke the illusion of knight and light, lords and ladies. The ghosts took one last step to a musicless pavanne and disappeared. Alone in the empty feasting hall, Sanchi heard the voice speak to him with reality's inescapable clarity. "What else would you expect Vergilius to shape, that ancient trickster? He began his career as a king's mountebank, you know. He sees things through other eyes."

Thick spears of juicy green stabbed up through the polished slate slabs of the feasting hall, shattering the rock. Sanchi was upended, feet splaying, as he flopped onto his back to meet the rich smells of a jungle floor. Spikes of new-sprung palm trees ripped the iridescent silk rugs to shrieking, squawking, flapping flights of parrots that soared up to perch among fronds and branches. Satin-petaled flowers, scarlet, pink, gold, and cream, all starred a heaven turned to winks of blue spied through bright chinks in the rustling roof.

A hand thrust itself before Sanchi's nose, a powerful hand with blunt fingers the color of burnished copper. "And you, little brother? Which eyes do you use to see?"

"Who are you?" Sanchi asked, hesitating to take the hand before his face but not pushing it away either. He boosted himself to his feet and stared at a world doubly changed. He was no longer the boy of memory, but his present self, ludicrously uniformed for a night on the casino floor. Persiles was gone, the tall splendor of the alien knight dwindled to this strange, small, bright-eyed being with hair like a brushstroke of black ink and skin the color of baked clay. He was naked, his body covered with carefully executed geometric patterns, his only ornament a small gray stone carving hanging from a cord of wild cotton around his neck.

"Who am I?" the man repeated. His teeth flashed white in easy laughter. "If I told you, the name would mean less than nothing. You no longer know me. Your heart leads you through more worlds than Persiles ever traveled. When will it lead you home?"

His smile was gone as suddenly as it had come. He bowed his head and removed the loop of cotton cord. The little gray stone figure twirled slowly in the air between the two men.

"We do not believe in the path that ends," he told Sanchi. "Always the forest opens our eyes to a new path. Sometimes it is only one that we have used before and forgotten. You think you yearn for knights and castles, for the hero others will worship, for the slayer of monsters. You forge a sword with your eyes."

Sanchi became aware that they were not truly alone in the jungle. Other eyes watched from the cover of the leaves. Shapes of many sizes, colored like sun and stone, earth and shadow, were ranged behind the nameless man. A salt breeze from an unseen ocean riffled the branches and sent them whispering names:

Yucahú . . . Huracán . . . Atabex . . . Itiba Cahubana . . . Deminán Caracarcol . . . Guahayona . . . Marohú . . . Boinayel . . . Yukiyú . . . other names as well.

A shell of stone closed overhead with a boom like thunder, clapping a cavern around them. Sanchi felt the cool touch of subterranean air, smelled the stale droppings of bats. His eyes strained for light in the darkness. A torch flared, held in a copper hand. By its light Sanchi could see strange figures scribed on the walls and ceiling. His guide stood with his back to the greater darkness of the cavern's depths, but a tongue of sunlight from the cave mouth lapped at Sanchi's feet.

"They wait," the man said. "Will you come?"

Sanchi backed away, moving for the sunlight, the open air. The man made no attempt to stop him. Sadness pooled in his eyes, silence robed him in dignity. The only sound for a long time was the nervous shuffle of Sanchi's backtracking feet over the cavern floor, the drip of water from the light-less regions, and the seductive rustle and sigh of distant leaves.

"Not yet," the man said at last. "Still you only see the sword." He threw his head back and howled, then flung his torch into the cavern's maw. Darkness devoured light, even the sunlight of the outer world. The earth shifted again, and Sanchi grabbed wildly for anything, any handhold he could find. His knuckles scraped against rock, he felt his white trousers tear as sharp stones lacerated his sides, and once, fleetingly, he felt the warmth of a hand close over his wrist only to have it slip away, cheated of a firm grip.

Luminous ghosts shared his fall. Misty armor caught flicks of light where no light could be and reflected an eerie dazzle into Sanchi's eyes. All the tales he had been taught in school of legendary heroes swam past—knights all, or swordsmen, conquerors, heroes ablaze with bronze, iron, steel. A blade spun in the blackness, just within his reach, but it spun so wildly that the odds were even Sanchi would seize its hilt or lose a hand to its edge. Still the whirling steel drew his eye, mesmerized him. He saw Persiles' face beyond the blade, saw the knight beckoning him.

*Take up your true weapon, Sanchi. You cannot be a squire forever.*

Mouth dry, he reached for the sword . . .

And screamed as the blue-white edge sliced down, sever-ing his right hand at the wrist. Blood streamed from the stump, turned from crimson to black, a dark river that itself bled clear, then ran into the limpid blue of a tropic sea.

Suspended in the river of his life, submerged in the heart of the mother-water, Sanchi floated in silence. He watched the mute ballet of multicolored fishes, the waving tendrils of sea anemones, the patient sea-road of the great turtles, the dreamless eyes of sharks. His soul felt the pull of an outrushing tide. Bubbles of air burst from his mouth. The ends of his hair lifted from his head to fan the waters above. His wound flowed red again, a gauze of blood dirtying the swimming world around him. Not so far away, too near, a gray-and-white shape turned its wedge-shaped head toward him with the eternal hunter's habitual interest.

A shout from above split the water. An ebony spear spitted the shark when its half-moon mouth was inches from

Sanchi's belly. Black hands plunged into the sea. A woman armored with bright shells and coral scooped Sanchi from the ocean and flung him onto the sand. With a battle-cry that might have summoned the dead, she brandished her recovered spear in triumph and strode away, walking the sky to where the sun was rising.

Sanchi pushed sopping hair out of his eyes with what should have been the stump of his wrist. The touch of his own fingers was only one marvel. Another was the cotton cord now tangled between them, the small triangular stone figure dangling from it.

"For you, little lost brother."

Sanchi saw the copper-skinned man squatting comfortably nearby, at the entrance to a circular thatched hut. Persiles was there too, standing beside him, holding the sword.

"Another gift," the knight said. "Use it better than you have used mine."

Sanchi stood up, brushed sand from his clothes and skin. "Persiles, what is this? A dream? One of Vergilius' spells? Where am I, really? What's happening?" He was whining like a frightened child, knew it, and despised himself for what he could not help.

The knight shrugged. It was an easy, natural move, unencumbered by armor. The sword was the only metal he carried. "You see what I mean, Sanchi? The eye sees, the mind interprets. The true eye sees inward, but it needs wisdom to understand what your Sight tells you."

"I understand that you're here. When you took me to Khwarema that time, it was a dead world, but we could still touch the people there. Is it that way now? Can I—?" He extended his restored hand timidly.

"Would you really touch me?" Persiles' Olympian gaze rested on Sanchi like a weight of guilt. "Would you allow it to yourself, when all these years you have pushed my memory away?"

"I never—"

"You did. Because you loved me, Sanchi. Because you could not read all the paths of love any better than you have read yourself. Who was there to teach you how? There was only one name your ignorance could give to a man who loved another man." The knight sighed. "Unless you learn to link the true eye, the heart, and the mind, your life will

111

be one long denial; your name for love, now and ever, will be death."

He thrust the sword into the sand and stretched out his arms to encircle the hut and the man squatting before it, the sea and the shore. "Here is beauty," he said. "Here is a land to love."

An iron breastplate unrolled from neck to hips over the knight's tunic. A backplate clanged into place behind. The bell of a *cabacete* helmet suddenly shaded his face, and a torch flared in his left hand. He drew the sword from the sand and chopped the squatting man through the ribs, then wrenched the blade free and tossed the torch atop the thatched roof. He fell to one knee long enough to yank a small plug of gold from his victim's earlobe, then held his sword high in triumph.

*"Ven, Sanchez! En nombre de Dios y Santiago! A nosotros los héroes la gloria!"* He signaled for Sanchi to follow and ran on.

Sanchi let him run. He rushed instead to the Indian's side, tore off his silly, sopping blue blazer, and tried using it to stop the flow of blood. It was useless. What stopped was the heart.

*Well, little brother, have you learned?* The voice came from everywhere, from sea and sand and jungle and the blazing hut. *This is what comes of forging swords. Have you chosen the path made for you to follow? Have you found your true weapon?*

Sanchi felt something small and cool touch his chest. His fingers found the little gray stone figure on its cotton cord, but he could not remember having put it on.

*A zemí, little brother; yours. Only a token. You are not alone if you realize what gift I have truly given you. I, Yukiyú.*

"What gift?"

A wind swept over the sea, whipping thicker froth in the shallows.

"What gift?"

The trees rustled louder and louder still, a whisper running into a roar that soon drowned out the crackle of the flames.

*"What gift?"* Sanchi was on his feet, fists clenched around the *zemí*, screaming at the sky and the sea and the dead man. "By all holy, *what gift?*"

"My question precisely," said Vergilius, and his words sent Sanchi lurching out of vision into the present world.

"Oh God." Sanchi leaned against the sorcerer heavily. "God, I gotta sit down."

They found a bench where Sanchi sat for some time, his head in his hands. Vergilius waited patiently, asking nothing, saying nothing, letting Sanchi find his own way back. Once he cleared his throat and remarked, "At least your hiccups are gone." He got no reply.

At last the younger man lifted his head and let out a short, husky breath. "God," he said again. *"Damn!"*

"You see why we have come together, Sanchi?" Vergilius said quietly. "Gifts call to other gifts. Just as many say that money finds money, need clings to need."

"All these years . . ." Sanchi could not get over it. "The Sight Persiles gave me, and I never—" He jumped up suddenly. "Hey, now I don't need to bother you to help me find 'Lonso!"

"Eureka," the mage said dryly. "Which would mean more to me if I knew who this person was."

In as few words as possible, Sanchi brought Vergilius abreast of his half brother's existence and unpleasant doings, so far as Sanchi himself had tracked them. He finished by saying, "Now all I have to do is search for his mind with mine, right?"

"You can try." A wad of matted cotton candy popped into Vergilius' mouth. The bag and box of candy were back in the sorcerer's lap. "On two conditions. One, that your half brother has a mind to find, and two, that a raw, untrained, unguided gift of the Sight would be capable of such a search."

"Untrained?" Sanchi's face fell. "Unguided?"

"Of course. You were given an uncut, unpolished gem. You can turn it into a treasure, or a handful of pretty pebbles if you abuse it. But no fear"—the sorcerer clapped him on the back—"I can train you, and try searching for Alonso on your behalf meanwhile. Chin up, Sanchi. Mastering the Sight is a lot like learning to ride a bicycle. A few tumbles that sting, but once you have the skill, you never lose it."

Sanchi cocked his head to one side. "When did you learn how to ride a bike, Vergilius?"

"I?" It was the sorcerer's turn to look abashed. "Ah—never. The spokes, you know, tangling things; training wheels at my age simply out of the question; more pressing things requiring my attention . . ."

He was still mumbling excuses as they left the arcade to get Sanchi to his job.

Elena used her passkey to open the door to the penthouse suite. The head of housekeeping had sent her up when the call came for maid service. Mrs. Beddow probably thought of it as a figurative rap across the knuckles, penance for tardiness.

"Take extra care," she'd said. "Do everything just so. Ms. Apeiron owns this place. She's got more money than God."

Elena couldn't help thinking of Ali Baba as she entered the suite. More money than God. Mrs. Beddow had almost genuflected when she said that. Would there be little heaps of dollar bills, spare change, chips, jewelry? Would the Dust Buster choke on a ruby molted from the Maltese Falcon?

She was disappointed. The draperies were all drawn, though it was a sunny afternoon outside. When she turned on the lights, she saw a sitting area like those in the lesser suites downstairs, only much larger. Down there as up here, the furniture was of higher quality than in the hotel's commoner rooms. It still looked as if it had been extruded from a Play-Doh Make Your Own Antiques Fun Factory. She set to work.

After the sitting area, she opened the master-bedroom door. The windows were covered here too, and flicking the light switch near the door did nothing.

"I disconnected the lamp on that switch. Don't be scared, honey. I won't be in your way. I'm the one called for maid service." A lascivious smooching sound followed.

The voice was familiar, but so out of place in that setting that Elena fought to believe the evidence of her ears. All her doubts were destroyed an instant later as another light clicked on; the lamp on the bedside table.

Naked and leering in the tumbled bedclothes, Alonso winked at her.

# CHAPTER THIRTEEN:
## Separate Tables

The sphynx perched on a plush blue stool that echoed the color of her sapphire necklace and indicated that she would like another card. The dealer complied, and laid a king atop the queen she had showing. Her hole card was a deuce.

"Bah! A fine way to spend a Friday night, losing to you. Someone else must have the luck tonight; it has abandoned me."

With a little hiss of pique, she flicked the impertinent cards away. None of the other players at the table had succeeded in capturing the wandering spirit of good fortune, but for the cachet of lingering near a celebrity like Ianthe Apeiron they continued to make their wagers. The dealer raked in the chips, maintaining his carefully guarded facial expression as the house won another round.

With an equally feigned grimace of annoyance, the sphynx watched her money feed back into the coffers of a casino hotel she owned and take the chips of all the other losers with it.

Gemma prowled one bank of slot machines under the cold blue eyes of Mr. Jorgensen. It seemed as if the slots had replaced the harem as the purview of females. Little old and middle-aged women predominated. The liver-spotted men among them had the unsexed look of Turkish eunuchs, black and white, to complete the picture. Loose flaps of flesh jiggled from nearly every arm upraised to pull a lever. Raggedly manicured fingernails snapped, to accompanying cries of indignation soon forgotten when a few coins rattled down into the trays.

Gemma shuddered. She hated being assigned the slot machines. A mirror held no fears for her, but a mirror of the future did. She closed her eyes and visualized Ms. Apeiron, so sleek, so graceful. And how old was she? No way at all to tell. For the rich there were a myriad ways to cheat age, to counterfeit youth up to the edge of the grave itself. For those not fortunate or smart enough to know the lie behind *Money isn't everything* there was this: the borrowed glamour of the casino floor, the borrowed thrill of quarters tumbling into a little metal pan.

Ms. Apeiron would not let that happen to Gemma. Not if Gemma served her well, not if Gemma learned to serve herself even better. Now Ms. Apeiron wanted Sanchez. How strange, the change in her from the rage she'd first expressed on hearing that the man had taken up with Gemma's other employer. Ms. Apeiron had slipped from hot anger to languid appetite regarding Sanchez. Was this something for which to thank Alonso?

Gemma doubted there was anything in this world for which one could thank Alonso, except leaving it. Still, Ms. Apeiron had stated her wishes, and Gemma must provide, but where was he? Gemma grew nervous. If he was out sick, it would mean delay. From what she'd heard, Ms. Apeiron's patience was either chancy or absent. From what she knew, Ms. Apeiron's ire was more dependable. The lady was used to control and brooked no excuses. Acts of God were for other people.

Then Gemma spied him across the floor. He was at the baccarat tables again. His dark, exotic good looks seemed quite in keeping with the reputation of the game. He could have been the prince of some affluent Third World nation, evaluating the game at the tables in Monte Carlo before having a plunge.

Gemma sighed. Such a shame that in reality he wasn't more socially appropriate for her. The same blending of blood that made him so attractive to the eye simultaneously made him unacceptable; a mongrel. On second thought, Ms. Apeiron had expressed an interest in the man. If she did anything to advance his lot high enough, perhaps Gemma's own unformed attraction would someday be justified, mongrel or not. It all depended.

For tonight, she had her orders.

Mr. Jorgensen did not try to stop her as she left her post. She assumed that word from Ms. Apeiron concerning her had come swiftly down the chain of command. Sanchez looked surprised to see her. Her pride winced slightly when he did not register pleasure as well.

"Before you ask, no, I'm not following you." She laughed deliberately. It had the desired effect of relaxing him. "I'm just the victim of a shift change. I don't know any of these people." A wave of her hand took in the other employees. "It's so good to see someone familiar. Especially you. Do you have a break coming up soon? Would you care to join me for coffee?"

He did, on both counts. As he and Gemma left the floor for Dolmades, she noted Ms. Apeiron's eyes following them. The lady was not displeased. She might be impatient, but she had encouraged subtlety in bringing Sanchez around to meet her. From the complacent look she wore, she approved of Gemma's tactics thus far.

"You know where he is?" Sanchi's hands tightened involuntarily around the cup.

Gemma's thick lashes hid her eyes as she gazed into her coffee. "I thought you ought to know. I'd have told you sooner, but I had only a glance at first. I wanted to make sure he was who I thought before I upset you over nothing. I didn't have to wait long for a good look. Ms. Apeiron takes him almost everywhere with her."

Sanchi gnawed his lip. "Damn. Damn it to hell, he's just a kid! She's breaking the law, what she's doing with him."

"I'm afraid you'd have to prove that." Gemma's voice was level, sympathetic. "And if he is happy, there's no hope of getting him to testify against her."

"But he's *living* with her!"

"Listen." She rested her hand atop his. It felt hot and dry and smooth. "Ms. Apeiron is one of the richest women in the world. If you try to prove your underage brother is living in sin with her, she can order up an apartment for him—good Lord, even a house!—and get any date she wants on the lease. On paper, he's living alone, a little priest."

He pulled away. A little coffee slopped out of his cup and sprinkled her hands. The napkin he shoved at her was compressed to a tight ball. "I'll bet she was the one who bailed him out of jail. What does she do, prowl the police station looking for kids? Too damned proud to cruise for trade? *Puta vieja sinvergüenza!*"

"Sanchez . . ." The lighting in Dolmades favored her fair coloring and fine bones, making her look all the more like a reproving angel. The look in her eye let him know that she understood Spanish, even those words.

"Sorry." He had the courtesy to look ashamed. Then, desperately, "Everything Alonso's done, gotten into since he came here, is all my fault. I was supposed to be responsible for him. If I'd've done my job right, he would never—"

His right hand went to his chest, touched something small and solid under his shirt. Gemma could see its mass as his fingers pinched it. She assumed it was a holy medal of some sort, which was odd. She had never picked Sanchez for a superstitious man.

"At least he's safe," she told him.

"Safe?" He made it into a joke. "How about when she gets tired of him? How about when she wants a new toy? He's only a boy. He thinks the world begins and ends inside his own skin. The first time he learns it doesn't shouldn't be as hard as she'll make it."

Gemma's lashes swept down again. "You sound as if you know what you're talking about." If he heard, he heard; she had uttered the words that softly on purpose, playing her own gamble with God.

He didn't hear; if he did, he had nothing to reply. The chips remained in the center of the table. "He's making a mistake he can't imagine." He seized her wrist. "I've got to talk to him, Gemma."

She turned her wrist in his grasp and slid back the hand until their palms met, fingers laced. "I'll help you, Sanchez." A gentle pressure on his skin while she willed her own warmer. "I'd do anything I could to help you."

Elena and Vergilius stood beneath a frieze of romping nymphs, figures of antique gold in high relief against a stark white marble ground. The sorcerer stood so still that he might have passed himself off as a male caryatid in afterfives. Only Elena's constant, insistent tugs at his sleeve showed that he was more flexible than painted marble.

"Do you see him yet?" she demanded. "Do you?"

"I would have said so, if only to save the material." He removed her plucking fingers from his arm firmly.

"I mean, do you *see* him!" Her voice dropped to a whisper. *"Telepathically."*

"You can speak in a normal voice. None of these people

care about your sanity." He indicated the Friday-night crowd at Dionysia. Everyone seemed to have somewhere urgent to go and no time to get there. Stationary as a pair of rocks, Elena and Vergilius had been jostled more than once. "No one is even paying attention to us."

"Including you, I see," she snapped.

"Elena, you are a beautiful girl, but a trial. For the second time today you have burst in on Mamacita and me during a very pleasant interview—*and* a good dinner, this time. This afternoon you haul her away from me, tonight it is my turn to be torn from her company. Do you fear I will seduce your grandmother? All this babble of Alonso! Suddenly it is so vital that we know where the stripling is, and what he is doing. If you and Sanchi had been this concerned as to his activities earlier, he might have stayed in his own bed and I might have finished some excellent *quenelles du saumon*."

"I'm sorry," Elena said, letting the way she said it tell him that she wasn't. "I just want to find Sanchi and tell him where Alonso is. I couldn't care less. The little bastard tried to pull me into the bed with him—"

"—and you learned a new use for Lysol spray disinfectant. You told me."

"Sanchi will feel better after he finds 'Lonso again, and then we'll have his full attention for dealing with the sphinx. That's what you want, isn't it? Or haven't you noticed how his mind keeps straying?"

A curt *tsk* escaped Vergilius' tightly pursed lips. "True. You are right, Elena."

"You sound as if it really hurt to say that. So come on—find him so we can tell him and take it from there. You use your mind reading, I'll go talk to his boss."

Elena's interview with Mr. Jorgensen did not last long. When she returned to the magician's side he greeted her with: "I hope you had better fortune than I. His thoughts are guarded. I cannot find him."

"Well, relax. Mr. Jorgensen told me he went off on break."

"Shall we follow?"

"No; no sense in chasing him through the hotel. He'll come back, and then we can tell him." Elena was smiling, relieved. "How long could he be gone?"

# CHAPTER FOURTEEN:
## This Boy

The bowl was gold, the blood was red. The pictures within were only suggestions of what was to come, yet the sphynx was a seasoned reader of such promises. Tiny diamonds winked at the tips of her nails, lacquered the hard, iridescent green of a beetle's carapace. The bowl was small—both gold and blood were dear commodities, and she sometimes played the game of frugality with herself—small enough to balance on a tripod she fashioned of the three midmost fingers of her left hand. The bowl was shallow, but deep enough to give her warning that Gemma was on her way with the one she wanted.

Oh, it had been masterfully done! That Gemma had the spark, the cold fire of pure mind inside, the infinite calculation that the sphynx admired. Those huge blue eyes, how nicely they could hold just one desire at a time, an obsession to kindle at the center of her life and burn there forever. That was where lesser humans failed. Their eyes filled with the many wonders of their world and they spread their arms wide to gather in so much, so very much.

What could they know of the one driving force that forges a life's purpose? To live one life for one reason—revenge, money, power—there was the key to mastery. But they divided themselves between heart and mind, soul and eye, the labor of their hands and the yearning of their spirits for what they could never touch or mold or shape to suit them.

There was a Riddle in it. Beneath the semblance of smooth human skin, her fur rippled and prickled with the forcibly restrained thrill of its anticipated making. She would meditate upon it, add it to the Riddle already forming in her barren loins, taking the place of the cub she would never bear, the child whose birth would mean world's end for the creatures whose kind had destroyed her own.

The time of that last Riddle was not yet. Too much stood

between her and the heart of the human world. How can you deal a mortal blow if you do not know where to plunge the blade? The filaments she wove were strong, but not yet strong enough. She had time.

But now she wondered . . . did she? Vergilius had followed her, found her, frightened her enough to make her send her minions after him. That had been a mistake. She should have let him come to her, attack on her own terms and territory. The very fact that he had forced her into such a raw, half-formed assault was the mark of her own weakness. The ghost-collar still chafed. How could she be mistress when one cowardly corner of her being still thought of a mere human as master?

The gold bowl was thin as a flower petal. It seemed to rise to her lips of its own lightness. She lapped it clean and dry. Soon she would meet the one Vergilius had chosen, after all these years. Why had he done it, what was there about that youth to be special enough to burst the walls of solitude the wizard had set up around the self-sufficiency of his magic? All the world as witness, the young man's brother was only so much meat. Yet they were both human, and of common blood. *Could* there be a difference?

If there was, she would find it. And then she would ask a Riddle.

The doorbell of her suite rang. She pinched the empty bowl into a wad of glittering metal and dropped it into the wastebasket beside her desk like a gum wrapper.

"Really, she's very nice," Gemma said as she pressed the porcelain button.

"I'll bet," Sanchi snarled.

Gemma rounded on him suddenly, for the first time letting him see a slip of temper crease that perfect eggshell face. "Listen, Ms. Apeiron didn't have to agree to see you at all. In fact, considering who she is, you could be looking at the want ads right now instead of at her front door. She could get you fired in a minute; and me too, for helping you."

"So the bitch is that rich?"

"You really were raised in the streets." The way Gemma said that, it was plain statement of fact, condescending pity, and burning indictment of all Sanchi's family at once. It cut, and the blood rushed to his face.

"Don't worry, I'm housebroken. I won't talk that way to Ms. Apeiron. I'm just—I just have to get it out of my system now, all right?"

Gemma softened. She sandwiched Sanchi's hand in a firm squeeze. "I understand. I'm sorry if I insulted you. Please believe me about Ms. Apeiron, though. She *is* nice. We might both be wrong about her and your brother. I ran some little errands for her, and she said I could call on her anytime, and here's the proof that she meant it."

The door opened on a silvery chain. A warm scent of lilac blew into the hall. "Yes?" Sanchi thought he saw a golden eye regarding him through the crack.

"This is the man who wanted to see you, Ms. Apeiron," Gemma said with a high, bright, cheerful voice like a little lapdog standing on its hind legs for a treat. "Sanchez Rubio."

"Ah, yes. Please come in, Mr. Rubio." The eye withdrew, the door opened. Sanchi had his first look at the magnificence of the penthouse suite. He stepped across the threshold without being aware of it. So much sparkled and gleamed. Another memory spread stiff wings and tried to fly forth to greet its younger mate. Gold. Jewels. Rich fabrics. A cathedral.

The dragon.

He turned at the sound of the door being shut and saw her. Above the smooth cascade of her satin robe was the bony mask of the dragon's skull.

The curve of the fangs, the gaping hunger of the empty eyesockets melted away to misty trails of ivory embroidery, japonesque curlicues of silver and white at the cuffs and hem and open neck of Ms. Apeiron's jade robe. She was motioning him toward a sofa, wearing the mild, noncommittal smile of empty social pleasantries. At his neck, the small stone carving felt colder. *Open the third eye, and see.* The *zemí* would not allow him the comfort of saying, *Well, it was only a dream after all*, or permit him to take refuge behind *It's a trick of the light* or *My eyes are playing tricks on me.* He saw what he saw, and he knew.

She had the look of the dragon. She was the sphinx.

*And here I am, without a goddam thing to protect myself with, let alone a sword to kill her.* Sanchi made himself smile as the sphynx settled beside him on the sofa in a swish of satin. Behind his idiotic grin lurked one last heartfelt reflection on his situation. *Oh shit.*

She poured a little wheat-colored wine from a decanter on the cocktail table before them. The little glass she pressed on Sanchi was the blue-white of frost. He declined, hearing himself mumble something about not drinking during working hours.

"But you must," she said. "I insist." Her accent turned the words to melody. "It is so much more civilized this way. I understand all about the exigencies of your job—truly, I regret that our dear friend Gemma could not join us because she had to return to the casino—but I assure you, I have given instructions for your supervisor to make of this night an exception in your case."

"You have?"

"Certainly. You did say that you had something of great importance to discuss with me. On the telephone, Gemma said that you were deeply upset. I am not a light-minded woman, Mr. Rubio. I did not get to be where and what I am by bowing to frivolous impulses. I know the value of swift, accurate information. As soon as Gemma told me of your wish for an interview, I had you investigated. From what I learned of you, I think you must be sincere, and your distress genuine. Oh, do not look shocked! A woman in my position does not remain there if she admits just anyone to her rooms. You will notice that we are quite alone. I have even dismissed my bodyguards. Would that be the wisest action for me to take if I did not know everything about you?"

"How much do you know?" Sanchi's voice was hoarse, his mind screaming, *No witnesses and all that money. She's a monster in her real shape—I've seen pictures. Lion's claws. Falcon's wings. Fangs. And a Riddle. The one gamble she takes, the Riddle. Oh boy, what was the sphynx's Riddle again? Right. Four legs, two legs, three legs equals man. But Oedipus answered that one. After all these years, she's got to have something new, and the Answer won't be something I studied in Western Lit 101. Son of a bitch, I don't even like doing crossword puzzles!*

\* \* \*

The sphynx forced herself to keep smiling at this monster seated so close beside her on the sofa that her flesh itched and her wings shivered with the urge to unfurl and clap her far from him. Behind the facade of human sophistication she was a nursling cub, trembling at thunder.

She was afraid of Sanchi.

*No wonder Vergilius chose such a one!* The ghosts clung to him, baring their teeth at her, daring her to move against him. Magic beat strongly in his blood, each pulse of the heart visible to her as it added a shade of brightness to the aura of power shielding him. What was worse, it was power with an alien stink to it, a potency the more dangerous to her because she could give it no name.

But it was power unformed, unfocused, untrained. He was like one newly blind, unaware of all that surrounded him, not yet able to use his other senses to piece out a world in the darkness.

*Untrained . . . Vergilius will see to righting that, if I let him. How long you waited for this, my master! To find such a one, to find your youth and your potential all over again, in a different skin. You are reborn.* Then the shape of the jest struck her, a spear of inspiration.

*Reborn . . . and mine. Mine as I was yours, Vergilius. In this new skin, this other self, you shall be mine.*

The sphynx sipped her wine. No time had passed. Sanchi's anxious question still hung on the air. "I am not fond of prying into the lives of others," she said. "My inquiries were only to find out whether I might trust you, the two of us being alone. Your reputation is enviable, Mr. Rubio; your ethical and moral standards above reproach. Perhaps you are only a great deceiver, but so far as your supervisors have been able to tell, you are a good man. That is what I know of you."

The words were without meaning, a soothing recitation of what any man would want to hear. She did not need her mind for such a conversation. She withdrew into the place where the servant thoughts awaited her commands and dispatched one to evade the guardian ghosts, to slip through the chinks in any hedge of power, to probe the naked self of this young man she wanted for her own.

The thought was swift and skilled, cunning and subtle. What it found, what it brought back to the sphynx's knowledge, was so simple she almost laughed aloud. Was there ever a soul that cried out so loudly to be enslaved? Such an easy chain to forge! This would be no challenge.

"Now, what did you wish to discuss with me, Mr. Rubio?"

She listened with polite attention as he hemmed and hawed his way around the matter of his half brother. He circled the subject with a coward's tread, yet she knew he was neither coward nor weakling. She bent her head as he continued with his tentative accusations, his meek inquiries all couched in the subjunctive and the conditional.

*I may be wrong, but . . .*
*You have to admit, things look as if . . .*
*It could be I was misinformed . . .*
*If he weren't so young, I wouldn't say . . .*

She burst into tears at the appropriate moment, and as he stared at her, horrified by what his tentative words had done, she made some minor changes in her suite and herself.

Her face was softer, the amber eyes darker and more tender when she raised them to his. "Forgive me." Huskiness crept into her voice. Her perfume faded, and a warm aroma of milk and cinnamon stole from her flesh to draw him nearer without knowing it.

"Forgive—?" He was badly confused.

"You are right, Mr. Rubio. I am the one who freed your brother. But wrong also. Though I know how it looks to you, to the world, I swear I am—" She wept anew.

He offered her her own wineglass and in his agitation took several short, nervous sips from his. She dispatched him to the bathroom for tissues. It was primitive, what she did next, but she saw no need to waste subtleties. While he was gone, three drops of a yellow liquid fell from the tip of one viridian fingernail into his glass and blended with the wine. It was only water condensed by magic from the very air around her, yet water enclosing the essence of a spell to weaken resolve and open the mind to the impulse of emotion.

When he returned, she dabbed away the tears. "I am sorry," she said with a little gasp, leaning closer, her shoulder brushing his chest. "I thought that all the ghosts were banished years ago, and my guilt with them." Her eyes shone. "You will think I am a madwoman, to speak of ghosts, Mr. Rubio. It is more fashionable in this country to mention guilt, unresolved psychological conflicts, mind-babble. But I am not of this land. Where I come from, the ghosts are very real."

Sanchi shifted uncomfortably beneath the gentle pressure of her shoulder. He had expected many things, but never for a monster to dissolve in tears and send him after Kleenex. Nothing felt right. Doubt made him antsy. He took another sip of wine and let its warmth ease the frizzing sparks running through his nerves.

*Open the third eye and see.* But what about when your own two normal eyes told you and told you that the third eye lied? That could happen, couldn't it? False visions? Imagination clouding the way to a true seeing? He had seen Khwarema that way, expectation warping truth. Maybe he wanted to find the sphinx so badly that he was becoming the maker of his own dragons. He could have been wrong, Gemma might not have seen Alonso, maybe it was all innocent, or a mistake, or both. He wished Elena were here with him. He wished Vergilius had trusted him enough to show him the sphinx as she was. He wished—

*Oh God, I wish she'd stop crying!* His head was aching. Only her words seemed to salve the throbbing pain that drummed itself against his temples. She was saying something, but it sounded muzzy. Spiderwebs blew from the immaculate crystal chandelier, silkworm strands wrapped a cocoon of air and space around him. He blinked a burning haze from his eyes and swam into the tears brimming in her own.

"—my son."

The photograph was framed in silver, the child was caught in the moment between last youth, first maturity, when immortality was still his birthright and death could never know his name. Sanchi saw a smooth face, a hesitant smile, black hair, skin the color of— *"Por qué no te ríes, Sanchito?" Papi shouted as he took that one last picture before Sanchi went away to live with his real mother again. "Give us something to remember you by! I will see to it that your Mama gets a print, too."* He held his hand up to the photograph, skin to skin. How strange.

Her son. Monsters didn't have sons, did they? Could they? Would they weep for them like this? But her son had died. Wasn't that what she was saying? The photograph with Sanchi's own face was folded to her bosom, so white, so warm. Sanchi could smell the milk-and-cinnamon scent stronger with his every breath, and when she bent toward him to shed more tears, he took her into his arms to drain the fragrance from her skin, her tumbling black hair.

"In prison. You can never know how harsh those places are. Here they are bad, but where he died . . . I blame myself. He was my son. He should have come first, but all I saw was time slipping from me, and the money, and the need to prove that I could be as good in business affairs as any man; never enough. He would thank me for leaving him so much wealth. He would be proud of his mama." Her hand brushed Sanchi's as she pushed her tousled hair away from her face. Her fingers clung to his as if by reflex. He thought he felt her bones burning incandescent through the flesh.

"—money. That was what I gave him, all and everything. Nothing. Another prisoner killed him before I could reach the prison, use my influence to set him free." Her laugh echoed up out of depths Sanchi could sense only inches from his own feet. "My precious *influence*. With death?" That laugh again, to rake across the pounding pain still ravaging his head.

"He was stabbed to death because he did not have a cigarette with which to buy his life; my son."

He mouthed hollow comforts, and all his heart ached for what she suffered. He reached for more wine with his free hand and found he had left the cup dry. Was it the wine that made her smaller, darker, her eyes a warm shade of brown like no other in the world for him? She was explaining how she came to free his brother—penance for the child she had come too late to save. Her life had become one long act of atonement, sackcloth beneath the silk, for his sake. She was begging him to forgive her, to understand, to pardon her for not being there, to let her make it up to him now.

Didn't he know who loved him best in all the world? Didn't he know all she could be to him, if he would only grant her that much forgiveness for the years they had lost and wasted?

*A boy stood atop the dead body of a monster and gazed down at a small, dark woman who knelt in the shadow of his* sword. *It was just as he had imagined it would be. She had come back for him. She was sorry.*

"Sanchi . . . *my son.*"

He never knew the moment that they rose from the couch and drifted into the bedroom. For an instant he felt something cold and hard pressing against his chest. Then soft lips stole his brief cry of alarm, and all was warmth and welcome and the dark.

And that same voice whispering in his ear, in his mind. *"I will not ask it yet, not yet. But oh, I will ask it of you, Sanchi! Of you and no other."* Laughter trailed ice behind his eyes. *"Now I truly have all the time in the world."*

# CHAPTER FIFTEEN:
## All the Aces

"How can you sit there playing so calmly?" Elena demanded. Her fingers dug into the back of Vergilius' chair while she wished for the boldness to make it his neck.

The sorcerer laid a finger to his lips, never taking his eyes from the red plastic shoe containing the cards. The hand he was playing with such solitary concentration at the baccarat table came up a loser.

"There. No longer so obvious. That should please Sanchi," he remarked. "I am not so old that I do not learn my lessons." He dismissed his loss with a twitch of the lips, then pushed away from the table and rose to take Elena's arm. She was too angry to protest when he steered her out of Dionysia and into the early-Saturday-morning boardwalk sunshine.

Gulls screamed and rode their private roller coaster over the sands. The girl and the magician leaned against the cold gray railings as if they were a pair of ordinary tourists. Only Elena's uniform made them stand out from the crowd. The wizard had learned more than one lesson from Sanchi, including the value of less outlandish garb for daytime wear. His habitual evening dress was swapped for a Kelly-green sports shirt and navy slacks. Little green whales spouted all around the embroidered twill belt at his waist. When he caught Elena glancing at them, he made real mist spray from their blowholes for an instant.

"That's right," Elena grumbled. "Wet your pants."

"Why are you so troubled, my dear? The day is beautiful. You are young. I think I detect an illusion or two still with you, but they are harmless and rather pretty things. What has you so upset?"

"*There's* a stupid question. What do you think? Sanchi!"

"Ah yes. Sanchi."

" 'Ah yes, Sanchi.' " Elena twirled an imaginary mustache as she mocked Vergilius' accent. "You act like you've got him tucked in your pocket, ready to flick out at me like the king of diamonds. Where *is* he, Vergilius? Why didn't he come back to the floor from his break last night?"

"You heard the young woman." Vergilius' eyes mirrored the Atlantic, held the flight of gulls. "She said he didn't feel well and went home."

"Then why wasn't he home when I called him?"

A shrug. "There are any number of explanations."

"Well, the only one I can think of is that maybe he ran into Alonso on his own and took off after the brat."

"Yes. That is one possibility."

"But not the one you're buying?" Elena's brows rose quizzically. The sorcerer remained noncommittal. "What do you think happened? Where do you believe he went, if not to chase down his brother?"

"Chase him down . . . and do what when he catches him?"

"I don't know. Talk to him. Reason with him. Ask him what the hell he's doing in some rich hag's bed."

"A hag. She is anything but that. You have never encountered the lady, have you?"

"Ianthe Apeiron? No. But I've heard about her. Good God, one person with all that money! I hear she never goes anywhere except as the filling in a bodyguard sandwich. It's easier to take a photo of Sean Penn and live than to snap one of her. But if she's as rich as they say and even halfway good-looking, why would she waste her time on something like Alonso?"

The sorcerer smiled. "There's a riddle."

The way he said it made Elena's breath come hissing in between clenched teeth. "No."

"But yes. Are you pleased? You did want to know our enemy."

"Ianthe Apeiron is the sphynx?"

"What use is there in concealing the fact any further? I would have told both you and Sanchi together last night, had we found him. I would not want him to hare off after his brother if the boy is indeed sharing that one's bed."

"But how do you know he didn't find Alonso last night? And the sphynx—oh God!"

"Calm yourself. People stare." The magician closed his hand over hers on the railing. "Regard the ocean, Elena. In its depths, mountains are born, chasms open, lives begin and end in blood. Yet the surface reveals nothing."

"Until a hurricane. Vergilius, I don't want platitudes. I want to know where Sanchi is right now and I want to know why you're so cool about it."

The wizard laced his fingers together on the boardwalk rail as if he knelt to receive communion from the sky and the sea. "Sanchi is your friend. It is good to be concerned for one's friends."

Elena's scowl deepened. "You'd better have something more than that to tell me."

"More. The very word. More than a friend, is he not?"

Her exasperation came out in one sharp breath and both fists hitting hard on the rail. "You know that! We practically grew up together. He was like an extra brother, and he was a sight nicer to me than my own brothers, sometimes. Some of them."

"So I have been told. Repeatedly. With much emphasis on the truth of it." The sorcerer cupped his hands, and a downy gull chick peeped out at Elena. Its feathers were the virbrant green of a freshly cut lime. In the magician's hands it grew to maturity in seconds and leaped for the sky. The other gulls saw it approaching and veered off, leaving it to hover miserably in the middle air, bewildered and alone.

"See the bird, Elena. He does not know he is different. He only thinks the world is unfair, or mad, or unable to understand his worth. He cannot see the truth. Sometimes the truth can only be seen outside the skin."

"Point made." Elena watched the weird gull as it dipped

and climbed, trying to approach the others. They fled, and a tether of magic kept it within a set compass, able to chase them only so far. She could almost feel it pull at her own neck every time the green gull attempted to pursue its terrified mates. "God knows why you want to make it this way, though, or what it has to do with my question. This is cruel."

"I regret it." With a pass of his fingers Vergilius caused the anomaly to disintegrate by degrees, its wings streaming away in pale green droplets of illusion on the wind. He shifted his eyes from the waves to her face.

"As I regret all of my words and actions, past and present, that cause pain. At times I do not realize how cruel they are, until I see the outcome. Like that poor bird, I live too close to the truth to see it. Like others. A green gull . . . a pretty conceit, a decorative touch to nature, until we saw the lone life it would lead. It did not ask for life, but you do ask for an answer. Very well. The young woman we spoke to last night is in my pay. She has brought me much reliable information since my arrival here. Perhaps some of it has helped to stave off the final encounter with the sphynx until I can be ready for it. I reward her well and have not been disappointed. Lovely, is she not? Beauty is often a key to knowledge denied others. Her name is Gemma."

"The one who told you Sanchi got sick?"

Vergilius looked solemn. "That is not precisely what she told me. Only what I chose to tell you."

"What?" Elena pushed herself from the rail. "Then what did she say? Where is he?"

"At this hour, so early in the morning, he is likely where he was the night before. In her bed."

"No." For the second time Elena uttered that word in the hush of disbelief, as if her own will could unmake what was so. She felt her stomach churn, bile creep up her throat. A nasty, knowing voice inside her head shrilled, *Like an extra brother, is he? Oh, sure! And this is how you felt when Bobby got married, when Manolo started bragging about getting laid!* Her eyes stung, but she forced the iron stubbornness in her bones to become a barricade that would let no tears fall.

The sorcerer spoke on. "She said he had used illness as an excuse to go ahead to her place and wait for her. She gave him the keys, but she had to finish out her shift or it would look too suspicious. Their supervisor is no fool. Gemma would not lie to me; she likes the pay in my service too well, and what is it to me with whom she sleeps? More, last night as I was walking home I caught sight of your Sanchi's half brother. The street was dark, but I could see well enough. He was leaning out the window of a fine car to talk with a small crowd of other youths. They gave him money, he passed out several plastic bags."

"Drugs." Elena came near choking on the word. "To think I called him a brat, as if all he's up to is robbing cookie jars. Alonso seems to have found his calling."

"Indeed. And Sanchi nowhere to be seen."

Elena's words came out with mounting difficulty, though she tried to turn the shake in her voice into a laugh. "No, I wouldn't imagine Sanchi would stand there to see that and not yank 'Lonso out through the windshield."

Vergilius was still observing her with a scientist's emotionless regard. He said nothing, but in his eyes was *So I was right. You do love him.*

Unshed tears were locked away for good as she glowered an equally wordless reply: *Yes! Now save your pity. I'll survive.*

"I have to get to work," she said, tugging microscopic wrinkles from her skirt. "You should have told me straight out where Sanchi was and saved us both a big, unnecessary go-around. I'm supposed to meet my family later this afternoon, and if I have to pull overtime because you made me late . . ."

"My apologies. I thought to spare your feelings."

Elena's smile was wistful. "First you make me admit I've got them, then you want to spare them. You'd make one wicked therapist."

"Another offense to my charge? Hmph. You must confess, you and Sanchi are not the easiest people to comprehend."

The sorcerer sounded so vexed that Elena couldn't help chuckling. "Well, that's not your problem. Want to know what is?"

"Not especially."

"Oh, no trouble. You're easy to read."

"So now you have that power?"

"Don't make me into a sorceress just because I know

people. I know you, anyway. You've been the near-immortal magician so long that you like to pretend you don't have anything to do with ordinary humans like us. The bad news is, you do; you're stuck. One person—the right one—and down comes the wall you took centuries to build."

"A wall . . ." Vergilius considered it. "I am not the only one."

"Of course not. You just knocked down one of mine. And God knows, Sanchi's got enough pulled up around him to make a city."

"Including the one that keeps you out." The sorcerer was sympathetic.

"The one *she* built for him!" Elena wanted no sympathy. It made it too easy for the tears to return. "Do you know why Sanchi's brother's the dirt he is? Do you know why Sanchi wishes he could be that little creep, even when he knows what kind of punk Alonso is? For *her*! For the love she gives 'Lonso that she never gave him, and never will."

Vergilius stroked his chin thoughtfully. "They are half brothers, of different sires, yet it seems to me they never shared a common mother either."

"You could say that." Elena leaned her back on the rail and watched all the different people strolling past the towering facades of the hotels, the low storefront honky-tonks of the boardwalk. Each of them was a living story she might never know, but there was one tale she knew too well.

"A lot of adults think little kids are deaf. We didn't have a very big apartment, and Papi and Mama and Mamacita always talked things out in the kitchen. I could hear every word. No secrets in our house, and almost none in our neighborhood. Sanchi's mother's name is Cruz. His father was some kid she went with in high school. He got her pregnant and that was it; goodbye. She had to drop out, her parents tossed her, only her big brother Carlos—Carlitos, Sanchi called him— only he would give her a place to stay. He took care of her and Sanchi, loved the baby, made it easy for them. Everyone said he was a saint.

"But everyone didn't know what Papi found out: how Carlitos always reminded Cruz about just how much she owed him, just how impossible it would be to pay back. She was a disgrace to the family, *mujer sin honra*, one step up from a whore. She'd better do just what Carlitos told her, keep his place just so, raise the baby the way he said, no back talk, remember what she was. If not, out."

"Fine charity." Vergilius did not look taken with the late Carlitos.

"Cruz couldn't say anything against Carlitos. One word, and she'd be on her own with Sanchi. She saw what happened to other women in her situation—no money, no education, no job, a child to support. Carlitos' place wasn't a palace, but it was about five times better than anything she'd be able to afford on welfare. He kept telling her she was maybe a half-step up from the gutter, and she'd die before she'd let him see her fall in all the way. So she stayed and she suffered and she took it all out on the one person who couldn't fight back. His father was long gone, but Sanchi was right there. Her life, his fault."

"Logic is not something they teach any longer, is it?" the sorcerer stated.

"Then Alonso's father came along. She loved him, he loved her. I don't know whether she even told him about Sanchi. She sneaked around behind Carlitos' back to see him, and one day she just up and ran away with him. My parents knew him; he was a decent man. He would've taken Sanchi in too, if he had lived long enough—loved him, maybe helped Cruz to see him as her son again, instead of Carlitos' favorite object lesson on 'the wages of sin.' *Jesús!* I'm sorry that man was murdered, but what a pompous bag he was!"

"I see." Vergilius checked the Rolex on his wrist. "And Alonso is all she has left her of that good man she loved. So much bitterness. She has been deeply poisoned, this woman Cruz."

"Then she's doing her damnedest to spread a little of the venom around," Elena said sharply. "If Sanchi had any sense, he'd forget she ever had anything to do with him and live a healthy life."

"Forget her . . . like that." The sorcerer's gaze was suddenly penetrating. "It is those capable of forgetting the hurts who will never know the true healing. Scars are preferable to the wound that festers, forgotten. There is no health there, Elena."

He reached into his front pants pocket for his wallet and extracted a printed business card. "It is no use debating this further. I must rest for a time, and you must get to work. If you find Sanchi first, here is where you can reach me."

Elena read the name aloud. " 'Rhett Roman'? You're really out to get me for that one, aren't you?"

"On the contrary, I have grown fond of it. Remember, call. And reverse the charges." He pushed off from the rail, crossed the boardwalk, and ambled down the ramp into the city streets without looking back at her.

"Call him," Elena muttered. "Why don't I just find that skinny bitch Gemma and have her call him? She's the one who knows where Sanchi is, not me." She tucked the card away.

Elena was still mulling over all the ways she could insert Vergilius' card into Gemma's sinus cavities when she wheeled her cart off the elevator at the penthouse level. Ms. Apeiron had called for fresh linen, and Mrs. Beddow decided that Elena had not quite worked off her black marks for tardiness from the day before. The new girl's vague protests only served to clinch the head housekeeper's resolve to ship her upstairs.

Elena didn't know which was the most unpleasant of the three sensations presently running through her mind. Envious thoughts of what she'd like to do to Gemma kept getting shouldered aside by the sinking feeling of how she would react if she ran into Alonso alone in the suite again. Even this had to cede to the icy dread of new knowledge: Ianthe Apeiron was the sphynx. This was no longer a penthouse apartment, but the Minotaur's labyrinth, the lion's den, the dragon's cavern. And what did Elena have by way of sword and shield? Bitsy bottles of Vidal Sassoon shampoo and conditioner and a clutch of San-i-bags.

*If she's there, will she know that I know who she really is?* For an instant Elena was possessed by the cowardly impulse to scurry back downstairs and tell Mrs. Beddow she quit. *And for what reason? What will I say? "Job? I don' need no stinkin' job."* Right. She stood firm, shaming herself out of such fears.

*No, how would she know? Even Vergilius said it wasn't easy to read my mind. If I can't keep my thoughts guarded well enough, I deserve what happens.* She rang the bell.

"Come in," a languid female voice called. "It is unlocked."

Elena opened the door and entered, cradling a stack of clean sheets. She forced herself to look at the woman seated on the sofa, watching an old Bogart film on television. The lady glanced up briefly. Her nose twitched once, as if she had the sniffles, and a doubtful look crossed her face. Elena tensed, evicting all betraying thoughts of Vergilius and the sphynx from her mind.

The woman's expression changed. A wide, hospitable smile warmed her face. Elena had never seen anyone so happy to get fresh bed linens. "Oh, thank goodness. Just go right into the bedroom, my dear."

Mentally Elena frowned, puzzled by such a reception. The sphynx didn't seem to mark her as an enemy, yet there had been an impossible hint of recognition in her look.

*Almost . . . as if she knew me from somewhere.* She entered the bedroom. *Could Alonso have said—?*

Someone was in the bed. The curtains were pulled back, the shades were up, the sunshine admitting no chance to say she was mistaken. It wasn't Alonso. She couldn't even seize the comfort of that convenient lie. He was awake, propped against an avalanche of pillows, leafing through a huge book of Greek myths with a childlike delight in what he read.

All that faded when he looked up and saw her.

"Elena . . ."

The only thought she had was: *Not Gemma's bed.*

She ran, still hugging the linens to her chest. She dropped them in the hall, abandoned them and her cart, raced for the stairway—the elevator would take too long to come. Her footsteps echoed behind her for five flights before she emerged on one of the lower floors and rang for a car. The tourists inside traded bemused looks—why would a maid be crying?—but not one of them said a word.

Sanchi pulled on pants, shirt, and shoes in record time, but not quickly enough. "Where is she?" he shouted as he burst out of the bedroom.

The sphynx said, "Shh," then added, "Don't you adore Mary Astor?" Only after he slammed out of the suite did she smile, turn off the television, and pick up the phone.

"This is Ianthe Apeiron," she said. "Give me Personnel. . . . Yes, have you a Sanchez Rubio on the payroll? . . . No, you don't. Not anymore. He's fired."

She hung up looking more than satisfied. No word would reach Sanchi about who was responsible for his losing his job. She would be there to commiserate with him, to offer every kindness, to suggest he take some time to think about where he must go now. She would stand by him while he did.

She would never do anything so blatant as offer him a job herself. He hadn't the stuff of his half brother for her less legitimate operations, and he had too much pride to accept employment from the woman he was sleeping with.

The sphynx regarded the closed door with half-dreaming eyes. Satisfactory; more. There was much in the man, and a mind so easily accessible that it cost her nothing to learn almost all its secrets. There was some small gray area where her probing thoughts could not penetrate, but it was so paltry—not worth her effort, really.

How many Riddles were in the man, and how easily each was answered! That little snip of a maid, for instance—the one who'd just gone tearing out of here—she was one. Sanchi loved her, but love ringed by a wall of fear, imprisoned by a child who had been hurt too much, too often.

It would stay that way. No hope now of Sanchi and that girl speaking, loving, joining, taking joy in one another. The sphynx had seen to that. Fortunate, how the girl had come in, been known. There was a strong smell of power about her as well. It had put the sphynx on edge, at first, until she recognized the maid from Sanchi's thoughts. *Of course. Just the remains of casual contact with him. That is all I scent on her. It can be nothing else. She is only a woman.*

The sphynx had been an avid student. Vergilius was always loud in his contempt for any so-called magics claimed by females of his own breed. Love potions and little gewgaw witcheries. The grand sorcery was for men and beings like herself; the gods' whim made her therefore that much superior to other female creatures. The sphynx had learned that much from the mage, and her sated pride declared such knowledge undebatably true.

The sphynx stretched her arms and went to the window. A good day's work, and barely noon. She licked her upper lip. The gods gave her favor. Tonight's hunting would be good.

# CHAPTER SIXTEEN:
## Reach Out and Touch Someone

On the bed, Mama held a bitterly weeping Elena close while José María and the boys hovered nearby, extremely ill at ease. They took turns casting longing eyes at the door connecting the two double rooms the family had engaged for the weekend, but that avenue of retreat was closed. No matter how poorly prepared they were to cope with a grown girl's tears, they had to endure. Mamacita was occupying the other room for her prelunch nap. Disturbing her was unthinkable.

"So . . . you said Sanchi did what?" Mike tried to stop the awful sound of Elena's heartbroken sobs by a direct question. Instead of an answer, all he got was louder wails from the bed and an elbow in the ribs from Manolo.

*"Que hay otra mujer, idiota! No lo oíste?"* The middle brother grinned. "Or don't they teach you anything worth knowing at college?"

"Gee, no, Manolo," Mike returned. "I guess I should've dropped out of high school like you."

"You little—"

*"Basta."* José María stepped between the two young men, his eldest, Roberto, moving like Papi's shadow if need for an extra pair of peacemaking hands should arise. Manolo and Mike glared at each other and put as much distance between them as the overcrowded room allowed, but neither thought of defying Papi.

José María sat on the other double bed and looked at his daughter. "What you tell us of Sanchi is disturbing, Elenita, but I would not call it worth your tears. He is a man. Men are as they are; they need—" Mama shot him a warning look. "—what they need," he finished lamely. "This woman lives in the penthouse, you say. She must be rich and reputable. If she and Sanchi—"

"José María, I've read many things, but nowhere did I

138

read that where she lives or how much money she has suddenly makes a whore less of a whore!" Mama's hot words came out so crisply that it took her menfolk a moment to realize she had actually used a term long forbidden them in the house.

"You know it's bad when mama says 'whore' straight out," Roberto whispered to Mike.

"I wouldn't want to be Sanchi now," Mike responded in kind. "And I don't care how much money this lady's got, she's bought the ranch if Mama meets up with her." They both exchanged sympathetic chuckles over the horrid and bloody fate no doubt reserved for the helpless Ianthe Apeiron.

Elena had finished crying. The surprise of hearing her mother speak so plainly did its part to shock her out of her tears. She sat up straight on the bed and accepted the pack of tissues Mama tugged from her purse. "I'm sorry. I'm making too much of all this." She blew her nose. "It's finished. I quit my job here today. I'll be coming home with you on Sunday."

Papi said "Good" and Mama said "Why?" almost simultaneously.

"Why is it good so suddenly?" Mama rose from the bed and stared down at her husband. She looked like the female equivalent of a bantam fighting cock.

José María cleared his throat unnecessarily. "Isn't it, *querida*? I thought it would be nice to have our girl home again. She has her own life to get on with, and this whole matter with Sanchi and the lady—"

Mama uttered a scornful laugh. "The *lady*! That's as far from the truth as your reasons for wanting Elena home. *Safely* home. You were not like this with the boys."

"With the boys? I don't understand," said José María, who, judging from the way he avoided eye contact with his wife, did.

"Elena, *you* tell the truth at least. Why are you crying over Sanchi? Just because some other woman has set a hook in him?"

"An evil woman, Mama," Elena amended, with as little ability as her father to meet her mother's probing eyes.

"Evil? Because she sleeps with him? No, no, don't goggle at me that way, Elenita; you look like a carp. I did not raise three sons in a convent. I know the world, I know men, and

139

I know you. Weren't you always the one holding forth at the table about how times are changing, women are the same as men? (Though, *gracias a Dios*, you never did more than talk such nonsense.) Then *this* woman does what you've seen your brothers do time and again—well, Manolo, anyway—and you are the first to call her evil!'

"Mama, you don't know what she really—"

"I know enough." Mama raised her hand, commanding attention. "Enough to know that either I am crazy or you, *m'hijita*, are in love."

Elena's face burned as Manolo's guffaws overrode the astonished whispers of her other male relations. Mama looked smug.

"I'm not." Elena only mouthed the words, hands clutching the edge of the mattress, her expression stubborn. There was another face hovering behind her father's, a face with knowing eyes the color of a distant sea. *Haven't we laid this Riddle to rest already?* Vergilius' specter looked infuriatingly amused, but right. In an audible voice Elena said, "You're not crazy, Mama."

"In love with *Sanchi*?" Manolo let out a whoop of derisive laughter.

"Manuel . . ." Whenever Mama used his full name, Manolo knew he had better cut the clowning. The laughter was short-lived, quickly buried.

"Elenita, is it so?" Papi asked.

"You sound as if she's going to her own funeral." Mama aimed an admonishing finger at her husband. "You should be pleased! This was your idea too, to have our Elena set Sanchi on the right road. Is he there? *De ninguna manera!* If anything, he's farther off the proper way than before. Another woman could walk away now, could say, 'I tried,' and give up. But this is *my* daughter! She loves him? Good! Then she will fight for him."

José María shook his head. "A girl fighting for a man . . . it is not the right way."

"The way that works is the right way!" Mama was adamant. Elena had never seen her mother so hard-ridden by any cause. She could not keep her admiration from showing. "I don't mean fight *over* Sanchi, like cats over a piece of meat. Fight *for* him, for his sake, whether her love is returned or not; fight because she cares, not for any gain."

Mama's eyes grew gentler. "As I would fight for you, *mi bien*."

José-María looked from his wife to his daughter. "I know you would. But if Sanchi doesn't love our 'Lenita, the hurt . . . *her* hurt . . ."

"I'll be all right, Papi," Elena said.

"No, *hijita*. Let someone else do it. He has hurt you enough already. Why must it be you? Come home."

Mama stamped her foot. "Again, 'Come home'? Are we all going to go home and hide under the beds? Didn't you hear her? This—this *griega* had her hands on Alonso too! A baby-stealer! And now she gets her claws into Sanchi? What has she done with Alonso? José María, I do not like how Cruz raised her sons. She trod them both down in different ways, but for the same reason: to feel superior the only way she can, lifting herself up by standing on their bodies. Even so—especially so—I can't abandon them; neither one. God knows they need someone to care what becomes of them."

"Come on, Mama, they're big boys," Manolo said. " 'Lonso more than Sanchi, some ways. They don't need a mommy."

Roberto scowled. "Who asked you?"

"Same one as always, man: nobody! Doesn't mean I don't have the right to be heard. I'll speak up if I want. Just because I didn't shine at school like you and Mike doesn't make me anyone less in this family. Does it? Papi, does it?"

José María sighed. Elena stretched out her hand and he took it tenderly, smiling at his daughter. "You are all valued the same, Manolo. There is no need to fight for what you have; only for what you must. Even now that 'Berto has a family of his own, his voice still counts for as much among us. Nothing can change that except your own wishes. We are together. But you forget: Sanchi was once a part of us, too. He still is."

Manolo made an impatient gesture. "He left years back and went to his own people. He's got a family."

"He has people who share his blood. Whether that is a family . . ."

The yearning in Papi's face for the lost one he had himself brought home drew Elena and Mama to sit beside him. He gazed from one to the other and summoned a fond smile. "Forgive me. You know how foolish I become over my strays."

Mama clenched her hand over his. "You are a good man." She said it so forcefully that only a fool would dare to contradict her. "We are all the true family Sanchi has." She darted a quelling look at Manolo.

"Hey, so I was wrong!" He shrugged. "I just meant we weren't, you know, *legally* related to him and 'Lonso."

"Leave law to the lawyers," Mike said.

"Get to be one first, big man," Manolo sniped back. "You're not even out of school yet."

"That's *it*!" Elena sprang from the bed and confronted her sparring brothers. "You two make me sick. All right, I'm going to stay in Atlantic City for as long as it takes to put Sanchi right. The rest of you, *vayan con Dios, pero que vayan! Que este lidio es mío.* Yes, I do love him—shut up, Manolo, or I'll kick you a good one—but that's not why I'm going to stay and fight for him. I'm doing it because whether he loves me or not, Papi's right: We're family. We don't stand by and let each other down."

The connecting door opened. Mamacita came in just as Elena finished her harangue. *"Pero qué pasa, niñitos?"*

"Elenita's crazy in love with Sanchi," Manolo answered. "Only he's—*ow!*"

Having proved herself to be a woman of her word, Elena flung out of the room leaving Manolo to nurse a severely bruised shin and Mama to swear that the girl never got that foul temper from *her* side of the family.

*Vergilius . . . I have to find him.* The same thought had chased Elena through every casino on the boardwalk, with no results. Noon was long past and she hadn't thought to stop for lunch. She sat down on the plinth of the statue of Hercules in the lobby of Caesar's to rest her aching feet. A young woman in uniform drifted over and politely asked whether there was anything she could do for her.

It was a question containing several others: *Who are you and why are you here and are you going to be any trouble?* Elena suddenly realized that she was still in her Dionysia maid's uniform, hardly the usual run of couture found in Caesar's, especially not gracing the statuary. She assured the lady she was just leaving, and did so.

Out in the street, she pulled the wizard's card from her pocket. It was worth a try. He had said that he needed to rest, and hadn't she told him herself that he was only human, like it or not? Her purse was still securely stowed in her locker back at Dionysia, but Vergilius had told her to reverse the charges. She went back into Caesar's in search of a pay phone.

There were a bank of them in the hall near the ladies' room. She punched 0, then the number, and waited. Instead of the dull buzz she always heard when waiting for an operator to come on, Elena heard a musical trill reminiscent of glass wind chimes. A husky voice, at once sexual and sexless, asked, "How may I be of service?" and sounded as if no service were out of the question.

"Uh . . . I'd like to make this call collect, station to station, please, from—"

Rainbows fanned before her eyes like a cosmic peacock's tail. The plain black plastic telephone receiver in her hand melted away into strand after strand of onyx beads that trickled through her fingers. Clouds of burgundy smoke wafted up from the floor, solid and yet yielding as the frothiest seafoam, lifting her feet, tilting her body, sinking her tired bones into the sweet seduction of a velvet-cushioned chaise. The rainbows ceased to dazzle; gilded oil lamps glowed from silver chains.

"—Elena Sanchez."

"I'll accept the charges." Vergilius nodded welcome from across a rosy marble reflecting pool where wax-cupped lilies drifted in their endless ballet. The music of lovingly plucked strings floated in the mellow light, with no sight of the players. On a table of turquoise glass and bronze wire beside Elena's couch were a bowl of ripe peaches, each the size of a grapefruit, and an array of creamy cheeses on a lapis slab. Wine awaited in a tulip-shaped glass.

The sorcerer reclined on a couch of more austere classical design, though its legs were banded with cabochon gems and the toga draping it was purple, sewn with golden bees. "You see what happens when they disband Ma Bell?" he said. "I never could get a connection like this in the old days."

Elena was in no humor for the mage's jests and had lost all appetite for the temptations before her. She made it her business to tell him shortly what she had just told her family. This time she shed no tears. She watched Vergilius' face darken, saw his eyes lose the mildness of untroubled waters, waited for the coming of the storm.

None came. "Hers," was all he said, and he lay back on his couch, covering his eyes.

"What?" Elena slung her legs from the comfort of the cushions and walked swiftly around the perimeter of the pool. She seized the sorcerer's shielding arm and forced him to look up at her. "That's all you have to say? 'Hers'? Like in a tennis match?"

"A match is just that," Vergilius slowly replied. "An even pairing. We were never that, the sphinx and I, though my vanity and her passing weakness let me pretend it was so for those many years. Don't you see, Elena? She has won the point and she will win the game. Sanchi was right. What do I know of empires or those who command them? How can I hope to defeat what I cannot comprehend?"

Too many things rose to Elena's lips at once. She wanted to shout some sense into the man, to rouse him, to shame him into action if she had to. Her mother was still an afterimage in her eyes, exhorting her to battle. Mama didn't even know the full peril of Sanchi's situation. *Would it change anything for her if she did?* Elena knew that the answer was no, and what sorcery did Mama have beyond the passionate knowledge that you didn't stop fighting just because it seemed the logical thing to do?

Sense therefore had nothing to do with it. She discarded all her practical arguments and walked away from the sorcerer's couch, pacing out the borders of the room. Midnight-blue moiré drapes dripped from every wall. She inserted her hand between one pair and drew them back, revealing tatty aqua paint, a cheaply framed seascape print, and a window through which she saw a marsh, a well-traveled roadway, the Atlantic City skyline, and the derelict pylon advertising the *Sea-Side Inn*.

"A motel?" she asked aloud. She turned from the window and surveyed the feasting hall that seemed to stretch away forever. Pale pink columns rose in a marble forest beyond Vergilius' couch, Corinthian capitals adorned with fresh flowers. At the far end of the reflecting pool was a broad dais hung with azure silk and cloth of gold, supporting all the accouterments of sorcery. An astrolabe glittered, laved in lamplight. A brazen tripod gleamed, its legs a trio of bare-breasted women who might have been the Graces. Slender-limbed tables upheld a selection of sparkling glassware, liquids and powders and granules of all hues contained in their swollen bellies.

"I like what you've done with the place," said Elena. She came back to Vergilius' couch. "Now let's do some more."

"How I let myself be talked into this . . ." The sorcerer shook out the trailing sleeves of his white robe and tied knots in the silk to keep them out of the way.

Elena caught them up from behind and pinned them to the back of the garment, baring Vergilius' arms to the elbow. "It was your own idea, really." She reached for a retort full of blue crystals. "You want this one?"

"Minerva, no! Put that back. *Gently.*" He made tsking sounds. "My idea. As if I wake from my nap every day and exclaim, 'What lovely spring weather! I think I'll harrow Hades.'" He gave her a penetrating look. "*If* I am capable of the spell."

"You are." Elena was chipper. She actually hummed as she cast a shopper's eye over the sorcerer's row of flasks, bottles, and beakers. None were labeled. "If you want me to pass you anything, describe it really well, OK? We don't want any Junior Chemistry Set explosions."

"No, we don't." Vergilius' tone was dry. "Especially since in your world, Cerberus would have no trouble at all securing employment in one of those old Japanese monster movies."

"Big, huh?"

"To us, Godzilla; to Cerberus, sushi. And we would have that creature to contend with if, as you so lightly predict, anything goes wrong. One does not disturb the honored dead of Elysium for flippancy's sake. We borrow the scattered dust of earth herself to re-form them shells to house their spirits. Two vortices of magic spin at once—the one a potter's wheel to make the vessel of clay that will hold what the other draws up from the netherworld. Great quantities of power must be tapped, and I am only one source; too, I have limits. I have no way of telling whether what I contain will be sufficient to raise the spirit we seek."

"Oh." Elena felt very small. "Will you—be hurt if you fail?"

"I have no way of knowing that either."

"Then don't." She said it quickly. "It's not too late to back out. We can find a way without—"

"Without help?" There was actual fondness in Vergilius' voice. "Ah, no, my little one. You have already convinced me of that. Your concern for me is touching, but listen to your own arguments sometimes. We have no other way. A fighter who lacks understanding of his foe lacks all. Truly it is as Sanchi said: Send a thief to catch a thief. And I can think of no greater thief than Caesar. Ruthless. Avid. Cold to any desires but his own. *There* is our empire builder. *There* is a soul to understand power, to know whence its sources spring and to dam them over with a practiced soldier's mechanical efficiency. It will take much to bring up such a one. I only wish Sanchi could be here to lend me some of the forces he contains."

"Sanchi? What does he—?"

Once spurred out of his lethargy, Vergilius was impatient to undertake the spell at hand. He set the brazier alight with a word, commenced measuring pinches and drops and sprinkles from various containers onto the burning coals. "Certain men hold great enchantments. Those who have studied such things can tap into not only their own sorcery, but the latent powers of those nearby. If I had Sanchi here, you'd see. Why, with him to draw on, this spell would be child's play." His abstracted air effectively tabled any fuller explanation for later.

There was no later.

Elena saw Vergilius' emerald ring descend as he dropped a final measure of yellow powder into the flames. The smoke made her cough, the cough caught hold and grew stronger, shaking her whole body. She heard the sorcerer growling a long litany of alien words. She heard Latin, and Greek, and other tongues she could not name, but all came as feeble echoes over the shuddering reverberations of her own hacks and gasps. Vergilius raised his voice to make himself heard. Through swimming eyes she saw him scowl at her, but she couldn't help herself. The strangest thing was that the paroxysms racking her were painless, though strong enough to make her head spin. Or was that an effect of the brazier fumes?

Tendrils of smoke twined themselves around her. The fire

146

in the brazen bowl danced through multicolored veils. The
pink marble pillars waltzed in time with the wind that whipped
the midnight-blue draperies into twirling scraps of cloth
yanked taut from the walls with gale force. Elena stopped
coughing and screamed as she was torn from her feet and
spun high in the air, past a ceiling that was no longer there.
Far, far below she saw a figure in white blurred by the
clouds of green and yellow smoke rising beneath his hands.
He was lifting a shield to the sun, its polished reflection
blinding. Even from so high, spinning so wildly, Elena could
see the shapes of youths and maidens, ships and trees and
more on the bronze ground.

The sorcerer used that shield of wonder as a housewife
would use a pot lid to smother a grease fire. He dropped it
without ceremony over the brazier, extinguishing the flames.
They died, the whirlwind stopped, and Elena fell. The ceiling slammed itself back into reality with the hollow sound of
Fred Astaire popping a top hat on his head as soon as she
dropped past it.

"I b-b-*beg* your pardon!" said the elderly man in whose
lap she landed. Nakedness did not become him, and indignation made him stutter. "I'll th-th-th-thank you to get off
m-m-me."

Gaping, Elena complied, pushing herself up with one
hand while the other groped upward on air until taken in a
companionable grasp. As she was both pushed and pulled to
her feet, she heard a reedy voice complain, "*She's* dressed.
And she's nobody. Why amn't I?"

Another, thinner and whinier, responded, "Gods don't
have to dress. *She* should strip naked to be like us. It's only
polite."

"Gods?" This voice was definitely a woman's, though
deep. "Surely you aren't going to start *that* tiresome charade
again, Bootsy? I thought we settled it in free debate centuries ago."

"There's no talking to him." This voice reminded Elena
remarkably much of Eeyore, the melancholy donkey. "He
never listens."

"Maybe I would if I heard anything worth listening *to*!"
came the whiny voice again.

Someone snickered. Elena saw a slender man with thinning hair make a lunge for the musty pad of paper and

minuscule pencil on the bedside table. The noble feasting hall was gone. In its place, she found herself in a cramped and stuffy motel room with eight naked men, one naked woman, and a uniform half-inch of dust over all. She didn't even want to begin thinking about what Papi would say.

"Vergilius?" she quavered. Then, louder, "Vergilius!"

Fierce rattling came from the bathroom door, then an inarticulate bellow and the sound of a domesticated thunderbolt blowing the door to splinters. Ragged and rumpled, Vergilius staggered through the gap and surveyed the motley gaggle of humanity disposed over every piece of relict motel furniture and several parts of the floor. The sole female among them jerked a tattered bedspread free and draped it gracefully over her small, dusky body, then retired into the background. The man with the pad scribbled and giggled.

The sorcerer's fist touched his heart, then opened as he raised his hand high.

"Hail, Caesar," he intoned.

"Thank you," seven of the gentlemen assembled replied.

# CHAPTER SEVENTEEN:
## Caesar Salad

"You should have specified," Elena pointed out.

"Certainly." Vergilius' lip curled. "Like selecting the flavor of my fancy at Baskin-Robbins. A snap of my fingers and I can have Caesar Butterpecanensis or Gaius Iter Lapidosus Caesar!"

"?"

"Rocky Road. Gods, if I'd only known! Look at them!" His beringed hand swept over the line of Roman couches he had conjured up, together with the recovered feasting-hall illusion. On each reclined a Caesar. The dark little woman and the man with the pad had declined such lavish seating on the grounds that they were not entitled to the imperial honors of the Eternal City. She sat stiffly on a straight-backed chair, he slumped in a Barca-lounger from the original motel that had slipped through the fast-fraying edges of Vergilius' conjury. The sorcerer's emerald ring appeared to bear out their disclaimers. Seven tiny diamonds—not eight, not nine—now surrounded the central gem, winking with malicious glee every time Vergilius studied his transformed jewel.

"I don't understand it," the sorcerer said for the fifteenth time. "I never thought I had the strength to draw up one Caesar, but seven—?"

"At least they're decent now," Elena said.

"Decent?" Angular and leathery from his years in the campaign field, Julius stared down his hawk's nose at the girl. "You dare suggest we were ever less?" His words had a cool hiss and bite to them, though his face remained as impassive as if he were posing for yet another triumphal monument.

"I mean you're covered up. You know." Elena waved her hands vaguely and prayed Vergilius would get them back on the subject of ice cream.

"And besides," the man with the pad chirped up, "no one can say that Julius Caesar ever acted outside the social proprieties. That little incident of his romance with the king of Bithynia was just legionaries' talk. And you're on record, O divine Caesar, as taking after a queen or two—in the sense of pursuing them, I mean—so no one can accuse you of not playing the man's part as well. You know how raucous military men can get. Or if it was true, it's not as if they weren't doing it themselves. Pressures of the campaign, no women, a long and glorious tradition approved by example by Alexander the Great him—"

"*Who* asked for your opinion, whoever you may be?" Julius roared. The cords in his scrawny neck stood out in high relief when he got angry.

Angry enough, Elena noted, for the scribbler's talk of Bithynian kings to be true.

"Me?" The little man covered his bosom with the pad, by now half filled with his chicken scratchings. "Oh, nobody. Nobody worth your notice at all, noble Caesar. Pray continue to speak. I find this all most fascinating." To prove this, he made several further notes before any of the assembled Caesars said another word.

"*I* know who he is." Stick-limbed but paunchy, with a

complexion close kin to Iter Lapidosus ice cream, the whiny-voiced Caesar on the fourth couch down gestured regally with one limp hand. "He's that funny little shade who was always trailing after us down there, listening in whenever any of us had a conversation. The name escapes me, but there's no reason for me to take up valuable brain space remembering nonentities. Which he is."

The heavyset Caesar with Eeyore's plodding voice laced his thick hands across his belly and intoned, "You have just taken up much time to say nothing and to tell us what we already know, Caligula. I would say that there is little danger of overcrowding what brain space you have."

"You *dare* to talk to me like that, old goat?" Caligula started up from his couch, hands contracting spasmodically around a yearned-for neck.

"You call me goat, parricide?" A warning rumble grated deep in Tiberius' chest.

"Oh, really," the dusky woman murmured. "Taking our Bootsy seriously. What next?"

"N-n-n-now, Tiberius." The stuttering Caesar whose lap had broken Elena's fall seemed terribly anxious to fend off any sort of confrontation. His movements were as jerky and awkward as his words, and a fine spray of saliva soon floated in the air around him. "I'm s-s-sure you don't mean that. He doesn't mean that, Ca-Caligula. N-not ab-b-bout your b-brain or being a pa-parricide. It's n-not as if you were his real so-so-son. You sp-sp-spoke quite to the p-p-p-point, my b-boy."

Tiberius and Caligula gave the poor distracted fellow a supercilious once-over, then exchanged looks of mutual disgust. Their shared scorn for the wispy old fellow had yanked the teeth from any incipient battle.

On the couch between Julius and Tiberius, a slightly built though strangely powerful-looking man enjoyed a good chuckle. "Poor Claudius," he remarked, propping himself on one elbow and regarding the stutterer. "Still obsessed with keeping the peace as the price of your own survival. When will you learn? The question is now moot, eternally tabled. We are all dead."

"We are *not*!" came an indignant squeal from the far end of the row. A slender boy with the most incredibly huge, dark eyes sat swinging his legs off the side of his couch and bouncing compulsively on the padding. He was as naked as when he'd first arrived from Hades. The plain white togae that Vergilius had provided as the simplest answer to the group exposure problem were not to this one's taste. Elena could still hear him sniveling because it was not silk, not tailored, and he was not, not, *not* going to wear a horse blanket, he'd sooner die. Julius had told him to drop dead and that had been the last anyone had heard out of the kid.

Now it appeared he had something to say. "If we are dead, why am I hungry? Why does that nasty woolly thing just make me break out all over my body in this atrocious rash which I simply know is going to drive me mad?" He leaped up and trampled on the discarded toga beside his couch. "*There,*" he told the abused material. "Serves you right, making a god itch."

"Don't take on so, boy," said the slender one. "We are all gods here. It's nothing to crow over."

"*I* was a god before I got to be emperor of your silly old Rome." The boy gave his toga an extra kick that pushed it into the reflecting pool. "*I* wasn't even *dead* and I got to be a god. *I* got married to a goddess. *I*—"

"*I* never heard of you," came the reply, delivered in the same loathsomely logical and unflappable tone as everything that particular Caesar had said so far.

From his place beside that obnoxious Olympian, Julius commented, "You know, Octavian, I think if a crab grabbed hold of your privates, you'd try to reason it into letting go. Calmly."

"Uncle, please." Octavian shifted himself to face the old campaigner. "I thought we settled this soon after I died. I am called Augustus now." He had on the young person's preferred expression of indulgence when addressing his hopelessly fuddy-duddy elders, even though Julius and Octavian Augustus both were now men in their later middle years.

"I shall call you whatever I please," Julius replied. "You jumped-up young pup."

"Well, if your memory's failing you that badly, do so with my blessings." Having nudged his relative back into line, Augustus rolled over again to settle matters with the cranky youth at the other end of the row.

"You claim to be a god, boy? And as such, better than the ordinary rout of mortals, I don't doubt. Ergo, one may assume that yon fellow there"—he indicated Vergilius—"is a being yet more potent and venerable than the gods, since he was the one to pull us from our Elysian rest back into the fleshly word. Yet by the very definition of the word, *can* there exist anything greater than a god? Are there degrees of almightiness? Or else one must conclude that you wanted to be here and used your divine powers to make it so, in which case one is forced to wonder why you did not similarly employ your postulated omnipotence to provide yourself with garments more to your liking."

The boy's wonderful eyes glazed over halfway through Augustus' exposition. He was a mouth-breather, too.

Julius snorted like his favorite steed. "Octavian, why did I waste time conquering an empire? I could have waited for you to jaw the Gauls into submission."

"Outtalk a Celt? Me?" Augustus smiled. "You must think I am a real god."

"Well, I am so too a god!" The boy had recovered. "I'm the sun-god on earth, Heliogabalus, and I'd like to see you try telling me I'm not. Because I *am*! Mommy said," he declared conclusively, folded his arms, and sat down hard on his cushions.

Something made a loud futtering sound. The fat man on the next couch over from Heliogabalus tittered.

"See?" he chortled. "I knew I could get it right if I practiced enough. Sounded just like a ripe 'un, didn't it? Never even moved my lips *so* much!" Simpering did not become him. His pendulous lower lip wobbled like badly set aspic. "And you thought all I could do was sing."

"No, Nero." Claudius' stutter had been replaced by a great fatigue. "The gods witness, there is *so* much else you can do."

"Only do it elsewhere, jackass," Caligula said.

"Far, far, *far* away from me, you atheist piggy!" Heliogabalus whacked Nero with a bolster.

Elena looked sideways at Vergilius. "This is going to help Sanchi and defeat the sphinx," she said, deadpan.

"It will," Vergilius replied. He didn't sound particularly convinced of it, though. Forcing out more conviction he said, "It must. The spell I sent sought power from below, power in human form. These men each ruled one of earth's greatest empires and wielded the power that accompanied that post. It matters not whether they were worthy to do so, only that we can and must harness their special knowledge of power to our own cause."

"Your cause?" Julius Caesar spoke up. The small blue eyes held a tiny spark of interest. This kindled brighter as Vergilius explained the reasons for his oddly successful summoning. When he ended, Julius said, "I see. Very well." He sat up straight and clapped hands to knees. "Now we talk terms."

"Terms? What terms?"

" 'What terms, *O Caesar*,' " Julius prompted. "You may call me 'divine Caesar' if you like, though the adjective remains problematical. What terms? Ours. We have something you need, as you yourself reveal. Information. Expertise. But why should we give it over? What will you offer in return? *Harness* our knowledge, would you? Harness us, you mean. I think not."

"Then think again, *divine* Caesar," Vergilius growled. Nero, Caligula, Claudius, and Heliogabalus trembled on their several couches. "The same magic that raised you up out of Pluto's realm can cast you back down!"

"Can it? Can *you*? When you so lately wondered aloud over how you'd managed to bring us out of Hades? Never question your own abilities where your adversaries can overhear. You make a poor strategist, Mage."

"Good enough, O Caesar." Vergilius gestured, and the draperies turned to glass. The full panorama of marsh and road and waterway was revealed, and the towers of the city beyond. Elena heard a collective gasp go up from all present, even the placid little woman sitting in such serene formality on her straight-backed chair.

"I will make no more threats I cannot fulfill," the sorcerer said. "I will not claim I can destroy you. In truth, I know not whether revenants such as you can be destroyed by ordinary means. Go, then. Make no pacts with me. You are free, all of you, to enjoy this new world. This unknown world. You don't need me to teach you its ways. You need no food, no shelter, no proper clothing, no resources, no guide. Oh, I am entirely dispensable to you. Why should we bargain at all? Go. The world awaits."

Nero's lower lip bobbed and quivered. He gazed out at the alien landscape and looked ready to weep. Caligula picked the edge of his toga to a ratty fringe between spidery fingers. Claudius fluttered his hands, mouth working, and looked relieved when Heliogabalus started yelping for his mother and needed a good slap to calm down.

By contrast, Augustus seemed to take no more alarm at the magician's ironic invitation than did his imperial uncle. Tiberius too remained calm, though it might have been no more than residual lethargy. Elena thought she heard him snore.

"Well, Mage, if that is how you wish it." Julius rose and marched to the wall of glass. "We shall go, and take what we have to offer with us. You think to affright us into submission? You forget that new worlds are nothing new to me, at least. Do monsters lurk in those sparkling towers? Each of us, in his own way, has dealt with monsters before"—he looked at certain of his companions meaningly— "even if it was only the monster in his own skull."

"You will never fit into this world, O Caesar," Vergilius said. "It will devour you alive."

A curt smile flickered over the conqueror's lips. "That honor belongs to the sphynx. A shame we could not reach an agreement to bring our skills to your service against her. Oh, well, seeing as one employer disdains us, we needs must find another." He shrugged. "We could always side with the sphynx."

Vergilius opened his mouth, closed it.

"Where is the portal in this wall?" Julius asked. "We must be gone." His whole bearing made it clear that he was prepared to take on Atlantic City and whatever lay beyond.

"You cannot—you would not—" The sorcerer looked to Elena for a suggestion. She lifted empty palms.

A twist of the magician's hand and the glass wall was opaque again. Julius looked sincerely disappointed.

"Sit down," Vergilius said heavily. "*Please* be seated, O Caesar. We shall talk terms."

"Bravo, Uncle," August drawled. "You haven't lost it yet."

The man with the pad asked Julius to repeat the part about monsters in the skull from his last speech and wrote it down, bubbling with all the optimism left in the room.

# CHAPTER EIGHTEEN:
## You Pays Your Money

Manolo squinted first one eye, then the other just to make sure he wasn't imagining things. "Yo! Hey, Sanchi, over here!" He abandoned the blackjack table and sprinted across the casino before one of the ubiquitous floor people could ask him whether they could help him lower his voice.

Sanchi leaned against a white-and-gold ship's wheel, part of Dionysia's yachting-party decor. He wore plain khaki chinos and a blue polo shirt. When Manolo got close he looked up, mumbled a pro forma greeting, and returned to studying his shoes.

"Hey, what's up?" Manolo asked. He sounded honestly concerned, a reaction that surprised no one more than himself. He'd never liked Sanchi. He'd always thought of the kid as Papi's spoiled darling, the little scrap of street sweepings who played up his poor-abandoned-waif routine to the full. If Mike or 'Berto had run into Sanchi looking this down and told Manolo about it later, he would have been first and loudest to claim that the kid was up to his old tricks. Seeing those empty eyes firsthand, though . . .

Manolo laid a startlingly gentle hand on Sanchi's arm. "Something wrong, man? Shouldn't you be, you know, in uniform? Or home sleeping? Or—" He wasn't getting any response, not even a look, not even an attempt to cast off his touch. It frightened him. "Sanchez . . . is it the woman?"

*"Who told you about her?"*

Manolo got all the reaction he could have wanted at about twice the sound level the Dionysia personnel had been instructed to tolerate. It didn't take long for Manolo and Sanchi to find themselves escorted out the boardwalk doors for a bit of fresh air.

"Lost your job, huh?" Manolo passed Sanchi a Coke from the snack-bar counter. "I been there. That's tough."

"My job . . . and Alonso."

*"Qué va?"* Manolo didn't share Sanchi's depression over the second of his declared losses. "What did you expect? The kid's still doesn't know how to use Kleenex, but when he finds out you're doing the job on his woman . . . Hey, I didn't even like sharing my socks with Mike and 'Berto."

"She didn't have to *tell* him!" Sanchi squeezed his Coke a mite too hard.

"Shit." Manolo studied both pairs of ruined slacks. "I got a mind to send the bitch my laundry bill. You're damn right, *hermano*. She didn't have to tell him. Which kinda makes me think she's one of these wacko women who get sick thrills out of how bad they can fuck up a man's head. You know, the kind that likes to play games."

"That's her; guessing games."

Sanchi shuddered. He could still hear her voice on the house phone, so compassionate, so tender, telling him to come right up to her suite. He had just gotten word from O'Connor that he'd been fired. No reason was given, but he could guess. You didn't play fast and loose with your working hours the way he'd been doing and get away with it. Dionysia was a serious business, run with as sharp an eye to maximum profits as any Wall Street firm. Excuses would only take you so far, and when the excuse was *The wizard made me miss my shift*, forget it.

He had called her, remembering the warmth, the comfort of their first lovemaking. If she was the sphynx, he could never see her as a monster. In her arms, all his old wounds had been washed clean. Afterward, though, a peculiar malaise had crept up on his sated senses. It was nothing he could name, only a queasy feeling that he had done something terribly wrong. New embraces chased such misgivings from his mind, but they returned in greater strength when she left him.

Elena's surprising him that way had made it worse. The guilt was a monstrous wave, crashing down over him, sweeping him away in a maelstrom of doubts and denials. Why had he done it? Why not? Why should he feel so awful now, yet so elated when he clasped her body to his, so transcendently happy when he lost all memory of himself and the world for the universe between her ice-white breasts? She was a monster, the legends said. In his room, getting into a change of clothes, he caught sight of his back in a mirror. The gashes were spaced too widely, went too deep for a human woman's nails to have made them. Did that make him a monster for loving her?

"I'll bet she set you up," Manolo was saying. "You tell her you want to talk, she says fine, right away she gets ahold of 'Lonso and makes sure he's there when you come in. Am I right or what?"

"Just like you'd been there, Mani."

*Alonso's face, ashen with fury. The sphynx sitting there so imperturbable, explaining that honesty was best. Let Alonso know that he was banished from her bed and who was the cause of his exile. "You must be cruel to be kind, is that not so, darling?" Her hand reaching for his, Alonso stepping between them, slapping her across the face.*

*Sanchi knocking his brother down, telling the boy to get the hell out, just as if that woman there were only Ianthe Apeiron and not a nightmare disguised. As if she needed his protection. "I'll kill you!" The mildest thing Alonso had said to him. He remembered thinking that the kid was looking good, well fed, well dressed, radiating hard-cash arrogance. The sphynx looked after her lovers well. "I'll kill you!"*

*And the sphynx, laughing as Alonso stormed out, strangely cold when Sanchi came to her arms. There was no scent of milk and cinnamon. Her breasts smelled of rock, the granite of shadowed crevices high on a barren mountainside. He found no more comfort in her arms, but the certainty that she had done all of this—used him, used Alonso—for her own purposes. The supreme manipulator, Vergilius called her. What hurt most was the fact that if she had taken him back with the old warmth, given him the special tenderness he craved, he would have jumped at her call. He left her willingly, but he could not leave her completely. He went down to the casino floor because he couldn't think of anywhere else to go.*

Now he could.

"Manolo, you know where Elena is?"

"I don't know, Sanchi. I mean, I do know, but I don't think it's so good for you to see her."

"Just for a minute, Mani. Just long enough to tell her I made a mistake and say I'm sorry. You think she'll listen?"

Manolo threw an arm around him. "To a man licking

dirt? *Chico*, I never met the woman yet wouldn't listen to that cut, then go buy herself the whole fucking album!"

"What are you doing *here*?" Sanchi demanded. All thought of apologies flew from his mind like a well-launched clay pigeon. The small hotel where they'd found Elena was a step up from her former lodgings, but belonged to the company of those leftover hostelries that lagged far behind the boardwalk-side gloss of the big casinos. A frantic air of desperate gentility pervaded the establishment, along with the smell of Pine-Sol.

"Screw that," Manolo said. "What's *that* doing here with you?"

Heliogabalus squealed and pulled the sheets up over his nose like the aging soubrette in a French bedroom farce. Elena told him to shut up in a voice suggesting that this was but the last in a long line of such injunctions.

"How did you find me, Manolo?" she asked. Before he could answer, she said, "Let me guess: Mama."

"Yeah, Mama. She told us that Mamacita's new pal, that Rhett Roman guy, took you on as sort of a gal Friday, you know? On the up-and-up, with Mamacita vouching for the man's good character, no monkey business, just a better job to keep you going here until we could get *this* sucker straightened out." He jerked a thumb at Sanchi, who was still too taken aback by the squirming vision in the bed to object to anything Manolo said. "And a hotel room thrown in for free. Neat deal. Too neat."

Elena started to steam. "There is no monkey business with me and Mr. Roman. This isn't the only hotel room he's rented. His—his special advisory staff arrived unexpectedly."

"Oh yeah? What does Tweety-Pie there advise him on?"

"This is—this is just one of Mr. Roman's relatives." Elena hesitated only an instant before dubbing the boy-emperor: "Sonny Roman."

"I *am not*!" came the indignant objection. "I am the living, breathing incarnation of the sun-god on earth, and I don't like you one little bit, you irreligious thing."

"So she'll wear a higher grade of sun block, Skinny," Manolo told him. To his sister he added, "Now you're a baby-sitter? Jesus Christ, Elena—!"

"Oh, ugh." Heliogabalus dropped the sheet to pout. "Competition. And *no* sense of style. Mortify this, give up that, *such* a tedious little sect. Now in *my* cult we knew how to show you a good time." He gave Manolo a slow visual evaluation. "You a religious man, darling?"

Manolo started to flip him the bird, them appeared to think better of what might be construed as an invitation. He pretended the boy was invisible, though a pungent smell of cheap musk oil radiating from the bed made this difficult.

"Listen, Mani, if I'd known it was you, I never would've answered the door," Elena said.

"Who were you expecting?" Manolo had trouble keeping his eyes off the boy in the bed. The sheets were creeping lower by the minute, and each inch they dropped was another one Manolo sidled toward the door. Sanchi stepped behind him and stopped his retreat without warning. Manolo jumped, then covered his edginess by shouting, "Goddammit, isn't there *one* cradle left full in this stupid town?"

"Mani, I'm not going to tell you again—" Elena's rising warning was interrupted by a loud pounding at the door, which swung wide open immediately.

"*How* am I supposed to create anything worth listening to without a lyre?" Nero demanded. He was still swathed in his original toga, but he had a shabby hotel towel plastered atop his head. Water dribbled down his jowls.

"I have been *waiting* for Augustus to do whatever it is one does with that telephone thing and have our room serviced, but he's been gone for hours, and I've had a shower, and I would kill for a *real* bath, and he hasn't brought back the telephone—you know, at least I could get some very interesting compositions roughed out by pushing those square bits on its face, but no harmonic capacity; I could die. Then he just *did* something to it so that I couldn't get a sound out of it at all—pinched its tail off, I think—and claimed he was going to see the room servants personally. Well, that was the last I saw of *him*. Maybe he's having them crucified," he finished on a hopeful note.

Manolo and Sanchi never stood more united than in the look they now fixed on Elena.

"I liked it better when you tried telling me that Rhett ran a traveling nuthouse," Manolo said. "I mean, I didn't believe that either, but next to the truth—" He regarded Heliogabalus and Nero with a mix of mistrust and wonder. "Monsters, wizards, Roman emperors like in those movies on Channel Five every Easter . . . This is is pretty heavy sh—stuff."

"Believe her, Mani," Sanchi said.

"Yeah, yeah, I do. You know, Sanchi, that stuff that happened when we were kids, the stuff you reminded me about with the dragon and all, it's amazing, but I couldn't remember a damn thing about it until you and Elena started talking. All of a sudden—*wham!*—it's like I never forgot it. I remember sitting upstairs, watching this mob on TV, hearing that they were marching uptown from St. Patrick's, heading for our place, wanting this guy Persiles, the knight, and God help us if we didn't give him up. Christ, I was crapping in my pants! I knew Papi wouldn't give up anything, never mind any*body*, to a mob. *Válgame Dios*, I knew we were all gonna die. You'd think something that big'd stick with you."

"Magic is change," Sanchi explained. "Sometimes the stronger the magic, the more violent the change it leaves behind. A dragon's pretty strong."

"I see. I think I do," Manolo admitted. "Like when you get a big shock, sometimes you get amnesia after?"

Elena smiled proudly at her brother. "Very good, Mani!"

Modestly he shrugged off the compliment. "Saw something like it happen once on *All My Children* and—Hey! Not with my sister, pervo!" He took a moment to swat Nero's hand as it tried a backdoor maneuver on Elena. She was seated between that particular emperor and Sanchi on the other bed while in his, Heliogabalus was establishing a meaningful relationship with the Magic Fingers attachment.

"That story about the nuthouse would have worked, except for him." Elena singled out Nero for a venomous stare.

"Yeah, that was incredible," Manolo said. "Trying to kill yourself, that's crazy, but when you stab yourself like that in front of witnesses and nothing happens? I mean, *nada*? If I hadn't seen it myself, man . . . You guys are immortal! Creepy. Magical, convincing, but creepy."

"I did it for love," Nero moped. "And what more poetic way to prove my undying passion for your beauteous sister than suicide?" He sprang up and struck a heroic pose, miming a dramatic dagger thrust to his own heart.

"Stinkbugs," Heliogabalus opined, his voice somewhat muffled by the mattress. "You already found out you couldn't be killed in any of the old ways, so you didn't have one thing to lose! Stabbing yourself with a nail file, anyhow . . . too tacky."

Nero's monumental underlip thrust out. "You seem to forget that I risked much to discover that I—that we—cannot die as formerly. Is this the thanks I get?"

The Magic Fingers shut off. Heliogabalus propped his face up on one hand. "Oooh, snitty. *You're* the one who seems to forget that the way you made this big fat hairy discovery, hooray, was trying to kill Augustus!"

The lip trembled, the chin beneath it aped gelatin in a mating frenzy. "How—how did you—? Who told—?"

Heliogabalus rolled on his back and kicked his legs in the air. Sanchi covered Elena's eyes until she slapped his hand down. "I *knew* it! I *knew* he was right! Goodness, and if he was right about you trying to kill Augustus, then he must be right about all the other things he told me too!" The boy-emperor shrieked with delight. "Oh, this will be worth every sester—every penny he'll charge!"

"*Who* is right? *Who* will charge *how* much for *what*?" Nero bawled.

Heliogabalus eyed the Magic Fingers meter box. "Give us another quarter and I'll tell."

"Suetonius?"

"Caius Suetonius Tranquillus, fair lady," said the gentle-man so hailed, looking up from his copy of the *National Enquirer* with real reluctance. "Please come in, all of you." As he rose from his chair to greet them, Sanchi saw him cast one last fond glance at the tabloid and heard him murmur, "Astonishing. So much to learn."

"You're no emperor," Elena said as the five of them trailed in, Heliogabalus bringing up the rear.

"My lady makes that sound like something of which to be ashamed." Suetonius inclined his head modestly. "I never laid claim to the purple, but our absent guide Vergilius has seen fit to assign me the divine Claudius as a roommate.

Alas, he too is absent or I would gladly perform the introductions."

"We've met," Nero said with stuffy disdain.

"So you did. Your stepfather, wasn't he? For as long as it took your mother to secure you the succession and cook up those poisoned mushrooms. Such a romp, Agrippina! Such a fine hand for creative hors d'oeurves, too. Spirited and ambitious to the end, despite all your efforts to—ah—send her to a well-merited eternal rest. And how *was* your dear mother when last you saw her? I never could catch up with her down there, and I did so want her recipe for those mushrooms. Just to flesh out the narrative *a posteriori*, you understand."

Nero backed off before Suetonius' cheerful assault of embarrassing facts. "Mother and I travel in different circles these days," he mumbled.

Suetonius clucked his tongue, then grabbed a handy pad and made further notes.

Elena waited until he had done scribbling to ask, "But if you're no emperor, what are you doing here?"

"Oh, getting quite a fine secondary educa— Oh, *I* see what you mean!"

"Vergilius said the spell he used was to call up a fount of power. If you don't mind my saying so"—Elena had to look away from Suetonius' bright eyes and cheerful face—"you don't strike me as being very powerful."

"Alas." Suetonius tried to look rueful, but too much mischief clung to the man.

"There's more than one kind of power," Sanchi said. To the little man he said, "I'll never forget the first time I read your *Lives of the Caesars*. My professor called it biography, but—"

"Sensational, was it?" Suetonius beamed, gratified. "A shade . . . scandalous?"

"A shade fictitious. You as much as said you were including unsubstantiated rumors, and some of them— You're a gossipmonger, Suetonius."

"I prefer to style myself an information broker. As you say, there's more than one kind of power, and if information isn't one, what is?"

"Whatever you are," Sanchi said, "you colored every subsequent Roman historian I ever read."

"Colored them gray, I hope." The imperial biographer looked pleased with himself. His elation tempered sharply as he glanced at Heliogabalus. "But there! In the midst of triumph we are brought low. O excellent youth! Why were you born to rule so long after my time? Only fourteen when you came to the purple, yet slain by the Praetorians a scant three years later for your outrageous depravities! At the tender age of seventeen. Excesses too much for the Praetorian Guard to bear? After some of the things *they'd* been and done? Ah, *vae*, who weeps for Adonis? Gods above and below, what meat I could have made of *your* sojourn on the throne!"

Heliogabalus made kissy faces at him.

"Scandal is power, too," Elena admitted.

"Yeah, anyone who says different should live to see a presidential primary," Manolo added, chuckling.

"A what?" Suetonius cocked his head.

"See, there was this politico and this bimbo . . ."

Vergilius opened the door of Suetonius' room without knocking and reacted with real surprise to find Sanchi there. He rushed forward, though whether to embrace the young man or backhand him was a momentary question. Elena took one look at the sorcerer's face and decided to prevent either. She tossed aside Suetonius' copy of Kitty Kelly's latest unauthorized celebrity bio and threw herself between the men.

She never could recall afterward what she babbled, but it must have been something pretty good and pretty fast, the verbal equivalent of ice-skating on oiled glass. She actually felt a dew of perspiration forming on her brow before she got the two of them settled on the beds.

"Very well," Vergilius said. "If you claim to have forgiven his treachery—"

Sanchi started up from his place beside Elena. It took a strong arm to force him back down, an effort she backed up by snapping, "Choose your words better, Vergilius. Sanchi would never betray us."

"Is that so. Perhaps it is. So he took to our enemy's bed in search of what? To learn her weak points? An admirable sacrifice."

"*Stop* that. Cut the sarcasm. You're partly to blame,

keeping her more of a mystery than she kept herself. If you'd have warned him about—*specifics*, not just muttering about empires and Armageddon and Riddles, he could have been on his guard better than—"

"No, Elena." Sanchi pressed her hand but would not look at her or at Vergilius. "What happened to me with the sphynx . . . I don't think there was a way in this world to prevent it. But as for treachery"—he lifted his chin to face the sorcerer—"I betrayed no one but myself."

Vergilius stroked his trim beard. "I believe you, Sanchi. From experience I know how . . . difficult it can be to resist her wiles, her enchantments, the illusions she weaves to enhance both. And did she ask you anything?"

Sanchi spread his hands wide. "No Riddle. I mean, I'm still alive."

"Then perhaps she only singled you out for the cruelties she could accomplish on both you and your brother. Caprice is her weakness, if she has any. Her feline nature at work, I suppose, tethering the falcon's implacable hunting instinct. She can be distracted. That is something in our favor." For the first time since he had come in, Vergilius relaxed and smiled at Sanchi. "I am sorry it cost you so much to learn so little of our foe." He spoke like one who had shared the same steep price for the same scanty lesson. "Welcome back, my friend."

Abruptly, the magician sat straighter in his chair, with the perplexed expression of a man who knows he has misplaced something but can't remember what. "Is Claudius in the bathroom?" he asked.

Elena and Sanchi clasped hands again, guilty children.

"Or Suetonius?" Vergilius pressed.

"We wanted a little privacy—" Elena began.

"—to talk about . . . what happened to me, you know, with the sphynx," Sanchi went on.

"Besides, Heliogabalus was making it hellish for everyone, carping about not having a thing to wear, and Nero said Augustus still wasn't back from room service—"

"—and we thought that maybe if Mani took them out and bought them some decent clothes they might shut up for five minutes—"

"Suetonius is very level-headed. He swore he'd help Manolo keep them out of trouble."

"He was getting a little worried about Claudius, too, and the man at the front desk said he saw some weirdo in a bedsheet who asked whether there were still such things as libraries—and you know that has to be Claudius—so he wanted to pop by and try dragging the old fellow out of the stacks before—"

*"Cease!"* No thunder rolled forth from the besieged sorcerer's sleeves, though Sanchi thought he caught a lick of heat lightning in Vergilius' eyes. "Are you telling me that they are all *out there*?"

"With Manolo," Elena repeated.

"We *really* needed to talk," Sanchi stressed.

Vergilius was not mollified. "Who in Pluto's miserable realm is this Manolo person? Another 'recruit' you'd force on me?"

"Are you referring to me?" Elena's temper prickled. "Manolo happens to be one of my brothers, and you met him with the rest of the family."

"You have at least proved your mettle, lady. Your brother? The lip of disaster is a bad place to practice nepotism. What qualifications has he to face a sphynx, or to shepherd Caesars?"

"Beats me, man." Manolo stood in the doorway, with all the rumpled, hassled, end-of-rope desperation of a successful commodities trader. A discarded toga was slung over one of his shoulders, and a livid bruise under his right eye was already starting to turn imperial purple. "I fucked up. They got away."

Vergilius began to clap his hands in dirge-time, a slow, ironic applause. "My question stands answered. Behold the one thing this team needed: a philosopher."

Manolo told him to do something not strictly Platonic.

# CHAPTER NINETEEN:
## Hide and Go Seek

Vergilius paced the confines of the abandoned hotel room and sent off his mental seekings recklessly, to all points of the known and unknown compasses. He picked up the distant glimmer of Sanchi's mind—would that boy never find the serenity to contain his own thoughts?—and that was all.

Where were the Caesars?

It was a mistake to have left them alone, he knew that now. Too often in these times he had awoken to find he had made yet another error in judgment. He could not even ascribe the failing to encroaching age. For Vergilius, age had been banished to the same dark cave that held death and dreams.

Dreams. Maybe that was it, the reason for so many weaknesses coming up on him so fast. The price his spells had demanded to suspend the slow erosions of age, the oncoming tide of death, was not the loss of sleep but the loss of dreams; common dreams. And dreams were imagination, and imagination often was survival.

*When she was with me, I dreamed,* he thought. *When she was mine, her dreams could become my own, a gift she made willingly. I think she even liked it, imagining that somehow the sleep-visions she projected from her mind to mine made me less the master, more the debtor.*

*Didn't they?*

He thrust all thought of the sphynx away, renewed his magical efforts to locate the wandering spirits. It was fruitless. Sanchi, Elena, and Manolo would have more luck afoot than he, for all his vaunted sorceries.

How could he have been so stupid? Having dredged up such a treasure trove, how had he come to leave it virtually untended? Pride again; always pride.

He had relied too heavily on fear to play the guardian's role. Though Julius spoke boldly of going out into the unknown city, the new world of *now*, that first Caesar was exceptional. The others were different, easier to make answerable. So Vergilius had thought.

Claudius trembled if you looked at him crosseyed; he was harmless, safe to match up with the unknown little man who always seemed to be writing something down. How had he dared to flee? Where would he venture to go?

Augustus had a reputation for loving responsibility, so he had been set to watch Nero. He was *supposed* to have taken his charge seriously. What had misfunctioned? Why had he abandoned his duty?

Tiberius was to keep Caligula in line. Some historians wrote that the melancholy lump of an emperor had been smothered on his deathbed by his designated heir. Caligula had been impatient to get on with the depravities that marked his reign, they said. If it was true, Tiberius would not make the mistake of trusting his weird nephew twice; an ideal guardian. Where was Tiberius now? Had Caligula managed to turn historic rumor into present fact? But no; Sanchi had told him that the Caesars could no longer be destroyed by mundane means. What, then, had happened to Tiberius? To Caligula, for that matter?

That left Heliogabalus, whose warding Vergilius had given to Elena, and Julius, who rather haughtily had given his parole that he would not go where he did not belong.

Now the question remained: Where would one like Julius Caesar admit he did not belong?

So they were gone, even the scribbler. Vergilius dispatched his helpers to look for them while he remained behind. Ostensibly he would use his enchantments to locate the lost ones. In reality he only learned more certainly by the minute that if he had once held the power to draw Caesars out of Elysium, he now lacked even the ability to lure them back to the Promenade Hotel.

*Wild power.* The thought floated over the sorcerer's head like a ghostly vulture. Faithful beyond death, it would never abandon its vigil of obsession and doubt. *It was wild power, more of it than you ever thought existed, that drew them back into this world. You know the facts of magic too well to deny it; and that is all you know. Wild power, but yours? Wild power, but from whence?*

Vergilius held his hands out for yet another inspection,

turning them slowly palm up, palm down. The emerald ring with its recently spawned encirclement of diamonds sparkled with cold reproach. *I am a wizard. It is my business—my obligation to* know! *Yet here I sit, still as ignorant of how I did it as this latest "helper" they have wished on me.*

For an instant the hovering thought flickered. Who did he mean by "they"? Sanchi and Elena showed their faces briefly in the mage's mind, Manolo's sponsors, only to be replaced by three women draped in finest white wool. Maiden, mother, crone; spinner, assayer, snipper, they had come slowly on in the sorcerer's traces down the paths of the years. Slowly, but steadily, to be eluded but never escaped.

It was a lie, what lesser men taught, that immortality must lead to tedium. For those unwilling to learn, those entirely wrapped in the mummy-bands of self, that might be true. In time one tired of the world within, grew morose, looked to death as relief and release. But for the real scholar? Each day of existence was adventure, mystery, delight. The learning never ceased. Death gained a renewed measure of terror as realization grew that all the richness and the joy of life would indeed have an end.

Maiden, mother, crone, they waited. Had they at last taken an active hand, not merely spinning, measuring, and cutting, but now twisting the strand of his days? Perhaps, like Caligula, they had grown impatient of their prey. He had evaded them too long. Even in the glorious variety tolerated in this world, his difference had finally been decreed an offense against their rule. His knowledge was what had kept him free of the final stroke of the shears. To know, to understand, to use knowledge and understanding according to their purposes, was to buy life.

Not to know was to die.

*And I do not know how I did it,* Vergilius thought, regarding the mocking ring one more time. The diamonds dimmed. That much he understood. If he had commanded the power to draw so many Caesars out of Hades, his ignorance of that power's source and aspects would not let him maintain their new lives indefinitely. Bit by bit the life force would ebb from them. If you do not know where the leak is, small as any pinprick, how can you stop it? Though the pierced vessel be as vast in its containment as the sea, yet it will drain itself utterly, in time.

Once more the impossibility glided into his thoughts, wearing a woman's face: *Elena?* But that was mad. Females, ordinary human females, held no power. Oh yes, some instinct that could be honed to a simulacrum of magic—the Cumaean sibyl spoke oracles, her words still woven into Vergilius' own flesh as she prophesied his fate all those centuries gone—but foretelling was simply the art of postulating a probable future gleaned from insight into the seeker's nature and from knowledge of the past.

*Wild power. It must have been mine. No one else was with me to draw force from but Elena, and she is a woman, magicless. Man is mind, woman heart, earth strength to sustain both. Magic is of the mind and instinct of the heart, each drawing on the strength of earth in distinct ways. Tripartite fact, inviolable in its truth. No one can change what is so. So the power was mine. It must still be within me. All that remains is for me to find a second time the wall enclosing it and open the gates.*

*But how?*

The sorcerer sat on the rumpled bed studying his hands as the light waned. He did not hear the door open or see the little black-haired woman until she was at his side.

# CHAPTER TWENTY:
## Veni, Vidi, Gucci

In a squalid little store where the stock in trade was the most tedious kind of pornography, two old acquaintances met as they happened to reach for the same copy of *Spurts Illustrated*.

"*Ave, Caesar*," said one in a voice steeped in theatrical irony but badly hampered by its perpetual whine. His imitation of a gladiatorial salute nearly pitched him off his six-inch spiked heels. He had to do a lively double-time step—no easy order in a satin skirt that tight—to keep from lurching forward onto a dump of *Lust and Leona*.

"Get stuffed, Bootsy," Heliogabalus replied. He sounded

more nasal than formerly, a change assignable to the safety pin presently protruding from his left nostril and the gold stud adorning his right. Jeans that were seventy percent air to thirty of frayed denim rode dangerously low on his hips. He had drawn a wailing Mr. Bill face around his navel, bared by the insufficiencies of a cropped orange tank top. Alas for the total effect, the ragged shirt flaunted a likeness of Wayne Newton.

Ever the coquette, Heliogabalus thrust his pelvis forward and demanded, "Like it?"

"You mean the clothing, or—?"

"Just a little something I threw together in town this afternoon. With the help of this *adorable* little man named Johnny—let's see, I'm awful with names, but I never forget a—Johnny *Crud*, that's it! He's in a band, the Chicago White Sux. I sat in on a session. Johnny says I could be one of the great untrained voices of our time; coloratura, whatever *that* is. But Johnny likes it." Heliogabalus blushed.

"Busy afternoon," Caligula remarked. He tugged at his fishnet hose. "I'm surprised we didn't meet before this. Where did you shop?"

Heliogabalus giggled. "Better ask with *what* I shopped. Honestly, the look on that precious man's face when I stopped stark still in the middle of the menswear aisle at K-Mart! Have you met Manolo? No? Well, you are in for a treat, love, believe me. All talk, but no foresight. Trying to make *me* wear polyester slacks! I ask you. Some things can make a wool toga look good. I would *not* go up to the cash register and buy them like a good boy, so I just dug in my little heels. Plowed right into my cul-de-sac, he did, then jumped back like he'd been *burned*! Well, I know an insult when I grab one, and I did, or I tried to, and Nero took his cue from me—though he doesn't look half bad in double-knits—and I shoved Manolo backwards while he took a wild swing and *connected*, can you believe it, and Suetonius—*there's* a man with foresight!—dipped into Manolo's pocket for his wallet and keys while he was lying there stunned and the three of us hotfooted it out before the guards could come and into the car and away!"

"Car?" Caligula's plucked and penciled eyebrows rose. "Which one of you has learned how to manage one of those things so fast?"

"No one," Heliogabalus replied. "But Nero got in a lot of practice on the way back to town. Nero and I split the money—paper, did you ever?—and that silly Suetonius said he just wanted these little plastic cards because they were so pretty. It didn't take *me* all day to swap those yicky pants for something that—that—" he searched for the right expression among so many new words—"that makes a *valid personal fashion statement.*" He pirouetted for inspection.

"Nice," Caligula commented. He tilted his head to weigh the merits of the boy-emperor's new hairstyle. Heliogabalus looked as if Sweeney Todd and Lizzie Borden had waged a hands-on battle over who should be the unique influence on the young man's tonsorial expression. Both lost; twenty-three tubes of Rigigel and a spray can of neon-green hair tint won.

"Nice?" Heliogabalus kicked the *L&L* dump petulantly. "That's all you can say? What ever happened to words like 'disgrace'? 'Abomination'? 'Putrid'? 'Corrupt'?" He groaned. "I'd even settle for an itsy little ol' common 'decadent.' "

Caligula straightened his Dolly Parton wig priggishly. "You'll have to do better if that's what you want."

"Better than all this?" Heliogabalus' gesture took in his whole tenue, including glitter-covered sneakers and the genuine dead parrot hanging from his chopper-chain belt.

"My sympathies, brother, but I haven't exactly been causing any major riots out there either." Caligula cast a scornful glance at the shop's proprietor, a blobby man with the charm and physical attractions of a silverfish. "Not so much as a second look when I came in. Not even a gasp when I hailed him in my normal voice. He told me I'd probably find the magazines I wanted in aisle ten and that my seams were crooked."

It was Heliogabalus' turn to survey Caligula from blond bouffant to open-toed ruby slippers and say, "Nice."

Caligula snorted. "If this is what I escaped Tiberius' keeping for, the Furies take it. This isn't even one of their major cities, yet no one shrieks, no one points, no one *looks* at me!"

"Too sad." Heliogabalus sighed. "If you can't make them puke in the provinces, what's the use, I always say."

"I was hoping for some fun—nothing major, just a little rape or maybe find the local barracks—but if this is how it's going to be, I'm going back to the hotel." Caligula teetered toward the door.

"Wait for baby."

Nero sat in the darkened theater, making a sour face at the screen. Was this the level to which the arts had sunk? Those gaudily dressed whores he'd passed on the streetcorner must be sisters to the Muses if entertainment was at this nadir.

This had to be a punishment of some sort. Nero knew punishment. His time in Hades had not been all empty symposia in the Elysian fields with his imperial colleagues. His reign and his life had occasionally overstepped the Hellenic ideal of moderation in all things, he had to confess it. Having his mother murdered, kicking his pregnant wife Poppaea to death, using pitch-dipped religious fanatics as torches to illuminate his banquets, he could see why Minos, Aeacus, and Rhadamanthus had taken him to task. For one thing, the stench and shrieks of those human flambeaux had put his guests off their dinner.

Mother always did say it was a shame to waste good food.

But then, who were they to get shirty with him? Everyone knew about how their mother, Europa, had been carried away, in every sense of the word, by a bull. If the beast turned out to be Zeus in disguise, it still left Europa's tastes in doubt. Maybe Nero had made yet another *faux pas* in bringing up the topic of *your mama was a cowgirl* just as the Three were about to decree his eternal punishment.

Eternal punishment was not necessarily the same thing as continual punishment, unless it was one of the cleverer ones, such as poor old Tantalus suffered. That tormenting predicament of being ever unable to reach such temptingly close food and drink had to remain without equal or duplicate in the annals of divine retribution.

Like every other intelligent being, the three Judges had some pretensions to art and did not like to repeat themselves in assigning penalties. Therefore, they relied on simpler agonies for the small fry, making sure that no punishment lost its original sting through familiarity. Nero himself had been wafted from pits of boiling oil to lakes of ice to charcoal grills to indefinite respites in the Elysian Fields made excrutiating because one never knew when they were going to end or what horror would follow.

One especially effective session had locked him voiceless in a room full of second-rate epic singers and third-rate critics, forcing him to listen to the outrageous paeans of the latter for the former. What hurt worst was the way each critic ended his litany of praise with "*Much* better than that hack Nero."

This theater just had to be an aboveground subsidiary of Hades, and that lickspittle Augustus must be in the service of the Three. Why else would he have given Nero pocket money and told him to come here and "take in a movie at the revival house"? Once a brown-nose, always a brown-nose.

Revival house, was it? An apt name for this edifice of subtle torments aimed at those so miraculously revived as himself. On the screen, a long-limbed man in outrageous garb cavorted through a downpour. Even poor mad Caligula had enough sense to come in out of the rain. Not this wight. He leaped, he soared, he capered over the puddled pavement and up the lighting stanchion, warbling a song whose message was patently obvious.

"Of course you're singing in the rain, idiot," Nero gritted. "Did you think you were dancing in the turnips?" He furiously crammed more popcorn in his mouth, too incensed to dab up the melted butter streaking his chin. Though he wanted to leave the theater, there was something hypnotic about the food available here. As in Hades proper, the tortures always had some hook to keep you going. Or why hadn't Tantalus given up aeons ago, sat down in the retreating waters of the lake, and told the Judges to go to—? Well, to somewhere else.

Nero fumed. He thought of Augustus again, and his own injured feelings. Fresh from his daring escape from K-Mart, at great personal risk to life and limb, he had separated from those ingrates Suetonius and Heliogabalus. The boy simply ran away, whooping and waving his share of the plundered cash as he plunged into a dingy hole-in-the-wall clothing shop. Nero had tried to stick with Suetonius—purely for the little gossipmonger's own security—but had his selfless offer of companionship rejected.

"We're free, divine Caesar. Why don't we use it to best advantage? Strike out on your own! No need to fear."

Fear? He? Nero? It was only by accident that he encountered Augustus at the dicing table in one of those towering buildings. Beneath flashing lights and over the clatter of plastic chips he told Augustus that he was ready to return to the hotel now and magnanimously offered to escort his keeper safely back too.

"Mercury, not now! The dice love me too dear. Here." Another wad of green paper was pushed into Nero's pudgy hands. "Go buy yourself a bodyguard if you're wetting yourself over a few blocks' solitary walk."

Nero stuck out his lower lip. Everyone at the table stared at him, which was as it should be, but only for the moment when Augustus deigned to note his existence. As soon as Augustus turned from him, attention turned too. It wasn't right.

*He* should be the one they looked at. *He* should be the one wearing those oddly flattering garments, smoky black, cool white, that Augustus had adopted. They appeared to be an adaptation of barbarian braies and tunic, like the suit Nero now wore. He had been content with his new gear until he noticed that Augustus' ensemble was better-cut, of finer goods, with what looked like a satin zone girdling his midriff. And how had the man come by so many gold rings?

Nero had had an exciting afternoon, but Augustus had had a profitable one. And, strange, the afternoon seemed to have *stretched* somehow.

"Are you still here?" Augustus sounded aggrieved. "Very well, if you must hang about like a blowfly, I'll be ready to quit in a couple of hours. Come back then." That was when he suggested the revival house.

A box of Milk Duds was chomped into oblivion as Nero reflected on the injustice of it all. Why, in his day he had been the cynosure of all eyes, and not just because he was the emperor! Everyone told him he had a wonderful voice, a real stage presence, a true talent for the composition and performance of high art! Hadn't he won every singing contest he ever entered? Hadn't he swept the board of prizes during his acclaimed tour of Greece? Had one judge cast a vote for anyone but Agrippina's son?

O Fame! It still meant more than mere riches, even in these degenerate days. Nero knew. He had picked up a copy of the *Star* on his way to the theater. No one in his right mind could claim that the men whose photos appeared therein were anywhere near the physical perfection of a sculptor's models. Oh yes, some did have rather impressive musculature, but those *faces*! The gap-toothed barbarian, the droopy-eyed pugilist, and that pathetic, balding redhead with a nose like a bucina—! None of them knew how to dress with any style, either. If a slave had shown himself so unkempt in Nero's presence, his next post would be head down in the manure pile. Why stop at half measures if you were that contemptuous of good grooming? Yet Fame had touched those men, and for all their shortcomings, people would never look away if they approached a gaming table.

"I'm the emperor," Nero sulked. "They should look at *me*. I'm the artist. I'm the only one with real style. I'm the ruler of the empire. I'm the—"

The first feature had ended while Nero nursed his grievances. The second film came on. A gaggle of that same breed of garish-plumed streetbird came into the theater, hastening down the aisle in hotpants and heels, hustling each other for a change.

"Come *on*, Monica, *move* it! I been waiting too long to miss this flick. I just *adore* him!"

"You're weird, Heather. The man is *dead*!"

"I don't care if he dead. I still love him. And he's not really dead. 'Long as there's music, he's not never dead!"

The third woman sighed. "Don't argue with her, Monica. This the same girl blew a stack on that trip to Graceland. And anyhow, we're here with her, so what's that make us?"

Monica picked her way into a suitable aisle and brushed off the seat fastidiously before plopping down. "I know, I know," she said. "We're all fools."

"No one's a fool when it's the *King*," said Heather.

They were scarcely halfway into the second reel of *Jailhouse Rock* when the Muses drygulched Nero with the blunt instrument of artistic revelation.

The *King*!

"There he is!" Sanchi exclaimed, tugging at Elena's arm.

"Are you sure? You never saw him, and from here I'm not sure if—"

"So we move closer. I'm almost positive. He looks like all his statues, only he's wearing one killer suit and I *think* . . .

a toupee?" He made a small mouth. "Huh. Who are those creeps with him?"

"If he's really Julius Caesar, I'd watch it calling his new playmates creeps. And even if you're mistaken, I've seen warmer smiles on a school of sharks. Oh well."

Elena started across the casino floor. It was at its most crowded and its most cosmopolitan, this being Saturday night. For once the baccarat tables were full. Dresses aglitter with sequins and faux gems, necks, wrists, and fingers sparkling with the real thing, for once outnumbered the polyester pantsuits. Trim midriffs belted by silk cummerbunds overruled beer bellies. Saint-Tropez tans had it all over liver spots, and the merchant princes of Hong Kong on pleasure bent, the gilded sheiklets temporarily free of their petroleum playpens, wrested majority rule from the pensioners and retirees out for a modest good time. Though Elena knew Dionysia better than the other casinos they'd already searched, and Sanchi was the native guide, it was still turgid going. It had been worse elsewhere, and much time had been lost.

Although . . .

Elena pulled up short, her path blocked by the crush in one of the blackjack aisles, and checked her watch. It couldn't be. She must have knocked it against a wall or a door or something. It still ran, but this just couldn't be right. "Sanchi, what time is it?"

He consulted his wrist. "Early yet. Not even . . ." It was his turn to frown and shake the timepiece. "It's working—the seconds are flashing—but how could it only be—?"

Elena's lips twisted. "They say time flies when you're having fun, but they never say a word about whether the reverse is true."

"But time hasn't stopped. Look around you!" Sanchi waved in the whole casino floor for Elena's consideration. "Vergilius might try freezing time to help us find the Caesars, but then we'd be the only ones moving in here."

"If Vergilius could freeze time at all," Elena said thoughtfully.

"Well then, who else could? Or would?"

She could see that he knew the answer to that, yet his eyes implored her not to say the name. Shame still burned in his face. She had tried to understand, and to forgive him with enough of her love to let him forgive himself.

She would not let him down. "The point is, no one has done it, with or without the power to accomplish it." There. The name need not be said. "So let's get on with what we were sent to do and take our watches in for repairs tomorrow."

They elbowed their way through the crowds with new fervor and a secondary purpose. They moved rapidly, both to reach Caesar and to escape the clinging doubt of time gone awry.

Their intent was noted before they reached his side, and noted in a most disturbing way. Of the five men surrounding Caesar, two were of the human mastiff breed whose every movement screams *muscle*. They stood nearly shoulder to shoulder with the divine Julius, and as Elena opened her mouth to address the whilom emperor, she saw one of them reach casually inside his Armani jacket as if to scratch his armpit. The old Mae West line sprang to mind, even though the pistol wasn't in his pocket and he definitely wasn't happy to see her.

"*Pax*," Julius said, moving his right hand ever so slightly. At once the overeager guardian's arm dropped back to his side. A smile twice as false as it was wide shone benevolence on Sanchi and Elena. "We're old friends."

Old friends and new retired to the Krater bar, where another of Caesar's flunkies slipped ahead to survey the room before giving a curt nod to signal all clear. As they all slid into one of the larger booths, Julius insisted that Sanchi and Elena flank him.

One of the three nonmuscle men objected. "Mr. Caesar, sir, I'm not sure—"

Julius treated him to an indulgent smile and a pat on the back. "You may rest assured, Peter, that these fine young people mean me no harm. Thank you for your concern, however. I shall put in a good word for you with Mr. Gianicolo. Ah, if I had only had gentlemen of your caliber around me ere this, it would have been a different story that March day."

"Yes sir, Mr. Caesar," Peter said. Elena got the impression that the man would have used the same cautiously respectful tone if Caesar had commenced munching the centerpiece of plastic grapes and silk ivy.

Lowering his voice so that his words reached Sanchi and Elena alone, Julius said, "It would break his heart if he knew that any assassination attempt on me here and now would only kill the two of you. I should regret that. Therefore, let us give suitable thanks that Tony and Patrick are reputed to be the best bodyguards in the family. Peter, Johnny, and Sal aren't amateurs either, even though their main duties no longer entail force of arms *per se*. We can speak in security. Briefly, though, Mr. Gianicolo is awaiting my recommendations on—ah—rechanneling the retail commodities markets in this city and environs."

"What commodities?" Sanchi asked, though his expression revealed that he had guessed and didn't like it.

"Come now," the divine Julius said. "You needn't look so upset. As you are a close associate of the man responsible for my—return to the business world, I am prepared to make you every assurance that your brother will not be permanently or *too* detrimentally affected by the projected changeover in recreational-substance vendors. In fact, considering the reputation he has made for himself already, I foresee no managerial-level pushback should he wish to continue in his present serviceperson capaci—"

"My brother's *dealing*?"

All five of Julius' new associates leaned forward at once, a neatly choreographed ballet, *Goon Lake*. Caesar himself made another of those minimalist shushing movements with his fingers.

"I would suggest discretion, my friend. My influence is already considerable within Mr. Gianicolo's organization, but even so—"

"A mobster." What Sanchi cut on volume he made up for on contempt. "One of history's greatest generals, a hero, a flaming legend, for God's sake, and all you can find to make of yourself in this world is a two-bit hood?"

"And so quickly," Elena murmured.

"You are very quick to condemn, young man." A tight little smile more like suppressed pain than amity twitched Caesar's thin lips. "I did not ask to be brought into your world. I and the others were summoned by your master, ostensibly to turn our experience to his own ends. An empire may best be undone by those used to thinking in terms of empires, and who better than I, who forged the heart of

178

Rome's domain? Yet when I set to my assigned task—Jupiter Capitolinus knows where those other lackbrains are; I expected better of Octavian—I am scorned."

"Explain slowly, then. Tell us how your hooking up with the mob, with the drug scene, how all that is going to help us overcome the sphynx?"

"How limited your vision is. You say 'drugs' and shudder like a maiden on her bridal night, when drug sales are the first volley *I* choose to launch against *your* enemy."

"She's no—" Sanchi shut up quickly.

Another of those pained grimaces tugged the conqueror's mouth. "Drugs are merely the initial front on which we shall attack her. Don't pretend ignorance of the fact that your brother's work in the field stems from her. It may take me some time to nose out all her sources of wealth and power, but I shall, and destroy them, one by one. This first encounter is on the field of battle, in the streets, to give me her measure as an adversary. I am fond of open combat, but I am also experienced in the subtler political arts. These too are well tended by my new friends." He indicated his five companions. They nodded, though they had heard nothing.

"Her empire is everywhere, I was told," Caesar went on. "She is, as you would say, well connected. Very well. So is the empire Mr. Gianicolo's group represents. Ample opportunity to cut her off on as many fronts as she may tend."

"Yes, but"—Elena spoke in a whisper—"what if your new employer finds out you're using his connections to serve a different master?"

No smile at all this time. "Caesar serves no master."

Elena started to reply, then something made her hold her peace. A misgiving danced at the corner of her eye. She looked more closely at the five men surrounding them. She hadn't bothered to give them more than a trifling glance—as criminals they were too dangerous to stare at, too despised to study. Still, she had picked up a sense of *what's wrong with this picture*? from that first cursory look.

Now she had it. Loyalty. It was there in their eyes, in their faces, for anyone with a mind to delve beneath the surface to see. Dogs gazed at Papi just the way these five were gazing at Julius Caesar. History spoke of how dearly his troops held him, how staunchly they stood beside him, swept into the wild forests of Gaul, crossed the English Channel to the wild shore beyond, left the Rubicon behind them and marched to what might have been traitors' deaths on the cross solely because *he* led them. His military prowess was a matter of record, but his irresistible personal magnetism was the bedrock on which the record rested.

"You've still got it, O Caesar," Elena said to herself, unconsciously echoing Augustus' earlier sentiments.

Suddenly she almost felt sorry for the unknown Mr. Gianicolo. Almost.

Caesar continued to address Sanchi, perhaps sharing Vergilius' noble Roman feeling that women were decorative and had some usefulness, but serious business discussions could get on well without them. "If you can control your lip from curling *too* much when you mention my name," he said dryly, "tell your master that he will hear from me after I have brought this little street skirmish to a successful end. We shall call it proof of my ability to deal with the sphinx on her own territory and terms."

"I've got the feeling that's not all you're going to call it."

Bad teeth showed. Though his new hairpiece was state-of-the-art, he obviously had not thought it necessary to consult a dentist during the whole of that weirdly telescoped afternoon and evening. "Perceptive. I shall also call it the first chip on the table. Having shown that my goods are genuine and valuable, I shall expect the mage to pay fair price for them."

"Which would be—?"

"Shall we say . . . life?"

Overlooked, ignored, Elena heard Caesar lay down his terms. He was not going back to Hades. He'd been there. The fact that he had discovered his new incarnation to be proof against the rude interruptions of bullets, poisons, strangling cords, daggers (especially daggers!), and the rest of Death's gewgaws made him even fonder of life this time around.

"My intelligence network informs me that Claudius has bolted. In his cowardly way he seeks to evade duty as well as death." Caesar gave a short laugh. "He will be disappointed. Tell me, you seem a bright lad: Have you not noted a certain . . . elasticity of time since our arrival in your world?"

"Yes. I was going to ask you—"

"Whether I had noted it? I'll pass over that insult to my powers of observation. Of course I've noted it! In Hades all we *have* to note is time! It stretches on and on, an infinity of nothingness which we seek to fill in with the insufficient ruses of mortality, like children emptying the sea with a spoon. Oh, I recognized the feel, the *taste* of Hades' own hours up here soon after I left your master's so kind care. I marked it from the moment I approached the first of Mr. Gianicolo's minions, with an eye to entry into his venerable organization. Events proceeded, time did not."

"It did; it just slowed around you."

"Exactly so. And when a thing stretches far enough, it spreads its substance too thin to maintain its original strength. It attenuates. It breaks. And all those who trust their weight to a thread pulled out too fine must tumble down into the abyss when the snap comes."

He motioned for Sal to refill his glass. "A strand that cannot bear the burden of many weights, however, may be more than enough to carry one. I am all the spirit that your master ever really needed. The others coming out of Hades with me was an accident. Accidents can be undone, if the motivation is strong enough. Tell this to the sorcerer: I, Caius Julius Caesar, will deliver your enemy into your hands. In return, he must deliver full strength of life into mine."

"If he can't do that?" Elena asked. Caesar regarded her as if watching an acrobatic dog. "Suppose the life you have now can't reach a violent end, but just . . . fades?"

"So it will, if it continues to be spread out among my imperial colleagues. Therefore the mage must find a way to—persuade them of the advantages eternal rest has to offer, and as they depart, transfer their newfound purchase on mortality to my account."

"You make it sound like laundering money." Sanchi smiled.

Not so Caesar. "That is my offer. It is generous. I shall not even attempt to force a reply from your master until I have taken the first victory over the sphynx. But ask him to recall, should he think my price too high, or too inconvenient, that a well-made toga looks well worn on either side."

They left the divine Julius with his new legionaries, outlining strategies for a drug war on cocktail napkins.

"That was the most elegant excuse for treachery I ever heard," Elena remarked as they left the Krater.

"Julius Caesar was never known to put anything ahead of the main chance," answered a familiar voice from among the potted ficus trees near the entrance. "If one side doesn't give him what he wants, he switches. I doubt he considers it treachery. His first loyalty always was Caius Julius Caesar; that never changes." Dapper in a lightweight navy-blue suit, Suetonius extricated himself from the greenery and bowed to them both. His obeisance snagged on the wires running from inside his jacket up to the plug in his right ear. "A fascinating interview," he said with an appreciative smile.

"You had the table bugged!" Sanchi accused.

"Who do you think is the intelligence network the divine Julius was so uppity about?" Suetonius retorted. "As a matter of fact, my fax sheet's picking up new subscribers by the moment. I never did see such a suspicious bunch of the walking dead. Every one of them wants to know where the others are. Without me, they'd be nervous wrecks, jumping at shadows, suffering from indigestion, headaches, neuritis, neuralgia . . . well, I'm very *good* at what I do."

"You know where the others are?" Sanchi sounded incredulous. "Where's Tiberius, for example?"

Suetonius slipped his hands into his pockets and rocked on his heels. "I'm not a mentalist, so don't expect me to pinpoint the man, but I'd say he's still closeted with the hotel doctor right in this very building. Once a hypochondriac, always a hypochondriac, except when he was being a pervert, and our friend Tiberius will get around to that soon enough. He likes them young and— Hold it." Suetonius tensed like a bird dog. He adjusted his ear plug. "Yes, that's it. Caesar shall forth. He's going after the sphynx right now, impatient to have his own mortality sealed. I'd suggest we all find Vergilius and inform him of Caesar's deal. He'll want to know, especially if the divine Julius makes good."

"Wait a minute." Sanchi grabbed his arm. "If this—this bulge in time is being caused by so many of you up here from Hades, aren't you afraid Vergilius knows? Aren't you worried he might want to get things back to normal and start by sending you back?"

Suetonius laughed with heartfelt humor. "Back to normal? With a *sphynx* in the streets? Even if he does want to knead time back into its proper shape, he'd never start with me."

"You sound sure of that."

"Who do you think was the first to buy a lifetime subscription to *Tranquilfax*?" The Amex Vendor's Copy Suetonius brandished said *Rhett Roman*.

# CHAPTER TWENTY-ONE:
## Remember the Ladies

The sphynx paced her suite in long, fluid strides, making taut, close turns just inches from the walls. She needed no watch to shake, no clockface to wonder at. She could sense the wrongness in time. It had the iron smell of the chain, the sour reek of the cage.

Whose doing was it? His? Astonishing. She was willing to wager all her hopes that he could not contain so much power. Stumbled over it, yes, a possibility. She had stood witness many times in the course of their centuries together when blind luck presented the startled sorcerer with a gift of power that he never understood and subsequently lost.

Blind luck. Blind justice. A blind prophet, a self-blinded king. The sphynx dissolved her human eyes to slit-pupiled shields of gold. How many oboloi would two such shining counters buy? How many dead men's eyes would the lesser coins weigh down, bearing the fare for Charon?

The phone rang. She refused to answer it. It would only be more bad news. Something was wrong on the streets. Alonso had been the first to tell her, still her devoted slave in spite of every humiliation she had visited upon him. His attachment was more than just what her spells had wrought. Even her powers had limits, and at the moment she was too beset by other problems to maintain an enchantment of physical addiction on two men at once. Even the weirding she had worked on Sanchi was spun out to gossamer. Her magics were cried for in other quarters.

If Alonso was still attached, it was a bond self-forged within his own spirit, a tie wrought of some need she filled. So be it. She was not one to question fortune.

Yes, Alonso was her good servant, her brave warrior. In the short time she had possessed him, he had handled his share of her interests well, trustworthy middle management to oversee the transfer of crack, cocaine, PCBs, heroin to the street, money to his mistress. He had even expanded the market, with a cunning eye for spotting a user at the casino tables, guessing the drug of choice—there were more left-over sixties relics in the world than the sphynx ever imagined, too circumspect to snort, too weight-conscious to bolt bourbon, and too terrified of time's passage to let the Woodstock Nation follow the Edsel into trendy Elysium. She had been doing a hell of a brisk business in Ward Cleaver ganja since Alonso came along.

But business was off. Alonso brought her the word as swift and sure as he brought her the dwindling profits. Time bent, stretched, pouched around her, and in that unnatural ballooning of the moments she saw rival sellers hustling her people off the streets. Some got hustled so far off that no one heard from them again. Shipments never made delivery. Cash and its carriers vanished.

She was furious. The night was hers. Who dared to take it from her? It must not happen, not now, not when the Riddle of world's end hung so near completion in the loom. The warp was set; it only wanted each of the seven weft threads run through to finish it. Seven Askings, each of which would add to her waning strength if incorrectly Answered, and then the turn of the final Riddle.

But to ask each of the seven required an investment of magic, a measure of her inner powers to be poured out into the channels she had dug through this world. Her holdings in land, her anchoring claws in finance, her discreet intrusions into politics domestic and foreign, her grasp of industrious vices to weaken her foes, and so many other rivulets of her own carving, all dusty as old bones without her powers to fill them brimful of destruction.

She could not afford to lose even one of her footholds. She could not risk losing the whole game for lack of one propitious turn of the cards. Above all, she could not spare much more of her inborn and acquired powers to defend conquests she thought already hers.

Someone was leaning on the doorbell. The sphynx's tail lashed visible, then vanished. Her talons flexed with pure vexation and were compelled to retreat into a woman's perfectly manicured fingernails. "Go away!" she shouted.

The pressure on the doorbell went on. The sound was an atrocious imposition on her nerves. She wished she had not dismissed her corps of attendants, so that one of them might go to the door now and teach manners to the impertinent creature on the other side. Vainly she cursed her own besotted addiction to solitude. Now she would have to discipline the interloper herself.

Ianthe Apeiron jerked the door open so viciously that it slammed into the wall behind. Her caller measured her with sardonic eyes. "So you are the monster out of myth," he said. "History has not been kind. You are lovely."

Under her rosy silk blouse, the sphynx felt short tufts of fur spring up between her unseen wings. They prickled with suspicion. The incredible had come to call on her, in all the arrogance of a conqueror's bones. She knew him even as she denied it, but he gave her no chance to wrestle with her own doubts.

"I am Caius Julius Caesar. Won't you ask me in?"

She found herself taking small, feline sidesteps as he swept past her and sat with magnificent ease on the sofa closest to the brandy decanter. There was no need to offer him a drink in the name of civilization, and less to probe the reasons for his reappearance here, in her den.

His economy and elegance of phrase were the despair of every nascent Latin scholar. In a few words he informed her that he was the cause of her present discomfiture on the streets, and also that it was no use trying to return to the status quo by means of murder.

"You see?" he said, drawing a small Swiss Army knifeblade across his bared wrist. No trail of blood followed the cut, and the gaping lips of the wound closed momentarily along a seam that disappeared. "You see?" he said again, and jabbed the same blade deep into his eye.

He laughed at how high she jumped. His amusement lasted as long as it took for the eye to heal itself, which was not long. "You see." The third time, it was not a question.

"If you think I can be killed more easily than you, O Caesar, you do not see at all."

"Why should I want to kill you?"

"You are one of Vergilius' works. He wants me dead, and the master's wish must be his creature's command."

Caesar bridled. "That for the sphynx's supposed wisdom!" He spat tidily over the sofa arm. "I am my own."

"Truly?" The sphynx appeared to relax and be interested instead of merely hostile. "So you too slipped your collar?"

"There was never any such on me. I am . . . the mage's partner, you could say."

"Ah." The sphynx slid sinuously onto the cushions beside the divine Julius. "And do all Vergilius' new minions assume such an independent air? He is slipping if he allows such autonomy."

"He cannot *allow* or disallow anything with regard to me and my colleagues." The sphynx grew still more fascinated as Caesar chatted on about the gleanings Vergilius had made from Elysium. "But his common servants," Julius continued, "they are another story. Especially that pretty pair of turtles even now conveying my offer to their master."

"Turtles?"

"Paired close as any mated pair of turtledoves, though I doubt there is a formal bond between them yet. Still, I am not blind. I could see the tenderness that passed from eyes to eyes."

Caesar spoke on, glorying in the bargain he had tendered Vergilius, the terms of which might be altered to suit the sphynx's service should she so desire. She heard his bombast only peripherally, caught up in a more private irritation.

*I did not finish with him, girl*, she growled at an absent Elena. *He is no one's but mine until I let him go.*

"So you would serve me gladly then, O Caesar?" she asked, full of the pert, charming harmlessness of a kitten.

"Or help destroy you just as gladly. That is up to you and Vergilius."

"To the highest bidder." He did not flinch as her glittering scarlet nail tickled his ear. "I see no problem there. I have it in my power to siphon you a full life in this world. I drank in all I could of Vergilius' knowledge before I left him and added it to my own inborn magic; I am more than a match for any promise he might make you. And I know the worth of a valuable ally."

She poured herself a brandy and added to Caesar's nearly empty glass, then raised hers in a toast. "I can throw in a publishing contract for your new *Memoirs* if you like. You *will* want to continue writing?"

"Merely to instruct the young."

"And not for any personal attention it might bring you? How refreshing. It might even be miniseries material. I know all the right people."

Wild hope kindled in the divine Julius' eye. "Joan Collins?" he implored.

"Why not?" She poured more brandy. "Seeing as it's you."

She contrived to snuggle nearer. There was a cold, dry scent blowing from the man that no amount of fine French talc or bitter-lime after-shave could mask. With the surgical precision of edged steel, it cut through the dull look of smugness presently making his face obnoxious. She knew the odor of ruthlessness, though she was sure he would call it political practicality. The greatest mistake anyone could make was putting faith in the human feelings of Caius Julius Caesar. No one needed to tell her where his first love and loyalty lay.

Fortunately, self-love too could blind.

The Riddle pulsed within her. It was one of the Seven she had worked so carefully to craft. The words were set, but they would be more than mere words by the time they rose to her lips. Power would throb from every vibration of the air when she broke the silence with the first Asking.

He felt the change emanating from her, but it came too suddenly for escape. He started as magic poured invisible from the slight and small-boned figure beside him on the couch and wrapped immobilizing cords around him at wrists and ankles. By instinct he tried to break free and gasped to see his arms and legs move easily. What her enchantment bonded was not this new physical form, but his restored soul. If he moved, he would tear himself apart.

"A formality," the sphynx whispered, her rough tongue darting maliciously into his ear. "You know how fond I am of ceremony. A rite of the old times to seal our bargain and give me the full measure of my new ally. How can you refuse? Indeed, you cannot. But it should be short work for a man of your intelligence."

"A riddle?" Caesar managed to keep his voice level, but

he spoke as one who did not know the full importance of any question the sphynx could put to a man.

Her laughter was throaty, stirring him in spite of himself. "I said you were bright. Now . . .

"Not the leveret, not the doe
Faster from the snare can go
Than this most elusive prize.
Most tightly grasped, it fastest flies."

She watched his face as she chanted the Riddle, as she felt her body weaken with the outflow of magic used to spin the weft-thread of its making. Dread coated her flesh with a clammy dew. *He is smiling! It was too easy! He knows!* He could kill her now, in the time of weakness that would come over her if he answered rightly. He could take that same ridiculous little knife and plunge it into her eyes and destroy her if the words she now saw forming on his upturned lips were correct.

"A formality after all," said Caesar. "How kind of you to riddle me on a thing with which I am so very conversant. What flies fastest the harder you grasp it? Oh, I know that indeed! Quite simple: fame."

"Quite simple," the sphynx repeated as her skin crawled and quivered. Silvery crescent moons sprang from her fingertips. Silk and linen clothing unraveled to their component threads as bright wings burst across the emperor's sight. A lamp toppled and shattered. Tawny fur rippled over coiling muscles and a whipcord tail lashed a marble-topped table clear to the far side of the room.

"But quite wrong."

She struck instinctively, in the exaltation of the moment, without bothering to wonder whether the all-pervading power of the Riddle would affect his demonstrated immortality. Oh, but how soon she saw that it did! No greater vulnerability ever wrapped a man than what he could not answer, than anything he did not know. Ignorance and death were closer kin than death and sleep. He died without a scream as her forepaws opened him. That much was disappointing. The sweet steam of his spilling innards intoxicated her. Her human neck bent with animal grace to let her lap the blood.

More disappointment. She licked air. Where so much

blood had spilled was only the wavering of a fast-vanishing scarlet ghost. Julius Caesar no longer lay split from breast-bone to belly on the sofa. A tiny diamond twinkled on the cushions, but by the time the sphynx had resumed the human fingers clever enough to pick up such a small object, the gem had become a nub of compressed ash that powdered between thumb and forefinger.

The sphynx licked her fingers clean with short, petulant dabs of the tongue. She had won, but she still felt cheated. Julius Caesar did not taste at all as interesting as she had hoped.

A secret half-smile touched her lips. He was only one. There were others, he had said; others Vergilius had brought back from Pluto's kingdom. There was the cause of time gone warped and awry, stretched as it should not be stretched. But one of them was gone. Time felt nearer its old familiar shape around her. The Asker had stumbled across an Answer. How could she help but grin? And as each one of the revenants was sent back to Hades, time would return to its true shape.

*And another thread will fly into the pattern on the loom. Seven Caesars, seven Askings, and in the end it will be you and I, Vergilius, and the final Riddle. You will answer, and the world of man will die.*

Ianthe Apeiron picked up the phone and made several calls of inquiry, then went to her wardrobe to select something appropriate to wear. She fixed on a pleated red silk chiffon confection by Valentino, though she supposed a nice safari jacket and skirt from Banana Republic would be more in keeping.

The hunt had begun.

# CHAPTER TWENTY-TWO:
## To Bury Caesar

Augustus felt it as he was on the point of fastening the strand of diamonds around the neck of a compliant showgirl who did not remind him in the least of his rather forceful mate, Livia. The necklace fell from his hands, trickled down the front of her dress into the deep V between her breasts. She giggled, said he was very sneaky and much too naughty and did he want to get it out and try again.

"No . . ." Augustus was sweating profusely. He blotted his forehead with a wadded handkerchief. "No . . ."

*Yes,* said the voice of the sorcerer so that only he could hear it. *Julius Caesar is dead.*

A stocky beetle the size and color of one of Augustus' solid gold cufflinks whirred into the lavishly furnished room and alit on the emperor's trembling hand. *Come.*

He ran out, following its crazy flight, leaving the bemused showgirl to fish up her own diamonds.

Tiberius felt it as he sat leafing through a collection of magazines whose so very young models could not quite lose the look of harried prey from their eyes. He was a connoisseur of pretty little ones, relishing memories of the days of his self-made exile on Capri where the imperial villa and grounds had been well stocked for his entertainment. Some of the young ones changed under his personal tutelage, acquiring a taste for the unnatural, becoming willing partners because it was always easier to pretend that they still retained some control, that they were human beings with wills of their own who honestly desired all the pleasures the omnipotent emperor wrenched from them body and soul.

He had told himself similar lies in the days when his mother, Livia, made him her counter on the board of the imperial succession. He nearly convinced himself that divorcing his beloved Vipsania was his own inspiration, not

Livia's order. The illusion of control was supposedly better than the reality of helplessness and the madness that followed in its train. He understood those strange children, for whom a simple game of let's-pretend became a matter of mental survival, though he never remained as fond of them as of the ones who never escaped into fictions and never forgot that they served him out of fear.

Tiberius enjoyed fear, but not like this; not when it was his own. The chill was sudden, the shock like a block of ice in his groin. He was certain he had contracted some rare affliction and was about to call the hotel physician again when the sorcerer's voice spoke inside his head and the golden beetle came to lead him away.

"He's not there? OK, thanks." Sanchi hung up the phone and faced Elena. "Vergilius gave up the hotel rooms in town and left a message for us. For you. He said to give him a call." He leaned on one of the pay phones near the casino floor in Dionysia and looked thoroughly bewildered.

Elena laughed and showed him the enchanted calling card the mage had given her. She explained its properties. "Now let me at that phone. We'll be with him at the Sea-Side Inn motel before you can say Ma Bell."

She edged him aside and picked up the receiver, punching in the number on the card as before. As she waited for a response, she turned to say something to Sanchi.

She was just in time to see him walking away like a man moon-touched, his arm linked in the arm of Ianthe Apeiron. The sphynx looked back and smiled at Elena. Her teeth were a lion's fangs.

"*Sanchi!*" The name tore from Elena's throat as the heart tore from her breast. She groped to hang up the phone before racing after him.

Her own cry covered the faint sound of wings. The golden beetle touched down on the back of her hand.

*No, Elena. Another needs you more.*

The walls of Dionysia blew away like mist as the walls of the wizard's lair rushed in to take their place.

"Why have you brought us back here?" Nero demanded, stamping his alligator cowboy boot. He gave Vergilius a no-mercy sneer culled from studying the King's own lips.

The light of hanging oil lamps was multiplied tenfold by reflection off the gold lamé encasing Nero like an upscale sausage. The rhinestone-traced self-portrait on his belt buckle could blind a man. He tossed the fringed end of a white silk scarf over his shoulder and in an accent half Memphis and half Milan declaimed, "I've got me a show to do."

"And *we're* warming the room up for him," Heliogabalus cried, wig-wagging a pair of jet-black drumsticks. He and Caligula had swapped Wayne Newton and Dolly Parton for iridescent green spandex suits and face paint thick enough to make a street mime wince. "Isn't that *exciting*? Snapped the gig right out from under the runny little noses of the Chicago White Sux. *And* stole their bass player. *That* for you, Johnny Crud, saying *I* look dumpy in spandex!" He stuck out more tattooed tongue than necessary at the absent fashion critic.

"We haffa g'bag," Caligula added. His words were partly blocked by the ill-starred gecko making a few last thrashes between his lips. Caligula removed the expiring reptile and repeated, "We have to get back. We've got our reputation to consider. Not only is Geeks Baring Gifts a *cool* band, but we're prompt." He pried open the gecko's mouth and removed a golden beetle, which he dropped disdainfully to the floor before chowing down.

Vergilius sat in a high-backed chair, clutching the armrests for real support, not show. The mage looked drawn and tired, his skin sallow, the flesh of his face sagging. At his side, regal in the simplicity of a white sheath dress and the drapery of a sheer linen kalasiris, the small, dark woman out of Hades rested a hand on his shoulder.

The sorcerer gathered breath that came out as a sigh. A second inhalation produced words. "Julius Caesar is dead, slain by the sphinx. If that was not cause enough to summon you, I await better suggestions."

"*Dead?*" Heliogabalus skirled. "But he's dead already. We all are."

"I will not chop words with you. Think of him as destroyed, then, if you pause to think at all."

"That can't be. We *can't* be killed!"

"By common means," Vergilius amended. "*Her* ways are anything but common."

"How do you know he is dead?" Augustus blustered, as if

the wrath once dreaded by an empire could change facts or cow a magician.

Vergilius did not even bother meeting Augustus' livid glare. "You felt it when it happened—the life force leaving Julius Caesar, flying into shards, lodging deep in each one of you. You lie if you say otherwise. I felt it, too: my magic bursting from him in death, seeking new shelters. They say that the earth trembles at the death of kings." He extended the hand where only six diamonds now glimmered around the huge emerald. The seventh place was a black, empty crater.

Tiberius ran his fingers back and forth over his lower lip. "One gone." He looked around the room and counted noses. "Five of us here, and *those*." He made short, nervous, waving motions at the dark woman, at Suetonius with his eternal reporter's notepad, and at the banqueting couch where a miserable Elena clung to her brother Manolo for comfort. "Where is Claudius? Why didn't you bring him? Is he . . . departed too?"

"Departed indeed; but no deader than before." Vergilius drew back his hand and studied the diamonds. "I *brought* none of you. I only called. I have not the power to do more." He looked to the dark woman, whose face wore a sweet serenity. "Do I, O Queen and Lady of the Two Lands?"

"No, my lord," she replied, and even through tears Elena recognized the look lovers give one another.

"The Two Lands . . . ?" Tiberius nearly rubbed his lip raw. "Egypt. By Venus, I never thought the legendary Cleopatra was such a swart woman."

The lady's heavy eyelids, thick with paint and kohl, did not even flicker as she looked at him. "If your thoughts weighed for anything more than dirty schoolboy musings, Tiberius, I would be concerned that you mistake me for her. I did not need to retake my kingdom on my back, to accept it as a lover's gift. I never loosed it from my hands, and these same hands set the red-and-white crown of Pharaoh on my own head. I am Hatshepsut, Roman, queen *and* king of Egypt in my time. Like you, I ruled an empire; unlike you, I did it well, and for the benefit of my people, not myself. Now be still. My lord Vergilius would speak."

Tiberius started to splutter objections. Hatshepsut raised her hands. A swarm of black flies materialized around the emperor, their merciless attentions soon teaching him that he was only an amateur when it came to greed. When she judged he had been sufficiently instructed, she crossed her hands on her bosom and the swarm tumbled to the floor, a cascade of lotus petals.

"Egypt." Augustus sounded speculative. "A land of many magics, according to Herodotus. In higher places than that poor old liar ever had the nerve to imagine, it seems."

"She's a sorceress, too!" Heliogabalus was ecstatic. "Don't *ever* fight a woman unless you're another, I always say. *No* real chance for survival otherwise, and I know what I'm talking about. You should have met my mommy and gran. Were you the one sent us these darling little buggies?" He picked up the one Caligula had discarded. Hatshepsut inclined her head. "I *knew* it. You do like to work with insects."

"Then the lady's going to adore working with you," Nero said sulkily. "Stop your babble, you little twit, or I'll see to it that Geeks Baring Gifts won't be able to get a gig warming toilet seats."

"Big man," Caligula sneered.

"The biggest." Nero regarded him with artistic hauteur. "I *am*"—he gave his pelvis a one-and-a-half Immelmann twist—"the *King!*" His arrogance died, and in more plaintive tones he asked Hatshepsut, "You *are* going to kill the sphynx for us?"

"No," the lady answered. "I cannot."

Before any of the surviving emperors could raise questions or objections, Vergilius spoke out. "Do you ask the impossible, O Caesars? The lady Hatshepsut is queen and sorceress, but first a woman. How can we match mere woman's magic against the sphynx? It would be throwing a life away."

"Better hers than ours," Nero retorted. "Since we know the sphynx can kill us, why should we continue the battle? *Your* battle? We're comfy here now. Why shouldn't we copy that old toad Claudius, cut and run to somewhere safe? Like Vegas."

"*A Caesar, run?*" Outrage shook the pillars of Vergilius' hall. All eyes swiveled automatically to Augustus, but that tuxedoed gentleman indicated that he hadn't said a word.

*"Are we mere women, too, to be relegated to the safety of the hearth when there is man's work to be done?"*

Heliogabalus emitted noises like a coked-up Yorkshire terrier. "*He* said that! *He* did, so don't look at *me*! I mean, I may be crazy, but I'm not *Caligula*!"

"Caligula?" Elena and Manolo both sat up straighter. To hear Caligula speak out so heroically was a sign either that the world was about to end or that some strange new madness had seized the normally pusillanimous emperor.

Whatever the affliction, it was catching. If Caligula declared himself ready for the fray, no one else would dare to lag behind. Augustus was first to vow that he would renew the battle his twice-late uncle had lost. Tiberius grumbled his own willingness, glowering at Hatshepsut as if challenging her to outdo a real man's courage. Though the Egyptian queen remained unmoved, the general excitement overcame Heliogabalus so thoroughly that he jumped up and offered to give the sphynx third-degree sunburns through his familial connections with the solar deity. Nero belted out an altered version of "Hound Dog" in which he very bravely called the sphynx some nasty names. All of the emperors marched out to their cars and broke several traffic laws in their haste to return to the front.

"Wild," Manolo said. "Caligula, that little sniveling creep. I wonder what got into him?"

Caligula let Heliogabalus drive the black-and-crimson van while he lounged on the chamois-covered mattress in back and reveled in self-congratulation.

He had done it. A jest almost as smooth-'n-creamy as when he'd stocked a brothel with the wives and daughters of senators, or bestowed the consulship upon his favorite horse. No, even better. He'd get more out of this than just a few good laughs.

He would live forever.

Oh yes, for once he saw his future with astonishing clarity. He was the only one who had really paid attention to what that two-bit thaumaturge Vergilius had been saying. Had he felt it when Julius Caesar died? Had he ever! First a blow, then a glow. For a second he thought he'd pushed immortality too far, trying to play electric guitar with his tongue (the act did need something sensational, and Heliogabalus kept bitching about how *everyone* was doing lizards).

Now he knew what that jolt had been: that portion of the mage's magic that had brought the divine Julius out of Hades as it split itself between the survivors and dug in. He was stronger for it. So were the others.

But the others didn't realize what was going on. They didn't know that the same thing would happen when the next of their number died, and the next, and the next . . .

*Until there's only me to hold all the life-force sustaining us here above,* Caligula gloated. *The others will die as Julius Caesar died—all but that gossip Suetonius, and the magician's black slut-queen with that tongue-knotting name. Those two are too clever. I may have to help them along.* He considered several sharp means.

Caligula smiled. He was always so happy to help out.


# CHAPTER TWENTY-THREE:
## Woman's Work


After the Caesars' grandiose departure, Vergilius tried to rise from his chair. Hatshepsut remained nearby, watching his efforts closely. She did not hover, nor register much apparent concern when the mage slumped back down, defeated, yet Elena forgot her own misery for a time as she noted the forcibly suppressed anxiety in the Egyptian's eyes.

"You!" Vergilius' pointing hand looked like a claw. Every vein was visible, even at a distance, and the skin was waxy. "Why do you linger?"

Suetonius flipped his pad shut and stood with an ease that mocked the sorcerer's weakness. "I thought you might want to hear some details on Caesar's death, O Magus."

The black mustache quivered with the smallest of smiles. "For your usual price, eh, Suetonius?" The hand that dismissed the offered report shook. "What need? A Riddle opened the doorway to a second death. The moment of Asking and Answer must leave one or the other of the two players vulnerable. If she did not know how to destroy you and the rest before, she knows now. And even not knowing, it would not have taken long before you all faded out of these new forms and back to Hades."

" 'It *would* not have taken long'?" Suetonius repeated. The pad was open immediately. "Forgive me, lord, but as a man of words, I can't help but notice that you're using the conditional mood there. Am I to assume that conditions concerning us have changed? That there *might* be the chance of our not simply trickling back into the underworld like so many spiritual oil spills?"

Vergilius showed no willingness to address the question. "You tire me. All of you. Go."

"But I have to talk with you," Elena objected. "Something has happened to—"

Hatshepsut stepped in to block the way to the sorcerer's throne. "My lord has asked us all to leave him. I will escort you to your cars."

"Cars?" Manolo said. "What cars? One minute I'm minding my own business, the next I hear this buzzing sound and this gold bug comes in for a landing on my wrist and—"

The only woman ever to be hailed as Pharaoh was not about to let such jabber go on for long. She raised her hands again, and a second aerosquadron of biting insects snarled in a black halo above her head, awaiting directions.

"Right. Out of here." Manolo was a faster study than Tiberius. He grabbed his sister's hand and was out the door before the queen could give him any encouragement.

Outside, in the weed-grown parking lot of the Sea-Side Inn, only one car waited. Walking carefully on account of the dark, Suetonius made his way to the vehicle and patted it fondly on the hood.

"It's only a Hyundai, but it's all mine. I wish you could see the color, but . . ." He shrugged away the unlit motor court, the dead neon sign, the feeble illumination offered by a sickle moon and the distant glow of the casinos. He slid into the driver's seat and turned on the headlights.

"Acca Laurentia's twice-blessed tits, where *is* your car?" he asked as they swept the empty lot.

"Like I was trying to say in there, we don't have one," Manolo answered. He looked at Elena. "I mean, I know *I* didn't drive here; did you?" Elena shook her head.

"Brought as well as summoned, then." Suetonius nibbled an ink-stained finger thoughtfully. "But Vergilius said he doesn't have that power. Either he's lying, or—well, friends, however you got here, I doubt you're leaving the same way. Can I give you a lift?" He opened the door.

It slammed shut with no one touching it. "They will not wish to depart just yet," said Hatshepsut from the motel walkway. A cat the size of a Great Dane attended her. The beast's tawny fur was as incandescent as its peridot eyes, making the gold hoops in its batlike ears dull by comparison. "But you will, Caius Suetonius Tranquillus."

The jovial gossipmonger took one hand from the steering wheel to salute her. "As my lady wishes." The cool delivery of that courtly phrase was lost in the spray of sand and dust his wheels kicked up as he tore out of the lot and onto the roadway.

"He fears me," the queen remarked. "What a pity."

"Hey, he's not the only one," Manolo whispered to Elena. "*Jesus*, look at the size of that furball!" The golden cat seemed to hear and understand. It lifted a lip to show off formidable fangs.

"Come with me," said the queen. From the palms of her outstretched hands, two glittering beetles flew.

"A scarab," Elena said softly to the one that tickled her hand with its tiny feet. "Mani and I *were* brought here." She stared at Hatshepsut. "By you."

The dark queen was shorter than Elena, with a royal bearing that added illusory inches to her height. Her straight black hair, glossy beneath a plain silver circlet, swung forward in wings as she bowed ceremoniously to the girl. "You honor me, lady. You have heard my lord Vergilius say many times how we women must not aspire to the greater sorceries, have you not? And my lord knows much."

"Much isn't all," Elena replied.

Hatshepsut's smile was especially brilliant against the rich color of her skin. Without further talk, she led them to a door at the very end of the walkway, far removed from the earthly entrance to the sorcerer's realm.

"Let me guess," Manolo hissed in his sister's ear just before they entered. "She's going to have the Astrodome in here."

He was off the mark by several dozen centuries. The

decor of Hatshepsut's private apartments made Vergilius' Roman banqueting hall seem like the *dernier cri* in interior design. All was Egypt: ancient, magnificent, gilded, painted, carved, timeless. Egypt, and magic. Elena smelled a blend of pungent spices, the bite of natron, and the fragrance of rare woods burning in a baboon-footed brazier. Rows of identical painted clay pots awaited their owner on the long, low stone table. Under the table, the wizened body of a sun-dried crocodile greeted guests with its gaping, leathery grin. The huge cat rubbed its back against the top row of yellowed teeth and purred. A statue of the ibis-headed Thoth watched over all, his reed pen eternally poised over a stone tablet.

"Reminds me of Suetonius," Manolo quipped. "Who is he?"

"Tehuti." The queen bowed as she spoke the deity's true name. "God of learning. God of magic. He who taught man the measure of time and the use of numbers. At the moment, he is not pleased. Time is twisted, and those with the learning to set it right are too blind to recognize those with the magic they must borrow. My lord Vergilius has wisdom, but the power lies in another shell." She looked straight at Elena. "What are you going to do about it?"

Elena's reaction to this calm assumption came as a surprise to herself. Instead of peeping *Who, me*? she only laughed in Hatshepsut's face. "If I had any magic in me at all, do you think I'd be here?"

"No." Nothing could move Hatshepsut from her monumental complacency. "You would be at the sphynx's throat. And you would be dead." The queen lifted her hands, thumbs touching, palms outward so that her face was framed by this suggestion of horns. A pale green bowl began as a twist of fireflies, solidified until it floated in the air between the two women.

"To have the magic is not enough, Elena Sanchez," Hatshepsut said as a yellow liquid poured itself up from the bottom of the bowl and thinned with radiant visions. "To have the raw power, the wild magic that is in your blood, is not enough to defeat the one who has stolen your love from you."

In the bowl, Sanchi stood in the midst of a tropical jungle, on the shore of a pellucid sea. The purity of the vision was so great that Elena could see the small stone image hanging from his neck. Around him swept the shapes of many gods. Elena knew them. All of the old tales Mamacita told at her bedside, all of the ancient legends born of the island, brought to birth out of the wombs of the slave ships, all of the old powers that still stood vigil over their copper-skinned, ebon-skinned children were there. They warded him, they awaited her. Their names whispered over the waves, out of the hidden caverns, and washed across the sandy shore.

"Are you as blind as Vergilius, little one?" the dark queen asked softly. "Do you think there is but one breed of magic in this world? We each hold our own—some great, some small—and each of these is but a mirrored spark of the greater sorcery that burns at the world's heart. Tend the fire, nurture the flame. Awake and link his learning to your magic so that you may win back your man."

With an angry cry, Elena struck the bowl away. It shattered on the floor. The golden cat padded up to lick the spilled liquid. "*Win* him back? Sanchi isn't a—a prize. I don't want all this talk and doubletalk about magic. I can see you have it, so why don't you use it? Vergilius is *sick*, not blind! He can't sustain all the spirits he drew out of Hell. He's your lover—why not help him instead of bothering me?"

"No one told you Vergilius was my lover."

"It's plain enough to see!"

"For one who knows how to look. That, too, is a power." Hatshepsut's full lips softened. "Intuition," she said. "Insight. What he would call the only magics women own. There is a difference between the spells each sex commands, but it has nothing to do with strength, merely nature. Ours seem weaker because they are less sudden in effect, not quite so autocratic. We gently shape the changes in reality; we do not coerce them."

"In other words, you haven't the power to destroy the sphynx."

"Not alone; nothing, alone. That is also nature." The queen sighed. "I did not take the sorcerer to my bed on a whim. Death is a great teacher of chastity. There is more to Vergilius than any eyes but mine can see. I sensed it soon after I stepped back into this world. He is my completion; can you understand?"

"Yes." Elena looked wistful. "Very well."

"You are not the only one wise enough to regard a man as something human—not as shield or prize, treasure trove or banquet table, monster or pawn. Any help I could give Vergilius now would shatter him. He has held his illusions so long that they are in the fiber of his bones; they must be gentled out. If I made my full powers manifest, I would seem as another sphynx in his eyes, and no woman." Hatshepsut spoke more intensely now, her face burning as she brought it nearer and nearer Elena's. "But if you too, with my guidance, were to put on the mantle of enchantment, then he might finally know that all the power in the world does not make a woman more or less than human. You must learn, Elena. You must accept my teachings. For your own sake, for Vergilius, for Sanchi, you dare not refuse, you must—"

Manolo wrapped his arms around his sister. Elena had begun to tremble. She was turning pale, with anger rather than weakness, and she shook her head violently, too upset to trust her words.

"Hey, leave my sister alone!" Manolo shouted at the Egyptian queen. "For someone who talks a big game about not forcing things, you can just back off Elena. She doesn't want to play witch, OK?"

Hatshepsut's tender mouth hardened. "A man who touches power is a master to be feared and honored for his wisdom; a woman who does the same is a warped and ugly thing of shadows. Has so little changed? Very well, Elena. Remain as you are, a dutiful child, a conformable woman, a fire banked in its own ashes. I can wait until you know yourself ready to learn the lore of spells, the means to control your own magic. I am Egypt, and Egypt is older than time."

Again the queen raised her hands, this time in valediction. The shards of the green bowl fluttered up, a cloud of butterflies, and lifted Manolo and Elena over the marshes, across the face of the moon, and back into the streets of Atlantic City.

# CHAPTER TWENTY-FOUR:
## A Turn of the Cards

In the sphynx's so-called library, Gemma sat with her hands knotted on her knees, fingers plucking at the buttery folds of a white satin gown. It was a dress out of her fondest dreams, the material flowing over her long limbs like water, the gold and blue metallic embroidery at breasts and waist so exquisitely done, the sapphire clip of snowy plumes on the single shoulder so perfect a finishing touch. It was costly, and fit her like her own skin; it felt like her shroud.

The odor of lilac in the room was stifling. She yearned to escape, but she had been told to stay where she was. She hadn't the courage to do otherwise, even though she felt as if she were going to pass out any minute. She wondered whether Ms. Apeiron would take her to task for fainting without permission.

The game of double-spy was not as much fun as it had been. Second thoughts multiplied and crept everywhere, unbidden, like cockroaches. She couldn't remember the last time she had seen her other employer, that mysterious dark man who reminded her so much of a stage devil. Had he just left, like that, without a word? That didn't seem like him. Whatever he thought of her—"greedy" and "ambitious" were the kindest terms he'd use, she knew—he was too instinctively courteous to vanish without the proper leavetaking.

But other people had vanished before. It was none of their doing. This was a city; such things happened.

Why did she feel as if the air around her was slowly turning into cotton? Ms. Apeiron had appeared at her elbow as she headed for her rest break and said, *I need you, Gemma. It's all right, it's all arranged.* Then not another word as they went up to the penthouse suite, as Ms. Apeiron tossed her the white gown in its glossy black box and pointed to the library. Gemma changed clothes and came out, only to be told to go back, shut the door, wait.

How long had she been waiting? She couldn't tell. Something was the matter with her watch. Maybe she was getting sick. The night seemed longer than it could possibly be, the minutes stretching out into the waste of darkness and distant stars. It was like the time she'd disobeyed her mother and gone on that haunted-house ride at the fair. All alone, terrified, her most deadly fear not of the ghastly sights or eerie sounds surrounding her, but that they would have no end.

When at last she heard that rapid knock on the door, she flipped her chair over backward in her hurry to get up and leave. "Come in!" It was a gasp of relief.

Ianthe Apeiron let her stand there until she felt the full foolishness of her recent terror and was shamed. Gemma saw how her employer's smile widened by the same degrees as the blush warmed her cheeks. A queer thought brushed her mind—*There are all sorts of vampires*—but then Ms. Apeiron said, "How lovely you look, Gemma. That color suits you. Now come, I need you." She followed like a lamb.

Ms. Apeiron shooed her ahead into an unlit room and closed the door quickly, blocking off the light spill from the sitting room. Even in the dark, even without knowing the layout of this suite so well, Gemma could tell it was a bedroom. Powders and perfumes struck top notes of delicate scent over the stronger smell of human sweat and the inescapably potent tang of industrially washed bed linen. Regular slivers of colored light from the signs atop neighboring hotels bent in bars across the back of whoever it was who now sat hunched over the edge of the bed.

"Ianthe?" Gemma's breath hissed in as a hand touched hers. She knew the voice that uttered her employer's name so wishfully. "You did come back!" It was piteous to hear. The lights snapped on.

Sanchi's startled reaction had no darkness to hide it. Gemma saw the pain of betrayal follow fast upon the confused flush mantling his cheeks as he dropped her hand. She made herself look away, but the only person she could face in that room was Ms. Apeiron, and the lady's taunting smile held too much promise of more pain to follow.

"Gemma." Sanchi started up from the bed. "What are you doing here?" His shirt was rumpled, several buttons

203

torn away, and his trousers were similarly creased and poorly fastened. In the light, Gemma saw further evidence of what must have happened here. At his throat was more than one mark, little nibbled roses, and the sign of scratches trailing down the open neck of his shirt. Someone had been avid, greedy. Several small components of a man's casual outfit lay on the night table and the chair near the bed. Even as Sanchi spoke to her, he fumbled for his wristwatch and knocked another item to the thickly carpeted floor.

"I brought you here as witness, Gemma," Ms. Apeiron said. "I want you to listen closely to everything I have to say to this man."

Gemma flinched in sympathy with Sanchi as Ms. Apeiron's glittering eyes fixed themselves on him. An invisible barb was set deep in the man's flesh, and there was nothing gentle in the way this woman tore it out.

"I am tired of your delusions, Mr. Sanchez, of your misguided obsession with me, and of your imposition on my good nature. You are making a grave mistake, bothering me; do not worsen it further. I may be only a woman, but I promise you, I am not without resources and I do not relish this—*warped* idea of courtship you have embraced concerning me. I thought that you might have gotten the message when I had you dismissed from your job here at Dionysia—"

"That was you—?"

She would not let him speak. "—but you persist in your false suppositions. You trail after me like a lapdog. I do not know whatever placed the notion in your head that a woman of my standing would even notice your existence. Perhaps you are mad. I am not a psychotherapist. I will not have you following me, persecuting me, gaining admittance to my suite without my knowledge or consent. If you stole a passkey from the hotel before your dismissal, I suggest you return it and we will say no more of the matter. But if I catch sight of you anywhere near me again, I will summon the police. That, on the official level. Unofficially, I have employees whose sole task is to see that I am not troubled by unwanted attention. They have many forceful arguments. Do I make myself clear?"

Gemma was shaking her head without being aware she did so. All of Ms. Apeiron's words, all the palpable lies, were delivered with the clear diction and dramatic, carrying voice of a stage actress. There was not a mote of truth in any of it, Gemma knew, just as surely as she knew Sanchez Rubio.

If there was madness at work here, it wasn't his.

"Ianthe!" Gemma heard the rough surface of a sob deep in his throat as he tried to grasp the woman's hand. "What are you saying? You *brought* me here! I was with Elena, but when you said you had to speak to me, I left her. Even knowing what you are, I trusted you that far, because of what you were—what you let yourself be with me. And when you brought me here, when I asked what you wanted, you—" A deeper color flushed his face. He would never specify, but Gemma had eyes. Ianthe Apeiron might look as austere and untouched as an ice sculpture, but this bed and this man had another story to tell. "It was like before; the way you said you wanted it to be forever."

"You're a liar." The name was tossed off as a matter of fact, nothing to upset Ms. Apeiron or make her raise her voice.

"And you are . . ." Sanchi's words trailed off. The controlled ferocity and despair left his body suddenly, at once, a burden slipping from his back. "I know what you are." It was calmly said. "Now I know. It's broken."

The reply came just as calmly. "May you have every benefit from such knowledge. I have been generous enough. Now get out."

He left without another word, pushing Gemma aside, avoiding contact with Ms. Apeiron as with something leprous. Only when the front door slammed behind him did Gemma realize that she was starving herself for air. Ms. Apeiron laughed lightly as Gemma took deep, thirsty breaths and sat down on the bed.

Her feet touched a lump on the carpet. She bent forward and picked up the little stone pendant. "This must be his," she said aloud, without thinking. "I'll try to catch him and give it back."

Ms. Apeiron's nails made five small, sharp arguments on Gemma's upper arm. "Let him go. I want you with me in the casino now."

"But I thought you only wanted me to witness when you—when you threw him out of here for trespassing."

205

Was she any good at playing a part? Ms. Apeiron's eyes flashed golden speculation over Gemma's face. Did she believe her?

"Surely you did not think I gave you such a lovely gown for that purpose alone?" Ms. Apeiron said smoothly. "No, there is another service I have in mind for you."

Alonso was waiting for them downstairs, with a brace of bodyguards. He grinned his appreciation as Gemma stepped off the elevator, and that lupine look filled her with revulsion. Time had stretched indeed. Minutes must have turned to years, or else some dark enchantment had aged him preternaturally. The only thing left of the youth he had owned when she first met him would be the birthdate on his ID. The fine dinner jacket looked like a clown's suit on him. He didn't even know enough to adjust the set of his shoulder holster so that the bulge was less noticeable.

Ianthe Apeiron gave him both her hands, as if greeting a dear old friend. "How well you look, Alonso! The night air agrees with you. And tell me, is all well on the streets again?"

"Perfect." He tried to turn the handclasp into an embrace, but she glided away, laughing.

"Ah, no! When I spoke of gratitude, I meant another reward." She swept her arm back and Gemma shuddered as its cool whiteness fell like snow around her shoulders.

There was no more reality as Alonso linked her arm with his. Gemma had named her wages on the day she thought that money could answer every question, and Ianthe Apeiron was going to pay them out, but every penny would be earned on that woman's terms.

*I could refuse.* The thought was a last bright temptation. *I could say thank you very much for a lovely evening, and I'll send the dress back in the morning, and the jewelry, and the money—as much of it as I still have—and I'll even change jobs, if I can. But I don't want what she has anymore. It's not for me.*

Sanchez was a good man. Her every instinct said so, though she thought she had buried instinct in favor of savvy years ago. The raw, random flexing of so much power— power to exalt a man, power to send him crashing down— that was the fabled bottom line of everything Ianthe Apeiron represented. She possessed enough money, enough power, enough beauty and sex and ice-cold wisdom to take anything she wanted, any time, from anyone.

But once she had taken what she desired, she didn't leave a human being behind. She left a husk.

*There are all sorts of vampires. Monsters. Humans who have turned inhuman. But I am still as human as Sanchez Rubio. I have to be. I can't feed on my own.*

She must escape. It wouldn't be difficult. In a minute more she could announce that she had to go to the ladies' room and vanish from there. They were at the roulette wheel, watching Ianthe Apeiron lose. Gemma tried to shift Alonso's hand from her rump. He pinched her cruelly and pushed a stack of chips at her with his free hand.

"Go ahead, baby. The night's young."

"I'm sorry, I have to—"

The old woman tapped Gemma on the shoulder before she could finish her false plea to be excused. "Pardon me, Miss, but could you please tell that lady I must speak to her?" Bright black eyes in a wrinkled brown face darted at Ms. Apeiron. "About Sanchi."

Why had Ms. Apeiron consented to hear the old woman out? Why had she insisted that the three of them go up to the suite, smothering Alonso's objections with orders to go play the slots and wait until he was sent for?

And why, why was Gemma sitting on the couch beside this strange, doll-like woman with her heavy Puerto Rican accent, hearing her call Ianthe Apeiron a monster to her face, while the lady so accused placidly passed lemonade like a serving girl?

"You must pardon me, Miss," the old woman said, sipping from her glass. "I am only here because my Elena, *mi niñita*, is heartbroken. Calling you a monster—you can see how upset the child is. You are rich. Sometimes the rich find their diversions in strange ways. What is Sanchi to you? Downstairs I saw that you—" She looked away from Ms. Apeiron. "That you have his brother with you."

"And you disapprove."

"If I do, if I do not, what is that to you? Nothing. But I am asking you as a human being, let the boys alone. You are young. You are a pretty woman. You will find other things to amuse you."

"Yes. I think I will."

Gemma sniffed her lemonade. No alcohol; a tiny taste confirmed it. Yet her vision was wavering. Was that Ms. Apeiron standing there before the old lady, or was she crouched lower than that? What were those gray smudges standing out in twin feathery wedges at her back, and what the sinuous golden shadow now twisting and flicking back and forth around Ms. Apeiron's feet?

A low rumble rolled through Gemma's ears, like the purring of a cat, only larger, more perilous. Her sinews reacted sympathetically as she stared at the second image of Ms. Apeiron, the image of melded beast and woman, muscles coiling tightly for a leap that must come.

The shadow of the spear fell across Gemma's lap. She saw Ms. Apeiron give a little jump backward, avoiding the edge. Gemma's eyes traced the line of the misted shaft from the dark spearhead up, up, into the hands of the tall black warrior woman who stood on guard behind their aged guest. Others stood with the warrior woman. Where had that eerie corps of protectors come from? Gemma watched their faces shift in and out of focus. The most disconcerting thing happened when she recognized one of their number as the model of the little stone carving Sanchi had lost, the one she still had in her clutch purse.

But time stretched itself out even further. The moment of their presence passed. The guardians faded as the illusion of wings and tail abandoned Ianthe Apeiron. *Was it real?* Gemma asked herself, and found testimony enough to both apparitions' reality in the look of fear and hate on Ianthe Apeiron's face.

Ms. Apeiron recovered her poise amazingly fast. "I am glad you came to me," she told her guest. "I apologize for the anxiety my—my selfishness may have caused your family. I will amend it at once. Life is full of so many great sorrows, we should not have to deal with small ones. Gemma, dear, pass the glasses. We shall drink to my promise."

How was it accomplished? Gemma never knew. One minute, the old woman was drinking fresh lemonade, thanking Ms. Apeiron for her kindness, wondering aloud that Elena had ever called such a lady monstrous—a little heedless, maybe, but when one is young and used to having one's own way—

And the next, she was dead.

"Yours are the only prints on the glass, Gemma," Ms. Apeiron said. "Yours and hers. No one else could have poisoned it. But I prefer not to rely on such strait means to keep your loyalty. You wouldn't really be happy running away from me. To be human . . . is that truly a prize worth having when I could make you so much more? I am the last of my line. There are all sorts of vampires, yes, but there are also all sorts of children. Children of the body; of the heart; of the spirit."

"I'm not . . ."

Ms. Apeiron shrugged. "So you say; for now. Well, we have time enough for that later. Call downstairs and have them send up Alonso."

Alonso was not horrified at all by what he found in the suite, even knowing who Mamacita was and what she had been to Sanchi. He would take care of things. The last Gemma saw of him for a while was standing in the doorway with that pitiful little corpse rolled up in a sheet and slung over his shoulder. He was asking her whether she was more impressed with him now, and Ms. Apeiron was smiling beneficently at them both, like a priest about to pronounce the final marriage vows. With a groan, Gemma sank to her knees and vomited bile all over the white satin dress.

# CHAPTER TWENTY-FIVE:
## Marvin Gardens While
## Rome Burns

Manolo jumped when the ragbag man came stumbling out of the storefront to claw at his sleeve. It was late, and showing no signs of ever getting around to being early. He'd been put through the wringer with the family—Elena in tears again, Mama shushing her so she wouldn't wake up Mamacita in the connecting room, Berto and Mike off somewhere having one last round on the slots before it was time to pack up and go home tomorrow, Papi minding them like they were still kids—and that left just Manolo there to be the man when Mama opened the door to check on Mamacita and found the old woman gone.

Who the hell was this degenerate? Manolo didn't have time to waste smelling Mad Dog 20-20 breath and digging spare change out of his pockets. But then the fuzzlump lurched into the boardwalk lights and called him "Mani!"

"Oh shit." Manolo got an arm under Sanchi before he hit the planking. "Shit, what the fuck happened to you, *hermanito*? She drive a truck over you or what?"

Sanchi started to laugh, high and brittle. "She doesn't have a license. Cats are color-blind." The joke must have been hilarious. He couldn't stop laughing.

Manolo gave him a good, short shake. "Listen, I'm taking you back to Mama's room. You need to come down."

Sanchi blinked at his foster brother. His breathing sounded raspy, but he was back in control. An inquisitive sniff and a long, penetrating gaze into his eyes told Manolo that there was no booze or junk at work in Sanchi's system, just plain misery.

"I can't go there. I don't need to. I don't want to. If Elena's there—*Válgame*, this is it for us, isn't it? The end for her and me. No way she'll ever . . . I walked away from her, Mani. The sphynx called to me and I walked away, like Elena was nothing, not even there."

"*Oye, niño.*" Manolo put his arm around Sanchi. "It's not over until *you* let it be. I know my sister, and I know you. You think she's stupid? How many times does she need someone to tell her that this isn't any ordinary woman you're up against?" He made a face. "Sorry. Bad choice of words. You know what I mean, though."

"Then I want to talk to Elena."

"Good luck. She's somewhere streetside, talking to hotel security right now. I'm covering this side of the casinos. Mamacita's gone for a midnight walk, God knows why. We're asking the guards to keep an eye out for her—fat chance, them picking one old lady out of the crowd, but it's the best we can do. We've got to find her, or find Papi and the guys to help us look. Want to go back to the room to wait for us?"

"I want a bathroom. Then I want to help."

Manolo slapped his foster brother on the back. "*A la caza, entonces, machito*. Let's find Mamacita. And if you-know-who gets in our way on this hunt, we'll see if she's got an answer to this riddle." The lights danced off the blade of Manolo's hunting knife for just an instant, long enough for Sanchi to see, not long enough to draw attention.

The sphynx stood over the body of Tiberius Caesar and purred like a kitten. She looked entrancing in that frilly blue dress with its eyelet-trimmed white pinafore. Her feet were bare, the shiny Mary Janes and white anklets with their pink satin bows and lace discarded in the corner. Her little-girl toes scrunched and wriggled on the carpet. She imagined she still saw him staring at them with those squinty, black, moist eyes. She had allowed the dead man some last frissons of pleasure to make him the more vulnerable to the Asking when it came.

She indulged in one last glance in the mirror above the bed where he lay, half his throat torn out. The gushing scarlet stream that had drenched her spoiled the effect of a child's rose-and-snow innocence. Her cheeks were smeared with gore, her seed-pearl necklace sticky, and the fall of blue-black curls wadded together at the ends, gummed with drying blood.

On top of the blankets were picture books: Sesame Street, the Care Bears, *The Poky Little Puppy*, Richard Scarry. Tiberius had made her sit on his lap and read them to her as soon as Alonso collected the payment and left. The boy had played his role perfectly—he could keep the money. The sphynx licked a hardening smear at the corner of her mouth. Under the sheets, the late emperor was naked.

He was fading now. Soon he would dwindle to that provoking diamond, which in turn would fall to ash. He was holding on to mortal form a little longer than Julius. The blood staining her face and clothes also faded. All that she had left of him was the memory of his fingers creeping up her leg, squeezing her thigh until she thought it appropriate for a real child to squeal and show fear. He told her to be still or she would be punished, enjoying her added fright. She went along with the game, pretending terror, slowly letting him cajole her out of it, taking the candies he offered and listening wide-eyed to the tales of wonderful toys and treats and games he promised—later, if she was good—until she asked him if he liked riddles:

> Take your turn,
> Watch me burn
> Without flame.
> What's my name?

He was willing to humor her; it added spice. He said she was a clever girl, but that hate was something he knew much more about than she. He wanted a kiss for guessing her riddle rightly and grabbed her by the back of the head, shoving her face toward his. He meant for her lips to meet his own, but she squirmed and her mouth fell wet and sharp against the wrinkled hollow of his neck.

The sphinx put off her child's body before she left the empty room. A lesser Riddle flittered through her mind: *Where is the name monstrous enough to lay to a creature that feeds on innocence?* For once the sphinx had no answer.

Augustus picked her out of the chorus line in the "Wonderful Wings" number. She yeeped as she lost one of her false eyelashes in his drink and was more than compliant when he suggested they consume all further libations in private.

"Oh, please let's. I just get so *flustered* when I make a *fawks pass* out where people can see." She attached herself to his arm in the expected predatory manner, rubbing her breast against his elbow and batting what was left of her lopsided lashes.

Augustus congratulated himself for continuing to be such a great judge of character. It would stand him in good stead when he finally faced the sphinx, just as it had let him second-guess Antony's folly and Cleopatra's tendency to panic. That won him Actium, and an empire. This would bring life.

Earlier he had experienced another of those cold shocks, like the one heralding his uncle's death. Which of his comrades had fallen? Claudius, probably. That meek little man thought hiding was always the way out of anything. Oh, a man could hide his way into a ripe old age, but what was the point? Life without experience was empty as death.

Augustus was more fond than most of living, and of all the small excitements that made it interesting. He was not a fool like Caligula, who shocked society and his own body past the point where either one would bear with his excesses much longer. *All things in moderation* was Augustus' motto. *That way you get to enjoy all things for so very much longer.* Simple investment strategy, really.

This girl didn't look as if she would understand the fascinating ballet of stocks and bonds, but she had all the rudimentary intelligence necessary for what he had in mind. Gods be thanked, he had had enough of smart women with Livia. If he had presented a diamond bracelet like this one to his late empress, she would have squirreled off to her rooms to comtemplate his motivation for the gift, the reason behind the cause in back of the impetus for said motivation, and the far-reaching political implications and repercussions that would ensue. Once he had given her an electrum fibula to fasten her winter cloak and she had told him not to expect her approval of the new tax scheme on Tuscan geese.

"Ooooo," was all this pretty creature said when he handed her the open velvet box. Then, coyly, "Get it on? My wrist." She giggled like an amok chipmunk.

As Augustus fumbled with the clasp, his new lady friend said, "You're *so* smart! I bet you could win a fortune on *Hollywood Squares.* They had this one question, I bet no one could answer it unless they got told the answer before they went on the air, which my girlfriend Maxi says they do, but I don't believe her. See, they asked Shadoe Stevens this thing, real cute, like a nursery rhyme, sorta:

"Never given, still received,
Whether asked for or refused.
Though unsought, still freely gotten,
Leaves the getter struck bemused."

Losing his temper with the clasp, Augustus growled, "Bemused, is it? I'm surprised they didn't have to send out for a dictionary. The only thing a man ever gets that he doesn't go seeking is death."

"Oooh, that's not the answer Shadoe gave," the girl shrilled. "But it does kinda go with what I've got in mind."

213

The slim wrist thickened and sprouted golden fur. Augustus dropped the bracelet.

Out on stage, Geeks Baring Gifts was dying. Not even Heliogabalus' original composition "Strangle You with Roses" was getting a rise out of the audience, and Caligula's mega-hyped climactic act of stuffing aquarium snails in all his facial orifices drew loud yawns.

"Invertebrates, bah," Nero opined. He slung his booted feet onto the makeup table in his dressing room and let the hoots and jeers of the crowd run in a delightful *basso continuo* beneath the soundtrack of the Disneyfest he was watching on the mini-TV. The door to his inner sanctum opened. A bony kid, sexless in blue jeans, work shirt, and wire-rim glasses, came in with a cardboard box of coffee and sandwiches.

"You order the pastrami?"

"You betcha, son." Nero reached inside his paisley rayon robe and folded a new twenty into paper-airplane shape, launching it casually backward over one shoulder. "Set her down any ol' wheres an' go buy yourself a good woman."

"Gee, thanks! You want mustard with it?"

"Thought they took care of that at the deli, boy."

"Well, it's not on the actual sandwich, there's a squeeze packet, but if you want I could fix the whole thing up for you. You want me to?"

"Don't bother."

"You wanted more than one pickle? I could get you an extra, no problem."

Nero sighed. A lesser artist would assume that the kid was ass-kissing in hopes of getting another fat tip. Nero was above such mundane speculations. Clearly here was a poor soul who had heard how the new King had wowed them at the early sitting, but who lacked the price of a ticket. He would linger and whine until he got that most cherished of gratuities, beyond mere petty cash, a song from Nero's own lips. The emperor stood up and melodically enjoined his fan not to step on his blue suede shoes.

The kid looked puzzled. "You want the pickle or what?"

"Son, what do *you* want?"

It was endearing, seeing a stripling blush like that. "Oh

gosh, I'm sorry. I really shouldn't have said anything, bothered you like—I—*I write songs!*" It was out.

Nero was flabbergasted first, sympathetic second. Show biz was hard, even for a man who had made such an inexplicably rapid climb as he had. Sitting in the dressing room, he'd felt two further body-blows like the one that had rocked him when Julius Caesar died. He was strengthened by them—literally and figuratively. He didn't know yet who was dead, but so long as it wasn't he, who gave a damn? He could afford to indulge the unfortunate.

"Go ahead, son. Only make it short. I got me a *show.*"

"Yes, sir." The kid was yanking wads of paper out of his work-shirt pockets like magician's pigeons. "It's—it's sort of a duet. Really jazzy. You get to improvise. Would you—care to join me? If you can do stuff like that."

"Boy, comes to sticking words together, I am *there*, as I am *always* . . . the *King!*"

Not a bad song. Too cute for Nero's tastes, the way one voice kept on asking silly questions like *Who loves you, baby, baby?* and *When your Daddy gonna let you love me?* Answering them fell to Nero's lot, and in modesty's name he had to admit that his answers really made the kid's musical questions look like chicken poop by comparison. Maybe he could buy rights to the song and fix it up properly. He was considering how low a price wouldn't be too obscene when the kid paused.

"Last verse coming now, sir!"

"Yo."

> Burning, pretty baby,
> Alone in your room.
> You gonna ask what devours
> With being consumed?

Nero didn't wonder why he heard that last verse so distinctly, though he never saw the kid's lips move. He was working on his response. He swiveled his hips, gave the invisible engineer's whistle a taut pull, and bellowed out,

"Oh yeah, don't you ask,
"Call me no liar,
" 'Cause if there's one thing I know,
"Babe, it's gotta be fire!"

215

There was a Pluto cartoon airing on the TV when the sphynx finished him. She spared a minute to appreciate the irony of good programming.

"Whad dow, Zuetodiuz?" Caligula inquired, puddling into one of the audience chairs. He took a few moments to clear his nasal passages of costars, then articulated, "What now? Turning into a music critic?"

Suetonius set his pad aside. "You felt it, didn't you?"

"Which one?" The mad emperor's lips crinkled. "Three, at least. Who do you suppose my lady has taken off now?"

"Your lady?" The pad was back in front of the tireless chronicler.

"*You* don't know? But of course you wouldn't. You're too common. You lack the scope of imagination that makes for true greatness. It's only a matter of time. There is purpose behind every death, each sacrifice she makes in my name. My darling sister Drusilla used to be just that thoughtful for my sake. Consideration is so nice to find in a wife, isn't it? Even we gods can't choose our relatives, but dear Drusilla . . ."

"You were speaking of the sphynx," Suetonius prompted.

"Hm? Oh, yes. The sphynx is not foolish or she'd never have lived this long. She plots, she plans, she manipulates the world by a thousand unseen strings, our supposed magician Vergilius included. And all for her master goal."

"Which is?"

Caligula looked frankly stunned. "I thought you had *some* insight. To marry me, of course! To claim as her lord and lover the only human being worthy to accept the powers she commands. She loves me. Otherwise, she wouldn't be killing off the rest of you. What other reason could she have and be sane? I'll be the only one left, with all the apportioned life you lumps are hogging safely back sustaining *me*, where it belonged from the first. Vergilius made a mistake, dragging all of you up out of Hades with me, but she'll see he makes no more. Speaking of mistakes, Nero's supposed to do his tatty little act now. Staying?"

Suetonius pushed his chair back and got up quickly. "Another engagement. My regrets, O divine—"

They both knew Heliogabalus' piercing shriek of distress when they heard it, even rifling in from all the way backstage.

"Huh," Caligula grunted. "I guess now we know one of the also-rans, anyway."

Suetonius begged to be excused, but as he did it in the imperial ear still occupied by a Helicidae squatter, his departure went unnoted.

# CHAPTER TWENTY-SIX:
## Into Morn

Sunday morning came at last. Sunday morning, cool and sweet with the breeze from the sea, the hush of gray streets finally fallen silent, only the light of a rising sun to paint colors on the sky.

They should have been on their way to church or having a leisurely breakfast or carrying the suitcases over to the bus stop to catch an early ride back to New York. Instead, José María, his wife, his sons of the body and the heart, all stood beside a cold morgue slab and told a stranger that yes, they did know the old woman lying dead upon it.

Sanchi tried to get close to Papi. There was no room. Mama was supporting him, her tiny body propping up his while Roberto and Mike and Manolo clung to him, sharing tears. None of them was there, as far as Papi knew. He was lost in a chill, dark place, and his mother was gone.

*"Ay, madrecita! Mamita mía, no te vayas! No nos dejes ya, querida!"* José María wailed where a stranger could see. He wept for his mother like a child.

*If that were my mother* . . . Sanchi shuddered, letting the possibility slip through his mind. How would he react? Would there be anything left of all the love that burned him hollow inside, anything from which a single tear could be wrung? He tried to envision it, and found he could not form her face.

*It shouldn't be so.*

"Where was she found?" Mama was asking.

"In an abandoned building. A—" The attendant paused, weighed how much of the truth to tell these people, made a decision. "—A shooting gallery. From what we can tell, she just went in there, maybe feeling sick or tired, and died. There's no marks on her, not a sign of—"

*"No más."* José María shook himself free of his sons and forced himself to stand alone. He shook hands with the man. "Thank you very much. Now, what must we do?"

The attendant took them out of there, into another room where there were forms to fill out. Sanchi couldn't stay. He walked out to stand on the front steps of the building. The streets turned light, and he let the fresh air wash him cleaner than he'd felt in days.

More than anything, he wanted Elena with him now. An empty want; she wasn't with the family, and no one knew where she was. Mama said she was glad; the girl shouldn't have to add this to her old grief. Mama looked right at Sanchi when she said that. They had pieced together something of what had happened. Mamacita must have overheard Elena spilling out the tale of Sanchi's betrayal, her pain. Mamacita would not be one to let such things just happen. She had gone out to see what could be mended, but she was old. The last gift of her heart to her darling granddaughter was too much for her to accomplish.

Mani had come to Sanchi's defense, making excuses for him, but his vague arguments quickly fell apart. *How could you explain what really happened to me,* hermano? *That something more than human used sorcery and my own weakness to make me her slave? But no more; no more.* The face Sanchi saw when he tried to recall his mother's was the face of the sphynx. He didn't know how or when it had happened, but he did know, again, that it shouldn't be.

"Hey." Sanchi turned. Manolo stood one step above him, his face dead. He kept his hands knotted in his pants pockets and jerked a shoulder off in one direction. "Company."

It was Suetonius, and for once the devout scribe had something besides pen and pad to occupy his hands. Sanchi tensed immediately when he recognized her: Gemma.

"There is something you must know," said Suetonius.

"Murdered . . ."

"Keep your voice down, Mani," Sanchi said, his own about to break. The four of them were ranged along the counter of a dowdy little coffee shop, chrome and Formica and yellowing neon ceiling fixtures. Gemma in her sadly stained evening gown looked as if she belonged in the booth with the quartet of tired whores, but the counterman didn't even blink when she ordered black coffee and the soundless tears started flowing down her cheeks.

"I'll keep it down," Manolo replied. "The same way I'll make sure that bitch keeps it down when I take my knife and slit her open from the belly up, slow. Like I'll kneel on her neck to make sure *she* keeps *her* voice down when she's screaming for me to end it fast." The knife in question was out of Manolo's pocket and cupped between his hands on the countertop.

"Put that away before you get in trouble," Suetonius said quietly. "You know it can't harm her." Manolo only growled.

Sanchi stroked Gemma's arm. "You didn't know what she was."

"Not the name for it." Gemma managed to gulp down a sob and smile at him a little. "A real monster. It seems easy to believe, now. So I'm not crazy. What she's done to the world—"

"She's not responsible for that, for time being warped like it was last night." He glanced at the big black-and-white clock above the green milkshake machine and saw no pause or let-up in the advance of the second hand. Much of the force that had been distorting earthly time was gone, reabsorbed into its proper place in eternity. That was something for which to be thankful. He wished there were more.

"I'm glad I know," Gemma said. "And I'm happier I told Mr. Caius what I saw." She gave Suetonius a grateful look.

Mutely, discreetly, Suetonius slipped Sanchi a slick new business card:

---

PLACIDO S. CAIUS
Information Systems
Mgr. & Pub.: TRANQUILFAX

---

"Telling me was not enough," the self-made manager and publisher said.

"I know." Gemma was staring into her coffee again. "But

if I believe what—what I have to believe about her, I can't tell the police. They will think I'm insane."

*"Goddammit!"* Manaolo slammed his fist down hard on the counter. The Formica chipped as the steel-capped butt of the knife struck it a lucky blow. "Can't tell the cops, can't depend on Vergilius, can't do sweet bloody fuck-all but *talk* about her? Hell with this. Hell with you if you're going to play safe and scared and piss in your pants the rest of your life. She killed her." He was on his feet. "She killed Mamacita. *Le mató a mi abuela, y por Dios, yo le voy a matar o morirme!"*

"Mani!" Sanchi leaped up, tried to stop him. Manolo pulled back a fist and lashed out, swinging wild, clipping him on the cheekbone hard enough to lay open the skin and tumble him back against the row of swivel stools at the counter. Manolo was out of there while Suetonius was still trying to untangle Sanchi from the forest of leatherette-topped seats. Both of them saw Gemma race away after Manolo.

*"Loca de remate!"* Sanchi shouted. "She'll never get him to come back."

"Let her go," Suetonius said. "In her eyes, she has much to atone for. Let her feel as if she's making some reparation for what she's done."

"Gemma?"

"The sphynx's Gemma. Vergilius' Gemma. I could use a lady of her capabilities. *Tranquilfax* is growing in popularity—the ultimate upscale information collation and dissemination organ for the greater Atlantic City region."

Sanchi took some paper napkins to blot his bleeding cheek. "Sure sounds more classy than 'scandal sheet.' But what did you mean about Gemma?"

"Information to the highest bidder. There went a young lady with what most people would call a healthy attitude toward self-advancement. Anything for money, short of her body. The trouble with plunging into indefinite pronouns—anything, anywhere, anytime, anyone—is that no one knows how deep the water is until it closes over your head."

"Not a bad metaphor," said the crisply suited older gentleman who had entered the coffee shop. "More effective if you'd foreshadowed the water motif in the first clause as noun rather than verb. Still, more respectable use of literary devices than one generally suffers through with journalists."

All Scottish tweed and Spanish leather, he moved in an aura of latakia tobacco and brandished a shooting stick for which he evidenced no actual physical need. Walking right up to Sanchi and Suetonius, he hoisted his rump onto a stool, tugged up his trouser legs to preserve the creases, and pertly asked, "Now, how may I help?"

"Telling me who you are might be a step in the right direction," Sanchi answered. He tried to push out from between the stools again. "Look, I'm in a hurry, my brother just lost his temper and stormed out of here—"

"—into the teeth of disaster. Let us implore the gods to extend him some protection. He does not realize the magnitude of the foe." Bright eyes and silver hair looked disturbingly familiar. "Tell you who I am?" The man looked tickled by the thought. He extended Sanchi a strong hand to be shaken and simultaneously used as a means up off the floor. "Tiberius Claudius Drusus Nero Germanicus—preferably just Claudius—afterward deified, but we can forget about that bit—Emperor, Pontifex, Consul, half a capful of other honoraria, and most recently professor of classical languages at Princeton University until *this* fella here ferreted me out." He clapped Suetonius on the back.

"We need you," Suetonius said.

"So you wrote. Can't quite get over how you managed to find me, but then you always were one to unearth what was best left buried."

"I thought Claudius stammered," Sanchi whispered to Suetonius.

"He did before," Suetonius assured him. "And when he was first alive, his more influential relations thought a stumbling tongue meant a stumbling brain. They called him an idiot. The idiot survived to take the throne while more impressive candidates ended up in the Tiber."

"Now the idiot's here to see what all this hooraw's about." Claudius rubbed his hands together. "Dead, aren't they? The others?"

"Most of them."

"I thought I felt something. Imagined it was just the faculty-club food. I rather expected there'd be a deal of puffing and snorting and bulling through, with that lot.

Julius was the sort to grandstand his way into the grave, no talking to Augustus, Tiberius was—" He shuddered. "Never mind. And Nero's got the mind of a bread pudding on his good days. Caligula's stark mad. I expect that Heliogabalus creature's a similar prize, since they seemed to get on so well. I didn't want to be there when they bungled it with the sphynx, individually or communally. I'll die for my own mistakes, thank you."

"You're not afraid?" Sanchi asked. This self-possessed fellow didn't at all match the image of Claudius the cringer, the coward, the timorous soul who lurked under beds and behind curtains and whose own mother called him a fool.

"Wouldn't be here if I were, would I? Simple logic. Now the field's clearer, we can get something decent done. Lead on." He waved his shooting stick at Suetonius.

"Let's go to Vergilius," Sanchi said. "Maybe he can locate Elena. I've—I've got to be the one to tell her."

On the way out, to quell the uneasiness he felt rising inside, Sanchi made himself strike up small talk with Claudius. "Princeton, huh? Not a bad place to hide. You didn't have to answer Suetonius' note, you know. You could've stayed there, safe."

"Safe?" Caludius laughed heartily. "In *Academia*? There speaks the voice of one who's never faced a tenure committee. Pack of young upstarts. Deconstruct Homer, will they?"

Muttering arcane invocations to the dark gods Hermeneutics, Anacoluthon, and Paregmenon, he marched on. It was publish or perish, and he'd done both.

# CHAPTER TWENTY-SEVEN: Take by the Neck, Shake Well

"What are you, crazy?" Gemma panted.

Manolo didn't answer, though his actions were making her question seem more and more rhetorical. With feet and fists he hammered at the locked penthouse door, howling foul names in two languages.

"You really must be insane." She yanked down her bunched-up dress, kilted high to help her scamper up the last few flights of stairs between the hotel proper and Ianthe Apeiron's private aerie. Manolo had managed to hijack the only elevator servicing this floor and had jammed it once he got here.

"Insane? How come? Because I'm gonna kill her?" Manolo tore his eyes away from the smug, sealed door. "I'm not doing this to play Charles Bronson, honey. The sphynx is a monster, and in every story Mamacita ever told me—even the ones about the old gods from the island—all it took to kill a monster was someone with a good enough blade and a good enough reason to want it dead. I've got both."

"In the *stories!*" Gemma shouted at him. "We're not talking stories! You come on with me now, before you fairy-tale yourself dead." She grabbed his arm, and when he tried wrenching it free she held on tight.

They were still tussling when the door opened silently. Alonso and six of the sphynx's very human bodyguards had an easy time disarming and subduing their imprudent callers.

"Who are these two?" asked the man who had clouted Manolo unconscious.

Alonso grinned. "Old friends. Hell, don't you remember seeing this bitch before?" He jerked his chin at Gemma. "Ianthe's going to be real happy to see them. Sometimes she likes surprises. She always likes gifts."

"Elena." The sight of her, robed in gold and blue, red and ivory, took Sanchi's breath away. In that moment, he forgot that he had just stepped through a motel doorway, paint peeling, one of the room numbers askew, the other missing. He had entered an alien temple, and he stood facing its lady.

Behind him, Hatshepsut and Vergilius stood with hands clasped, watching his every reaction. "It cannot be easy," the magician murmured, "discovering that your lover is a witch."

"That word." Hatshepsut snorted daintily and pinched Vergilius' finger. "Have you learned nothing?"

"Have *you* not learned that there should be no onus attached to any word touching the use of the powers for good?"

"*Should be* is not *is*. Ignorance sees to that. Let it be, my lord. He is no ordinary man; they are well matched."

"As are we." The emerald's glow bathed their united hands in a warmth of the heart, the kindling of lonely centuries.

The polished silver lake of vision—a perfect circle of the moon's own solidified light, upheld by a bronze tripod—glowed before Elena, swimming with sights she had not yet commanded into fixed form. Sweet gums burned in a little clay dish on the table behind her. Another clay vessel waited to one side, a low, wide, shallow dish filled with strange dried leaves beside which rested a long, hollow cane and a carved, high-backed stool. Sanchi remembered another such seat, in a waking dream from which he had returned wearing a small stone token.

He touched his neck. It was bare. Had the gift, too, been an illusion? Or had he betrayed his blood once too often, become unworthy, and the gift been taken back into the dreams out of which it came?

He saw such dreams now, moving through Elena's eyes as she gazed into the silver mirror. The ghosts of the jungle and the cavern, of the shore and the sea, all floated at her back like wings. He could feel the powers surrounding her, emanating from her, and the answering strength in his own body. He was pulled toward her, inexorably as the moon called to the tides. Soft carpets and mats of scented rushes hissed beneath his feet as he approached.

But something stopped him. Something flashed between them, cold and white and hard. A smile. The sphinx's living presence barred his way, wings snapped wide, a cautionary paw lifted to the human lips, mocking.

"Elena . . ." Her name in his mouth had become a plea for salvation.

"Hush," said the Egyptian queen. "No need to disturb her. She knows you are here."

"She knows more than that," Vergilius said sadly, "if you mean to tell her that Mamacita's death was murder."

"She knows?" Sanchi looked at him sharply

"She came to me before it happened, ready to accept all that she was," Hapshepsut said, "and all that my training could make her. I weep that it was the first vision she mastered; a very hard time of learning for her, poor child."

"She was the source of wild magic I tapped when I sent my spells into Hades," Vergilius said. It sounded as if such a confession were being wrung from him under painful compulsion. "A woman, so young, holding so much . . . I still cannot understand it."

"Believe first, then understanding will follow," said the queen. "You and I are old, Vergilius. We cling to each other half out of love, half out of familiar sympathy. Our world is long departed. Tribes and breeds of man rise, flourish, pass, like the flowers in their season, the Nile in its cycles. So, too, do breeds of magic. Theirs is young"—her arms bridged the air between Sanchi and Elena—"young as this land, and full of the potency of all things youthful. Ours holds the wisdom of age. Both spring from the true heart of this world. Elena's formidability lies in how ready she is to bind age to youth, our wisdom to her power. Time is folding back into its true shape, yet she and I were able to do much toward training her talent in the expanded moments left us."

From the doorway where he and Claudius lingered, Suetonius cleared his throat and asked, "The fewer of us left alive, the faster time returns to what it should be?" His new Mont Blanc fountain pen hovered expectantly over a fresh page.

"Time knows what time should be," Vergilius said. "Only man has set a grid of fixed intervals over the flow of happenings. Another of our toys; it keeps us amused, busy, happy we are accomplishing something *real*. Somewhere, someone who loves us very much is watching all our play, and laughing."

Sanchi retreated to confer with the mage and the dark queen. "Elena . . . is she in some kind of trance? She doesn't seem to know we're here."

"There is nothing more sinister at work than concentration," Hatshepsut reassured him.

"The assignment was simple," Vergilius added. He showed Sanchi his emerald, now ringed with only three living stones.

*In the silver mirror, a boy in a lurid costume, but a face like curdled milk. He sat in a battered bentwood chair, twiddling a pair of black drumsticks. Near him, tables with pots of powder and cream. Ordinary mirrors framed with light* bulbs. Cinder-block walls painted over with sickly green paint. Yellowed letters and tattered telegrams stuck between mirror and frame, forgotten. Dulling black-and-white eight-by-ten glossies taped to the walls and the door with curling, crackling, amber cellophane.

Beside him, the sphynx, entrancing in aquamarine watered silk and a white fox wrap that crept up over one shoulder and trailed the ground behind her like an obese caterpiller. The albino Russian wolfhound attending her on its matchstick legs was a nice touch.

"Well, when will we have a deal?" Heliogabalus demanded, petulantly shying one drumstick at the wolfhound's anorexic rib cage. The beast yelped and fell sideways, tripping over its own grotesquely elongated limbs. Heliogabalus snickered and threw the second stick at it harder. It could only whimper as he hit its tender nose.

"You still haven't answered my question," the sphynx said, contriving to sound as blasé as the boy-emperor.

"Why should I?" he countered. "I don't see what it has to do with you becoming my manager."

"Don't you?" A kid-gloved hand smothered a tiny yawn. "I thought Alonso explained it all to you. I like my clients to be sharp. Sharper than you seem. If you don't see the connection between my question and my agreeing to handle your career . . ." She pushed back her chair.

"No, no, wait a second! Alonso is such a wonderful person. He explained your procedures so marvelously well—said you were a little eccentric, but your track record, the class of clients you represent, the chance to show them what a real performer like me can bring to the entertainment industry—and Bootsy's gone totally off his conk, anyhow, no working with him anymore—and I wouldn't want darling Alonso to think he'd made a mistake about me. I do so look forward to working with him. And you, too, of course."

"The question—?"

Heliogabalus sucked his finger. "Run it by me again, love? It blipped right out of my tiny little mind."

> Vast and empty, deep and wide,
> From the void where nothing dwells,
> Yet from nothing, substance made.
> What can work this queen of spells?

*The finger came out of Heliogabalus' mouth with a champagne-cork \*pop\*. "If you want to make something out of nothing, you should be managing Bootsy. Lies, darling. The only way to make something out of nothing is lies, lies, lies. But in your line of work . . ."*

*The silver mirror washed with blood as Heliogabalus learned the sphynx's true career path.*

Another diamond winked out.

Elena's legs folded under her, and she sat down with a loud outrush of breath. Sanchi had his arms around her, his face so full of anxiety that she had to hold his hand especially tight, a promise. "I'm all right. Really. And Sanchi, I'm so glad you're—"

He kissed all protestations from her lips.

"You see?" Vergilius raised one black brow. "I'd say he took it all very well."

"Is it o—o—over yet?" Claudius' stammer returned with the stress of waiting cap in hand for sorcery to have its say. "C—can we talk?"

"We must," Vergilius said. "Come near, both of you." Claudius and Suetonius entered Hatshepsut's realm circumspectly. What Elena had seen in the silver mirror was quickly communicated to everyone there.

"Which leaves Caligula," said Claudius. "And m—me."

"Not for long," Elena said, resting her head against Sanchi's chest. "I saw him with her, in another vision, at the gambling tables. He was hovering around her, making a pest of himself, slithering away from her bodyguards or grabbing them by the—grabbing them and dancing off whenever they tried to catch him. She looked irritated. He'll be next."

"When?" Hatshepsut asked sharply. "Was it a vision of past, present, future?"

"It must be future," Sanchi said, pointing to the twin diamonds still twinkling on the sorcerer's ring.

"But how *near* in the future? Is it something we can prevent?" The queen rounded on Elena. "Did you note a clue of light, of dress, or have the good luck to mark a clock anywhere in the vision? We may yet be able to save him!"

Elena shook her head. "I'm still learning how to maintain the visions I receive. Everything I have goes into sustaining them. I'm afraid that if I try to look more closely, for details, I'll lose them altogether."

"Why save him? Caligula's second death in itself would be small loss," Vergilius said. "I called the Caesars out of Hades to learn the uses of power, and its undoing. From him, all I could learn would be how power undoes a mind already weak. I feel my strength return all the more with each of the spirits the sphynx sends back to Pluto's care." Affection lit his face as he regarded Hatshepsut. "There is only one for whom I would gladly barter all the powers left me, if it would buy her life."

"It must not be," Hatshepsut said decidedly. "You have played draughts with time and fate for too long. There is a world at stake, not just the whims of one man's heart, however dear they are to me. Will you not see, my lord, that each spirit she returns to Hades goes by way of a Riddle? That each Asking without Answer adds to *her* strength more than to yours?"

"When something evil does your work for you, it is still evil," Claudius contributed. "Much as I—much as I nourish no great fondness for my nephew, I would not have his death add to our enemy's power. We must act, Master Vergilius. The time to hide is over—trust me there; I am an expert on the subject."

"We attack? How?" The magician did not look optimistic. "With what? As you say, she has been adding to her powers while I have been drained of mine through my own blindness. If I had only recognized what Elena could do— what magic a woman might master—she would not still be so rawly trained by this time."

"Let's not waste any more time talking might-have-beens," Sanchi said. "Look around you and see what you've got, Vergilius." He beamed with confidence as he took stock of his companions. "*Nombre de la Virgen*, we didn't have half this muscle when we took out the dragon!" A second thought dimmed his smile. "I wish Mani had waited to join us here instead of charging off. God, let him be alive."

"The lad speaks well," Claudius said. He puffed out his chest. "Now when I invaded Britain—"

"You had technologically and strategically superior forces to hurl against the aboriginals," Suetonius commented. "The instruments of this battle are not shortswords, but spells, and the sphynx has us at a loss there."

"What? Even with Vergilius and *two* female mages?"

"One barely trained," Hatsepsut said. "And—I must be honest—the magic we command may not destroy, but only shape and channel."

"Well, you could shape the sphynx into a guppy; I'd call that progress," Claudius huffed.

"O divine Caesar," Suetonius said smoothly, "have you never heard it said that when force of arms alone fails, strategy often evens the balance?"

"What's that? Of course I have! What are you up to, Suetonius? You've got that sly look on you. What do you know that I don't? Where have you been sneaking about?"

The gossipmonger sighed and cast demure eyes at the Egyptian queen. Hatshepsut laughed. "My surprise is a surprise no more, thanks to this woodworm. I should be paying you to withhold information as well as to produce it. Very well, Suetonius, we will show them."

She left Vergilius to stare with the rest as she took Elena's place before the silver mirror. Rippling reflections of light swam over her dusky skin as her words turned solid silver to glittering liquid. At the moment that was like no other, she plunged both hands through the mirror's surface and drew out a shining band of gold.

"A collar for a *very* dangerous beast," she said. "Not to bind her, but to mute the strength of her spells and keep her from summoning up all the destructive magic she may have to send against us. With this around her neck, we will have our chance to bring the sphynx down. We must be ready to use the opportunity well."

"Which, to this reporter's mind, leaves one classical question," Suetonius said.

"Who will bell the cat?"

# CHAPTER TWENTY-EIGHT: Chains

"Nervous?" Sanchi asked, leaning against one of the massive square pillars of the Egyptian colonnade. The Kennedy Memorial was a black shape beneath the curving roof, a single white flower laid before it.

"A l—little," Claudius admitted. He tweaked his bow tie for the thousandth time and slapped the pocket of his dinner jacket where the enchanted collar lay, wearing the guise of an earthly necklace. The pocket opposite contained an identical piece of jewelry, a temptingly rich confection of diamonds and emeralds. Vergilius knew the sphynx's weakness for those gems, bright as stars, verdant as cats' eyes. He had woven the spell of seeming over Hatshepsut's gold collar.

"Just make sure you bring her back here before you put it on her."

"J—j—j—just pray I d—don't forg—g—get which necklace is which, Sanchi."

"You'll remember. A Caesar never forgets."

"We can f—forget about *this* Caesar, when this is over. I'm going back where I belong."

"You're kidding. You'd *want* to be dead again?"

"What am I now? Don't stare so, lad. Poor Caligula was the maddest of our lot, but I am quite sane. I've had my life; why be a hog about it? Magic can make changes in the way the world goes, but only for a time. The urge to set things back to rights is strong, and there *is* a greater force that knows the true *should be* of creation. We do our best to muck it up—magicians and unmagical alike—with our wars of words and swords and spells, but eventually the mess we make gets tidied away. Until we make the next one."

"Vergilius has lived for centuries, and he doesn't seem to have a hard time with the idea."

Claudius patted Sanchi on the back paternally. "For a great magician, Vergilius is an incredibly slow study. But I think he has learned his lesson now. Can't you read the weariness in him, Sanchi? No matter what he may say, his eyes reveal how deeply he longs to leave a world he knows too well. Where's the scholar's challenge when nearly every answer's known? He lived on because he so feared the loneliness of death, never seeing how lone his endless life had been. Now that he's found her, however, the passage does not seem so dark or the land beyond so dismal. She will comfort him in the journey. Love answers fear wonderfully well."

"You wouldn't want to live even a little longer?"

"In this world?" Claudius laughed. "Not that it's a bad one, just not mine. Anyway, I was nearly as bad a hypochondriac as Tiberius, my every sneeze a disaster. With your improved knowledge of medicine and ailments, I'd never have time to enjoy living. I'd always think I had something or was on the point of catching it. Poo. At least when you're dead, you can stop worrying about your health." He consulted his watch. "Th—think she'll be at the tables by this time?"

"Sunday night? Yeah, it's about right. We're all in place. You're on."

"Banzai," said the emperor.

The sphynx was contented. Finally she could play without having that deranged gadfly nipping at her flanks, buzzing in her ear about how they would rule the world together. He was insane, useless to Vergilius, harmless to her, hardly worth destroying except for the relief of his guaranteed absence. And his death had added to her power, though there was no challenge in a Riddle asked of a lunatic.

It warps the world, affects the eye,
Does all without a touch.
Where is that master shaper
Whose strength can wreak so much?

Caligula took umbrage at the question. She was like all the rest of them, he accused. She, too, was out to get him. Dabs of foam speckled his lips. She was unworthy to share his bed and body. His deified sister Drusilla was the only woman who deserved the honor, who ever really understood how wonderful he was, how special. He would show her! He knew what she was, all about the myth of Oedipus and what happened when the Riddle was rightly answered. He would answer it now, just to show her with whom she was trifling, and then he would kill her and take all her power for his own and use it to bring his adored Drusilla back to life, his bride and queen. *That* would teach her to make fun of the divine Caligula, asking him a Riddle whose answer was—there could be no other—*madness.*

Drusilla would not come to him. He was dispatched to her, and the sphynx went back to roulette.

There was not much casino business on a Sunday night. Dionysia was calm, recuperating from the frenetic atmosphere of Friday and Saturday. Those who played tonight were either jet-lagged foreign money, or native American high rollers coasting to a gradual stop. The sphynx had leisure to mark her partners well, and it did not take her long to single out the silver-haired man who kept placing stack after stack of chips on 41.

He was expensively dressed; she was interested. A subtle motion of her hand dismissed her bodyguards as she changed seats. "Your lucky number?" she asked.

"I used to think so." He sounded meek and self-effacing, though all those piles of plastic told her he could afford to be anything he damned well pleased.

"Your age, is it?" She smiled mischievously at him through steepled fingertips.

"You're a flatterer, young lady." She was, but he didn't seem to mind. Soon they were talking more than playing. Soon he confided in her about his less than satisfactory relationship with the young woman he had wed in an uncharacteristic burst of imprudence. Soon he showed her the necklace he had purchased as a gift that, like others before it, would not be appreciated by his bubblegum bride. The sphynx saw the emeralds and her mouth watered.

It did not take her long to become his friend, or to hint at more. He did deserve more, didn't he? When he suggested a stroll on the boardwalk, she agreed. The moonlight made everything so romantic. The stars reminded her of the diamonds in that slim velvet box. In the shadow of the lotus-topped columns, after many insincere demurs on her part, much insistence on his, he fastened it around her neck.

And the scream of her betrayal made every light in Atlantic City go out.

"Sekhmet's fire, what has happened now?" Hatshepsut grabbed Elena's hand as the blackout clapped down. They were hidden beneath the boardwalk, there to await a signal from Vergilius. Needle lines of neon from the hotel signs above had been their only source of light, bleeding through the boards, painting the women's faces for war. Gone, now.

"Make a light!" Elena whispered urgently.

"I cannot create, only summon, bring, channel, change."

"We have to get out of here. In the open, we can see by the moon." Elena dragged the queen with her out onto the sand. The young moon did little more than to give indistinct shapes to things. The colonnade was a block of lighter shadow against the monolithic black of the Convention Center. All the figures on the boardwalk looked alike.

"Where is Vergilius?" Hatshepsut's cupped hands filled with a golden glow as twin armies of scarabs poured from her sleeves. They took to the air in a cloud of stars and made a comet's tail against the night.

"What are you doing?" Elena forgot all about any respect due her teacher. She seized Hatshepsut's arm so violently that the little queen staggered. "When they find him, *she'll* find him."

"When they find him, I will go to him, and nothing *she* can do will keep me from fighting beside him." Kohl-rimmed eyes burned into Elena's paling face. "Did you think I meant to keep to his plan, to let all the danger be his? Will I let him shelter me, out of love, and venture losing all that love again? Man's magic, woman's spells, they are the Question and the Answer. There is your last lesson, child. Learn from it while you can. Here." She closed Elena's fingers around a small, cold object. "A gift for an apt apprentice; use it with a master's hands."

The gentle sea breeze whipped itself into a wind as words of a changing spell from the queen's lips bridled it. Elena saw white robes flash into the sky, following the flight of the golden scarabs.

She opened her hand and saw the silver statue of the cat-goddess Bast. It thrummed, warm with purrs as fragile as a honeybee's breath, and its electrum earrings danced.

\*    \*    \*

*"How dare you? How dare you work such evil against me?"* The sphinx's hysterical shrieks made Claudius cover his ears. He had never cared for scenes. She yanked and tugged and jerked on the collar, but it would not budge.

"I w—wouldn't call things e—e—evil if I were you," he said, a trifle preachily.

The sphinx was in no mood for moral lessons. "I'll kill you."

"Y—you'd *like* to ki—ki—kill me, but you c—can't. N—not with a R—Ri—Ri—Riddle, can you? First the que—question, then the k—k—k—kill. That's how you did it with the others. And even if you d—did stump me"—Claudius' stammer subsided as he observed the sphinx to be securely bound, making no overt moves against him—"how would you kill me? That c—collar won't let you shift shape. You're stuck as a wo-woman forever, now."

"Nothing binds me," the sphinx snarled. She reached within herself for the spells of skinshifting, willing back her wings, her claws, the fangs she longed to clash together through this nasty little man's neck.

Nothing happened. Her consternation erupted in a wounded yowl.

Claudius chuckled. *"Quod erat demonstrandum.* Really, my dear, you should have husbanded your powers better. The collar dims them, but you tossed away *lashings* of magic with that little tantrum you threw when I got the better of you." He waved at the extinguished city for his own satisfaction, not caring whether the gesture was visible to her or not. The blackness was quite terrible, really, he mused. All sorts of skullduggery might go on under such favorable cover.

The sphinx's cry of outrage had been swallowed in the rising tide of bewildered human voices on the boardwalk and the streets, and how long before the cries of less deserving victims started up? The predators always recovered fastest in the wake of disaster. Such a pity. Where *was* that wizard?

"Here, Sanchi." From behind the pillar, Vergilius stole up to slip the emerald ring onto Sanchi's finger. "Go to her now. Demand the Riddle. Answer—oh, Answer it truly, and the gods guide your words! Do not be afraid; even if

234

you mistake the reply, the collar will not permit her to kill you. But it will not be so. I will stand with you, and give you the proper Answer, and then—then focus all the power within you through the stone, and destroy her."

Sanchi saw green fire creep over his hand, and the lone twinkle of a single diamond. "Take it back, Vergilius. I'm not the one to kill her."

"You must be. For what she did to your Mamacita. For what she has done to you. For the sake of breaking the last chain binding you to her, you must be the one."

Sanchi could swear that in the darkness he saw the wizard's eyes burning blue-green. He raised the emerald's blaze to their fires and slowly drew the ring from his hand. "And what about the chain she has on you?" he asked. "Do you really want me to have the glory of the kill, Vergilius, or do you just want me to do a job you've lost the stomach for? I was her lover for scarcely a day; you had her for centuries."

"Impudence . . ."

"Elena is the one with the power," Sanchi said. "What I had—if I ever really had it—" he touched his bare neck—"I forfeited."

"Very well." The ring was snatched from his fingers. "The squire eternal. How proud your Persiles would be to hear you now!"

Sanchi let Vergilius' spleen wash over him like water. He knew that the wizard was fighting a greater enemy inside his own skin, in memories. He would not add to it. "Persiles was born to win by the sword; I am Sanchi."

"Sanchi. Is that all you are? It is better to play the good and modest servant, always declining the *honor* of battle, than to call yourself an honest coward." A hard grip closed on Sanchi's wrist. "You might have been a man; you are only a shell. If you will not use what is in you, at least I will take what I can. Whether you share your power gladly or not, I will take it and use it to drive the sphynx into the sea!"

Vergilius yanked Sanchi between the covered avenue of columns to where two figures waited in the dark.

"Take off my collar, old man," the sphynx said low. She knelt before the emperor, but there was nothing servile in that pose. Even trapped in human form, she looked like a lion crouching for the spring. "Take it off, and you may live."

"Assuming that's what I want, aren't you?" Claudius had turned smug, but not completely so. He still gave little jumps of alarm each time a particularly disturbing noise individuated itself from the general blackout rhubarb. Physically, he was calm; emotionally, he had ruined six pairs of moleskin trousers while wishing for Vergilius to come.

"Oh, you want to live. You are greedy for life, like all your kind. You tell yourself pretty lies about not fearing death, but you shun it while you can. Hypocrite."

"Here! There's no need to get insulting."

"I am your prisoner. I am, as you said, only a woman now." Her hands lay atop the silly little evening bag in her lap, nervously kneading the clasp. "You are right; I could not kill you even if you did answer wrongly the Riddle I have crafted for your doom."

"For me?" Claudius sounded as flattered as if the sphynx had just confessed to planning him a surprise birthday party. "Just for *my* doom? Oh, surely not. I know your tale too well, my dear. You didn't chivvy up a new Riddle for every wanderer with the bad luck to take the Theban highroad."

"That was then." Was that a hint of sarcasm in her voice? "This is now. Yes, Claudius the scholar, the author, the little man who hid behind his books as behind so much else! What a shame that I shall never know whether you also hid behind a mere reputation for intelligence. This Riddle of mine that is yours alone was woven for an educated man."

Curiosity made Claudius fidget. Were those footsteps he heard, stealing closer? Friend or foe? All this fine game would be up once Vergilius and the rest arrived, though they might have slow going in the dark. What *was* that smear of gold in the sky out over the beach? What were those voices, fierce in carefully muted argument, behind him? What was that scuffling sound coming nearer across the planks?

Soon he would have eternity back, and no need to worry over questions. No risks, no change, nothing—his one regret—nothing new to learn.

Well, and why not let her ask it? She'd made it just for him. Why waste it? Why not prove to her that there was more to his erudition than hollow reputation? Not like some of those cardboard *Wunderkinder* at Princeton! And no risking unexpected death at all, for she was firmly bound in female shape now. Wouldn't that be a treat, to return to Hades as the only other mortal man to answer the sphynx's Riddle! Even among the drowsy poppy fields of Elysium, a sometime laurel tree still grew.

"Ask it," he said. "And hurry. I think I hear them coming."

What is this sweet gift sublime
That the gods for men devised?
Life without it is but time.
'Tis most precious where least prized.

He felt the shackles close on his spirit the moment her Riddle seeped into his mind. Claudius realized how truly Hatshepsut had spoken when she said that the collar damped but did not destroy the sphynx's power. The binding was weak, but it was there. Panic rose in his throat. Was he now joined to her forever, like a birthcord-tethered embryo in its mother's womb? When the sorcerer came, in his fury, would Claudius too be blown into whatever scattered state enraged magic would blast the sphynx?

The old instincts surfaced. *Escape! Hide!* And the sphynx's voice was a presence in his brain, saying, *There is only one escape, Claudius: the Answer.*

*She can't kill me. Can she?* He trembled as desperate thoughts rattled through his head. *How silly; of course she can't. She can't turn into a monster and slash me with her claws or tear me with her teeth. She's only a woman. I—I shall be safe again once I answer.*

"Y—y—you are qui—quite right, my dear," he said haltingly. "Th—this riddle was m—m—made for me, a s—subject I know in—in—intimately." He sent a sheepish smile into the dark. "I th—thank you for all your t—t—trouble, but the answer is h—h—health."

He heard a click—the evening bag opening—and then a funny noise, like a party-popper's string being pulled.

The gun wasn't big, but the bullet was big enough to drill a neat hole right between Claudius' eyes.

# CHAPTER TWENTY-NINE:
## Suspicious Minds

The sphynx watched as Claudius' body melted down into a diamond that became a pinch of ash. It was a vanishment she had witnessed six times before, but this one gave her a great deal of satisfaction. The dark was no impediment to her vision; feline eyes might change appearance in the skinshift, but they always retained their function. *How fortunate it should be so*, she thought as she stroked the petite gun. *I am only a woman, and a lady must have some means of self-preservation in these wicked times*.

"You have accomplished nothing," said Vergilius, seeming to rise from the same dab of ash that had been Claudius. "You are still a captive."

The sphynx sprang from her knees swiftly, backing away from the wizard. The gold collar shed its own radiance, illumining the haughty planes of her face from below. Instinctively she snarled, a parody of the beast's fearsome grimace when translated to a woman's lips. "Whose captive, Vergilius? Yours again?"

He tried to come nearer, but there was something unseen in the way. She laughed when he encountered the invisible barricade. "Keep your distance, O my late master. I am not wholly powerless. The last thing I want is to feel your fumbling hands on my body again. You must kill me at a distance, if you can, for I will kill myself sooner than submit to your degrading touch."

"You are mistaken." Vergilius was hoarse as a gore-crow. "The only desire I now feel is for your death."

"So passionate? What has changed you? In the heat of our wildest couplings, you were only partly there. I always felt that my loins were somehow the gateway for you to step out of your rutting body and play Aristotle: the detached observer, the annotator of lust, the scholar of sex."

"Ask it." The suddenness of the order startled the sphynx.

238

"Ask it?" she echoed. Realization dawned. "Ah. The Riddle. I am to Ask and you will surely Answer, and then you have the privilege of slaying me. Wouldn't that be pat? You must excuse me if I turn less than cooperative."

"You must Ask it."

"You are a powerful magician, my lord Vergilius. You ride spells of coercion and compulsion, but here"—she touched the invisible wall she had set up between them—"is where they shatter."

"I give you as much of a chance to kill me as I have to kill you. I might not have the proper Answer to give." So he spoke, but he did not sound as if he doubted the outcome.

The sphinx raised her hand. The glow from the collar cast blood-red shadows into her cupped palm. "By the Styx I swear, by the black river whose ultimate obliteration binds men and gods and more than these, I swear that this night you shall have Riddles enough from me, and I shall demand the Answer."

She swung her head from side to side, like a lion sifting the airs of the plain for the scent of its prey. "Come out, brave ones! Come and stand beside him, your master, your lover, your friend! I know you are here. The darkness holds no secrets from me. I am collared, but the chain is long. Come out, for I promise you that this man will be very glad of any help you can lend him."

"Leave them!" Vergilius shouted, but it was too late. The sphinx caressed a sphere of air and formed it into plastic brightness. The shining globe rose to touch the roof of the colonnade. Sanchi was first to step into the wide circle of light it spun. Hatshepsut followed, bringing her own brilliance in an armor of gold scarabs clinging to her gown. Elena lingered on the borders of the dark, creeping shyly nearer to Sanchi until she could slip her hand into his.

A silver statuette warmed between their clasped palms.

"So . . ." The sphinx's smile was unpleasant to see. "After so long, to find so many allies."

She clapped her hands.

"Let me go, you son of a bitch!" The indignant shout came from the beach.

"Mani!" Sanchi and Elena knew the voice and cried out that name at once. Together they bolted for the boardwalk railings overlooking the sands and strained their eyes to see him, but could only make out moon-silvered waves and indistinct hummocks of shadow on the shore.

"Do allow me," said the sphynx. The globe of light writhed from perfect sphere to amoebic form, extending blunt limbs of illumination into the night. Just beyond the lee of the colonnade, past the boardwalk rail, the shining pseudopod stretched, pulling away the curtain of darkness.

The shadows were men. There were more than thirty of them, the sphynx's faithful servants. Some flaunted the formal wear requisite for Ianthe Apeiron's bodyguards, but most still held to tight jeans, faded T-shirts, the creak of leather jackets, or the easier movement of their tattered denim and khaki counterparts. The protean light shone clear enough for Sanchi to see every patch of stubble, the webs and rims of blood overlying once-healthy eyes, the puckered brown of old scars, the slim red trail of needles, the green and black and rust of bared tattoos. They were alley spawn, street things, the predators that Claudius had spoken of so academically, from the safe distance of *It wouldn't dare touch me.* Metal gleamed, zippers and spikes and blades and the cooler sheen of gun barrels. They had come onto the beach in silence stolen from the confused wake of the blackout and had bided there for the signal from their mistress.

In the front line, in the deadest of all dead centers, Manolo and Gemma stood, wrists bound with baling wire. Frosty moonglow and the ailing yellow sheen of the sphynx's conjured light dappled Alonso's wintry white suit and the palm-length blade he laid against Manolo's throat.

*"Hola, hermano; qué tal?"* Alonso's warped grin was the blade of a reaper's scythe, drinking pleasure from the pain he inflicted as he pressed the knife a little harder into Manolo's flesh, drawing out a bloody thread. Sanchi shuddered to see what his half brother had become.

"Even when I play the fool enough to be tricked by a mudworm like Claudius, I am not entirely stupid," the sphynx said. "Insurance; everyone should invest in some. Those two guarantees you see there were obliging enough to make me a gift of themselves."

Sanchi glimpsed Vergilius as the sorcerer joined him at the railing. "Gemma . . ."

The sphynx's crackling laughter was crushed ice. "See, my late master? Though fate has sent us off on separate roads, still we retain enough in common to patronize the same hirelings. And Gemma *was* good at what she did; until she lost her nerve, the gods know why. I hoped to make much of her. I still might."

"Release them," Vergilius rasped.

"Release me," the sphynx replied.

"Never."

"Then I will have them killed."

"I will blast the hand that tries it."

"How many can you destroy at once? You forget, I know your magic; *and* your limitations. With enough opposition, you cannot both attack and defend on a large scale. Do you remember poor Tri? He and his handful would have been enough to remove you, had he cherished my gift more dearly. Even without the means to mute your power, as you have hampered mine, my followers can overwhelm you with numbers alone. Oh, you might be able to protect yourself, but what of your friends?"

"His friends are not helpless, demon," Hatshepsut said. Her voice rang out bravely. The glittering armor of scarabs had twirled itself back into the golden threads shot through her ornate sash and kalasiris from which her change-spells had first called them. She stood with Vergilius and the others at the railing.

The sphynx sneered. "You stink of strong magic, woman, but I can wash you clean of it. That crowd on the beach is but a small sampling of the people I command in this city alone. And in the world? Nothing prevents me from walking away, collar and all, and making a few phone calls. Ah, the comforts of technology! You may have stopped me from destroying your breed with the Riddle, but human as I am, I still have the capability to set in motion forces of your own forging which will be the end of humankind. With this difference: It will not be as quick or merciful as the Riddle, wrongly Answered."

"Then Ask it!"

The voice was not Vergilius'. Sanchi had spoken, tearing his hand free of Elena's, unwittingly taking the Bast-cat with him as he lunged forward to wave a defiant fist in the sphynx's face. His knuckles brushed the invisible barrier and encountered resistance, as he had supposed. The shock came to both him and the sphynx when the jellied air strained and parted, and his hand lurched through to strike her jaw a sharp, glancing blow.

The sphynx staggered, eyes volcanic. Her fingers touched her bruised jaw only for a heartbeat, then the little gun was back in her grip, its second round firing. The bullet exploded in midair. Vergilius lowered his hand. "I can protect my own," he said.

"For how long?" the sphynx snarled. "Against how many?" Her words were for the sorcerer, but her eyes never tore free of Sanchi's face. Now she spoke only to him. "What are you, boy? What do you conceal? I have known you, body and mind, heart and dreams. I have read your most shameful hungers and fed them full. I have made you answer my slightest call for the mere promise of sating those hungers again. You should be broken to my rein, dancing at the end of my tether. Why are you free? What gives you the power to breach my spells?"

"Is that your Riddle?" Sanchi asked.

*"Riddle!"* It was a screech. "If that is the coin I must pay for an answer, very well, it shall be! Vergilius!"

The sorcerer bowed with cold formality.

"I call on you to be oath-taker and oath-maker. I will Ask the final Riddle of this man, and no other. Swear now as I will swear, by the Styx and by your soul's saving, that he shall be the only one to Answer what I Ask."

"That oath would suit you, would it not?" Vergilius folded his arms. "Ask me, and you face the wisdom of centuries. Ask him, and you Ask a babe."

"And if I Ask no one, still I will be able to destroy. I thought you were a gambling man, O my late master. A chance for the world's salvation bet against the death of a single man seems a fair wager to me. Will you play?"

"Let him," Hatshepsut said in the sorcerer's ear. "Even if he answers wrongly, he may yet escape death. The collar holds her in that shape, and between us we can shield him from any human means of death."

"Can we?" Vergilius wondered aloud. "The moment of the Asking and the Answer is a time out of time. The laws of nature and of magic hold themselves suspended. All things are possible. The dead have died again in such moments—you know it. *Will* we still have the ability to lend him more shelter than our own bodies, if his Answer is wrong?"

"Even so," said the queen, "I would give him that much."

"No one gives me anything I don't want," Sanchi said. "That includes your permission, Vergilius. Take the oath."

"Has anyone ever told you that your ears are too big?" the sorcerer muttered. As the sphynx had done before, he swore. Hatshepsut took a similiar oath of honor's most binding power on a magic-wielder, and Elena, reluctantly, at the sphynx's insistence. When they were done, the sphynx herself swore.

"How I wish we had a little sherry, to seal our bargain with a sip," she mused. "So civilized. Or some lemonade. Come to the beach; let us have this settled."

"Why not here, where we are?"

"Why, for your own safety, Sanchi. Surely your master will tell you that Styx runs deep beneath the earth, and earth must touch our feet for the oath's full strength to hold. You should thank me for my honesty." She kicked off her high heels and padded down onto the sand, where her minions still stood ranked in the darkness. The glow floated with her, following like a pet balloon.

Sanchi had taken no oath, but he removed his shoes anyway. He was chary of any claims the sphynx might make to fair play, yet what choice did he have? He must go where she led. He kept his senses all the more alert, wondering from which quarter her treachery would spring.

Behind him he heard a rustle of surprised voices, and no wonder. So long as the conjured light had stayed in its place, under the colonnade, it might have been mistaken for an auxiliary lamp; there were some in feeble operation near the hotels, struggling to offset the total dark of the sphynx's rage. But when this light moved, when it traced one woman's steps, even the self-absorbed passersby stopped gabbling about pickpockets and hotel package refunds and gathered along the length of the boardwalk to watch.

"Say, isn't that the rich bitch who owns Dionysia?"

"What bitch? Her name's Ianthe Apeiron, and she's got more money than God. I read all about her in *People*."

"So what'd she do, buy her own private sun?"

"Shut up, you don't know nothing. I saw loads of light-up gadgets like that advertised in the Sharper Image catalog."

"The fucker is *flying*."

"You maybe expect a woman like her to use a flashlight?"

"Oh, come *on!* Microchips, dummy. You think there's something you can't do with microchips?"

"So how come she's waltzing right up to that bunch of rough trade, huh? I had a light to see by, I'd get so far from that scum you'd never—"

"Oh shit. The skinny one's got a knife on somebody."

"Where?"

"The one in the pimp suit. Hey! Anybody call the cops?"

"Somebody musta. Now clam it, wouldja? I wanna see what's going down."

"Shove over!"

"Oh, my God, Phil, would you *look* at the dresses those other two women are wearing? Nummy."

"Who's the guy in the black suit, with the beard and mustache?"

"I think it's Doug Henning. I heard he cut his hair and grew a goatee. Maybe this is for TV, a special, you know? Maybe he's gonna make all those punks disappear."

"Where's the cameras?"

"Didn't I read they were maybe bringing back *Candid Camera*?"

"Read it where? In *People*?"

" 'Sa difference?"

"Well, inquiring minds want to know."

"Those bimbos his assistants?"

"I always liked David Copperfield better."

"I bet that's a rubber knife."

"Your mama."

The sphinx and the rest walked well out on the sands, almost to the ocean's edge. Sanchi was close behind her, within the compass of her light. Vergilius, Hatshepsut, and Elena tried to walk with him, but the light itself seemed to define the boundaries of her fending spell. It held them at a distance, though it let Sanchi pass. The sphinx's own troops trudged after, Alonso in the forefront to hustle and harry the two captives along.

At last the sphinx stopped, raising her hand. The shining globe overhead began to whirl, spinning ever faster on its axis, the poles gradually flattening, compressing the mass of light, until its form was more disk than sphere. As it spun, it widened, and as it widened it repulsed Vergilius, Hatshepsut, and Elena farther into the darkness. The sphynx's men appeared to feel the same outward pressure. They withdrew from the widening ring of light, their hostages being shoved back with them.

"Hey!" Alonso shouted, watching his comrades' retreat. The light flooded over him without effect. "Hey, where are you going?" He blinked in the brightness, then stared across the arena at his half brother's back.

Over Sanchi's shoulder, the sphynx nodded. "Now," she said.

Sanchi heard the brush of running feet on sand and turned too late. The knife flashed down as Alonso shouted his triumph.


# CHAPTER THIRTY:
## In the Blood

The dull shock of pure impact rocked Sanchi sideways, and the harsh sensation of steel grating over bone made him wince with revulsion. He had been almost alert enough. *Almost.* Alonso's knife sliced down and was diverted by his left shoulder blade as he wheeled and leaped away. It gashed open his shirt and flesh but missed the veins and arteries of the neck, the soft places between the ribs.

*Only a kid,* Sanchi thought wildly, feeling blood trickle down his back, warm and sticky. *A weak kid. Thank God. If he'd have been any stronger*—adios, ya. *Small favors . . .* There was no immediate pain. That came later, lancing white and red across his eyes when Alonso made his second lunge and Sanchi dodged. His bare feet hit the packed sand hard, jarring his whole body. His left arm was numb, useless, his right hand still clenched tightly around that small silver cat. He held fast to it without being aware, as if it were a relic of saner times. It was all he had, and what was the use of it? He would do better to drop it and throw a handful of sand into his half brother's eyes.

" 'Lonso! Are you crazy? What the hell are you—?"

"Shut up, Sanchi, Sanchito, *hijito de mi alma, de mis entrañas, tesoro de la casa,* golden boy." Alonso chanted the terms of affection as if they were a roll of curses. "Too good to live, everyone's darling, *angelito,* only son worth having, only lover worth her while, *bien amado, adorado,* all the brains, all the luck, all the love, none for me, nothing left for me, not with Ma, not with her, nowhere, no one, *God damn you, couldn't you leave anything for me*? Nothing but what I take, but I can take away more than you ever dared to dream, Sanchi, Sanchito, *hermano,* my precious brother . . ."

Sanchi saw yellow fires in Alonso's eyes, vertical slits where human pupils had once been. How had the change begun, how far could it go? Was this truth, or illusion brought out of fear and pain? The sphynx was watching. She was the only other living thing inside the bowl of light her magic had created. In the outer dark he saw Elena's desperate face pressed against the unseen barricade, her fingers clawing at what she could never tear aside.

"Your oath, monster!" he heard Vergilius shout. It sounded as if the sorcerer were calling from the height of an isolated tower, the wind whipping his voice away. "Is this its keeping?"

"I swore to Ask him the Riddle," the sphynx replied. "So I shall . . . if he is alive to hear it." She shrugged with feigned helplessness. "Am I responsible for the actions of my servants?"

"By all the powers ever made, I will make you responsible!"

"If you can, Vergilius; if you can."

Alonso leaped, and again Sanchi dodged. His ankle twisted on a hillock of sand, folding his leg beneath him. A jagged scream ripped everything to raveled pain as he fell, rolling onto his wound. He forced his left hand into service, grabbing sand and flinging it as hard as he could. The toss went wide and weak, scattering ocher grains in a harmless cloud. Alonso jeered, and kicked grit into Sanchi's eyes with much more devilish effect.

Spitting, rubbing the sting away, Sanchi felt more blood flow down his back. He cleared his eyes enough to see Alonso make a sharp, vicious feint. A mad roll to the right made him gasp and groan, but Alonso just laughed, jabbing in the blade as Sanchi came to rest precisely where he'd been herded. The slash carved deep into his upper left arm, a cut meant to hurt and taunt—*I could have killed you with that one; next time, I will.* A red stream washed into Sanchi's folded palm, pooled beneath the silver figurine.

Alonso stood over his half brother, his rumpled white suit so lightly sprinkled with red that only a keen eye could see it. The sweat stains were more prominent than the misting of Sanchi's blood. "This time, *hermano*," he said, breathing hard, gathering himself for the last thrust. *"Y no adios; al Cuerno."*

Not to God; to the Devil.

Sanchi crossed his arms in front of his face, cloth and skin streaked scarlet. *Elena . . .*

Scarlet and silver flared from his palm, sudden life burst from his childishly clutching fingers. They splayed out like an exploding milkweed pod, curled back too late to reclaim the creature that had leaped forth. Paws reached out, claws spread, silver teeth gleamed as the Bast cat arced its slender body over the sands. In its flight it grew from tiny statuette to leopard's size and with fangs and talons struck Alonso down.

Behind the unseen wall, Elena's fists were knotted, her face exalted as the wild magic in her veins leaped out to fill the queen's gift with raging life. *For Sanchi, life,* she thought, in the small, bright space of self-awareness that the magic left her. *Protect him, save him, defend him!*

She could feel herself being pulled against the barrier by the force of the enchantment flowing from her body. *He* called to her from the other side, summoning her in the name of their shared wonder: one gift in two bodies, magic divided, seeking to be whole. But the body itself could not pass. Though she was with Sanchi, soul and self, she could not physically pierce the boundaries the sphinx had raised between them.

*It doesn't matter,* she thought. *As long as I can help him, it doesn't matter whether I can reach him, touch him—oh, even if the price is never to touch him again, let me save him now! Nothing more matters.*

A warm presence kissed her mind. *Well chosen, my daughter.* Hatshepsut's face was the ghost-image of breath blown against a frosted windowpane. *Do not fear; that price will not be demanded. See, you have done enough. It is over.*

\*   \*   \*

Alonso lay in the sand, his throat torn, alternately gasping for breath and groaning when he drew one. Sanchi knelt beside him, gently took his head into his lap. The huge silver cat rumbled with purrs and tried to rub its bloody muzzle against his unwounded shoulder. He shoved it away.

"*Hermanito.*" In memory, Sanchi saw his mother holding a cherished infant tightly to her bosom, a little woman willing to stand against the dragon that demanded her baby son in sacrifice. *The dragon is dead, but it looks as if he'll have his sacrifice at last. Oh, 'Lonso, what went wrong?*

"Why don't you finish him?" the sphynx inquired. She studied the brothers with a scientist's curiosity, at a judicious distance from the Bast cat. "He'll be forever dying if you don't, and if you have some grand, heroic idea of fetching him medical help, forget it. I can't prevent your comings and goings, but I can seal out anyone else. Go on. Kill him. It's the kinder of the two choices left you."

"Two?" His own voice was hollow.

"I could heal him. Remove the collar, and I will."

"I don't believe you."

"Then he dies. And out there, the hostages die too. I only swore to set you the Riddle, fairly. I did not name a time. I can wait. Do you see my servants out there? They are less patient than I. They are getting nervous. They do rash things when under pressure. They've seen your brother— their friend—fall to a monster's jaws. Your sweet pet has frightened them; dangerous. How can they know they won't be next? It would be just like them to cut their losses." She smirked over her own choice of words.

"They know what you are? The spells you can work?"

"They are ignorant. They have a mole's idea of the stars. Any of my actions that they cannot explain in terms of their small, sordid reality they quickly deny, or snarl into a knot of comforting lies." Her lips twitched. "Why? Are you afraid they'll burn me as a witch if I heal him? Don't. He will rise hale and hearty at a touch from the full strength of my spells, and they will find a way to explain it afterward.

"If you grant your brother life, Sanchi. If you free me."

Elena saw what he was about to do. She screamed his name and had the sound echo to her ears from the wall of light and shadow. Vergilius saw too, and joined his shout of warning and interdict to hers.

Hatshepsut spread her hands in a gesture of resignation. It was not theirs to prevent this thing.

The snap of the collar's clasp coming undone was a thunderclap. The gold circle split, and Sanchi felt all the sphynx's suppressed powers come rushing back into her like a tidal wave. It battered him away from her, bowled him across the strand.

The city surged with light. The people on the boardwalk and the beach blinked madly, blinded. It did not last long. They were able to see the impossible take place down by the water's edge.

The sphynx embraced the glare fearlessly, gladly. Full freedom seized her with bacchic ecstacy. Her own tame disk of brightness shivered down into a black bubble and burst under the assault of streetlight and neon. She threw back head and arms, rejoicing. Sheets of silvery gray light rippled from her back and snapped to the solid form of wings. Her hands curled into golden paws, her-human dress was torn apart from within by the thrust of her marble-smooth, marble-white breasts. The lion's roar and the hunting hawk's shriek blended in untamed cacophony with her laughter. Under lights too brilliant to permit the salve of lies, she grew in size until the protruding tips of her talons rested at half Sanchi's height. She lashed her tail against the steel supports, and a section of the boardwalk crumbled.

Her paw came down to end Alonso's pain. Sanchi could not shield his eyes in time to avoid the cruel sight. Her claws raked out and slashed the Bast cat to ribbons of smoke.

For the first time, her servants and her most casual admirers got a look at the real Ianthe Apeiron. The hardened punks had a more highly developed survival instinct than the aficionados of *People*. They ran first, knocking Manolo and Gemma out of their way. The men and women on the boardwalk gaped a little longer, then fled too.

As Sanchi collapsed on the sand, he thought he heard a plaintive whine fading off in the distance:

"Are you *sure* it's not something with Doug Henning, Margie?"

"It's a goddam Steven Effing Spielberg production, Bobby Lee. Now move your F/X *ass!*"

249

# CHAPTER THIRTY-ONE:
## Freeing the Stones

Hard hands, gentle hands, closed on Sanchi's battered body. He protested, but any struggle made his wounds hurt more. They hauled him to his feet. He mewled like a starving kitten. Even the sound of their voices gave him pain.

"Get up, Sanchi."

"Sanchi, you can't lie there."

"Be careful with him."

"Try to get the wounds clean of sand. Ah! That must be an agony. More care, Vergilius."

"You take him. Hurry. She will remember us soon, and I must face her then."

"Not alone, my lord."

"Your place is with him. Go."

"*Careful!*"

"Hey, would *someone* out there maybe stop mauling my brother and cut us loose?"

Sanchi felt a small body wedge itself under his arm. "Lean on me." Elena's breath was sweet and heady. It made his sight swim, like rich wine too rapidly gulped down. He closed his eyes, riding the sound of that voice into dreams. Before the darkness closed over him, his smooth descent was broken by a shrill cry of alarm. "He's collapsing!" He wanted to tell her that no, he was all right, only tired. He wanted to rest. Let the Riddle wait. The sphinx had other things presently on her mind.

Cool wind cleansed his face. He smelled the salt air, but saw only penciled lines of light in a matte-black sky.

"Don't move, Sanchi." A head blocked out even those puny stripes of brightness. "Elena said you have to lie still."

Satin stroked his cheek, wonderfully smooth, but full of a revolting sour smell. He grumbled and turned his head away. Sand got into his clothing from every angle, irritating him further. A tender hand pushed hair out of his eyes.

"Here. Drink this. Manolo stole it just for you."

"Mani—" He pushed himself up on his elbows and was pushed right back down immediately for his troubles. A straw poked him periously near the eye before he helped his nurse find his mouth. Iced Coca-Cola eased an arid throat. His eyes came to accept the shadows just when his ears made him aware of the sounds of battle. He was under the boardwalk, his head in Gemma's lap.

"No more." He shoved the cup away. "You're free! You and Mani—you're OK." He grabbed her hands, too distracted to notice immediately that there was no more pain in his movements; a weak ache of knitting flesh was all.

"Sanchi, you've got to lie still."

"I can't. Where is he? Where are the others? What's that noise?"

"It doesn't involve you anymore. You can't fight again, or all the queen's work will come undone."

"The queen's work . . ."

"Your wounds closed up for her like—like—" She had to smile at the only comparison she could summon. "Like Ziploc bags. We dragged you under here while Vergilius held off the sphynx. Manolo ran away and broke into a snack bar to bring us water, and that drink for you. The queen worked on you as quickly as possible, Elena helping her somehow. It was so strange; Elena just sat there beside you, not touching you, not touching the queen, but it seemed as if the healing came from her."

"And now? Where are they now?"

"Out there, on the beach. Let me help you onto your side. You can see from here."

He wished he could not.

The sphynx was a monument of living magic, a bulk of fang and claw, outstretched pinions blotting out the moon. Where she moved, gouts of sand spewed up behind; valleys were carved into the beach by her talons. Her tail switched back and forth and the sands were swept clean of all tidal debris. Her featureless breasts with their too-taut, too-white skin gleamed like a brace of polished skulls.

And against all this might, four people stood isolated on the sand: Hatshepsut with eyes downcast, unreadable; Elena holding herself immobile as any Egyptian statue with the effort not to show fear; Manolo, with the street-crazy look that said anyone, any*thing* tried to hurt his sister, he'd rip it apart barehanded or die; Vergilius. Green fire ringed them, a warding blaze whose leaping flames still looked pitifully meager, the merest glint in the sphynx's eye.

*Magician . . .*

Sanchi heard the word distinctly in his mind. From the way he felt Gemma tense and saw the other four stiffen, he could tell that though the sphynx addressed Vergilius, she did not care to hide her thoughts. She had come fully into the open; there would be no more masquerade, no waiting for a ripe moment to strike. Her hour had been thrust upon her. They had forced her hand, and must play it out before the night ended.

*Where is he, Magician? The Riddle waits, and world's end with it. Seven threads have fallen across the loom to weave the final Asking. Seven, none yet rightly Answered, and he must Answer all.*

"He needs to Answer none!" Vergilius was draped in shimmering blue robes, blue the same sea-change shade as his eyes. The emerald ring on his upraised right hand swelled with power. He rested his left on Elena's shoulder and seemed to draw strength from that contact. The green fires ringing them crackled with tawny lightnings.

*Remember your oath, Magician.*

"Better than you do yours. Trickery and deceit, ruthlessness and treachery—"

*Why not name me human and be done?*

"You did not scorn to use humans when it suited you. Where are they now, your faithful ones? Can it be that even you cannot offer them gold enough to serve a monster?"

*Men have served monsters before this, for less than gold. Let the fainthearts run; I do not need them any longer. I am strength and mind and victory. I need no one! Bring him to me, Magician. I would end the game. Now, or you will see that not even dread Styx can bind me from smashing this city into rubble.*

She screamed like a stooping hawk and bounded sideways toward the boardwalk. Gemma gave a thin cry as the ground shook with the beast's loping tread. She covered her mouth with her hands and leaned forward, bending low over Sanchi, but he could not tell whether it was to shield him with her own body or to hide her eyes from the sight of the sphynx's onrush. He saw titanic paws strike the earth less than three yards from his haven, then veer off.

The sphynx paused in front of the Kennedy Memorial beneath the Egyptian colonnade. One swipe of a forepaw knocked the topping slabs clear off their supporting pillars. She whipped her wings open, and the booming reverberations shattered windows in three separate hotels. Showers of fractured glass jingled down.

*Where is he, Magician?*

Sanchi tried to struggle up, but Gemma was in a good position to pin him down at once. Something small and hard fell from the neckline of her dress, swung out on a thin cord and struck him in the nose. The pain was too trivial for more than a nominal protest, but even that died when he recognized the gray pendant shape.

The cord snapped as he wrenched it from Gemma's neck. "My *zemí*!"

She was able to smile weakly, rubbing her neck. "I would have given it back, if I'd known you were that mad to get it. I was holding on to it for you."

"Where did you—?" He bit off the question, for shame, and made his hands into a protective shell around it.

His cupped hands tightened sharply as another sound of toppling masonry reached him. The dust of ruined stone and concrete sifted down through the boardwalk planks.

*Where is he, Magician? His life is bound to mine by the Riddle; I may not slay him until the Asking is done. He still lives—I feel his breathing spirit like a thorn! Before world's end, he must be first to die. Give him up! Must I walk into the city's heart, crush a thousand, ten thousand, in the wreckage of the buildings I will pull down seeking him?*

"You will not," a woman's voice said. From his shelter, Sanchi saw the little Egyptian queen wave her hands above a small arc of the wizard's wardfire and turn flames to flowers. She stepped through, and resealed the spells with another gesture.

The ground shook again. The sphynx came trotting eagerly back from the boardwalk to intercept the queen. At such a size, the perfection of her human face lost all claim to beauty. The moon was weak and small, but honest enough to bring up every curl of lust and bloodthirst on those precisely cut features.

Hatshepsut did not wait for the monster to reach her. The white-and-red double crown of Upper and Lower Egypt was on her head, the vulture and the cobra enthroned on her brow, regally defying conquest. She did not see the wardfire burn low behind her as Vergilius cried out for her return to his safekeeping. She spoke the words of power, of summoning, of transformation into the night, and a phantom of molded air lifted from her shoulders to fly across the path of the moon.

Woman's magic. It fell upon the ruins of the colonnade, draping a diaphanous veil of changing over the black monument within. Stone shuddered against stone. Blocks moved as earth was reshaped. The face on the memorial statue melted like wax, remade itself in time to join human head to lion's body, shake off a light coating of dust, and stride forth to meet the enemy in the full strength and glory of Egypt's sphynx.

Hatshepsut's creation lacked wings, but had the larger, more muscular body of the male lion. The raw power innate in his every movement reduced the female sphynx's late display of force to a kitten's tantrum. He opened his mouth and roared, showing fangs that dwarfed his enemy's own. The female sphynx saw his birth and was aghast, unable to move. Now, as he came toward her, rocking the earth, roaring for her death, she cringed. Forepaws and hind paws folded under her. Her belly and breasts dragged the sand, and she shrank from him, her tail poured out limp and lifeless behind her. She dipped her head low, begging for mercy with her eyes.

The Egyptian sphynx loomed above her. His face was as inscrutable as the moon. The broad planes of cheeks and brow and lips registered nothing human beyond the fact that they were a man's. She made small placating sounds deep in her throat and kneaded the sand. His forepaw cuffed her head hard enough to send her tumbling and stain the single lock of gray hair with crimson.

"Terrified," Sanchi breathed. "She's terrified of him. But—but he can't kill her."

"Why can't he?" Gemma asked. "Look at his size! He drew blood. He can tear her apart."

"No." Sanchi spoke as one who knew. "He can hurt her, beat her, drive her off, but only one thing can open the way to her death." He clutched his *zemí* more tightly. "Sphynx against sphynx, the Riddle. If she Asks, and he Answers, it's done."

"But if he doesn't know—"

"He knows the Answer; there's no way he can't. I always thought that creatures like those were only the products of human imagination. I let myself forget that at its worst, without compassion guiding it, imagination can be older and darker than the blackest sorcery. All the evil we've done— there's an old, warped wisdom behind it that we've poured into our worst creations. War and murder and cruelty weren't made with the world. Neither were they." He nodded toward the beach. "The lore of Egypt is ancient, and must hold the Answer she fears to hear. Look; she knows it. She's trying to get away."

The Egyptian sphynx saw through her ruse. She was making for the sea. He would not permit it. A magnificent leap carried him over her, placed him between her and the waves. Foam lapped at his flanks as another roar shivered the air, and a single word blasted through the sound.

*ASK!*

Another powerful buffet backed up the command. Sanchi saw blood mar the perfect whiteness of the sphynx's breasts.

*Ask* . . . Her all-pervading thoughts were a sigh. She closed her eyes and lifted up her head. Couched on the sand, her forepaws dug in deeply until she was the living parody of her opponent's traditional pose at Giza. *Very well. You shall have your Riddle, my lord. Hold, while the weaving forms. Your indulgence awhile yet, noble master.*

The wind was blowing in from the sea. Sanchi could smell the heavy animal scent of both monsters, but abruptly a new note crept into the breeze. It was a thick scent, penetrating, disturbing in the extreme. A shallow breath of it made his whole body tingle. He was desperately trying to lay a name to it when the wind shifted and carried its fragrant burden out toward the water.

"Ai, no!" Hatshepsut cried as the breeze drifted past her. She reached out as if to snare the wind and send it back from sea to shore, but a rough grunt of pain from the sphynx she commanded made her stop.

255

"He holds all her magic," Sanchi hissed. "That must be it. She can't run any other spells unless she lets go of him, and then—"

"I thought magic was—I don't know—always more of it there for a sorcerer to use," Gemma said.

"It's not. If it were, she and Vergilius could've smashed the sphynx to powder and we'd all be back in the Krater having a drink right now. Say, did you smell that? The change in the air?"

Gemma wrinkled her nose. "I'll say I did. God knows what it was. It reminded me of how my cat used to get before I had her fixed, but—"

"Oh no."

The impossible conclusion galvanized him. He tore away from Gemma's futile graspings and scrambled out from under the boardwalk with less dignity than an unearthed hermit crab. In the open, the beach appeared to stretch away to an incredible distance; the water looked leagues off, and the land undulated wickedly while the distant water held the rigidity of poured glass. The sphynxes were golden toys he could pick up with one hand.

Except his hand was closed around a small stone object, and his legs were rubber beneath him. He took a step and fell to his knees, then crawled on because the sky was trying to slide itself under him and whirl him away into the moat of stars.

Through the spinning world he crawled. Once he felt hands tug on his shoulders, but he shrugged them off as hard as he could, striking out backward with his left arm. He heard a gasp and felt wetness trickle down past his elbow to pool between his fingers. It made the sand cake up under his hand, which annoyed him, but at least there came no further attempts to pull him back.

Green fire burned against the waves. A woman crowned with red and white and gold shriveled to a moth's size with weeping. Two beasts with the heads of human beings scraped the night bloody with their amorous growls of demand and invitation. He was coming nearer to the sea. He could almost smell the brine through the reek of rut cloaking those two monsters.

The Egyptian sphynx's nostrils flared at the sweet promise of welcome and surrender so gracefully offered up to him from liquid eyes and sinuously treading haunches. Assured victory added to the hauteur of his bearing. He entered the female as any conqueror of old would take a fallen city, without respect, without humility, because it was his by right to use as he willed.

Sanchi was nearest when the wail of torment came. Amber eyes with slitted pupils flooded his mind with their heartless ridicule. Thoughts meant for the male—face no longer impassive as throes of anguish racked him—lapped cool and mocking in Sanchi's brain.

*Your Riddle first, my lord, and then if you survive it, the final Asking: Whose is your life, where the control? Who reigns to rule your self and soul?*

The male thrashed, held fast, and the Answer burst from him with all Hatshepsut's power in it: *\*YOU!\**

In the spate of outrushing power, Vergilius' wardfire was snuffed like a paper match. The sorcerer screamed as the emerald on his finger split into four shards that pattered across the sand, feebly glowing. He flung himself down to gather them back, Elena and Manolo with him.

Sanchi felt a tiny kiss of cool stone touch the fisted hand that cradled his *zemí*. He wanted to call out to Vergilius and tell him that he had found a portion of the shattered emerald, but the aftermath of the Egyptian sphynx's Answer hung in the air, a ringing sheet of beaten bronze that sucked all possibility of other sound from the air.

The female sphynx was beyond the merely possible. *No*, she said, freeing herself of the male's weight with a fastidious shake of her hindquarters. *Not I; yourself.* Already draining pale, the sphynx of Egypt did not have to wait long for the homage of a deathblow.

The living sphynx swung her head slowly around. She saw Sanchi, lying spread-eagled on the sand.

*Ah. There you are.*

# CHAPTER THIRTY-TWO:
## The Riddle of the Sphynx

With both hands, Vergilius clung to a pebble that resembled green beach glass. Still on his knees in the sand, he looked as if he were praying to the sphynx. "Don't touch him," he rasped. "Let him be."

*As my late master wishes.* Her thoughts were greater thunder than any spoken words. *You know I do not need to touch; that, I disdain.* The huge head swayed to follow the path of Elena as the girl ran across the sand to pull Sanchi into her arms. *Touch is for your kind.*

The sphynx's thoughts and Vergilius' words both made Sanchi's head throb. His world had stopped tilting, but he still suffered from the aftereffects of that sensory rollercoaster ride. Elena's worried face and anxious questions echoed against one another until he felt as if some supernatural trickster had submerged him in clear gelatin. He heard and saw everything garbled and blurred, from very far away.

He had to say something. She would keep staring at him with that anguished expression until he did. More than anything, he wanted to spare her pain, to make her stop fretting for him. "Look," he said with a bland, cheerful smile as his right hand folded back from the *zemí*. "I found it." The other hand also uncurled, though more slowly. "This, too. Tell Vergilius he can calm down now." Blood-damp sand caked around the fragment of emerald.

"I'll tell him."

Why did she sound on the point of tears? What was the matter? "I didn't kill Alonso. I didn't make the little cat grow. I don't even know how it happened—"

"It doesn't matter," she said. Her hand touched his re-opened wound and he saw her face tighten in concentration. "It doesn't work." Was Elena angry at him? "I tried, I really tried to focus all my power through the stone the way

Vergilius did, the way the queen can, and it won't work for me!" Her voice rose in frustration.

He saw a second bit of shattered gemstone glint green between her fingertips. He wanted her to take comfort; he didn't want her to cry. "Maybe it takes more, Elenita." He hoped she wouldn't mind if he clasped her hand with his, the one so gritty and sticky.

*Sanchi . . .*

His name was an icy blade that sheared away the comforting lies of a mind gone wandering. With no gradation of return, his senses cleared to merciless acuity. The same trickster spirit whispered that if the sphynx no longer hid herself from the real world, she would brook no one else a place to hide.

He sat up, still holding Elena's hand. Together they helped each other to stand. The sphynx filled the waning night, only the ocean rivaling her infinity of power. Still, he could not help but see, from the corner of his eye, how Vergilius and Hatshepsut now also stood close as ranked soldiers, awaiting what they could not change. A streak of white ran and stumbled into his line of sight—Gemma, racing to join Manolo at the side of the two magicians.

The sphynx observed Gemma's approach and did nothing to prevent it. As if he stood inside the monster's brain, Sanchi knew that she no longer dealt in trivial deaths. This was the time of the Riddle. This was the balance of world's end, or world's winning.

He led Elena forward, until they were close enough to touch one of the sphynx's tufted toes. "I'm ready," he said.

From here, he could hardly see her face. The leonine chest curved up and bowed out above him as gracefully as the prow of a sailing ship. The massive breasts seemed an insulting interruption to so much purity of form, a bulbous shelf of shining whiteness that blocked sight of the monster's expression. A blue-black curl dangled down over one tawny shoulder in a thick, tight coil. The huge pinions were tucked back against the body, yet Sanchi thought he saw a loose feather dangling from one wing.

*Send her away*, the sphynx said. One claw unsheathed itself, singling out Elena. *You must have no help in this*.

"I won't say anything," Elena answered, "but I won't go."

*I will seal you to that.* The sphinx tilted back her head, and the lone gray lock of hair poured down over her shoulder like a ground fog. Seven individual strands of hair separated from the tress, rising into the air, floating to the ground. As each touched, it spread its substance wider on the night and took the semblance of a ghostly man. Little by little, each phantom's features set. In tunic and toga and triumphal wreath, with the cunning shortswords of the legion in their hands, the seven Caesars had been riven from Hades once more.

Sanchi recognized them immediately. Their faces were their own, but emptied of all the human traits that had made each one hateful or comic, noble or vile. They were distinct entities, yet all part of the same being. Even foolish little Heliogabalus, whose experience was no battlefield but the bedchamber, looked confident of how to handle his sword.

*They are mine now,* the sphinx informed him. *A word from her, and she will lack the tongue to utter another.* She settled herself comfortably on the sand, her hindquarters kneeling over with a dull thud as she lazily stretched her body out behind her. The black paw pads on her hind feet were visible.

> *Tread the threads and walk the weave;*
> *Knowing, learn, and learning, grieve.*
> *Summon each to shuttle's call,*
> *On the loom I weave them all.*
> *Sevenfold of seven lords,*
> *Debt unpaid by wit or swords.*
> *Hear them, Man! And then decree*
> *What the Riddle wrought must be.*
> *Take the Question from the dead,*
> *Then you have my Riddle read.*
> *Seek the pattern, find the key,*
> *Know the Riddle, Answer me.*

The words of the chant bubbled up from the marrow of Sanchi's bones. He could not see whether the sphinx's lips moved to articulate them or know for certain whether she had willed them into his mind. The seven spirits made a wreath of swords around him and Elena, feet blowing like smoke over the sand as they slowly circled. With the hand holding the *zemí,* he reinforced the grasp he already shared with Elena. She gazed at him gratefully, and with only that look and a smile told him that she was not afraid of the circling ghosts.

And as each phantom emperor passed, he spoke to Sanchi. From mouths dark and hollow as the cavern of his waking dream, each repeated the Riddle of the sphynx, the separate thread of Asking that had been his doom. Paradox and puzzlement, subtlety of intent, all the specific sorcery of words' congenital deceit ran like a common thread through the seven Riddles. Sanchi thought he saw an actual thread begin to twine itself into being just beyond the ghosts, a finespun thread that lay in a floating noose around them all and only waited for his Answer to pull tight.

A thread . . .

There was heat in his hands. Sand and stones clinked and grated over each other as Elena pressed her fingers more snugly into his. The blood from his reopened arm wound was only oozing sluggishly now. What had run down into his hand was turning more and more viscid as it dried.

He was only half conscious of the kindling warmth. His mind was filled with dead men's voices: *What flies fastest when hardest grasped? What is gotten without being given? What burns without a flame? What devours without consuming? What warps the world and affects the eye, yet never touches either? What makes substance out of void? What is most precious where least prized?*

Their whispers darted in and out of his ears, like snakes' tongues. Each repetition was another cord that bound him closer to the moment of the Riddle, stripped him farther down than the bone, right to the center of his soul. The sphynx's amber eyes put out the moon. Her wings were the clouds from which the lightning would fall that must cleave the world like the sorcerer's lost stone. The dead men spun around and around, a ring of shadows, and whispered their Riddles again and again and again—

—until she said, *Stop,* and the world changed.

"Stop, youth. Where are you going?"

Sanchi paused in his tracks, though for all he knew the voice hailing him from that niche beneath the hill's rocky outcrop could belong to a bandit. There was many such on the roads these days. Still, he stopped. The day was hot, there was little shade, and his feet were paining him worse than usual. He was naked except for his sandals and a very short chlamys pushed out of the way over both shoulders. His pouch of provisions and waterskin were attached to the thick traveler's staff he carried. In necessity, he could use it against attack and had already done so, as the dried blood staining one end of it showed. If this hidden questioner was alone, there was no immediate peril in roadside courtesy; if not alone, what use would flight be anyway?

"I am going to the king's city," he called. "And you?"

"I rule the king's city," the voice answered. "Where I am, there stands the gate. If you would enter, you must come near."

What could *that* mean? It sounded like a riddle of sorts. He was not in a humor for nonsense. He longed for cool water and a place to rest, if only for a little while. He was an exile, a being without privilege of place in this world. All the home he had known had been taken from him at the whim of some force that could not be comprehended but must be obeyed. All he had was himself, and at times that seemed to be the greatest riddle of all. Cursing the pain in his ankles, he trudged over the next rise in the road and came face to face with the monster.

She smiled when she heard his hasty prayer, uttered at sight of the tumble of human skulls beneath her paws. "Are you afraid, youth? Do you think I will kill you outright? Oh no, that is for your kind to do—to slay without question. I am more civilized. Do you gamble? Will you play with me?"

His fists clenched around his traveler's staff. Odd lumps dug into his palms—irregularities in the wood, he assumed. The creature was smiling at him. Her forepaws flexed, her claws making a chalky sound as they skreed down to gouge white stripes into yellowing bones. He knew that no true choice came with her invitation.

"Ask," he said.

"But I have," she replied. "Many times—did you not hear them? If not, it is all one to me. And now it is your turn. Treat it well. In the span of this universe, I shall Ask no other Riddle." Again the bones shrieked under her raking claws.

Not death nor fire, health nor fame,
Hate, lies, madness . . . Speak its name!

Was that all? There had to be more? What manner of
answer could he give her? The heat was terrible. It was
making his head ache so badly. He wondered what would
happen if he turned and ran back the way he had come.
Would the beast pursue? With those wings and a lion's
strength she could catch him easily. Besides, he could not
move. His staff had driven itself into the dirt as if determined to reroot, and his hands were as fast to the wood as if
he were being forcibly seduced by the nymph of the vanished tree. The lumps under his hands felt sharper, dug
deeper into his palms, and rocked slightly when sweat slicked
his skin. And oh, how hot they felt! It was like cradling live
coals.

He must win free. He must break the spell that forced
him to stand frozen here on crippled feet while a hidden fire
consumed his hands.

There was one escape. Only one. Wait. Think. Open
heart as you open mind.

Answer.

The fire in his hands flared as the monster opened her
mouth to roar an end to time.

Answer.

*Answer.*

*ANSWER!*

"Love."

He said it quietly. The Answer hung in an iridescent
dewdrop of sound against the night.

So very simple. So clear. So less-than-clever. Was that
really all he had to say?

*And how much more of an Answer was "Man"?*

His hands were burning. Elena's hand must be too. He
looked at her, but she was staring past him.

"Oh, Sanchi . . ."

No ghost lunged forward to uproot her tongue. The ban
of silence was broken, the ghosts gone. Yet some undeni-
able presence still hovered on the sea air. Sanchi heard
many footsteps rushing up behind him, felt a strong hand on
his shoulder.

*"Ay, hermano! Que lo has bien hecho de veras!"*

"Master . . ." The crown of the Two Lands bowed before him. The dark queen, hands folded across her bosom, saluted the victor.

"Now," the sorcerer said hoarsely. He knelt before Sanchi in the squire's place and on the crook of his arm offered him a bronze blade out of an elder time. A fragment of emerald burned sullenly on its pommel.

"A . . . sword?" Sanchi made no move to take it. In his memories, another blade whirled. Armor glinted in tropic sunlight. A simple hut burned behind the body of its master.

"How else will you slay her?" The magician jerked his head to where the sphynx still lay at ease. Her lazy posture was a shell, a brittle sham. Shock iced over her eyes. She did not seem so huge as when she had first posed the Riddle. A dark stain was spreading out on the sand beneath her, black waters from below rising slowly, and at her back the tides of earthly ocean rolling in.

"No," Sanchi said. "Not with that."

"You must!" Vergilius pressed. "If you don't—"

"She's defeated. There will be no more Riddles. What harm can she do?"

"What harm—?" The wizard choked out a burst of dry laughter. "Haven't you learned?"

"Vergilius . . . I'm not the one to use a sword."

*Use it, Man.* The frost of first surprise had shattered. The sphynx was up, on her feet, tail making the air crack with every furious twitch. *The Answer gives only the chance, not the right, to slay me!*

*"Dios y la Virgen!"* Manolo exclaimed. "Quick, give *me* the sword. Sanchi can't swing it anyhow, with his arm cut up like that." He didn't wait, but snatched the bronze blade from Vergilius' keeping and started for the sphynx.

"Manolo, come back!" Gemma cried.

"Idiot," Vergilius muttered. He cupped his hands to his mouth and called, "Come back, you fool! You can't touch her with that!"

"Why not?" Sanchi asked. "I Answered her. She's vulnerable now."

Vergilius rounded on him in cold rage. "Only for a time, and only to *you!* She can fall to your weapon and no other. The time pours itself out on the sands. Do you see the blackness bubbling up in her shadow? The river of death rises, the Styx seeps into your world to receive what only you can give it. Sanchi, if you don't—"

But Sanchi only half heard the mage's words. Still clinging to Elena with both hands, he saw his brother—more his brother than his lost blood kin—saw Manolo charging like the fool Vergilius called him right into range of the sphynx's fury.

He did not think. Heart called straight to hand, and all the fear of loss, the yearning love within him flung out through his fingertips as he shouted, *"Hermano, no!"*

Green fire, gray heart sprang from his hands and Elena's. Two fragments of a wizard's gem melded like flaming wings to a little carved talisman that leaped from the womb of their explosively parting palms. Wild magic soared across the night, streamed from flying stone. On the transformed rock, etched features came to life, stretched to a warrior's grin to welcome battle. Gray stone grew like the young corn unfolding from its seed, putting out arms and legs the color of copper. Muscles stretched, and a spear sprouted miraculously from one hand. Black hair in which a multitude of new stars sparkled trailed behind. A birth-shout and a battle-cry opened twin caverns between the stars.

"I am your strength, I am your sword, I am the enemy of Huracán, the evil one!" Tattooed feet beat out a dance on the sand, a hypnotic rhythm that made Manolo turn from his death, made the sphynx's skin ripple as if with a sudden chill. "I am the spark in your blood, Sanchez Rubio, the special flame of world's heart magic in your keeping. *Haieee, I am Yukiyú!"*

And answering cries came down, poured like rain from the tattered sky. Sanchi looked up, and Mamacita's voice was in the beat of his heart, telling the old tales . . . *and all there was or ever will be in the world—sun and moon, beasts and birds, men and dreams—all came rushing out of those two caves in the high hills of Puerto Rico. And Yukiyú—child of the great unseen, unknowable one, the loving creator of all things whom our ancestors named Yucahú—Yukiyú led all of those who would stand with the forces of good against Huracán and the powers of evil.*

They fell from the sky in the finery of battle, summoned by their *cacique*, their commander. Not all were copper-hued. Sanchi saw the glow of burnished ebony skin, and echoes of other stories, other gods stepped out of memory.

*Ay, Sanchito, so many tales I could tell you! Tales of the black gods of Africa, too, because their blood also runs through our island: Ogun, Oxumaré, Exu the trickster, Yansen the woman-warrior who rules the dead, all these . . .*

All these were there, the gods of ancient iron, of storm, of death, of the deep forest, of the ancestral waters; the gods of the man who perished in the slave ship's hold, the gods of the man who died in the mine, toiling beneath the surface of a land once his. They had seen monsters with human faces before, and they were all hunters. Good gods to call now, when it was time to hunt the lion.

They formed the curving horns of a bull and let Manolo slip away between them. He stared as legs taller than young trees passed him by to either side, a forest going to the war. The shining wonder of their plumes and beads, the jangle of their gold and iron and shell ornaments left the neon signs and blue-white streetlights of the city looking like dirty-wicked clay lamps. The sphynx crouched, hissing. She slashed at the woman-warrior with a thought-swift paw. Yansen laughed, and the first casual jab of her spear drew blood.

The sphynx pulled back her head like a snake waiting to strike. The old gods stamped a scornful dance into the earth and changed the bull's horns to a crab's relentless pincer. The sphynx yowled and spat, snarled words that were curses of great power, and made mad, abortive rushes at the closing collar of spears. The curses were only words to these hunters sprung from the union of Sanchi's blood, Elena's wild magic. They drove her to the water's edge, urging her on with small, taunting pokes from their weapons.

The black Styx waters followed her retreat solemnly from below. The upwelling pool of last oblivion edged out until it joined with the silvered foam of incoming waves. One rose up taller than the rest, and on its crest rode Atabex, who birthed the waters, and Janaina, lady of the sea.

Moon and spears and wave crashed down together.

They sat on the sands and watched the dawn, blue and gray and gold as the banners of a departing army. They did not look like anything but a crowd of friends who had gone larking on the beach at night and had managed to elude the muggers. The three ladies all wore long, lovely gowns; their escorts were somewhat more eclectic in their choice of dress. There was a bottle of wine chilling in ice, six glasses, and—a riddle—four pieces of green glass laid jigsaw-wise together in their midst.

A policeman who strolled by, doing his duty, was offered a cup of the Falernian. He suggested that it might be time for them to be moving along. The oldest of the three gentlemen—very dark, with a diabolically suave beard and mustache—agreed with him wholeheartedly, took the hand of the small, regal lady, and promptly vanished without even the theatrical courtesy of a puff of smoke.

The other two couples did not wait for the policeman's stammers to devolve into questions. They moved on, leaving the detritus of their party behind. The scruffier of the two remaining men did pause long enough to scoop up the four green lumps. The policeman tried to call them back—that ice bucket looked much more valuable than bits of broken glass—but they kept walking. He started after them and kicked the abandoned wine cooler over. Ice spilled and gold glinted.

He picked it up. He knew what it was at once, having seen all the right movies. It was a Roman helmet, complete with scarlet horsehair crest. The bottle and the glasses had melted into the sand as neatly as the ice, but the helmet stayed.

He put it down gingerly and walked off in the opposite direction, his mind already forming the proper selection of comforting lies. By the time he cleared the beach, he had wrought a transformation on the helmet that Vergilius might have envied: It was only an empty Kentucky Fried Chicken bucket those wacko tourists were using to ice down the cheap white wine.

On the boardwalk, an army of maintenance men were sweeping up vast quantities of broken glass and talking like experts about the effects of sonic booms.

# Epilog

Elena had just gotten the vase placed where she wanted it—on display, yet out of reach of little hands—when they came home.

"You're early," she said, taking a sleeping José Alonso from his father's arms. "Did it go so badly again?"

Sanchi looked abstracted. He followed Elena into the nursery and watched her put their child to bed before he said anything. When the door was pulled to, he said, "She held him. And she kissed me."

"And Papi? What did he say?"

Sanchi shook his head. "Papi couldn't come this time. He called while we were there—something about Manolo going off to Greece for inspiration . . . I don't know. What possessed Mani to get into *philosophy*, for Chrissake—"

Elena shrugged. "It's his money. What gets me is why he didn't sell off the whole four pieces of the emerald and keep all the profits for himself."

"You don't know your brother too well." Sanchi embraced his wife, smiling. "The cash from just one quarter of Vergilius' emerald is more than enough for him, he says, even with college tuition up where it is."

"Yes, but a trip to Greece, too? That runs into—"

"She's paying for that." The gentle smile became a mischievous grin. "Her contribution to the future of pure academics, *she* claims. Support your local philosopher. And the fact that she's gone over there with Mani—all on the up-and-up, of course, separate cabins on the cruise ship—"

"*Cruise* ship?"

"Sshhh, don't squeal like that, you'll wake Joselito. Yes, *cruise* ship. You don't think a woman like Gemma would go all the way to Greece without taking an Aegean cruise, do you? She's entitled. The way she invested her share of the jewel was like a real magician's trick: making one emerald

268

multiply like it was a pair of rabbits. She does know the market. Maybe we ought to ask her about investing—"

"Ask her first what she thinks she's doing, taking my brother with her on the *Love Boat!*"

"Elenita, haven't you got it backwards?" Sanchi chuckled. "In the first place, it's the brother guards the sister's honor, and in the second, Gemma knows just what she's doing."

"I'll bet," Elena grumped. Then her worries for Manolo's virtue were shelved as an earlier thought returned. "So Papi wasn't there? Just you and Cruz—I mean, your mother— and you said she—?"

"She kissed me when we left." Sanchi gazed back into the recent past as if wondering how much of it was a dream. "Without Papi there to stare her down or force her to talk to me directly. He's had to do that less and less, lately. Since he wasn't coming, I thought she'd beg off altogether. But when she answered the door, Joselito started squirming to get out of my arms, yelling, 'Nani! Nani!' You know the way he does when he sees her?"

"I know what you've told me."

"That's another thing. She asked me why I don't bring you around next time. She asked it while she held the baby on her lap. The little *condenado*, he ran so fast to reach her once I set him down that he tripped over the doorsill and fell. Then you should've heard the screams!"

"From Joselito? Was he hurt?"

Sanchi had to keep her from going back into the nursery and waking the child to check for injuries. "Him! He's part springs and the rest rubber. Hey, you know why he howled; he always works best with an audience. And Mamita, yelling too, at me, telling me I don't know how to mind a baby while she picks him up and starts stuffing him with cookies, fruit, *turrón*, a dentist's nightmare . . ." Sanchi stopped. "Mamita," he repeated, as if his own words had taken him by surprise.

That was when he saw the vase. Elena assumed an annoying air of mystery as he picked up the slim-necked, silver-footed amphora and turned it over and over in his hands. A frieze of creamy white figures in low relief girdled the Wedgwood-blue belly—Wedgwood-blue, but never manufactured by that venerable house. The artistic directors would sooner resign than allow any design so anachronistic to emerge unsmashed from their factories:

Three women in long Doric chitons stood in counsel over a shining silver thread. It ran from the spindle the youngest held, through the measuring hands of the matron, and trailed down, awaiting the snip of the shears wielded by the eldest. Sanchi touched their faces warily with the ball of his index finger. So small, yet the representation of each feature left no room to mistake the resemblance: Elena, Hatshepsut, Mamacita.

Past them stood a man in Roman garb pouring out an invisible libation into a tripod brazier. Even in profile, Vergilius looked commanding. And beyond him, around the vase's delicate curve, was a naked child holding a winged horse by the bridle while another man, this one in modern dress, bowed to offer him a sword. The child's face was the only area which the potter's hand had obscured, but as for the man—it was like looking into a mirror.

"Where did you get this, Elena?" He got the words out with difficulty.

"It was delivered this morning, with this." She handed him a store-bought card to welcome a new baby, with the elegantly scrolled addendum: *Better late than never! So much dirt, so little time. Fondest regards, Placido S. Caius.*

"Suetonius," Sanchi said, amazed to recognize the old gossipmonger's earthly alias. "But where did he spring from? I thought—"

"My God, look at the time!" Elena wasn't listening. She pushed past her husband and threw herself down in front of the television set, nearly wrenching the dial off getting to the right channel. Sanchi came in just in time to hear:

". . . truth to the rumors that Bruce and Jessica have split the house, the cars, and the Shar-Pei right down the middle. On other fronts, those who know predict the Playboy Mansion West going *muy* mondo condo in the not-so-distant, despite denials from you-know-Hugh. Meanwhile, this reporter is happy to announce that advance sales on his modest unauthorized bio, *Kitty Kelley: Life Sentence*, bode well for the upcoming multicity promo tour. A free four-week subscription to *Tranquilfax* will be given if you buy five copies. Do your Saturnalia shopping early."

On screen, Suetonius set down his notes and gave the

familiar thumbs-up sign-off as the cameras cut to the weather report.

Sanchi couldn't tear his eyes from the set as he seated himself beside his wife. "He's still here? But when Vergilius and Hatshepsut went, didn't he—?"

"Magic passes," Elena said, "but gossip goes on forever."

"Yeah. I heard a rumor to that effect."

### *About the Author*

Esther Friesner was born in Brooklyn, NY. She received her B.A. from Vassar and her M.A. and Ph.D. from Yale, where she taught for several years. Now a full-time science fiction and fantasy author, she has published short stories and poems in *Asimov's, Amazing,* and *Fantasy Book*, and is the author of nine fantasy novels. She currently resides in Connecticut with her husband and two children.